THE BIG BAD WOLF

As it came closer I realized it wasn't an ordinary timber wolf. This animal was easily twice the size of any wolf I'd ever seen and had a distinctly human intelligence shining in its eyes.

I didn't stand a chance.

It bit through the pine-needle rope and shook its head, scattering the needles all over the ground. The rest of the needles instantly fell away and the trees halted their brutal assault.

I raised a bloody, trembling hand, not sure if I'd just exchanged one predator for another. "Please," I managed to gasp between the quick, shallow breaths that were all my punctured lung would now allow. "Please . . ."

In response, a soft shimmering light encased the wolf, and where the beautiful creature had stood, now crouched a man, his ice-green eyes still glowing. As he gently lifted me into his arms, I cried out, pain engulfing me.

"It's all right," he said softly, cradling me against him. "You're safe now."

I looked up into the grim face of my rescuer, now recognizing him. How could I not when I'd seen his face on "Wanted" posters and in the *Tale* news so often over the centuries?

As pain and nausea sent me careening toward a dark abyss, his name drifted to me:

Seth Wolf.

Books by Kate SeRine

RED

THE BETTER TO SEE YOU

Published by Kensington Publishing Corporation

The Better to See You

A *Transplanted Tales* novel

Kate SeRine

KENSINGTON
PUBLISHING CORP.

www.kensingtonbooks.com

KENSINGTON BOOKS are published by

Kensington Publishing Corp.
119 West 40th Street
New York, NY 10018

All Kensington titles, imprints, and distributed lines are available at special quantity discounts for bulk purchases for sales promotion, premiums, fund-raising, educational, or institutional use.

Special book excerpts or customized printings can also be created to fit specific needs. For details, write or phone the office of the Kensington Special Sales Manager: Attn.: Special Sales Department. Kensington Publishing Corp., 119 West 40th Street, New York, NY 10018. Phone: 1-800-221-2647.

eKensington and the K with book logo Reg. US Pat. & TM Off.

ISBN-13: 978-1-60183-025-8
ISBN-10: 1-60183-025-4

First Electronic Edition: February 2013

ISBN-13: 978-1-60183-174-3
ISBN-10: 1-60183-174-9

Printed in the United States of America

For Z. L. S.
Sun, moon, stars . . .

ACKNOWLEDGMENTS

Thanks to my family, friends, and fans who make all the hard work worthwhile! To Alicia, Alexandra, and the rest of the team at Kensington—your guidance and encouragement have been invaluable! And many thanks to Nicole, my ultra-fabulous agent whose awesomeness knows no bounds.

I also want to express my gratitude and appreciation to my mentors: John Selvy, Jonathan Smith, Dee Goertz, Kathy Barbour, Marshall Gregory, and Lee Garver. Although it has been more years than I like to admit since I sat in your classrooms, I still carry with me the wealth of knowledge you imparted. Thank you for sharing your wisdom and for inspiring generations of students to be better scholars, better writers, and better citizens of the world.

Prologue

Magic's a funny thing. It's seductive, addictive. There's no bigger rush than harnessing the elements and bending them to your will, experiencing that orgasmic release of energy as a spell bursts forth and alters time, space, reality. . . .

But the thing is, just when you think you've got magic under control, you come to find out it's actually controlling you.

And, once upon a time, a brash young fairy found this out the hard way.

Up until then, she'd been unstoppable—arguably the most powerful and talented fairy ever born, guardian to an ancient magic to which only the most gifted beings were privy.

She was also an arrogant, egomaniacal snob who needed a major smackdown.

And when that came in the form of a cosmic sucker punch from Aladdin's genie during a magic duel, her epic failure cast the characters from the land of Make Believe into the world of Here and Now, leaving those who'd once idolized her stranded in an unfamiliar place with unfamiliar realities.

Suddenly, the It Girl of legend was the most despised Tale this side of Make Believe, a pariah cast off by her own kind. Stripped of her titles, her name, her wings, her very essence, she was forced to scrape and bow and kiss ass just to get by—

Ah, to hell with it.

There's no point in trying to sugarcoat it. This is *my* story. *I'm* the fairy whose sucktacular judgment and giant ego got all us Tales into this freaking mess. And I've been paying for it ever since. 'Cause if there's one thing Tales are good at, it's holding a grudge.

I'd give you my true name, but you wouldn't know it. My family was so pissed off by what I'd done, they had my name stricken from record long ago, erased from the collective cultural consciousness of the Ordinary humans who'd once spoken of me with reverence and awe.

These days I go by Lavender Seelie. And after nearly two hundred years of being shunned and reviled, I've had enough of the hackneyed, bullshit story of my so-called life.

Time to turn the page.

Chapter 1

The flames climbed higher and higher, licking at the night sky with malevolent glee as they devoured the Baroque-style mansion that had been so painstakingly recreated by James and Cinderella Charming nearly a century before.

Although I mourned the destruction of the priceless works of art and other opulent extravagances inside, I had to appreciate the poetic justice of the situation. With my help, a beautiful young woman had risen from the cinders to become one of the most pampered, petulant, puerile princesses ever to grace the pages of a fairytale. And now, thanks to me, her world had been reduced to ashes once again.

"You bitch! You stupid, crazy bitch!"

Ah, and there was the reason why. . . .

From my seat on the garden bench, I calmly turned my gaze from the conflagration to the raging man in gold lamé bikini briefs and a silk smoking jacket who was straining against the hold of two much taller Investigators from the Fairytale Management Authority.

"I'll fucking kill you for this, Lavender!" he screamed, his voice cracking. "You're going down, you half-assed fairy!"

"Bring it on, half-pint," I called back, emphasizing my lack of concern with a syrupy sweet smile and a one-finger salute.

If James Charming had looked like he was going to have an

apoplexy before, my fuck-you-very-much response to his threats now made him look like his head was going to explode. A strangled scream of fury burst from him as he surged forward, but a shadowy black figure in a fedora and trench coat swooped into his path, stopping him dead in his tracks.

"Back off, Charming," warned Nate Grimm, the FMA's lead detective and part-time Reaper.

For a brief moment, James looked like he might balk, but then Nate's girlfriend, Tess "Red" Little, strolled toward James and lifted a single dark brow, daring him to start something. Knowing well her reputation as a bad-ass, James ducked his head a little into his shoulders and cast a murderous glance my way.

"Why don't you escort Prince Charming here over to Enforcer McCain and let the kid take his statement?" Red said to Nate, her hand skimming lightly over his back as she passed, a simple, unconscious gesture of familiarity and affection that spoke volumes about her love for the enigmatic Reaper. The look he sent her way in return was so heated it put to shame the fire raging in the background.

Red's confident, cocky half-smile was still on her lips when she turned away and headed in my direction. She sat down next to me and leaned back, casually draping her elbows over the back of the bench. "How we doing over here, Lavender?"

"Couldn't be better," I assured her. I laughed a little maniacally, which probably did little to negate James's claim that I was one big sack of crazy. "This has to be one of the best nights of my life!"

Or, at least, of the last couple hundred years, I added silently.

Having served as fairy godmother to Cinderella and her crooked, philandering, asshole of a husband hadn't exactly been the carefree life of ease and contentment I'd signed up for. When I thought about the magic I'd wasted to bring those two together, it made me want to puke. But those days were officially over, thanks to my little pyrotechnics display.

Red shifted positions on the stone bench, leaning forward to rest her elbows on her thighs. With a sigh, she clasped her hands together and stared at the flames for a moment before turning her head to peg me with a don't-bullshit-me look. "So . . . wanna tell me how we came to be having a multimillion-dollar campfire tonight?"

Red was the FMA's best Enforcer even on a bad day. Since solving a series of grisly murders committed by an Arthurian enchantress named Sebille Fenwick a little over a year ago, she'd been promoted to Assistant Director of the FMA—whether she liked it or not, from what I gathered, and in spite of the scandal that resulted when Sebille's corpse disappeared right out from under the FMA's noses. So I guarantee Red didn't get to where she was without having a finely-tuned bullshit detector. I had no doubt she'd know in a hot second if I wasn't being straight with her.

Plus, in addition to the fact that I knew she could clean my clock without breaking a sweat if she wanted to, she'd once seen me at my lowest of lows and still had made the effort to be my friend—not a common occurrence for either one of us. I wasn't about to piss on that by lying to her.

"James attacked me and I panicked," I told her simply. I cast an embarrassed glance her way before adding, "My magic's been a little hard to control since I've been sober."

"So you weren't drinking at all tonight?" she asked, her tone daring me to lie to her.

I shook my head, feeling damned proud to be able to do so. "I made a promise to you. I've kept it."

She gave me a nudge with her shoulder. "Sorry. Had to ask."

"Yeah, I know."

"So, what set him off?" she prompted. "I know James is a total prick, but I've never seen him become violent. Why'd he come at you?"

I pursed my lips with a quiet puff of air.

Here we go. . . .

"Do you read the *Daily Tattletale*?" I asked, referring to the tabloid newspaper we transplanted Tales couldn't seem to get enough of.

She grunted. "Not if I can help it. Why?"

I cleared my throat a couple of times and ran my hands through my bobbed violet hair. "Well, there's a weekly gossip column in the paper that dishes all the dirt on the Tale elite—information that could only have come from an insider."

Red grinned. "Okay, now *that* column I've read. It's freaking hilarious!"

"Yeah, well, tomorrow's edition will feature none other than James Charming and his lovely wife."

Red's brows shot up. "And you know this how?"

I grimaced a little. "Because I wrote it."

Her quiet chuckle was edged with something that sounded like pride. "No wonder James looks like someone's walked over his grave. How'd he find out about the article?"

I groaned. "Cindy. I thought I'd give her a heads-up about what was coming—you know, for old times' sake. Technically, she's still my ward, so I felt I owed her that much."

"She's treated you like a slave for hundreds of years, Lav," Red pointed out. "You don't owe her anything."

"I took an oath," I mumbled. When she gave me a disapproving look, I added, "It's a fairy godmother thing. Anyway, considering what James has put her through all these years—what he's put *me* through all these years—I figured she'd be happy to see him get his. And, honestly, *she* didn't look too bad in the article, aside from being outed for the plastic surgery she's had—which really isn't such a secret anyway. I mean, come on—she looks like she could suck a duck through a garden hose."

Red tried unsuccessfully to smother her grin. "But she didn't see it that way?"

I shook my head. "I really thought she'd be loyal to *me*, that she'd come to my defense and be proud of me for finally getting my life together and trying to make up for letting that little son of a bitch walk all over us for all these years. But she went bawling to James the minute I told her, terrified that the article would ruin their precious reputations. And you can see how well *he's* taking the news."

Red shrugged. "Well, if the entire Tale world was about to find out that my empire had been built on extorted magic, I guess I'd be a little freaked out, too."

"That's not all he's freaked out about," I muttered, glancing over to where James continued to fume, pacing a path in his perfect grass while Cindy wailed uncontrollably. But before I could fill Red in, a woman with buttercup yellow ringlets came toward us, her expression one of weary irritation.

"Ordinaries," she grumbled, jerking her head toward the human firefighters still attempting to battle the blaze.

"What'd they say?" Red asked.

The woman ran her hands through her ringlets, then clasped the back of her neck where her tension seemed to be knotting. "I told them James and Cindy confirmed the fire was started by a candelabra set too close to the curtains."

"Will there be an investigation?" Red asked.

Ringlets shrugged. "A cursory one, I'm guessing, but nothing we can't handle."

"Thanks, Trish," Red said. "I owe you one."

She gave Red an acerbic glance. "You owe me about a million." She then turned to me and offered her hand. "Trish Muffet," she said, her penetrating green gaze making me feel like she'd known me for years. "Forensics—and, apparently, Damage Control."

I shook her hand sheepishly, fully aware of what a mess I'd made of things. The one cardinal rule we Tales were supposed to obey at all costs was to blend in and let none of our human brethren—the Ordinaries—discover the truth about us. There were laws the FMA had put into place in order to protect us from the Ordinaries—and to protect them from us. And I'd managed to slip up big-time by bringing our little family feud out into the open. "Thank you for your assistance, Ms. Muffet."

"Will the Charmings go along with the story?" Red asked, rising to her feet. "Or are they going to be a problem?"

Trish nodded. "I think Nate's got that under control. Can't promise James won't press any charges, though."

"Charges?" I echoed. "For what? That little shit attacked *me*!"

Trish gave me a knowing look. "He claims you used your magic to, uh, significantly reduce the size of his manhood."

Red's head snapped toward me, her eyes wide. "Did you really shrink his dink?"

I didn't flinch. "He had it coming."

Red exhaled a low curse.

"I'm going to have to take your wand, Lavender," Trish said, producing a plastic evidence bag. "I'm sorry."

I shrugged and handed it over, the tip dangling precariously where James had attempted to break it when he'd come at me with a gun, threatening to blow my brains out. "Be my guest. It's not working right anyway. I was only planning to make him impotent. But I can't say I'm disappointed that the spell went awry this time."

"Don't worry," Red told me, clasping my shoulder. "We'll sort this out. If anything, it sounds like you have grounds to press charges against him for attacking you. Do you *want* to press charges?"

I crossed my arms over my chest, lifting my chin higher. I was officially done with being the obedient little fairy who never questioned her orders. James and Cindy Charming had cured me of that. "Damn right, I do."

She gave me a tight nod, then turned to Trish. "I'm going to get Lavender out of here. Tell Nate I'll see him back at home, will you?"

Trish gave a mock salute, then headed off to talk to the rest of the Investigators on the scene. As soon as she was out of earshot, Red turned to me, her angry gaze edged with concern. "This is a dangerous game you're playing, Lavender."

I frowned at her, surprised by her sudden admonishment. "I thought you, of all people, would be proud of me for standing up for myself. If it wasn't for you encouraging me to write my own story, to be true to myself, I'd still be buried in a bottle, drowning my sorrows, and kissing the ass of that little bastard."

Red grabbed my arm and began leading me toward a 1940 Lincoln-Zephyr parked beyond the Ordinaries' fire trucks and the black SUVs that belonged to the FMA.

"I *am* proud of you," she assured me, "but James Charming has a lot of really crooked people in his pocket. When the shit hits the fan, he's going to make life hell for you."

"Like it hasn't been already?" I drawled.

"Yeah, well, at least you're still alive," she shot back. "And seeing how he was just threatening to rectify that, I'd feel a lot better if we got you somewhere safe until I can sort all this out."

"I don't have anywhere else to go," I told her. "I've never lived anywhere else in the Here and Now."

"What about family?"

Oh, God no!

I shook my head. "They made it very clear after our relocation that I was no longer welcome among them."

"Then you can stay with Nate and me," Red said, digging car keys out of the pocket of her black leather trench coat. "Gran and Eddie are on safari in Africa, but I'm sure they wouldn't mind you crashing at our place for a while."

"Thanks, Red," I said, sincerely touched by her friendship. "But if you think there's a possibility that James could try to retaliate, I can't put you and Nate in danger—especially in your condition."

Red stopped dead in her tracks and pegged me with a frown. "What condition?"

I gaped at her, wondering if she was evading or truly didn't know. When I said nothing, she opened the car door and muttered, "Get in."

When she got in behind the wheel, she sat for a long moment, staring out the windshield in silence. Nate must have instinctively felt the heavy weight of her gaze upon him because his head snapped around in the middle of a conversation with one of the other Investigators. He frowned and headed toward the car.

"Shit," Red muttered under her breath. She rolled down the window when he tapped on the glass.

"You okay, sweetheart?" he asked softly, leaning down to rest his forearms on the car door.

She nodded and grabbed his lapel, pulling him close for a hard kiss. "I love you, Nate," she whispered. "I love you so much."

He glanced at me, then turned his attention back to her, his frown deepening. "I love you, too, baby. You sure you're okay?"

She nodded again. "Yeah. Yeah, I'm good. I just . . . we need to talk later, okay?"

"Sure," he said, caressing her cheek. "I'll wrap things up here, and then you've got me all to yourself." He gave her another kiss and headed back to oversee the last of the investigation.

"I'm sorry," I said quietly. "Fairies can't help noticing these kinds of things. You have a certain glow about you that's impossible for us to miss. I thought you already knew."

Red shook her head, her expression blank. "No, I didn't know. I had no idea."

I reached over and gripped her hand. "Well, now that you know, you see why I can't stay with you and Nate."

She let out a mystified sigh, then gave herself a shake. "No, I *don't* see why. I'm *still* an Enforcer, Lavender. I'm *still* the Assistant Director of the FMA. And I'm *still* your friend. This doesn't change anything."

"Then be my friend and find someplace else for me to go," I insisted. "I don't just need to hide out for a while, Red. I need someplace where I can start over. It's time for me to live my own life and be the person I was meant to be."

She stared at me for a moment, her robin's-egg blue eyes boring into mine. Then she took a deep breath and let it out slowly. "There's a place I know of that's good for Tales trying to make a fresh start. It's called The Refuge."

I nodded, encouraging her to continue. "That sounds promising."

Her gaze narrowed and she worked her mouth from side to side as if debating the wisdom in her suggestion. "Don't take this the wrong way, Lav, but most of the people in The Refuge are starting over because they couldn't cope with life in the Here and Now. I don't know if they'll be all that happy to see you, seeing as how it was your spell that brought them here."

My laugh in response was bitter. "Like I'm the belle of the ball now? Trust me, Red, I can handle a few hard feelings."

"Maybe," she said slowly. "But I'd feel a lot better if you had someone looking after you—at least at first."

She reached into the inside pocket of her trench and withdrew a small black notebook. She flipped it open and scribbled something quickly. "Here," she said, tearing out a sheet of paper and handing it to me. "This is the address of a friend of mine."

I looked at what she'd written down and frowned. "This is in Washington State. I don't have the money for a plane ticket."

She gave me a cockeyed smile as she started up the Zephyr. "Luckily, being the Assistant Director of the FMA comes with a few perks."

Chapter 2

I spent longer than I should have in the hotel's shower, my emotions vacillating between being proud of myself for finally having the courage to break away from the Charmings and being flat-out panicked over what the hell I was going to do now.

I'd told Red I needed to start over and live my own life, but I honestly didn't have a freaking clue what that meant. I'd been depending on someone else for so long, I didn't even know where to start.

I'd allowed Red to take me back to the house she and Nate shared with her Gran so that I could get some sleep before boarding the FMA's private jet for the four-hour flight to the Pacific Northwest. Seeing as how I had pretty much nothing to my name, Red had offered to take me shopping—but not wanting to put her through what I could tell would have been a special kind of torture, I told her I'd just borrow something to wear and buy everything else I needed when I reached Seattle.

Smiling at the remembrance of the unabashed look of relief on her face, I pulled on the yoga pants and T-shirt I'd borrowed from Red's Gran. But my smile faded into a grimace when I saw my reflection in the mirror. Not only did the bright pink T-shirt do nothing to tone down my violet hair and eyes, but the ensemble was also a little on the cheery side for my tastes. Red had offered to let me borrow

something of hers, but I had a good four inches on the diminutive Enforcer and so had opted for something out of Matilda Stuart's closet
instead.

As grateful as I was, I was going to need a wardrobe of my own.
STAT. And seeing as how I'd pretty much charbroiled my cash cow
the previous night, that left only one alternative.

I turned on the faucet again, building up the steam in the room.
When the mirror had clouded over once more, I blew out a sigh, re-
signing myself to what was coming. "Here we go."

My call through the mists connected on the second try.

"Poppy Seelie," came my sister's cheerful voice, her smiling face
suddenly appearing in the steam on the mirror. "How can I—Oh. My.
God. I can't believe it! Is it really you, Lavender? I am so totally
shocked to be hearing from you—"

"Poppy—"

"—'cause I was, like, totally expecting someone else. There's this
Tale I met at Ever Afters the other night that is—oh, my God—so to-
tally hot! Are you calling about what happened last night? Mom and
Dad already heard and are beside themselves. You should have heard
Mom—"

"Poppy, could I—"

"—she was all like, 'I can't believe Lavender is bringing shame to
the family again.' And I was all like, 'James Charming is a total asshole,' and—"

"Poppy!" I snapped, breaking in before she could go any further.
"I need to talk to Dad."

My youngest sister cocked her head to one side, her bubblegum
pink hair swishing about her chin with the movement. "Dad? Why
would you want to talk to Dad? He's totally grumpy in the morning.
I'll get Mom instead."

"No, no, no, no, Poppy!" I called urgently as she ducked out of the
gateway I'd opened in the mist. "Don't get—"

"Lavender? It *is* you!"

I forced a smile. "Hey, Mom."

"Poppy told me you were calling, and I just couldn't believe it,"
my mother said, her hands fluttering about like frantic little birds.
"What have you gotten yourself into *this* time? Do you realize the

Tale network is buzzing with the news that you burned down the Charmings' mansion?"

Great. So much for them going along with the cover story. . . .

"How could you be so vindictive after all they've done for you over the centuries?" She paused long enough for a dramatic gasp. "Are you in *prison*? Is that why you're calling? Do you need us to bail you out?"

I tried hard not to roll my eyes. I really did. "No, Mom," I told her, forcing myself not to clench my teeth as I said it. "The fire was an accident. James attacked me, and—"

"Those poor, poor dears," she interrupted, shaking her golden head and sending up a tiny cloud of fairy dust that would've brought a fortune on the black market. "I don't know what to make of this, Lavender. I really don't."

Wait for it. . . .

"Where did we go wrong as parents?" she gulped, practiced tears shimmering on her cheeks. "How did we manage to bring up such a careless and thoughtless fairy? We gave you everything! And such talent—even the ancients were jealous of your gifts. And you've squandered it all. Squandered it! It is simply too much for my frail heart to bear!"

I didn't even bother trying not to roll my eyes this time. "Yeah, I know—I'm a huge disappointment, I broke your heart, I tarnished the Seelie name," I said, having committed my sins to memory long ago. "Save the histrionics, Mother. You're playing to an empty house."

She huffed, her golden eyes flashing with anger. "Well, forgive me if I lack your ability to so easily forget what you've put this family through."

"Trust me," I drawled, "I couldn't *possibly* forget how ungrateful and irresponsible I've been when you remind me *every single* time we talk." Before she could go on to the next line of our customary melodrama, I quickly added, "But don't worry—I've left town and won't be coming back. Now, could I *please* talk to Dad?"

She blinked at me in utter astonishment, thrown off by my changes to the script. "You've already gone?"

I nodded, bracing my arms against the bathroom vanity. "Isn't that what you've wanted since the genie incident? After the relocation, you made it very clear I was no longer welcome."

"But I didn't say I never wanted to see you again," my mother said, her expression hurt. She shook her head, her chest beginning to heave again. "First my darling boy was lured away by those horrible Shakespearean Tales and now—"

"Rob was a grown man, Mom," I cut in. "He had his reasons for wanting to go live with the Willies." *Not the least of which was an overbearing, melodramatic mother.*

"And if that wasn't bad enough, he changed his *name*," she hissed, her timelessly beautiful face twisting in disgust.

Denying one's heritage by casting off a name was among the worst offenses a fairy could commit. Even so, my brother had been eager to sever his ties to the Seelies and live a life of his own choosing. Something I could totally relate to at the moment.

"And he chose such a horrible substitute," she raged on, her fair skin flushing. "It completely lacks the finesse of—"

"Is that my little Lavender?"

I sighed with relief at the sound of my father's booming voice. When his face came into view I felt a twinge of regret for what I was about to do. "Hey, Dad."

"I'll take it from here, Mab," he said to my mother, pressing a kiss to her temple. My mother looked mildly irritated to have her drama interrupted, but my father gave her a gentle nudge, sending her on her way. As soon as she was out of hearing, he turned back to me and gave me a loving smile. "Hello there, petal. How are you holding up?"

"Been better," I muttered with a grimace. "I'm going away for a while, Dad—at least until things blow over. But I don't think . . ." I took a shaky breath. "I don't think I'll be back."

My father's normally sparkling blue gaze seemed to go flat at the news. "We can work this out, Lavender. Whatever trouble you've gotten yourself into, I'm sure that I can pull a few strings and see to it that everything is quietly swept under the rug."

I shook my head. "Not this time," I insisted. "I don't want this trouble with the Charmings to hurt your business."

Soon after our relocation, my parents had created a fairy dust business that supplied and managed all of the various distribution clinics. If not for my father personally overseeing the sale of the highly addictive substance also known as Vitamin D, we'd have a much higher rate of overdose and abuse than what we currently faced. I wasn't about to let anything jeopardize the progress he'd managed to make in that regard.

But he swatted my words away. "To hell with the business. You're my daughter."

I smiled, grateful for his unwavering love in spite of all my failings. "I appreciate that, but you know Mom doesn't feel the same way."

He huffed, having to admit I was right. And as much as he loved me, his devotion to my mother knew no bounds. "Well, then, what *can* I do to help you?"

I grimaced, hating that I needed to ask for help of any variety. "I lost everything in the fire. If there's any way I could—"

He held up a hand. "Say no more. No daughter of mine will be left homeless and penniless."

"No, Dad, that's not what I meant," I said quickly. "I just need—"

"Tell me where you are staying, petal," he interrupted. "You will receive a delivery within the hour."

The sparkle had returned to his eyes, and I knew trying to rein him in would be a losing battle. I rattled off the name of my hotel, then kissed my fingertips and pressed them to the mirror as the mist began to dissipate and my father's image drifted away.

Exactly one hour later, a severe-looking man wearing a black suit and sunglasses stood at my hotel room door, his shoulder-length red-gold curls pulled back in a tight ponytail at the base of his neck. The only concession to his fairy heritage was the silver lapel pin he wore, which bore my father's insignia. If I hadn't known him already, I would have thought he looked more like Hollywood's stylized version of an assassin than a fairy—which probably wasn't that far off the mark.

I offered him a warm smile. "Hello, Gideon."

"Ms. Seelie," he said with a tight nod, his voice devoid of inflection. He reached into his breast pocket and took out a small bundle. "Your father said that if this wasn't sufficient, he could send additional funds at once."

I shook my head. "I'm sure it's fine. Thank you."

He then took from his pocket a key ring and held it out to me. "Your new Jaguar is downstairs in front of the hotel. Your luggage is in the trunk."

I shook my head. "I didn't ask Dad for any of that."

"Your father insisted I see to your every need." He reached into the empty air beside him and withdrew a suit bag. "Perhaps you would prefer to change. Your current ensemble is decidedly not your style."

I grinned, grateful that he still knew me so well even though I'd been away from my mother and father's court all these years. "Thank you, Gideon."

He nodded and turned to go but paused to glance over his shoulder. "Good luck, Lavender," he said, a hint of warmth coming into his voice. "There are those of us who still wish you well."

I put my hand on his forearm and let my fingers slide down until they brushed against his. "Gideon . . ."

But before I could offer the long overdue apology that rose to my lips, he gave my fingers a squeeze, then quickly strode away, vanishing into thin air before he reached the end of the hallway.

Trying not to dwell on yet another painful reminder of all I'd screwed up and focusing instead on the fact that I still might have a friend or two among my own people, I unzipped the suit bag and quickly changed into the long, formfitting, gray knit skirt and black V-neck sweater Gideon had brought. At the bottom of the bag were black tights and a pair of lug-soled black biker boots just like the ones I'd had to leave behind at the Charmings.

Of course they would be. Gideon had the uncanny knack of being able to anticipate the needs of others—sometimes even before they knew it themselves. That's what had made him indispensable to my father.

I was folding up the bag when a flash of silver caught my eye as it slipped out onto the floor. Frowning, I bent and picked up the delicate chain. Hanging at the end was a pendant I recognized well. The elongated triskele knot with a moonstone at the bottom had been worn by every Seelie woman for as long as memory. Whether a gift from Gideon or from my father, I couldn't tell. But I understood the message. Regardless of my past, I was still a Seelie. And I should never forget that.

I fastened the chain around my neck and took a deep, bracing breath, wondering if I was making the right decision.

I had no idea what to expect once I arrived at The Refuge. Red had explained that it was a Tale colony started around fifty years ago as a place where Tales could live openly without fear of discovery. However, in recent years, it had also become the home of Tales who thought the FMA's many rules and regulations were too restrictive. The FMA was willing to turn a blind eye to the colony as long as its residents stayed out of trouble. Consequently, Red had warned, the inhabitants were an interesting mixture of characters. Still, something in the way my heart fluttered told me that my future was at The Refuge, and that it would be a future far better than any I could've possibly imagined.

As I felt the first faint flicker of hope in over two hundred years, I grasped the pendant around my neck and rushed from the hotel room, eager to leave my past behind and embrace the new life that awaited me.

Chapter 3

The sun was beginning to sink below the horizon, filling the sky with magenta and violet as I came around one particular bend in the road, giving me a breathtaking glimpse of snowcapped mountains against the setting sun. I blinked several times, clearing away the salty blur that had suddenly come into my eyes.

Get a grip, Lav, I admonished, feeling ridiculous for growing teary-eyed over a simple sunset.

But then I shook my head, not willing to push away such an intensely emotional moment. I'd sat in that damnable castle of a mansion for so many years, surrounded by the superficial beauty that money could buy, I'd lost touch with the power that fueled the very essence of my magic. It was no wonder my spells had gone to shit over the years. James was right at least in one regard—I *was* a half-assed fairy these days.

But that was going to change. And I was never going to let it happen again.

For the rest of the three-hour drive, I soaked up every ounce of loveliness I encountered, even after the sun had slipped quietly away, leaving darkness in its place. The longer I drove, the more remote my surroundings became. And as I made the final turn onto a long, winding logging road, my GPS gave out completely, the signal lost.

"Damn it," I muttered under my breath, straining to see in the darkness.

I flipped on my high beams and slowed the car as I made my way along the rough road. Too bad Dad hadn't given me a Jeep instead of a luxury car. I cringed with every pothole I hit, waiting to hear the car bottom out.

I'd been on the logging road for the better part of an hour, traveling deeper and deeper into the woods when the rain started. What began as a light drizzle soon changed into an autumn storm, the powerful winds buffeting my car and swaying the trees that lined my route.

"Fabulous," I spat, fighting to maintain control of the car as the dirt road turned to mud.

Where the hell was this freaking house anyway? I was beginning to think Red had given me the wrong address when I finally caught a glimpse of a light a hundred or so yards away. At the same moment, I hit another bump in the road that sent my Jag sliding toward the trees.

"Son of a bitch!"

Panicked, I overcorrected, sending the car into a spin. I fought to regain control and managed to keep the car from slamming into the trees but not in time to miss the jagged tree stump that jutted up from among the thick ferns lining the road. The impact rocked the Jag as first one tire and then another raked across it.

I sent up a juicy string of curses as my car jolted to a stop. "God-*damn* it," I yelled, slamming the heel of my hand against the steering wheel. I peered through the windshield at the light I'd seen earlier. Suddenly a hundred yards seemed miles away.

The rain was still pouring down, but I couldn't just sit there and wait for it to stop. It was October and who knew how cold it would be here in the middle of nowhere now that night had fallen. I didn't even know if my father had sent me a coat. Of course, even if he had, by the time I rummaged around in the trunk for it, I'd be so drenched it wouldn't be worth a whole hell of a lot.

With a sigh, I realized I was just going to have to trudge through the rain until I reached the house and hope that someone was actually home. I turned off the car and grabbed the keys. Then, taking a deep breath, I threw open the car door and grimaced as the cold, stinging rain struck my face. I'd only gone a few feet before my clothes were soaked and hung heavy on my body, my skirt clinging to my legs and tangling around my ankles. My hair was matted to my face, the tips of my bangs hanging in my eyes. The wind continued to howl, chilling me to the bone.

Wondering where the hell my sunshiny optimism was now, I groaned and stomped through the mud, bitching a blue streak about my super-duper future totally ditching me. But then a sudden awareness of another presence prickled my skin beneath the chill of the rain, jolting me out of my pity party.

My head whipped toward the trees in time to see a hulking black form lunge from the underbrush. It landed squarely in front of me, startling a scream from me as I stumbled backward, narrowly avoiding its enormous claws.

What the hell?

I caught only a glimpse of the horrific, deformed features of the creature before I pivoted and bolted back to the car. Before I'd gone more than a few feet the creature bounded over my head and landed in front of me, once more blocking my path, a smug grin draping its terrifying maw of razor-sharp teeth.

Shit.

My mind raced, searching frantically for a spell to hurl at the winged beast, but I drew a blank as panic took over. Short on options, I sprinted toward the dense cover of the trees, hoping like hell that the massive creature wouldn't be so damned confident if he had to chase me on foot and making a mental note to thank Red personally for this unbelievable cluster fuck she'd gotten me into.

As I ran, I curled my hand into a fist and jerked my arm upward, calling upon my mastery of the surrounding flora. Instantly, tree roots sprung up from the ground. They snaked along the forest floor, tangling together behind me to create a barrier. But the creature broke through them with a roar that drowned out the thunder.

My panic rising, I muttered a spell under my breath, asking even more of the trees. By some miracle, they actually responded, the branches swaying and bending, hacking at the ground. I heard the creature let out a yelp from not too far behind me. He'd been hit—

hopefully hard enough to hold him off until I could put some distance between us.

But that would've been too easy.

I was just leaping from a rotting tree stump when a tree branch caught me around the waist and hurled me back toward the monster. I landed in a tangle of underbrush, but aside from a sore ass, was unharmed. I scrambled to my feet again and took off, now dodging the branches that were becoming even more brutal in their attacks.

"Not me, you idiots!" I yelled, rolling out of the way of a particularly vicious Douglas fir. "Him! The creature!"

But I might as well have been talking to a—well, a *tree*.

Now, not just the trees were on the attack but the ferns and moss were getting in on the action, wrapping themselves around my feet as I hoofed it through their wilderness home. Even my most basic magic—the magic I'd mastered as a child, for chrissake—was on the fritz.

Son of a bitch. It fucking figured.

My lungs burned, each rapid breath searing them with a million tiny flames as I blindly zigzagged through the wild growth of the forest, branches scratching my hands and face and tearing at my clothes as if working in tandem with the living nightmare pursuing me. The creature's massive body crashed through the underbrush behind me, bringing my doom closer and closer with each stride.

At the sound of my pursuer's angry snarl, I hiked up the hem of my skirt and ran faster, my biker boots digging into the thick bed of ferns that covered the forest floor, propelling me forward.

Shit, shit, shit.

I was losing ground fast.

Hoping the damned thing couldn't corner well, I dodged to my right and leapt over the rotting trunk of a fallen western hemlock and landed in mud that came up over my ankles. I tried to keep going, but the heavy muck sucked greedily at my feet as if it, too, had been affected by my jacked-up magic. With a strangled, panicked cry, I lifted my knees, my thighs burning with the effort, and managed to pull myself free.

I glanced over my shoulder and muttered a curse under my breath at the precious seconds the mud had cost me. I heard the beast gaining but still couldn't get a bead on it under the blanket of darkness that covered the moonless night. Unfortunately, my imagination filled in what my eyes couldn't see, which made my terror that much worse. My heart pounded, the furious thumping filling my ears like a staccato death march.

Lost and disoriented, I had no idea in which direction my car waited now. I tried to call upon the light nestled deep inside my soul, the fairy light that had been mine at birth by virtue of my parentage, hoping it could maybe at least guide me to safety without blowing something up. But the magic that had turned the woodland into a do-or-die obstacle course now failed me completely, fizzling out with a sputter. And I found only horror and hopelessness in its place.

Hot tears made their way to my cheeks as I felt the heavy presence of my pursuer just a few yards behind me. He was toying with me, forcing me to play this sadistic game before his final strike. I pumped my legs, my sobs catching in my throat as I waited for the searing heat of teeth or claws to pierce my flesh.

Closer. Closer.

Oh, God...

The great claws ripped into my side, tearing open my skin as it lifted me from my feet and flung me through the air in a high arc. I slammed into a tree and felt my ribs give with the impact. What little breath I still had shot out of me with a groan when I hit the ground. My head was still spinning as I tried to scramble to my feet, falling to my knees twice before righting myself. Thank God I was a Tale—if I'd been an Ordinary human, that blow alone could have killed me.

I put my hand to my side and felt the warm, sticky ooze rapidly growing under my sweater and tried to limp away, but the creature now had the scent of my blood and was prowling toward me. Its approach was no longer the rapid footfalls of a predator pursuing its prey but the slow, careful creep of a beast preparing for the kill.

Not yet ready to submit, I forced my feet to keep moving, trying desperately to ignore the hungry snuffling and snorting that warmed the autumn air around me.

"*No*," I growled, my vision beginning to blur. "Not like this. I'm *not* dying like this."

Just ahead of me, a wide ribbon of darkness wound through the ferns, cutting off my path. With my last ounce of strength, I sprinted forward and dove for the other side of the ravine, somehow clearing the yawning blackness below. But as I landed, my ankle twisted beneath me, sending a lightning bolt of pain up my leg and into my spine as the bone snapped with a sickening crunch.

The scream that erupted from deep in my gut burned my throat and set off an explosion of light in my head. I tried to drag myself forward but collapsed before I'd gone even a couple of feet.

It was over.

I was going to be torn apart here in the middle of nowhere by some winged demon-dog. I'd never have the chance to start over. I'd never have the chance to prove I was more than just a colossal failure in every regard—as a daughter, as a woman, as a fairy.

I couldn't believe my unbelievably shitty luck.

Shaking violently from the pain wracking my body, I lay there, the raindrops mixing with my tears as I sobbed and watched helplessly as pine needles gathered together, creating a thick rope that wound itself around my arms and torso, pinning me to the ground.

Briefly, I wondered how people would remember me after I was gone. Would they speak the name *Lavender Seelie* and think of the fairy godmother who'd once wielded almost unparalleled power and skill? Or would they remember only the screwed-up fairy who'd ruined their lives when that same power had betrayed her?

After several agonizing moments, I finally heard the creature leap across the ravine and snapped out of my last-minute pity party, fear and panic once more flooding my veins.

There was no point in trying to summon my magic now—it had deserted me, that was pretty freaking clear. I just hoped like hell my death would be quick.

The creature prowled toward me, its massive bulk a mercifully indistinct silhouette, and I swear I thought I heard it chuckle, the sound sending chills down my spine. Then from behind me came the whisper-soft padding of paws on the underbrush. In the next instant, a great white wolf leapt over me and slammed into the shadow-creature. The two rolled end-over-end in a tangle of claws and teeth, coming to rest with the wolf on top, its lips peeled back in a vicious snarl.

I turned my head for a better look just in time to see the wolf grab the creature's throat in its teeth. The beast's howl ended abruptly as the wolf gave a powerful shake of its head, tearing out a large section of the demon-dog's throat.

The wolf flung the chunk of flesh into the underbrush then cautiously padded toward me, its head down between its shoulders, sizing me up. As it came closer I realized it wasn't an ordinary timber wolf. This animal was easily twice the size of any wolf I'd ever seen and had a distinctly human intelligence shining in its eyes.

I didn't stand a chance.

It bit through the pine-needle rope and shook its head, scattering the needles all over the ground. The rest of the needles instantly fell away and the trees halted their brutal assault.

I raised a bloody, trembling hand, not sure if I'd just exchanged one predator for another. "Please," I managed to gasp between the quick, shallow breaths that were all my punctured lung would now allow. "Please . . ."

In response, a soft shimmering light encased the wolf, and where the beautiful creature had stood, now crouched a man, his ice-green eyes still glowing. As he gently lifted me into his arms, I cried out, pain engulfing me.

"It's all right," he said softly, cradling me against him. "You're safe now."

I looked up into the grim face of my rescuer, now recognizing him. How could I not when I'd seen his face on "Wanted" posters and in the *Tale* news so often over the centuries?

As pain and nausea sent me careening toward a dark abyss, his name drifted to me:

Seth Wolf.

Chapter 4

I blinked my eyes, slowly coming out of the thick fog that had enveloped me, obscuring half-remembered dreams of horrifying winged creatures and a beautiful white wolf.

I put a hand to my aching head and groaned, wondering how much I'd drunk to produce such a massive hangover. But then I remembered I hadn't had a drink in over a year. And as soon as *that* barrier of denial was breached, the rest came rushing back to me in a flood of graphic, bloody images.

With a gasp, I bolted upright, instantly regretting the sudden movement when a white hot lightning bolt of agony shot through my ribs. Closing my eyes against the pain for a moment, I pressed my hand to my side and swung my legs over the edge of the bed.

My brows snapped together in a frown.

Bed?

I looked down, confirming I was, in fact, sitting on a bed, my bare legs hanging over the edge, my toes just touching the hardwood floor. I smoothed my other hand over the down-filled duvet. It was simple but of decent quality.

Where the hell was I?

The last thing I remembered was looking up into a handsome face that was taut with concern.

But whose?

I slid the rest of the way off the bed, crying out as my right ankle raged against the sudden pressure. Tears sprang to my eyes, but I blew out a long breath and limped cautiously toward the bedroom door.

When I reached the threshold, I peeked around the doorframe, surveying what appeared to be a living room. The room was dark but for a fire in the hearth and a few oil lamps that cast a soft amber light upon the room. I hobbled out of the bedroom as quietly as I could, my heart pounding as I searched the thick shadows for any sign of my host.

Convinced I was alone, I let out a long, relieved sigh.

"How'd you find me?"

Startled by the sudden voice, I spun around, my weakened ankle giving out under me. I landed in an undignified—and half-naked—sprawl, cursing under my breath to keep from screaming. I groaned as I tried to right myself while struggling to keep the hem of the men's button-down I wore from completely destroying the modicum of modesty I had left.

I'd managed to push myself up into a sitting position when one strong arm slid behind my knees and another went gently around my waist. A moment later, I was settling onto a worn but sinfully comfy sofa.

"Sorry," the man said, his face unreadable as he stared down at me with those amazing green eyes. Even now they glowed a little in the light of the oil lamps, giving him the appearance of a predator. "Didn't mean to scare you."

"You're Seth Wolf," I blurted, scooting back a little on the sofa, the weight of his gaze making me uneasy. As if having a pissed-off prick of a prince and a vicious demon-dog after me wasn't bad enough, now I was trapped in the lair of what was rumored to be one of the most dangerous Tales in the Here and Now. How the hell had he come to be in the forest during the attack on me anyway? And, maybe more importantly, what was he planning to do with me now?

His eyes narrowed as if I was the one who was a threat. "Why were you looking for me?" he demanded, his shoulders hunching over a little, just enough to show me he was on his guard, ready to attack if provoked.

He was dressed only in jeans that sat low on his hips, giving me a good look at his lean physique. His beautifully sculpted bare chest rose and fell in a slow, even rhythm. He was on his guard all right, but he was in perfect control of every muscle, his body a potent weapon he could unleash the moment he perceived a threat.

"I wasn't looking for you," I said, my throat suddenly very dry. The effects of adrenaline pumping through my veins, no doubt. The sudden increase in the pace of my heartbeat had absolutely nothing to do with the primal sexiness of the man standing over me. Really.

"No one comes back here unless they're looking for me," he insisted. "And very few people know where I am. So how the hell did you find me?"

"Look," I said, pressing deeper into the pillows, "I had no idea you lived here. Trust me, if I *had* known I would've turned right back around. I'm not keen on being your next hot lunch, pal."

His face twisted into a grimace of fury and disgust. "Why the hell would I save your life if I was planning to kill you?"

I gave him a wry look. "Ever read *Hansel and Gretel*?"

He shook his head slowly with a bitter laugh. "Yeah, I've read it. In fact, I know them personally. But I can guarantee you, princess, if I wanted to take you down and gobble you up, you wouldn't even see it coming."

I blinked at him, wondering if that was a threat or just a statement of fact. Figuring I'd better try to smooth things out a little, I cleared my throat and lifted my chin a notch higher.

"Listen, thanks for saving my life and for not—you know—*eating* me and everything. I appreciate it. Now, if you just tell me where my clothes are, I'll be on my way."

"I burned them," he said. Before I could gasp in horror, he added, "They were shredded and soaked in blood. Except the boots. They're by the door."

I glanced toward the front door and saw my biker boots sitting on a mat, completely devoid of mud and looking as good as new. I frowned, curious as to why he'd bother cleaning them for me. "Uh, thanks, but I'll need more than your shirt and my boots to wear. And you'll need to call me a cab. Or a tow truck. My car blew a couple of tires."

He crossed his arms over his chest. "Phones are still down from the storm."

"Still?" I repeated. "How long was I out?"

"About twenty-four hours."

I gave him an irritated look. "Then use your cell phone."

"Don't have one."

"You've got to be kidding me," I muttered, swinging my legs off the couch. "This just gets better and better."

I stood up, careful of my ankle this time, but before I could take a step, he was blocking my path, his body so close to mine I could feel the warmth of his skin. I had to resist the urge to reach out to him and let my fingertips experience that warmth a little more up close and personal.

"Sit down," he ordered, his eyes flashing.

"Excuse—" I coughed when my voice caught in my throat. I gave myself a mental shake and tried again. "*Excuse* me?"

He leaned down a little closer, his expression growing harsh. "Sit. Down."

"Screw you," I spat, giving him a hard shove—which really was totally pointless. He didn't even budge. But I was hoping it at least showed I wasn't about to take orders from *him*, of all Tales. "I'm leaving."

I tried to go around him, but he stepped with me, his arm circling my waist when I wobbled on my feet. I struggled to escape his hold, but his grip only tightened, making me wince when my ribs protested.

"I didn't spend five hours massaging your shattered ankle to make sure it healed right just to have you overdo it and fuck it up again," he ground out through clenched teeth, his face so close to mine that tendrils of his longish, wavy, golden brown hair tickled my cheek. "Now sit that pretty ass down on the couch before I tie you to it."

Something about the smoldering fire in his eyes and the heat of his body pressed into mine made me think that being tied to his sofa could be one hell of a fun idea. But then I reminded myself that this was the same guy who not so long ago had been the suspect in the most brutal Tale slayings in the Here and Now. Even though he'd been cleared of those murders, he wouldn't have been a suspect in the first place unless he'd done something at some point to get on the FMA's watch list.

So, instead of taking him up on the tantalizing offer of a little experimental bondage, I dropped back down on the sofa and sent a furious glare up at him.

With a shake of his head, he sat down next to me and pulled my legs onto his lap, careful not to jar my ankle. Then, with gentle hands, he began to massage the bruised and swollen skin.

"Your ankle seems to be pretty much back to normal," he told me, his tone clipped. "In a day or two you should be able to walk without too much pain."

Trying to distract myself from the way his hands slid so tenderly up my calf and back down to my ankle, I asked, "So, why aren't you naked?"

His hands instantly stilled and his brows shot up. "Pardon?"

"Oh God, that's not what I meant!" I cried, the words spilling out in a rush. Humiliated, I put a hand over my eyes and grimaced as I amended, "I was just curious why you were still fully clothed when you transformed back in the woods. Most werewolves I've met have to strip down before they go all wolfy."

He frowned at me. "You don't know my story?"

I shrugged. "Just what everyone else knows about you and Red Little. Why?"

He turned his attention back to my ankle, his brows pinched together still. "I wasn't born a werewolf," he said after a moment. "I was cursed. My transformations are magical—not natural."

I waited for the rest of the explanation but none came. Fortunately, being a magical being, I understood the distinction. It was no different from when I transformed one creature into another—every part of the creature was absorbed into the spell and reverted back to the original form when the transformation was reversed. I studied him for a moment, curious to know the rest of the story behind his curse, the mere mention of which had so blatantly deepened his already dark mood. But sensing he was eager to move on to another topic, I asked, "So, what was that thing that attacked me anyway?"

He shrugged. "Don't know. A hellhound maybe."

"A hellhound?" I repeated, frowning. "Do you have a problem with those in this area?"

"No," he said, his own frown growing darker.

"Maybe it was summoned to find a lost soul," I suggested. "I've heard of the FMA sometimes using them for that purpose."

Seth shook his head. "Don't think so. We haven't had anyone pass in a long time."

I raked through my knowledge of hellhounds, trying to come up with some other reason for my attacker to be roaming around in the woods. "Perhaps it was looking for something else then—like a . . . a treasure of some sort—and I just stumbled into its path."

He grunted. "Maybe, but it looked to me like it was pretty intent on taking you out—not trying to just scare you away." He pegged me with a pointed look. "Anyone you know who'd want you dead?"

I swallowed hard, wondering where on the list to start. James, of course, was the first one who came to mind. And I knew he'd had his fair share of shady deals with wicked witches and nefarious necromancers over the years when I'd balked at performing the darker magic he'd needed. But there was no way he could've found me that quickly!

Could he?

When I didn't immediately respond to his question, Seth turned his attention back to my ankle, my silence no doubt telling him all he needed to know. He rolled my foot, keeping the ankle from getting stiff. I winced, sucking in air through my teeth. In response, he muttered something under his breath.

"What was that?" I demanded.

He met my gaze and calmly blinked long, golden brown lashes at me. "I said you're being a baby."

I made an indignant noise in the back of my throat. "Well, if I'm such a bother, why didn't you just take me to a hospital instead of bringing me here so you could whine and bitch about taking care of me?"

He gave me a look that clearly conveyed I was a total moron. "If you hadn't noticed, I'm not living in the cradle of civilization. We don't even have an *Ordinary* hospital within an hour of here. The closest Tale clinic is in Portland, Oregon."

I felt my cheeks growing warm from both irritation and embarrassment. Of course there wouldn't be a Tale clinic in the area—the colony of Tales in The Refuge wasn't even officially recognized by the FMA. No wonder he thought I was an idiot.

Still.

"Well, there's no need to be an asshole about it."

His eyes flashed. "Maybe I wouldn't be an asshole about it if you'd show a little gratitude instead of acting like a spoiled brat."

I pressed my lips together, holding back the "eat me" I was tempted to throw back at him. Considering who I was talking to, it might have been misconstrued as an invitation. Instead I said, "All I'm saying is that there has to be some kind of healer around. You could have taken me there."

"I could have," he admitted. "But you probably would've bled to death by the time we'd gotten there." Before the shock of my near-death could sink in, he added, "Besides, I've taken care of worse. I've had my own fair share of injuries over the years, that's for damned sure."

"You don't strike me as the kind of guy who'd be stupid enough to sit around and wait to get shot," I told him, a little disappointed when he slipped out from under my legs and propped my ankle up on a plump pillow.

He gave me a bitter smile. "When you're hunted while both a wolf and a human, someone eventually gets lucky."

Something about the despondent resignation in his voice tugged at my heart. "Listen," I said on a long sigh, "I think we might have gotten off to a bad start. So let me try again. Thank you for saving me and for treating my wounds."

He stared at me as if trying to decide whether I was being sincere. Finally he said, "You're welcome."

I extended my hand, offering a truce. "By the way, my name is Lavender Seelie."

His face filled with disgust. "Seelie? You're a *fairy?*"

He spat the word as if it was acid on his tongue.

I blinked at him, retracting the hand he'd ignored anyway. "Yes, I'm a variety of fairy," I confirmed. "That term is technically just a catchall for various types of magical beings, though—*sidhe*, leprechauns, pixies. Why? Does that matter?"

He grunted. "It just figures. I try to be a nice guy and rescue a damsel in distress and she turns out to be a fucking fairy."

I couldn't help gaping at him. "I beg your pardon?"

He leapt to his feet and began to pace around the rug on the floor. "And not just *any* fairy, but I recognize the name. You're the same damn Tale who stranded us here in the first place."

"Well excuse the hell out of me!" I shot back. "If you have such a problem with my kind, why didn't you just leave me in the woods to die?"

He stopped and gave me a puzzled look as if wondering the same thing. "I didn't sense any powerful magic in you."

Nice. Rub it in.

"Besides," he added, "how was I supposed to know who you were? You don't *look* like a fairy."

I crossed my arms in a huff. "Well you don't *look* like a dickhead. Guess looks can be deceiving."

He cursed under his breath and pulled his hand down over his face.

"Hey, I get it," I told him. "You were cursed by someone magical and now your life is one big woe-is-me parade. You don't trust any Tales with magic? Fine. But, guess what, pal? Considering your track record, I can guaran-damn-tee that I don't trust you either."

He stared at me for a moment, his face blank. Then with a clenched jaw he ground out, "Are you hungry?"

"What?"

"Are you hungry?" he snapped. "Simple question."

"Are you inviting me to dinner?"

"Jesus, lady—I'm asking if you want some fucking food!"

"You mean, you aren't planning to toss me out on my 'pretty little ass' now that you know I'm a fairy?"

He sighed and sat down on the arm of the sofa. "Of course I'm not going to throw you out—you're injured. I'm not a monster."

I lifted a brow at him, letting him know the jury was still out on that one. When his eyes narrowed at me I said, "How are you planning to cook? I thought the power was out."

"Only the phones are down," he said. "I just like the oil lamps. Now, do you want something to eat or not?"

I shrugged. "I guess I could eat." But then a horrible thought struck me. I leaned forward a little and whispered, "Do you have to go kill something?"

He leaned toward me, narrowing his eyes. "No," he whispered back. "I actually keep food in the fridge. I've even been known to use a fork on occasion."

Nice, Lavender. Could you be more of a snobby bitch?

"I'm sorry," I stammered. "It's just that . . . well, you know . . ."

He rose from the couch and headed toward the kitchen area of his cabin, giving me a great look at his broad shoulders and trim waist. I hastily wiped my hand across my chin, making sure I wasn't drooling.

"You know," he called over his shoulder, "not everything you've heard about me is true."

I could relate, probably more than he realized. "Well, I've heard you're an incredible chef," I said, craning to see over the half-wall dividing the kitchen from the rest of the cabin as he bent to grab pots and pans from the cabinets. "And now that you've mentioned eating, I'm seriously hoping *that* part's true."

He straightened and arched a brow at me, his deep voice going a little raspy when he said, "It's *one* of my talents."

My stomach did a little flop and a very lonely—and extremely naughty—part of me couldn't help wondering if I'd have the chance to discover those talents firsthand. . . .

An hour later, Seth set a beautiful plate of poached salmon, wild rice, and steamed veggies in front of me and helped me scoot my chair closer to the table. Then he unfurled my napkin with a snap and draped it across my lap, his fingertips brushing ever so lightly across my thigh.

Feeling my face growing hot, I turned my eyes down to the plate and dug in. The flavors exploded on my tongue, so delicious I couldn't help the little moan that slipped past my lips.

"So were the rumors true?" he asked, watching me closely.

I nodded. "God, yes! This is incredible."

Satisfied that I was enjoying my meal, he sat down next to me and began to eat as well, his expression still stormy but growing calmer. When he'd finished off the majority of his dinner, he reached for his glass of wine and leaned back in his chair, regarding me closely.

"So, if you aren't here looking for me," he began, breaking the silence, "why *are* you here?"

I glanced at the glass of wine he'd set before me, temptation to give it a try making my hand shake a little when I reached for my glass of ice water instead. "I needed to get away from Chicago for a while," I told him with a shrug, not eager to share the sordid details. "Red thought The Refuge would be a good place for me to hang out for a while."

"Tess sent you?" he asked, frowning. When I nodded, he laughed, shaking his head. "I should've known."

"Should've known what?" I asked around a mouthful of baby carrots.

"You're not in The Refuge," he said, tossing his napkin on the table. "It's about five miles from here as the crow flies."

I shook my head, confused. "But she gave me an address. This is where the GPS brought me. It must be closer than that. She told me the person who lived at the address would look after me until I got on my feet again. She said it was a friend of hers—"

He offered me a tight grin and spread his arms. "Guess who."

"You've got to be kidding me," I said, my voice flat.

"Trust me, princess, I'm not thrilled about it either," he shot back. "I'm not exactly the nurturing type."

I thought about how tenderly he'd massaged my ankle, helping the bones slide back into place, which was so at odds with the harsh, detached person he seemed determined to be. Regardless of which was the true Seth Wolf and which was the construct, he'd made it pretty clear he was ready to be rid of me at the earliest opportunity.

I slumped a little in my chair. "I'm sorry. I'm sure the last thing you need is some half-assed-fairy-on-the-run dropping in on you." I wiped my mouth and set my napkin aside as I pushed my chair back. "I'll leave for The Refuge first thing in the morning."

He grabbed my arm as I got to my feet and held me there for a moment before finally lifting his eyes to me. "If Red sent you to me, I'm not going to turn you away," he assured me, his voice gruff. "I owe that woman one hell of a lot. I'm not about to turn her down if she needs a favor—even if she didn't bother to actually *ask* for one." When I opened my mouth to remind him how much he was supposed to hate me, he cut me off, adding, "Besides, I've got being on the run down to an art. My guess is Red didn't think there'd be anybody better than me to look out for you—at least for now."

My eyes stung with tears, whether from disappointment that I wasn't really at The Refuge yet or from the sudden pity in his eyes, I couldn't tell.

He stood and grasped my shoulders. "I'll look out for you like Red wants. I'll even do what I can to help you get set up in town. But it's probably best if you don't stick around me for too long—no matter what Red thinks."

I frowned at him. "Why's that?"

He sighed and released me, stepping back to put some distance between us. "Because trouble has a way of finding me. And I won't put anyone else at risk. Not ever again."

Chapter 5

When I awoke the next morning and limped into the living room I was surprised to see several suitcases stacked there. They didn't look familiar, but the monogram stitched on each clued me in that they were the ones my father had provided. At some point Seth must have dragged them all in from the trunk of my car.

"I thought you might want some breakfast," Seth said from the kitchen. "I hope you like bacon. I made a shitload of it."

I laughed a little and made my way to the table. "I love bacon. Thanks."

The table was already set with scones with clotted cream and blackberry jam and two steaming cups of coffee. A moment later, Seth brought over a serving dish of bacon and a plate containing what was the most beautiful omelet I'd ever seen.

"Dig in while I take a shower," he said, grabbing up one of the cups of coffee.

"You aren't going to eat with me?" I asked, wondering why I felt so disappointed.

"I ate a couple of hours ago," he explained. "I thought I'd let you sleep."

As he hurried off, I took a bite of my omelet and realized why he had been such a celebrated culinary talent back in Chicago. By the time he returned, I'd polished it off as well as half of the bacon he'd prepared and two of the delectable scones. I couldn't remember when I'd last eaten so much.

I took my time showering and slipping into my clothes. When I finally emerged from the bathroom, Seth was standing there waiting for me, his hands shoved deep in his pockets. He was wearing a deep green button-down over a Band of Skulls T-shirt, and when he looked up at me his eyes were even more vibrant than I'd remembered. The effect was devastating, damn it all. I wasn't sure how it was possible, but he actually looked as hot fully dressed as he did half-naked.

His gaze followed me as I grabbed my boots and sat down at the kitchen table to put them on. I winced as I tried to pull my boot over my still-healing ankle and paused, planning to give it a minute before trying again. But then I heard Seth sigh and he knelt before me, gently sliding my boot on and lacing it up for me.

"Not exactly a glass slipper," I mumbled, flushing a little.

"I'm not exactly Prince Charming," he muttered back, tying my laces in a double knot. When he finished buckling the straps, his hands paused, his fingertips lingering on my skin for just a moment too long. Then he abruptly rose to his feet and took my hand, pulling me up with him. "I have something for you."

When we reached the front door, he picked up a beautifully carved cane, the handle whittled into what looked like a sprig of lavender.

"Where did you find this?" I asked, smoothing my hand over the wood.

"I made it," he said. "When you were first recovering. Thought you'd probably need it for a little while."

I pointed to the design he'd carved. "What made you choose lavender? You didn't know my name yet."

He tapped his nose with his index finger. "No, but your scent is a mixture of lavender and spring sunshine. It's not strong like perfume, but it's there." He then motioned toward the door, offering me a smile that was surprisingly shy. "Your chariot awaits."

When I saw the vehicle Seth intended me to ride in, I tried hard
not to look too appalled. "This is a pickup truck," I pointed out, hoping my voice didn't sound disdainful.

He opened the door, which groaned and squeaked in protest.
"Yep. Climb in."

I surveyed the numerous dings and dents in the truck body—the
rust spots that edged the tire wells, the peeling white paint that had
gone dull with age—and couldn't quite help wrinkling my nose. "Are
you sure it runs?"

"Of course it runs," he shot back. "Now, if you want to go to The
Refuge, get your ass in the truck."

I blinked at him, astonished at his audacity. "I beg your pardon?"

"Either get in the truck or flitter-fly your way to town," he said,
wagging his fingers at me.

I felt the heat rising in my cheeks. "I can't flitter-fly my way to
town," I mumbled peevishly, wagging my fingers back at him. "I lost
my wings."

"You *lost* your wings?" he repeated. "How'd you manage that?
Aren't they attached or something?"

"I didn't *misplace* them," I snapped. "They were removed as a
punishment after the genie incident. Didn't you notice that when you
were, you know, cleaning me up the other day? I can't imagine you
got me out of my clothes and into your shirt with your eyes closed."

Now it was *his* turn to flush, which was disarmingly sexy.

"I've never seen a fairy naked," he grunted. "How the hell would I
know what your wings are supposed to look like?"

"You wouldn't," I chuckled, enjoying his discomfort immensely
and hoping I could figure out a way to embarrass him again just to
catch another glimpse of his ears turning red. "They're made of the
very air around us—only other Seelies can see them."

He gave me an exasperated look. "Then why even ask?"

I gave him a smile that I knew was a little flirty. "I was just curious how closely you'd looked."

He flushed a darker shade of red.

Success!

"Like you said," he muttered, "I couldn't have taken care of you
with my eyes closed."

I blinked at him. "And?"

He suddenly had the look of a cornered animal. "You know you're beautiful," he said, the words tumbling out over one another. "You don't need me to say it."

My heart fluttered. "I was only wondering if you'd noticed the scars on my back," I stammered, a little breathless. "I wasn't insinuating . . . I didn't mean . . ."

As my words trailed off, his guarded gaze met and held mine for a long moment, an awkward, tense silence falling between us.

"Anyway," I finally said, my voice barely above a whisper, "my point is I can't fly."

He abruptly looked away, then cleared his throat a couple of times. "Well," he said, squaring his shoulders, "I guess you have no choice but to ride in the truck then." He opened the door wider and bent at the waist, sweeping his arm toward the inside of the cab. "World's waiting on you, princess."

Whatever it was that had happened between us just a moment before dissipated in an instant. "Stop calling me that," I spat. "I'm not a princess." But as soon as I said it, I had to amend, "Well, okay—actually, I *am* technically a princess because my mom is Queen of the Seelies, but I haven't lived like a princess in over two centuries."

He raised his brows, evidently begging to differ.

I huffed. "Okay, fine, so I've been living with royalty since then, but I wasn't really—" I bit off my words, thinking of all the luxuries I'd enjoyed with the Charmings. Couldn't really deny I'd been living the high life even if it was actually a gold-plated piece of shit. "Just get out of my way already."

I hiked up my skirt and tried to haul myself up, but between the cane and my ankle, I was having a rough time of it.

"Want some help?" he drawled. In spite of his offer, I got the impression he much preferred watching me struggle.

"No!" I barked. "I'm not totally helpless, you know. I *can* take care of myself now and then, thank you very much."

I tossed the stick inside and tried again, this time hopping right up—courtesy of a hard shove from a certain werewolf's hands on my ass. The look I gave him in response just made him chuckle.

We'd driven a couple of miles in silence before I finally said, "Sorry for being, you know, *testy* back there."

"Testy?" he repeated. "Not the word I would've used."

"You know, I'm trying to apologize," I huffed. "If you could stop being an ass for two seconds, I'd tell you that I didn't mean to bite your head off earlier!"

He stared straight ahead, not saying a word. For a moment, I wondered if I'd offended him. But then he glanced my way with a look of feigned innocence. "What?"

"You have nothing to say?" I asked, not bothering to keep the exasperation out of my voice.

He blinked at me. "About what?"

"About my apology for biting your head off."

He shrugged. "I don't mind a little biting now and then," he drawled. "As long as it's in the right places."

I blinked at him, trying to ignore the thrill that lanced through the center of me at his words. "Are you . . . are you *flirting* with me?" I asked, my voice a little breathier than I would've liked.

He sent a sheepish glance my way. "No," he said quickly, looking decidedly uncomfortable. "No, of course not. Why would I be flirting with you?"

My God, he was incorrigible. I was beginning to see why Red had fallen so hard for the guy back in the day. One moment he was cold and harsh; the next he was so adorable I wanted to jerk the pickup over to the side of the road and cover his face with kisses. Considering all the guy had no doubt been through, I could understand the cold and harsh part, but it was when he let me have little glimpses of what he probably once was that he was both charming and heartbreaking.

From my very first glimpse of Seth, I'd seen he was oh-my-God handsome in a rugged, formidable sort of way. But there was a vulnerability there just below the surface that was immensely intriguing. It was something he tried to hide behind a gruff exterior, but it was as if the true gentleness of his soul couldn't help peeking out now and then. As I sat there studying the harsh lines of his profile, from his long eyelashes, to the slight hook of his nose, to his sharp chin, I suddenly didn't want to let him push me away. I wanted to know more, see more of the man Seth Wolf truly was. And I wanted him to see me—down to the deepest, darkest recesses of my heart, for good or ill.

What the hell was that *all about?*

Pushing aside thoughts that I knew were all kinds of crazy, I cleared my throat a couple of times. "Seth, I—" Suddenly, my stomach plummeted at warp speed, cutting off my words and threatening to make me yack right there inside the truck cab. I groaned, doubling over. "Stop the truck."

Seth whipped the truck over to the side of the road and threw it into park, a dark frown creasing his brow. "I sense it, too."

I looked around, not entirely sure what had sounded my extrasensory alarm. There was magic nearby, that's all I knew. And it was powerful. Dark. Forbidden.

Without a word, I opened the truck door and slid down, taking my cane with me. Seth was at my side in an instant. He sniffed the air, then cursed under his breath. "Death," he announced. "Recent, too. Maybe only about eight hours old."

"But not a Tale," I muttered, my hand coming up to grip his bicep. "Otherwise Nate Grimm would be here."

We headed toward the source, Seth keeping me tucked a little behind him, his arm held out in front of me as if to shield me from harm.

"Son of a bitch," he hissed suddenly, burying his nose in the crook of his elbow.

I caught sight of the body at the same moment and stumbled back a few feet, completely shocked by what I saw.

Lying in the ditch not far from the road was a nude man, his body carved up like a coroner's botched autopsy. He'd been completely disemboweled from the looks of things, and there were crude markings all over his skin as if the killer had taken a dull knife to him, carving designs into his flesh. There was so much blood, though, it was tough to see if there'd been any sort of purpose to the designs or if they'd been just random cuts to torture the victim before finally putting an end to his misery.

"Jesus," Seth breathed. "What the hell?"

"Could the hellhound have done something like this?" I whispered.

Seth shook his head. "They tear you apart, they don't slice and dice."

"We need to report this to the FMA," I told him, forcing down the bile that rose in my throat as I backed away.

"Not the FMA," Seth argued. "Not yet. I'll call it in to the sheriff of The Refuge."

When we reached the truck, Seth snatched up the CB, calling in the murder to whoever was on the other end. Not twenty minutes later, a nondescript black SUV pulled up behind the truck, and a tall, barrel-chested man in black fatigues and plain black ball cap got out. He swaggered over to us, his massive biceps straining the arms of his black T-shirt. When he reached the truck he took off his sunglasses and pegged Seth with a suspicious glare.

"Wolf," he drawled, looking down his nose. "Hear you called in a dead body."

"Thought you'd want to know about it," Seth told him, his shoulders visibly tensing up.

"Am I going to have any reason to drag your ass in?" the man asked.

"He didn't do this," I interjected, stepping closer to Seth. "He's been looking after me for the past couple of days. The man in the ditch has only been dead a few hours."

"And who might you be?" the man asked, his eyes narrowing.

"My name is Lavender Seelie—"

He guffawed, cutting across my words. "Well, I'll be damned! Never thought I'd see you in these parts, Ms. Seelie."

I glanced at Seth, who just shrugged his shoulders.

"I'm sorry," I stammered. "Do I know you?"

The man held out a massive paw of a hand. "Name's Tom Piper. Well, *Sheriff* Tom Piper now." When I tentatively shook his hand, he explained, "You once helped me out of a bit of a situation back in Make Believe when I stole a pig to feed my family and was about to be beat all to hell by the villagers—"

"Oh, you're *that* Tom!" I cried, making the connection. "Tom, Tom, the Piper's Son. I remember you now. Wow—last time I saw you, you were just a skinny, scrawny little guy." I surveyed the towering, burly bear of a man whose handsome face and kind gray eyes were hardly recognizable as the same teenage boy I'd rescued all those centuries before.

He pumped my hand enthusiastically. "It's so good to see you again, Ms. Seelie. I never got the chance to thank you properly for all you did. If there's ever anything I can do—"

"How about you take a look at the stiff in the ditch?" Seth interrupted, his tone bringing Tom up short.

I shot Seth a chiding glance, then gave Tom's hand a final squeeze. "We should let you get back to work. Why don't you and I catch up later over coffee or something, Tom?"

"That'd be right nice, Ms. Seelie," he said. Then he went with Seth to take a look at the body.

A few minutes later, Seth returned and helped me into the truck without a word, sinking even deeper into his surliness. We rode the rest of the way in silence until we reached the edge of a little town that looked like it had been transplanted directly from the pages of a fairytale along with us.

There appeared to be just one main street running through the town with several smaller streets that branched off along the way. Numerous brightly colored clapboard buildings crowded in along the tree-lined route, squeezing in among one another to maximize the limited space.

Seth pulled into a parking spot in front of a particularly colorful Victorian-style building painted yellow and orange and gray with intricate white latticework that reminded me of the distinctive row houses I'd seen in San Francisco on a trip I took with Cindy several years before. On the storefront window was painted the name of the business: DAS GINGERBREAD HAUS.

I glanced at Seth. "You can't possibly be hungry again."

"I'm not here to eat," he grumbled. "I have to go to work."

"You work here?" I don't know why it hadn't occurred to me that he might have a job, responsibilities other than me to deal with.

He nodded then glanced up and down the street, looking a little uncomfortable. "Look, I don't know what you were planning to do once you got here. . . ."

I shrugged. "Neither do I, frankly. Go ahead and do what you need to do. I guess I can just take a look around or something."

His gaze flicked down to my ankle.

"Don't worry." I laughed. "I'll take it easy. The cane helps. A lot."

He smiled at this and nodded. "All right. But stop back in the restaurant now and then. Let me know you're okay."

"Got it." When he continued to stare at me, his brow furrowed in a frown, I offered him a smile. "I'll be fine, Seth. It's broad daylight." I gestured with my arm at the businesses beginning to open up for the morning. "There are plenty of people around if I need anything."

He put his hands on his hips, surveying me a moment longer. "Are you sure?"

"Yes!" I insisted. "Now go on. Really."

He pressed his lips together, then stepped forward and took my hand. He turned my palm up and placed the keys to his pickup in it. "If you get too tired, take my truck and go back to my cabin."

I didn't have the heart to tell him there was no way in hell I'd drive that piece of shit to his cabin. I'd rather hitch a ride with the Boogeyman. And that dude's one creepy son of a bitch.

Instead, I curled my fingers around the keys and gave him a tight smile. "Absolutely."

He smoothed his thumb across my closed fist and edged a little closer as if there was something more he wanted to say. But then he gave me a terse nod and went inside the restaurant, leaving me standing alone on the picturesque little street and wishing like hell that he'd come back and stand that close again.

I knew I was grinning like an idiot as I started making my way slowly along the sidewalk, peeking in store windows as I went. I was probably three blocks down when a squat little house with chipping white paint and crooked shutters across the street caught my eye. Next to the front door was a little hanging sign that read: THE DAILY TATTLETALE. J. G. SQUIGGINGTON, PUBLISHER.

"No way." I chuckled, amused at the irony of finding the secret location of the tabloid newspaper that had brought me to The Refuge in the first place. Of course it would be here! Where else would Mr. Squiggington be able to safely publish his rag without outraged Tales showing up on his doorstep demanding retractions and apologies for sharing private—and often damaging—information about them?

It was as if destiny had stepped in and showed me what I was supposed to do here in The Refuge. I'd needed a sign and I'd received one. Literally, as it turned out.

A few moments later, I was letting myself in the front door of the *Daily Tattletale*'s office, determined to meet face-to-face the man who'd changed my life. I don't know what I thought I'd find inside—scads of reporters busily pounding out sensationalized stories about the Tale bon ton? Whatever I'd been expecting, it sure as hell wasn't what I was looking at now.

In the little sitting room were a couple of mismatched, dilapidated armchairs and a ragged, threadbare area rug that looked like it might have been on the floor of a bank lobby maybe a hundred years ago but had been stored in a moth-ridden attic for the better part of its life. And there were no reporters anywhere to be seen. In fact, there didn't appear to be anyone there at all.

"Hello?" I called, beginning to wonder if anyone was even in the house.

I heard a soft, feminine twitter and a moment later, a busty bottle-blonde tottered in on stiletto heels, hastily buttoning her blouse. Her skirt was so tight it was a miracle she was able to move her legs at all. But maybe the fact that her skirt was hiked up too high to have risen there on its own afforded her a little more mobility than usual.

And, I realized, she was an Ordinary. Each Tale has a particular . . . *vibe* . . . that is instantly recognizable to another Tale. It wasn't even something we had to look for—it was either there or it wasn't. That was how we could pick each other out in a crowd or know when one of us had come over. She didn't have the vibe and so was completely and totally Ordinary—and completely out of place in a town full of Tales. How the hell had she ended up *here* of all places?

"May I help you?" she asked, a little breathlessly.

"Who the hell is it, Brie?" came a shout from the other room. "It better be goddamn important!"

I started to back toward the door. "You know, I'll just come back another time."

The blonde rolled her eyes. "Don't worry about him," she whispered, waving away my concerns. "He's always a little grumpy until he gets his morning nookie."

"Wow," I said, not really sure what else to say.

She giggled. "I know! So, how can I help you, sugar?"

"Really," I demurred. "I can come back later. I was just going to introduce myself to Mr. Squiggington. I've been writing for his paper for the last year or so, and—"

"Jesus Christ, Brie! Who the fuck is it?"

Brie rolled her eyes and grabbed my hand, pulling me after her. "C'mon. You might as well meet him now. He won't let it go until he finds out who's here."

She dragged me down the hall to what had probably been the master bedroom at some point in the house's history but was now an office, complete with a massive desk and leather high-back executive's chair that would've made William Randolph Hearst green with envy.

Sitting in the chair was a lanky, fresh-faced teenager, his black hair slicked straight back, a thick cigar held tight in his teeth. "Who the hell is this?" he demanded around the cigar. Then, not waiting for an answer from Brie, he pegged me with a narrowed gaze. "Who the hell are you?"

"I'm Lavender Seelie," I said, still a little baffled that the person behind the infamous publication looked barely old enough to shave. "I...uh..."

"Spit it out, honey," he grumped. "Ain't got all day."

"I've been writing a column for you," I blurted. "The weekly gossip column."

His mouth turned down in a contemplative frown. "No shit?" He waved Brie out of the room, then gestured to the wooden chair across from his desk. "Have a seat."

I hobbled over and sat on the edge of the chair, not quite sure I wanted to settle onto it completely for fear of what it might have been used for besides sitting. "I, um, I'm new to The Refuge, and when I saw your sign I wanted to come in and introduce myself."

He grunted. "Not quite what you imagined, I bet."

I gave him a tight smile. "Not exactly."

"Yeah, well, trust me—I'm not what I imagined either." He stubbed out his cigar in an ashtray at his elbow. "You have any idea what it's like to look like I'm a fucking fifteen-year-old kid? I was twenty-five when I outted that stupid fucking emperor for prancing around naked, and the dumbasses who told my story called me a kid. A kid! Didn't matter to them that it wasn't true as long as they got their story. Who's gettin' the last laugh now, eh?"

I forced a little chuckle, feeling guilty that I'd made the same assumption based on his appearance.

"Damn straight," he said, punctuating his words with a tight nod. "Can't do shit about this baby face, though, no matter what I try. Do you have any idea how hard it is to get laid when women think you're just this side of puberty? Took me months to convince Brie to sit on my face."

My eyes went wide at the *seriously* unwanted information. "Oh. God." I lurched to my feet, ready to bolt for the door. "You know, it was great to meet you, Mr. Squiggington, but I think I'll just—"

"So, you got a job yet?" he cut in.

I blinked at him. "No."

"Probably gonna need one," he said, opening his humidor and taking out another cigar. He rolled it between his fingers then brought it to his nose, inhaling deeply before continuing. "You can work for me. Pay sucks, but it'd probably be enough to rent you a room at Old Lady Patterson's place. She's got a shit pot full of kids, but at least she's not living in a fucking shoe anymore, you know what I'm sayin'?"

My mouth opened and closed as I tried to figure out how to respond to his proposal without running away screaming. "Thank you for the very kind offer," I said at last, "but I kind of cut myself off from my sources. Permanently. I don't think I'd be able to supply the same kind of stories I did before."

"Piss on that," he said with a shrug. "That piece of shit tabloid I print is just to pay the bills."

I pressed my lips together to keep from asking how well that was working out for him.

"My thing is hardcore investigative reporting," he continued.

"I've got something in the works right now, gonna knock the Tale world on its ass. But I can't follow leads if I'm stuck here behind my desk. I'm already too busy making up shit for the *Tattletale,* and now these fuckwits want a town paper? Fuck off!"

I jerked back a little at his vehemence. "Mr. Squiggington—"

"Let's cut the bullshit and get right down to it," he interrupted, leaning forward and wagging his cigar at me. "I need someone to cover the news here in The Refuge. Nothing too exciting. Probably a bar fight now and then. Or maybe an argument over trash collection or some other tedious shit like that. But, hey, if they're buying, I'm selling, you know what I mean?"

I shook my head a little, baffled by the entire experience. "Uh . . ."

"If it's too boring, just make some shit up," he continued. "No one will know the difference—and it might liven things up a bit around here."

"I'm not going to lie, Mr. Squiggington," I insisted.

"Fine," he said with a shrug. "Be a Goody Two-shoes and stick to the truth. But be sure to tell it like a lie or no one'll believe it."

I started to nod but couldn't quite bring myself to, and I felt my brows furrowing at the decidedly strange conversation.

"So, what do you say?" he demanded, snipping off the end of his cigar. He stuck it in his mouth and lit it with the flick of his engraved silver lighter. "You want a job or what?"

I quickly mulled over his offer. J. G. Squiggington was a lewd, irascible, unscrupulous letch, but he hadn't batted an eye when he'd heard my name. He had to know my history as well—if not better— than anyone else, and yet he'd offered to give me a job before I'd even hinted that I needed or wanted one. There had to be something re- deemable beneath Mr. Squiggington's rather sleazy exterior. And be- sides, it's not like I had many other options. I was in what was pretty much the Tale equivalent of the Witness Protection Program—except I wasn't entirely sure how protected I would be here or anywhere else if FMA Director Al Addin decided to throw my ass in prison for a while to teach me a lesson about shrinking the penis of a fellow Tale. I'd certainly never call someone a "little dick" again when my magic was acting up—that was for damned sure!

"All right, Mr. Squiggington," I said, deciding to do what I could to fit in at The Refuge and blend in like I'd failed to do among the Ordinaries. "I'll give it a go. On a *trial* basis."

"Great," he said, pulling open his desk drawer. He tossed a small spiral notebook on the desk. "Here you go. There's a town meeting tomorrow night at seven o'clock. Should be boring as shit. Have fun."

Chapter 6

I had a spring in my step despite my limp as I made my way back to the sidewalk. I couldn't believe it—I'd been concerned about how I would be received in The Refuge because of my history, but so far I'd run into an old friend who was also the law in town and had been given a job.

And then there was Seth.

I still wasn't sure what to make of him. I just knew I couldn't wait to tell him about my new responsibilities. The thought of him possibly even being *proud* of me left me grinning like an idiot. And more than a little . . . fluttery. I almost felt like I could fly again even without the benefit of my wings. I mean, my God—how long had it been since I'd actually given anyone a reason to be *proud* of me?

My unexpected jumble of emotions regarding Seth Wolf also left me more than a little distracted. So distracted, in fact, I didn't even notice the little tyke who ran right in front of me. I bumped into him, sending him tumbling onto the sidewalk, and almost joined him when I stumbled quickly to keep from trampling him.

His angry wail tore at my heart. "Oh, honey, oh," I cooed, kneeling down beside him. "I'm so sorry. Are you okay? Where's your mommy?"

He looked up at me with wide, tear-filled eyes, his bottom lip poking out in an adorable little pout. "She's in the store," he hiccupped, pointing at the window of a butcher shop. "She won't let me go in there."

Probably for good reason.

"Well," I said with a smile, "how about I walk you down there to wait for her? I'm guessing she'll be looking for you."

He nodded and got to his feet, slipping his chubby little hand into mine, looking up at me through long, dark lashes. "My name's Gareth," he said, his tears now forgotten. "What's yours?"

"My name is Lavender," I told him, grinning down at the little guy, who was maybe five years old, and wondering if a more adorable child had ever been born. He was dressed in short pants and jacket like the children in Make Believe often wore, reminding me so much of home, it was as if I'd never left.

"You're very pretty, Lavender," he chirped, skipping beside me now. "You look like a princess."

"I *am* a princess," I told him in a faux whisper. "A *fairy* princess."

His already wide eyes went even wider and his hand tightened around my fingers with barely restrained excitement. "Really?" he gasped. "Mommy says we don't have any princesses in The Refuge. But I told her there had to be a princess somewhere 'cause I'm a dragon slayer, and everybody knows a dragon slayer needs a princess to rescue!"

"It's a good thing I came along then," I told him.

At that moment, a woman in a decidedly antiquated long yellow dress with teal piping and a matching bonnet exited the butcher shop and glanced up and down the street, clearly panicked, but her expression changed to one of relief when she saw Gareth. She rushed forward, and dropped to her knees in front of the boy, hugging him and covering his face with kisses.

"I was so worried when I looked out the window and didn't see you," she admonished, her voice carrying a very distinct Make Believe accent. "Where did you go?"

"I wanted a sweet," he said, his eyes beginning to brim with tears again.

She kissed him once more, then turned her eyes up to me. "Thank you for walking him back to the store," she said. "I have such a problem with him wandering off!"

"My pleasure," I told her, winking at Gareth. "He's a darling boy."

She lovingly smoothed his auburn curls. "Yes, he is," she said softly. "He's all I have. My husband did not come over with me."

"I'm so sorry," I said, meaning it.

In all the years since the initial relocation, no one had ever been able to figure out why some Tales came over and others didn't. The heart-rending pain this caused to those affected by my screwup was something that kept me awake at night. On the worst nights, I could still hear the horrific wails of sorrow I'd witnessed that first day. The grief of my fellow Tales still haunted me, an omnipresent phantom of guilt that reminded me of the harm I'd caused. For decades I'd tried to blame the genie for everything that had happened, claiming to be just as much of a victim as the rest. But in my heart, I knew the truth. And trying to escape my conscience had driven me to the bottom of a bottle. I could only imagine the toll it took on those who'd actually lost the ones they loved.

"Have you been here long?" I asked.

The woman stood and smoothed the front of her dress, her manner becoming rather distracted. "I cannot say," she replied, rather dazedly. Her gaze darted around the streets that were growing a little busier now that the morning was wearing on. "I really . . . well, I have lost track of the days. I sometimes am a little confused, you see. I miss my husband so desperately. . . . He isn't here, you know. I haven't seen him in a while. . . ."

I frowned, sensing something off about her demeanor. Her absent-mindedness made me glance toward Gareth, who was even now following a fat spider as it crawled down the curb. "Perhaps you need someone to help you look after Gareth," I suggested, nodding toward him. "He seems like a busy boy."

She nodded, her gaze vaguely darting toward the boy but not noticing his growing distance from her. She gave me a slight smile, then pressed a hand to her cheek. "I think . . . I think I may need to lie down," she murmured. "I am feeling very warm."

I narrowed my eyes, taking in her flushed cheeks and noticing for the first time the glassy, listless look in her eyes. It was a look I'd seen too many times to count. She was hopped up on fairy dust, probably taken at first as a mild sedative to help her cope with her relocation. She was clearly an addict now. Her listlessness and unfocused gaze made perfect sense. She was going through the first stages of withdrawal. If she didn't get a fix soon, there was no telling what kind of hell might break loose.

"Could I help you home, Mrs. . . .?"

"Peep," she said, beginning to walk in the opposite direction from her son. "Bo Peep."

"Nice to meet you," I told her, forcing the irritation out of my voice. I took hold of her arm and gently turned her around, guiding her toward where Gareth was now squatting, watching a line of ants cross the sidewalk. "My name is Lavender Seelie, and I—"

She abruptly halted and turned her unfocused gaze on me. "Lavender Seelie?"

I nodded, glad she was having at least a few lucid moments.

"This is your fault," she said, her voice a hushed monotone. "You did this to me."

I blinked at her, taken off-guard by the sudden switch in her attitude toward me. "I know," I told her, not able to deny the charge. "I'm so very sorry. It was a horrible accident."

She pulled her arm from my grasp. "An accident?" she repeated, her voice growing louder. "An *accident?* You ruined my life! You ruined *everyone's* life!"

Out of the corner of my eye I saw a head peek out the door of the nearest store. "I can't apologize enough for what you have been through," I said, trying to keep my voice even. "I know this hasn't been easy—"

"You have no idea!" she shrieked, her voice edged with hysteria. "How could you possibly know what it's been like? I lost *everything*! *Everything!"*

People were coming out onto the streets now, eager to see what was going on as Bo Peep hurled not-unwarranted accusations at me. Knowing well how dangerous a situation like this could become, I tried to edge away, but bumped into something and glanced over my shoulder to see several people had gathered behind me, cutting off any escape route.

"Mommy, what's wrong?" I heard Gareth ask. "Why are you sad?"

"Ask this *horrible, evil* woman," she screeched. She was shaking now, her eyes wild. It was tough to determine which was more at work—her heartbreak or the fairy dust.

Gareth turned his dark eyes up to me, his look of betrayal cutting me to the core. "But I thought you were a princess?"

Ah, God.

"That's Lavender Seelie," Bo Peep announced, pointing an accusing finger at me, her hand trembling violently. "She's the one who did this to us! She's the one who ripped our lives apart!"

I glanced around at the faces in the crowd, beginning to feel that particular brand of uneasiness that went along with being stuck in the middle of a situation that could go disastrously wrong at any moment.

"You don't belong here," came a deep, angry voice that held the hint of a German accent. The speaker was a rotund man with thinning blond hair and a florid complexion, his beady eyes reminding me of a rat's.

"Get out before we make you get out," ordered another member of the crowd, a woman this time, her pretty, heart-shaped face twisting with rage.

"I'm sorry," I said, my voice a little weaker than I would have liked. "I never meant to hurt anyone. It was all a mistake. Please, I came here to start over, just like you."

"Not like us!" spat a towering man in a flannel shirt, denim overalls, and work boots. He took a menacing step forward, sending a panicked spike of adrenaline through my body.

Before I could stop it, a rush of magic burst forth, shattering the street lamp nearest me and showering the street with shards of glass. The crowd covered their heads with a collective, startled yelp and backed off a little.

"She's attacking us!" an elderly woman charged, grabbing Bo Peep and Gareth and dragging them back a few feet.

"No, no!" I said in a rush. "I swear, it was an accident. Please, I wouldn't hurt any of you intentionally—"

My words were cut off as a robin perched nearby exploded with a startled tweet and a puff of feathers. Then another—a blackbird—exploded, causing those present to gasp in horror and revulsion.

"Jesus Christ!" someone cried.

Oh, shit.

I was totally losing it. The stress and fear of the situation were taking control. I had to get out of there before one of the Tales standing too close burst apart like the birds and the lamp posts.

"Look, look," I said, dropping down and gathering up the mass of feathers. "I can fix it. It's fine. See."

The feathers came together slowly in a horrifying amalgamation of brown and black feathers and tiny legs in all the wrong places. "Oh, God, oh, God," I muttered, as both beaks began to chirp in frantic, confused cries that were pitiful and nightmarish at the same time.

A little girl in the crowd screamed and began to cry, "Mommy, Mommy, make her stop!"

"It's okay," I said, holding up my hands to quiet her. "I can fix it! Really, I—"

But before I could try to rectify the hot mess of horror that would no doubt haunt the nightmares of all those present for years to come, a viselike hand grabbed my upper arm and jerked me to my feet. It was the farmer in the flannel shirt and overalls. Another townsperson grabbed my other arm and together they began dragging me from the sidewalk into the street.

"Stop, stop!" I cried, struggling to break free, the cane Seth had made me falling from my grasp. "You don't understand. If I panic I can't control my magic. It'll become worse! Let me go! Please, I don't want to hurt you!"

"Let her go!" I heard Gareth yell. A moment later, he rushed forward, brandishing my cane, and whacked it against the farmer's shins.

The farmer instinctively swung his arm, catching Gareth across the cheek and sending him sprawling. Rage fueled my magic like white-hot lightning. Bolts of purple flame shot out in wild, zigzag arcs, burning the hands of my captors and shattering several streetlights and more than a few car windows. As alarms started to wail, I broke free of the crowd and rushed to Gareth, then pulled the little boy into my lap, hugging him close to comfort his tears.

"She has my little boy!" Bo Peep screeched. "Someone kill her before she hurts my little boy!"

Three of the men surged forward, looking like they intended to carry out Bo's request, but suddenly a massive white wolf was in front of me, his hackles raised, his fangs bared. A deep growl resonated from his chest, audible even over the cacophony of the car alarms.

The men slid to a halt, eyeing Seth warily.

The shimmering light I'd seen the other night now encased the wolf again. Seth rose to his feet, squaring off against the townspeople. "Back the fuck off."

"She doesn't belong here, Wolf," Rat Eyes explained.

"That's not for you to decide, Hansel," he shot back.

The elderly woman now stepped forward, her approach a little less threatening by comparison. "Be reasonable, Mr. Wolf," she said. "Have you seen what she's done? She's *dangerous*."

Seth's hands curled into fists at his sides. "As I recall, Mrs. Patterson, every single one of us has had some trouble along the way, or we wouldn't be here. Lavender's no different."

"She *is* different, *mein Freund*," Hansel told him. "Look at the destruction she has already wrought."

"Because she was threatened," Seth insisted. "You were trying to hurt her. What did you expect her to do? Besides, it's not up to you who stays at The Refuge. Only the mayor can decide that."

"He's right," Hansel called over his shoulder to the others, albeit begrudgingly. "We can bring it up at the town meeting tomorrow night."

Seth gave a nod. "We'll be there."

As the townspeople glanced between one another, Seth edged closer and crouched down beside me, slipping his arm around my shoulders. "Come on," he whispered. "Let's get you the hell out of here."

"I can't leave the boy," I whispered back, rising to my feet. "His mother's hopped up on D. She isn't able to look after him."

Seth cast his gaze down to Gareth's tear-streaked face and cursed under his breath. "It's not our place, Lavender."

"Like hell," I snapped, picking up Gareth and hefting him on my hip. "What happened a few minutes ago is nothing compared to what I'll do if they try to take this boy away from me right now."

"Fuck," he groaned, running a hand through his hair and casting a glance around the crowd. A few of the people on the fringes had already started to wander away, apparently deciding the fight wasn't worth it. Bo Peep was pacing back and forth on the sidewalk, mumbling to herself and twisting a lock of hair that had slipped out from beneath her bonnet. "We'll talk to Tom about it. He can figure out what to do."

I nodded. "Fair enough."

Seth bent and snatched up my cane, his eyes taking in the remaining townspeople, watching for even the slightest movement. He kept his arm around my shoulders, helping me limp down the street, his gaze constantly scanning the surrounding area.

My heart ached a little for him as I witnessed firsthand the effects of constantly being hunted. He must've never had a single moment when he was truly relaxed and at peace. Suddenly, my being snubbed by the other Tales for all these years didn't seem nearly so horrible. At least up until this most recent episode, no one had actually gone as far as trying to take me out.

When we reached the end of Main Street, we turned onto a side street and walked another two blocks before we reached a chocolate brown Queen Anne with a black, wrought-iron fence enclosing the little patch of yard.

"This is the sheriff's office and jail," Seth explained, opening the gate for me and glancing around as he ushered Gareth and me inside.

A few moments later, we were sitting in the sheriff's office— which was literally a single room of his house—waiting for Tom to arrive. Tom's wife, a lovely ginger-haired Tale named Eva, brought in a plate of chocolate chip cookies and a glass of milk and sat with Gareth at a little round table, chatting with him while he ate.

When Tom still hadn't arrived by the time Gareth had polished off his snack, Eva said, "I think I'll take this little darling outside to play. Do you mind?"

I shook my head, offering her a smile. "Not at all. Thank you, Mrs. Piper."

"Eva," she said, placing a hand on my shoulder. "Please call me Eva. Tom has told me about you, about what you did for him. I never thought I'd actually meet the woman who saved his life. He's quite a fan of yours. I'd like nothing better than for us to be friends."

I gave her a grateful smile. "I'd like that very much, Eva."

As soon as Eva and Gareth had left the room, Seth pivoted toward me, his eyes that cold green fire I was beginning to realize blazed up when he was righteously pissed off. But, maybe—

"What *the hell* is wrong with you?"

Yep. Totally nailed it.

I huffed and met his angry gaze. "Nothing is wrong with me. I told Bo Peep my name and she went off the deep end. Did you see her when we left? She didn't even notice we'd taken her son with us!"

"I'm not talking about trying to protect the kid," he snapped. "I'm talking about your magic going apeshit. You were blowing up *birds*, for fuck's sake! What the hell is that all about?"

I turned away, staring at a sepia-tone photo of Tom Piper and Wyatt Earp hanging on the wall. "I told you I was a half-assed fairy."

"I thought you were being sarcastic!"

"I wish." I took a deep breath and let it out slowly. "I've had trouble controlling my magic ever since we came over," I explained. "I think I felt so guilty about what happened I lost touch with my fairy light."

Seth shook his head. "Fairy light?"

I looked up at the ceiling, trying to figure out how to explain it. "That's what we call the center of our power, our innate abilities. When we first came over, I think I was blocking my abilities because I'd lost faith in myself, my power. A little over a year ago, Red gave me a kick in the ass and made me see I seriously needed to get my shit together. But my inability to control my magic has been even worse than before."

"And?" Seth prompted.

"And I lost it the other night," I told him. "Burned down James and Cindy Charming's house and divulged a lot of secrets that could bury James. Oh, and I accidentally shrank his penis."

Seth choked, his eyes bugging out a little. "You can do that?"

I cringed. "Yeah."

"Shit," he exhaled, his expression that particular look of horror unique to males of any species when there is a perceived threat to their most prized appendage.

"Anyway," I continued. "James threatened to kill me for what I'd done, so Red sent me here." I turned to face him, the intensity of his gaze catching me a little off-guard and stealing my breath, so my words were little more than a whisper when I added, "To you."

"To me." Seth regarded me for a long moment, his expression growing increasingly perplexed the longer we held each other's gazes. Then he lifted his hand and ran his fingertips along the curve of my jaw until he reached my chin.

He was scowling, though, as if he didn't quite understand what was happening any more than I did. Then the scowl faded, his expression becoming one of wonder.

Holy shit, he was going to kiss me.

I could see it in his eyes, in the way his lids grew heavy as he dropped his gaze to my lips. And I wanted him to. My God, how I wanted him to. I wanted him to kiss me and never stop. My heart was pounding as he slowly drew me toward him.

"Sorry to keep you waiting!"

Seth and I jumped apart like two guilty teenagers as Tom came in, and I could feel my face flushing fiercely. But if Tom noticed anything, he had the grace not to say a word.

"Finally got that body dropped off to Doc to take a look at," Tom informed us, taking a seat behind the desk.

"Doc?" I asked, turning toward Seth. "I thought you didn't have a clinic in town."

"We don't," Tom assured me. "There's no way in hell any of us would trust Doc to deal with the living. Can't really do any harm, though, if they're already dead."

My brows shot up.

"You know the saying, 'An apple a day keeps the doctor away'?"

Seth supplied. When I nodded, he said, "Didn't you ever wonder why you'd *want* to keep the doctor away? Well, Doc's that reason."

I turned wide eyes back to Tom, but he just offered me a kind smile. "Now, Eva tells me there was a little dustup in town today. Want to fill me in?"

When I'd finished telling Tom about the incident with Bo Peep and the other townspeople, his kind smile had been replaced by a troubled frown.

"I've known for quite a while that we have a fairy dust problem in town," he admitted, "but I haven't been able to figure out where they're getting it. No one's willing to talk. If Bo Peep is in as bad shape as you say, I'll have to take her into custody and lock her up to detox before she starts with the hallucinations and other side effects."

"What about her son?" I asked. "I got the impression there was no one else to look after him."

Tom leaned back in his chair, mulling over my question. "Well, now, that's an interesting story. Bo didn't have a son when she came over. In the ten years she's been here, I've never seen her pregnant. In fact, little Gareth just showed up one day a year ago—about a month before Seth got here, I reckon."

"And no one thought that was odd?"

Tom nodded. "Bet your ass I thought it was odd. Did a full investigation, ran his picture through the Tale registry. Found no evidence that the kid had ever existed. Hell, I even checked the Ordinaries' missing persons database in case he'd belonged to one of ours who'd maybe accidentally come to the attention of the Ordinaries. No hits there either."

"So you just dropped it?" I asked, trying not to sound accusatory.

"Not much else I could do," Tom said on a sigh. "He had all the appearance of a Tale, but no one knew anything about the boy. And he seemed to be loved and cared for staying with Bo—God knows she needed something to hang on to to keep her grounded. I knew she'd been a D addict before she came to us but she seemed to straighten up once Gareth came into her life."

"Looks like she's fallen off the wagon," Seth pointed out.

Tom nodded. "Damn shame."

"What will happen to Gareth?" I asked. "Who will take care of him?"

"I reckon he can stay with Eva and me," Tom told us. "At least for now. Eva loves the little guy. And we haven't been blessed with any children of our own."

I felt a huge weight lifted from my shoulders. I honestly couldn't think of a better situation for the little boy. I had no doubt that he would be well cared for and dearly loved while he was part of the Piper household.

The streets were fairly quiet again when we left Tom's office. By the time we reached Seth's pickup truck, only a few shoppers and businesspeople made their way along the sidewalks, and a few even cast a friendly smile Seth's way.

"I'd better go inside and see if I still have a job." Seth sighed, running a hand through his hair.

"This isn't *your* restaurant?" From what I'd heard back in Chicago, Seth had been on the verge of taking over one of the best steakhouses in the Windy City. I'd just assumed he'd opened up a restaurant here when he'd arrived.

He shook his head. "No, and my boss is the guy who was ready to run you out of town."

Das Gingerbread Haus.

"Hansel," I moaned. "I'm so sorry, Seth. I didn't mean to put your job in jeopardy."

He shrugged. "Wouldn't be the first time I've lost a job." He opened the truck door for me and motioned for me to climb in. "I'll see you when I get home."

I glanced at the truck, remembering my earlier vow and weighing it against the wisdom of staying in town. "Maybe I should come with you and smooth things out with Hansel," I suggested. When Seth looked mildly horrified at the thought, I added quickly, "Please, Seth. Let me try to help. You've saved my ass twice now. It's the least I can do."

He grimaced, ready to protest, but I darted forward and pressed a kiss to his cheek. "Good. It's settled."

I hobbled toward the restaurant before he could stop me. And when I cast a smile at him over my shoulder, I was more than a little gratified to see him still standing by the pickup, a somewhat bemused expression on his face. But then a slow smile curved his lips and he slammed the truck door. I thought I even heard a quiet chuckle as he followed me inside.

Chapter 7

I dropped onto Seth's couch, completely exhausted, my ankle throbbing. "You know," I grumbled, "when I told Hansel I wanted to make amends for keeping you away from the restaurant, I didn't expect him to have me wait tables."

Seth's eyes twinkled with amusement as he sat down next to me and lifted my injured leg onto his lap. "You did great," he told me, carefully removing my boot. "I think Hansel might even consider offering you a full-time job, if you're interested."

I swallowed hard as he began to massage my ankle, his soft touch making my stomach twist into knots. "I already have a job," I said, more than a little distracted. "I'm going to be covering local news for the paper."

Seth's hands went still. "You're going to be working for Squiggington?"

I nodded, grinning. "Yeah, isn't that great?"

"I don't like that guy," Seth snapped. "He's a total prick. And he'll screw anything with a pulse."

"Jealous?" I teased.

Seth's expression grew stormy. "I don't give a shit who you sleep with," he said quickly. "That's your business."

"I was just wondering if you were jealous of his getting so much tail," I stammered, "not about me sleeping with someone else." As his gaze darted to me, I quickly amended, "I mean *someone*. Not someone *else*." My giggle was ridiculously shrill.

Oh, my God! *What was* wrong *with me? I'd turned into the village freaking idiot.*

When he gave me a look that pretty much seconded that, I continued in a rush, "Anyway, I'm not planning to sleep with him, just to write about completely innocuous local events like town meetings and bake sales."

Seth just shook his head and turned his attention back to my ankle before I could fully read his expression.

"You know, I thought you'd be happy for me," I huffed. "The salary's not great, but I should be able to afford to at least rent a room or something. I'll be out of your hair before you know it."

"I told you I'm not throwing you out," he muttered.

I leaned forward and placed a hand on his. "I appreciate all you've done for me," I told him when his gaze met mine. "But I need to find my own way. I need to prove to everyone that I can do this on my own."

He shook his head slowly. "It's no wonder you and Tess are friends," he said, his voice edged with bitterness.

I frowned at him. "What's that supposed to mean?"

"You're so damned determined to prove you don't need anybody."

"And what about you?" I shot back, extricating myself from his tender grasp. "You sure have the whole emotionally dead loner vibe going for you. At least my emotional range consists of more than just pissed off and apathetic!"

He hissed a string of curses under his breath as he launched himself to his feet.

"Where are you going?" I asked, a little uneasy.

"Out," he spat, storming to the front door and jerking it open. I flinched as he slammed it shut behind him.

Damn it.

With a sigh, I got to my feet and hobbled over to the door, hoping to catch him. But when I pulled it open, he had already vanished into the night.

* * *

It took me a few seconds to realize where I was when my eyes snapped open. But then I remembered that I'd dozed off on the couch while waiting for Seth to return. The oil lamp I'd left burning had gone out and the fire in the fireplace was little more than smoldering embers, leaving the house in almost complete darkness.

Still not sure what it was that had jolted me awake, I sat up slowly, allowing my eyes to adjust to the darkness as I searched the shadowy corners of the house. When I found only silence, my skin began to prickle with apprehension.

I pushed up to my feet and slowly crept through the living room and kitchen, finding no one there. "Seth?" I called in a whisper. "Is that you?"

Nothing.

The door to the bedroom was partially closed, so I moved toward it. Taking a deep breath, I eased it open slowly, scanning the room.

Empty.

What the hell?

Now seriously on edge, I made my way to the bathroom, muttering a whispered curse as the floorboards creaked just outside the threshold. I swallowed hard and reached my hand inside the doorway to flip on the light.

The moment the light snapped on, a murderous snarl sent me stumbling back. I tripped over the edge of my skirt and ass-planted with a startled scream. But the scream was cut short by the warm breath of the beast whose snarling muzzle was nearly touching my cheek.

Instinctively, I swung my fist, catching it across the snout and startling it enough that I could scramble out from beneath it. When my back hit the wall, I searched frantically for an escape. It was only then that I noticed the creature wasn't another hellhound sent to murder me, but a massive white wolf, its fur matted and bloodied. The wolf shook his head, recovering from the blow I'd delivered, and crouched low, ready to respond to my attack.

"Seth!" I yelled, holding up my hands. "It's me! It's Lavender!"

His snarl abruptly stopped and the next moment, Seth the man was scrambling toward me on his hands and knees and gathering me into his arms. "My God, Lavender," he murmured, burying his face in my neck as he held me close, his breath coming in labored gasps. "I'm so sorry. I didn't—" His words died on his lips as he pulled back and took my face in his hands. "Are you okay? Did I hurt you?"

I shook my head, my heart still pounding. "No. You just scared the shit out of me!"

He released me and dropped down beside me, resting his back against the wall. When he let his head fall back in relief, I saw the reason his fur had been bloody. He had a deep gash across his chest that ran from his left shoulder to his right side, exposing the bright white ribs beneath.

"Oh, God," I gasped, scrambling to my knees and pressing a hand to the wound to try to stanch the bleeding. "What the hell happened?"

He winced, hissing in a breath through his teeth. "I'll be fine," he ground out. "Just need to bandage it up."

"Bullshit," I snapped. "You need stitches. Your ribs are showing, for fuck's sake. We need to call that doctor from town."

Seth shook his head, but the movement made his eyes roll back into his head. I slapped his face with my free hand, jarring him back to consciousness.

"Tell me how to help you," I ordered. "Tell me what to do."

But it was no good. He'd lost a lot of blood—a good portion of it was now all over my clothes, I realized—making it difficult for his body to heal as quickly as a Tale should from such an injury.

My mind raced, trying to figure out what to do. There was no way I could drag him into the truck and drive him to town before he bled to death. He'd mentioned a healer lived nearby, but I had no idea where the hell to go. That left pretty much one option.

Shit.

I hurried into the kitchen and threw open the cabinet doors until I found a bowl, then grabbed a dishtowel and a paring knife sitting on the counter from breakfast. I rushed back to Seth's side and gently eased him down onto the floor.

My hands were trembling violently as I shoved up my sleeve and picked up the paring knife. Visions of how many ways this could go horribly wrong came rushing into my head, but I pushed them away, needing to focus all my thoughts and energy on the magic that would save Seth's life.

I held my forearm over the bowl and took a deep breath, blowing it out slowly and trying to still my other hand. Then I closed my eyes and began to murmur the words my ancestors had passed down to only the most powerful fairies of each generation. The magic was sacred, dangerous, unspeakably powerful. And, at its essence, questionable. It was what many would consider dark magic. And it was expressly forbidden except to the chosen Guardians, which meant I'd be in seriously deep shit if anyone found out I'd used it again after my guardianship had been revoked.

I opened my eyes and looked down at Seth, his face now frighteningly pale as his life seeped out of him. And suddenly I didn't give a damn what happened to me as long as he lived.

The first symbol I carved in my skin began to glow as the blood trickled into the bowl. Then the second. And the third. With the fourth symbol, the blood I collected began to boil in the bowl, congealing into a thin paste. The blood sacrifice had been accepted.

I sighed in relief and lifted the bowl, my hands no longer trembling, the words on my lips growing louder as my confidence returned. I held the bowl over Seth's ragged wound and slowly poured the blood paste along the gash, starting where it was the worst. Instantly, the blood and tissue began to sizzle and cauterize, sealing the wound and stanching the flow of blood. In a matter of seconds, the skin began to knit together once more.

I sat back on my heels, watching as the spell progressed. As soon as the skin had healed, the color began to return to his cheeks and lips as the blood I'd given him began to replenish what he'd lost. He would still be weak for a few hours, but with both my fairy blood and my magic coursing through his veins, he'd be feeling as good as new by morning.

I reached out and smoothed his hair from his brow, leaving a streak of blood on his forehead. He stirred slightly but didn't waken. Then I bent forward, intending to brush a kiss over his cheek, but instead, I pressed my lips against his. Just a brief kiss. Such a little thing, really. But it sent such a lightning bolt of heat through me, I gasped and fell back on my ass, startled by my own response.

Completely weirded out by how deeply the stolen kiss affected me, I quickly gathered up all the evidence of the magic I'd performed before Seth woke up and discovered what I'd done. I then set to work cleaning up what blood I could from Seth without dragging him into the shower—a tantalizing thought, I grant you, but I'd much rather Seth be conscious if we were planning to get all hot and steamy together.

I dragged him over to the rug and put a cushion under his head before stoking the fire and bringing it back to life. Once he was comfortable, I set to work cleaning the floorboards. As I scrubbed the floors clean, my thoughts turned to what it was that might have attacked him.

Was it another hellhound? Or had some other creature been sent to kill me? Of course, I couldn't even be sure that it was James who'd sent the hellhound in the first place. Now that I had a moment to seriously consider the matter, something told me that if James had sent an assassin to take me out, it wouldn't have been in the form of a hellhound. He struck me more as a car bomb kind of guy.

But if *I* wasn't the hellhound's target, then who was?

I paused in my scrubbing and glanced over my shoulder to where Seth lay in front of the fire. Could *he* have been the one the hellhound was after? Seth definitely wasn't the most popular guy in The Refuge from what I'd seen, but he wasn't exactly persona non grata, either. They *feared* him, but they didn't appear to *hate* him. Why the hell would anyone be going after him?

I shook my head, none of it making any sense.

First a hellhound attack. And then an Ordinary body dumped on the side of the road leading to The Refuge. Just a coincidence, of course. Had to be.

Still, as I stripped off my blood-soaked clothing, I decided that first thing in the morning I was going to talk to J. G. Squiggington and see if he'd heard any good town gossip that might give me something to work with. Then I was going to ask Tom if I could take a closer look at the Ordinary body. By God, I was going to figure out what the hell was going on if it killed me.

Chapter 8

"I can't believe how great I feel."

I glanced over at Seth as he drove us into town and forced a smile. "I'm glad you're healing so quickly. You were in pretty bad shape last night."

He shook his head. "I have to be honest, for a few minutes there I wasn't sure. . . . Well, I guess when I passed out, my system just really kicked into gear."

I nodded, feigning ignorance. "Guess so . . ."

"But you know what the craziest part is?"

That my magic actually worked?

I shook my head. "Nope, sure don't."

"In all the times I've been injured, I've never felt this fantastic after I healed. It's unbelievable! I mean—"

"So what happened anyway?" I interrupted, trying yet again to divert him from the subject of his miraculous recovery.

His brows snapped together in a frown. "Mountain lion."

Bullshit.

I knew Seth was lying to me. I'd seen him take down a demon-dog like it was nothing. There was no way a mountain lion could've bested him. But I wasn't going to push him on it. Not just yet.

When we finally pulled into the parking spot in front of the restaurant, I practically leapt out of the truck. But before I could make a break for it, Seth was blocking my path.

"Hey," he said, shoving his hands into the pockets of his jeans, "I never said thank you for what you did last night."

My stomach clenched. "What do you mean?"

He took a half-step closer to me, his eyes trained on the ground. "When I came at you, you could've taken off and left me to die." He lifted his gaze and came in another step, now only inches from me. "I appreciate your sticking by me, Lavender."

I wondered how appreciative he'd be if he knew that I'd used magic to heal his wounds. And not just any magic—the same perilous magic that had landed us here in the first place. My conscience couldn't take it anymore. "Seth—"

"Have dinner with me tonight," he interrupted. And then he gave me a smile so sexy, so unbelievably, heart-stoppingly gorgeous, my attack of conscience was instantly forgotten.

"Of course I'll have dinner with you," I said, rolling my eyes. "What kind of freeloader would I be if I wasn't eating all your food?"

Seth actually chuckled, then took my hand and raised it to his lips, pressing a kiss to my fingertips. "So that's a yes?"

"That's a yes," I replied, grinning like an idiot. But then I suddenly remembered the town meeting. "Damn! I have to cover the town meeting and throw myself on the mercy of your mayor to see if he'll let me stay."

Seth's brows drew together in a frown. "Shit. I forgot about that."

"You'll come with me, won't you?" I asked, my fingers tightening around his.

"Absolutely," he assured me, giving me that smile of his that made my knees weak. "Then when we get home, I'll make you a dinner you'll never forget."

"With dessert?" I breathed.

He leaned in a little toward me. "Like nothing you've ever experienced before."

I swallowed hard, wondering if his idea of dessert and mine were anywhere close to being the same. If the look in his eyes when he pulled back again was any indication, my vision of whipped-cream-covered bliss wasn't far off the mark. I was on the verge of asking how we might incorporate chocolate syrup into our evening, when the door to the restaurant burst open.

"Wolf!" shouted an über-fit, ultra-tan, and muscular woman with incongruously girlie golden curls decorated with little pink bows. "Are you working today or should I have Hansel kick your ass to the curb?"

Seth gave me an exasperated look. "Looks like I have to go."

I glanced over at the woman, sizing her up. "Is that . . . *Gretel?*"

Seth snorted. "Yeah. And if you think Hansel's a hard-ass . . ."

"What the hell happened to her?" I gasped.

"Got hooked on 'roids about ten years ago when she and Hansel were really pushing their fitness line."

"Fitness line?"

He laughed in a short burst. "Remember the Cookie Diet that was big for about a minute? Well, Hansel and Gretel started the Candy Diet. Had a huge following among the Tales for a while until an FMA investigation found out the candy was essentially just a really sweet and tasty version of speed. It was causing stimulant psychosis or something in the people taking it. There was a huge scandal, they were indicted by the FMA and after having to fork over most of their fortune in restitution, they came out here to start over."

I frowned, racking my brain for some scrap of memory about the whole incident, but nothing came to mind. "How the hell did I not know any of this?" But the answer was clear to me the moment I'd uttered the question. I'd been living it up on the bottom of the bottle diet. I wasn't paying attention to much of anything at that point.

"Wolf!" came Gretel's gruff shout. "You're five minutes away from my foot up your ass!"

"You'd better go," I said, releasing his hand and taking a step back. "She looks seriously pissed off."

"She always looks that way," he groaned. "Want to come in and have some coffee?"

I shook my head. "Nah, I'm good. I'm just going to check in with Squiggington, then see how Gareth is doing with Tom and Eva."

"Try to stay off that ankle," he warned. "You might not need the cane today, but it could still be pretty weak."

"I'll be fine!" I laughed. "Now go before you get in trouble. I'll pop in for lunch if I can."

"Wolf, goddamn it!"

"Coming!" Seth shouted, then turned back to me and gave me a wink. "See you later, I guess." He jogged toward the door, pausing just long enough to offer me a final wave.

As soon as the door closed behind him, I let out a long, sad sigh. Suddenly the beautiful autumn morning didn't seem nearly as bright as it had just a moment before.

I made my way down the street toward the *Tattletale,* offering cautious smiles to those I passed. A few Tales actually returned the courtesy and even gave me a timid wave in greeting. More often than not, though, my efforts were met with a cold, indifferent stare.

I was relieved when I reached the *Tattletale* office so that I didn't have to mingle with any other potentially hostile Tales. For all his faults, at least I knew where J.G. stood when it came to being associated with me. But when I opened the door and stepped inside, a spike of adrenaline hit me, alerting me that something was horribly wrong. A preternatural silence filled the air, making the hair on my arms rise.

I started to call out for Brie or J.G. but bit the words off before I could utter them. Instead, I slowly scanned the reception area, looking for some clue why warning bells were going off inside my head. There was no sign that anything had occurred that would warrant such uneasiness. And yet . . .

I crept down the hall toward J.G.'s office, my apprehension growing. I quickly scanned each room as I passed, but found nothing wrong in this part of the building either. When I finally reached his office it was a completely different matter.

Inside, it looked like a cyclone had struck. Papers were strewn everywhere. Drawers had been pulled out, their contents emptied onto the floor. Furniture was overturned, torn apart, cushions shredded with what looked like massive claws. And there was blood. A lot of it.

With a startled gasp, I whirled around and rushed for the front door, not needing to see any more. I slammed the front door behind me as I raced down the steps and ran as fast as I could to Tom's house, hoping like hell he was there. By the time I reached the house, my ankle was shrieking in protest, but I ignored it as I dashed through the gate.

"Tom!" I yelled, pounding on the front door. "Tom! It's Lavender!"

Seconds later, Eva opened the door, her eyes wide and frightened. "Lavender? What's wrong?"

"I have to see Tom," I said in a rush as I shouldered past her. "It's urgent."

She nodded. "Okay, honey. We're just finishing up breakfast. I'll get him. Go ahead and have a seat in his office."

I started toward the office door when I caught movement out of the corner of my eye. I whirled around but laughed in relief when I saw it was just little Gareth. "Oh, my gosh, kiddo!" I gasped. "You startled me!"

He gave me a sunshiny grin and rushed toward me, throwing his arms around my legs and giving a squeeze. "Hello, Lavender! I heard you calling for Sheriff Tom. He's eating pancakes."

I lifted him up and gave him a big hug and a kiss on the cheek. "Did you eat some pancakes, too?"

He nodded enthusiastically. "They were yummy!"

"So, are you liking it here with Sheriff Tom and Mrs. Eva?" I asked.

He put a little arm around my neck. "Oh, yes! They are so nice to me. And Mrs. Eva gives me lots of hugs. I think she wants me to be her little boy."

My smile faded just a bit. "What about your real mommy? Won't she be sad not to see you again?"

He shrugged. "Bo Peep wasn't really my mommy."

"No?" I said, wondering if the little guy might remember how he'd come to The Refuge. "And where is your real mommy? Maybe we can help you find her."

He let out a very big sigh for one so young. "You can't find her. No one can."

My heart shattered for the poor little angel. If Gareth had been there for close to two years, he must have been only three or four when he'd arrived. And who knew what he'd been through before he'd shown up in The Refuge.

I forced a smile. "Well," I said, trying to make my voice cheerful, "you never know—"

"G'morning, Lavender," Tom called as he strode into the room, still wiping his mouth with a napkin. "Eva said you had an urgent matter to discuss with me."

Apparently seeing the grown-ups needed to talk, Gareth gave me a kiss on the cheek and a squeeze around the neck before wiggling out of my hold and scampering into the kitchen to join Eva.

"Sorry to interrupt your breakfast," I apologized to Tom as he led me to his office. As soon as he shut the door and took a seat at his desk, I quickly explained what I'd seen at the *Tattletale* office, careful not to leave out any detail.

"Holy hell," Tom muttered. He grabbed up his black ball cap and strode toward the door. I got to my feet to follow him, but he held his hands up in front of his chest. "Whoa, now. Where do you think you're going?"

"With you," I said matter-of-factly.

He shook his head. "I'm afraid I can't allow that, Lavender. What if the attacker is still there?"

"Then you'll need someone to watch your back," I retorted, crossing my arms over my chest. "I'm not staying behind, Tom. Now, we can stand here and argue about it, or we can go figure out what the hell has happened!"

He shook his head. "All right. But do exactly as I tell you and don't touch anything."

I huffed and checked the clock on the wall in the *Tattletale's* reception area. I'd been standing there for close to thirty minutes while Tom went through the house, one room at a time, checking out the residence and gathering what evidence he could find. I'd hoped to go through the house with him, but he staunchly refused, insisting that I stay just inside the front door so I couldn't contaminate the crime scene.

"Contaminate the crime scene," I mumbled for what had to the thousandth time. "You've got to be kidding me! Like I would just—"

A strangled cry from the second floor cut off my complaint. Not waiting another second, I bolted up the steps. "Tom!" I cried, gasping for breath as I reached the landing. "Tom, are you okay? Where are you?"

"In here!" he called back, his voice strained.

I raced down the hall toward one of the bedrooms but came to an abrupt halt when I caught a glimpse of what had made Tom cry out. Gagging, I covered my mouth and whirled back out of the doorway. Leaning back against the wall for support, I squeezed my eyes shut, trying to banish the images of the carnage I'd seen, but that just made it all the more vivid.

A moment later, Tom came out of the bedroom, his face pale with shock. "I'm going to call in the Doc," he mumbled. "Stay out here."

Not needing to be told twice, I nodded as he strode down the hallway toward the stairs. I didn't need a second look. What I'd seen was clear enough. Someone—or something—had entered the house overnight and murdered J.G.'s girlfriend. Her naked body lay splayed out on the bed, arms and legs tied to the bedposts. Like the body Seth and I had found the day before, Brie's body had been mutilated with countless cuts. But unlike the man we'd found, her head had been severed and lay on the ground where it had been cast aside.

But perhaps the most gruesome sight was the gaping wound in her abdomen. It looked like her ribs had been pulled apart by two monstrous hands, splitting open her abdominal cavity. And where her innards should have been was just an empty crater. All of her organs had been removed—not with the surgical precision like that employed by Jack the Ripper, but savagely, viciously, and, I imagined, while she was still alive.

Even in the remembering, my stomach retched, and I had to swallow several times to force the bile back down my throat before the contents of my stomach joined the gore on the floor.

What seemed like an eternity later, a scrawny, hunched little man with a hawklike nose and squinty, cold blue eyes skulked down the hall toward me carrying a tattered black leather satchel. He wore a long lab coat that probably once had been white but was now dingy beige. He cast a suspicious glance my way as he passed, sending a shiver through me.

Good God. No wonder no one wanted the doctor to pay them a visit! I'd never encountered someone so undeniably creepy. He looked like he'd stepped right out of a low-budget horror film. But what was perhaps the most disturbing was that he appeared excited to be called to the scene of such a crime, those cold blue eyes sparkling with a morbid glee.

Tom gave me a sorrowful look and squeezed my shoulder briefly as he followed the doctor inside. Too rattled to stand any longer, I slid down the wall and brought my knees up to my chest, curling into a ball of quivering fear and revulsion as I listened to the doctor's nasally voice detail the crime scene.

"—*decapitation . . . torn off . . . eviscerated . . . broken ribs . . . exploding outward . . . symbols carved into skin . . .*"

My head snapped up.

Symbols?

Taking a deep breath to steel myself, I stood and peeked around the doorframe, making sure to keep my gaze above Brie's severed head. "What kind of symbols?" I asked, my voice quaking.

Tom and Doc both turned toward me, Doc peering over his spectacles to peg me with his icy glare. "I have no idea," he admitted. "I've never seen anything like them. Whether they are ritualistic or just a form of torture, I cannot say."

I straightened and swallowed hard. "May I take a look?"

"What the hell would you know about anything, girl?" Doc demanded. "Seen many carved up corpses, have you?"

"A few," I lied. The total was more like two—and both had been since coming to The Refuge. I smoothed the front of my skirt, then blew out a cleansing breath before approaching Brie's body, my hands balled into fists at my sides.

When I was within about a foot of the bed, I couldn't go any further. I stood there, shivering uncontrollably until I felt the weight of Tom's arm come around my shoulders. "You don't have to do this, Lavender," he said softly.

But I did. I needed to know. Even though a part of me already guessed what I was going to find.

I took another step closer and wrapped my arms around my torso as I bent forward to take a closer look. The first symbol I looked at was poorly done, amateurish, hardly recognizable. But the second and the third were all I needed to see to know the truth. I recognized them immediately—though to most Tales they'd look like nothing more than random designs.

"Have you seen anything like this before, Lavender?" Tom asked. "Do you know what they are?"

Of course I did. I'd used several of the symbols just the night before to save Seth's life. I started to confess as much, when a sudden thought struck me. The townspeople of The Refuge were already looking for a reason to send me packing. If they discovered that I knew the kind of magic that someone else was using to murder people, what would keep them from suspecting that I was actually the one doing it? After all, the first body hadn't shown up until I'd come to town, as far as anyone knew.

No, I'd have to figure out who was doing this before I shared anything with Tom. I liked and trusted the man, but for all his gratitude, he was the law in The Refuge and he had a duty to perform. I wouldn't ask him to choose between that and a debt he believed he owed me.

I shook my head and backed away from the carnage. "No," I told him. "I'm afraid I don't know these symbols."

Tom sighed and removed his baseball cap to run a hand over his crew cut. "Shit. I'd really hate to have to call the FMA about this one." He put his hat back on and crossed his arms over his chest, staring down at Brie's body. "Finding a butchered Ordinary outside of town's one thing. It's another to have one right here on Main Street. This kind of problem could bring a lot more attention than we'd like to have."

I frowned, just as concerned about bringing in the FMA as Tom was. But at least the fact that Brie was an Ordinary explained why The Refuge wasn't already crawling with Investigators. If Nate had known about her death, there was no doubt he would have alerted the FMA's director, Al Addin, to what had happened.

"So, how did an Ordinary like Brie come to The Refuge anyway?" I asked.

"Met up with J.G. when she was working as a cocktail waitress at the casino a few miles up the road," Tom replied. "Moved here about a month later. It's a shame. She seemed to actually care about that murderous little bastard."

"You can't possibly think J.G. did this," I scoffed. When Tom gave me a speculative grimace, I shook my head. "There's no way. Why would he? What did he have to gain?"

This time it was the doctor who answered, his eyes gleaming with a manic light that made me uncomfortable. "Perhaps it was a crime of passion. Or a mental defect." A far-off look came into his eyes. "Maybe he is *psychotic....*"

Tom strode toward the bedroom door. "Well, I guess we'll find out when I track him down and haul his ass in for questioning. In the meantime, this crime scene is off-limits."

He waved his arm toward the hallway, motioning for Doc and me to leave. We made our way down the hall and into the reception area and were heading toward the front door when it suddenly swung open with a bang. There, framed in the doorway, was a strikingly handsome man with wavy blond hair, his athletic physique set off to perfection by the impeccably tailored Armani suit he wore.

I stopped dead in my tracks when I saw him, my mouth falling open.

Holy shit.

The man cocked his head to one side when he saw me, clearly as surprised to see me as I was to see him. He took his shades off and regarded me for a moment with golden eyes that sparkled with a sinfully charming mixture of intelligence and mischief.

A slow smile curved his lips. "Well, I'll be a motherfucker."

The shock that had turned my feet to lead suddenly dissipated at the sight of his smile. I ran to him and threw my arms around his neck, hugging him so hard it was a miracle he could breathe. But when I finally released him and looked up into his face, he was beaming down at me.

"Hello, petal," he said softly before pressing a kiss to my forehead.

There were tears in my eyes when I sniffed, "Hello yourself."

"I'd introduce you, Lavender," Tom said from behind us, his tone perplexed, "but I see you already know Mayor Puck."

I wiped the tears from my cheeks. "I know this pain in the ass better than anyone," I said, still finding it hard to believe that Puck was actually standing there in front of me. "He's my big brother."

Chapter 9

I waited outside on the porch while Tom and Doc briefed Puck on the details of Brie's murder. When they came out to join me, Puck cast a sidelong glance my way, then put his shades on, hiding the apprehension in his eyes. He reached into his suit pocket and withdrew an engraved gold cigarette case and stuck a rather delicate-looking brown clove cigarette between his lips.

"Seal off the building," he barked. He patted his suit pocket, looking for a lighter. "Do whatever investigating you and Doc need to do, but I don't want the FMA poking their noses into our business." Frowning he added, "Any of you got a light?"

With an irritated sigh, Tom fished a silver lighter out of his pocket and tossed it to Puck. "I'm not equipped to deal with this kind of investigation," Tom protested, although his voice was the usual even calm as he watched Puck light up. "It's going to take a little time to sort all this out." When Puck handed the lighter back, Tom waved it away with an impatient swat. "Keep it."

"Thanks." Puck took a long draw on the clove cigarette and blew the smoke out in an intricate spiral. "So what do you want from me here, Tom? I'm not going to let the FMA barge into our town declaring authority and fucking up everything we've managed to build. Now, I want you to figure out what the hell is going on and put a lid on it. I think two dead Ordinaries and two missing Tales is quite enough, don't you?"

"Two?" I said, frowning. "Who's missing besides J.G.?"

Tom sighed and put his hands on his hips. "Bo Peep. I went looking for her yesterday to put her in detox, but she's disappeared. Doesn't seem to have taken anything with her either."

"She could be a danger to herself and others if she is going through withdrawal," Doc added, his tone sounding a little too eager to me.

"She hasn't been right in the head since the whole sheep incident back in Make Believe," Puck snapped. "But aside from some serious abandonment issues, she's harmless. Your priority is keeping these murders under wraps. Is that clear?"

I glanced between the two men, sensing the obvious tension there. Tom's jaw clenched and he looked like he wanted to argue the matter further, but with a disapproving shake of his head he said only, "Yes, sir, Mr. Mayor. I'll handle it."

Then Puck turned to me and gave me one of his broad smiles, his irritation instantly vanishing. "What do you say I treat you to some coffee, little sister? We have a lot of catching up to do."

No shit we did.

I followed him to the black Ferrari parked at the curb and got in when he opened the passenger door for me. A moment later, we were parked in front of Das Gingerbread Haus.

I turned toward him, puzzled. "You want to have coffee *here*? Why didn't we just walk?"

He grunted dismissively as he took a last drag on his cigarette before stubbing it out in the sand-filled cauldron outside the restaurant. "Are you kidding? Like I want my car parked outside that asshole Squiggington's place. People might think I actually believe the bullshit he puts in his paper."

I blinked at him. "Okay, you're clearly not a fan, but still . . . I mean, the guy's missing. Aren't you even a little concerned that something's happened to one of your citizens?"

Puck's smile came too easy. "Same old Lavender," he said with a laugh, shaking his head. "You were always busting my balls about something. Now, c'mon—I'm not worth a good goddamn until I've had my third cup of coffee."

Once again, I was taken aback by the quaint charm and hominess of the restaurant. I don't know what I'd expected, but considering the gruff demeanor of its owners, I guess I was anticipating something stark and modernistic. But it was warm and inviting with a Bavarian theme to the decor that reminded me of the cafes I'd seen in European skiing villages.

The moment my brother came in, two young women in traditional German folk attire came scurrying over, their cheeks flushing brightly. These must've been the waitresses that had left Hansel high and dry the day before when I'd been pressed into service. Seeing them now in their jaunty—and decidedly over-the-top cheesy—little outfits, I was grateful I'd managed to escape *that* additional indignity at least.

"Good morning, Mr. Mayor," chirped the girl with the long, white ponytail, clearly smitten with The Refuge's elected official.

"We haven't seen you in a while," said the other girl, whose short, green, spiky hair reminded me of the ferns that grew so densely in this area of the Pacific Northwest. She gave my brother the once over, the hungry, sexual look in her eyes so blatant, I had to glance away before I threw up.

But Puck took it all in stride, of course, used to that kind of reaction from his scads of fawning admirers. "How about one of the best tables for me and my guest?" he said, putting an arm around each of the women and tucking them close as we entered the dining room.

Once we were seated in a secluded little corner, he whispered something to each that made them giggle and scurry off.

"Well, nice to see you haven't changed a bit in all these years," I drawled. "Are you sleeping with both of them, or are they just hopefuls sitting the bench?"

He winked at me as he tucked his shades into his suit pocket. "Let's just say my service to the public has no limits."

I muttered a curse under my breath and rolled my eyes, but there was no point in being disgusted. My dear brother, Robin Goodfellow Seelie—or Puck as he called himself after he defected to the

Willies—had a way with women that put the great lovers of history and myth to shame. Casanova looked like nothing more than a horny teenager by comparison.

And with such a fantastic and impressive history, Puck deeply resented that in spite of his many appearances in folklore and fairy-tales, *A Midsummer Night's Dream* was the story for which he was best remembered. And, to add insult to injury, his more carnal talents had never been chronicled at all for the public to enjoy. It irked him that he'd been cast as little more than a servant to Oberon and not the randy, bed-hopping lothario who'd seduced just about every one of the Willies' heroines at some point since his association with them.

I'd never had the heart to tell him that his diminished legend was due to our mother's censorship. Much as she'd sanitized my history, she'd stricken all *his* exploits from record for fear of Puck bringing shame to the Seelies. But now it seemed he was making his mark on The Refuge without the matronly oversight he'd had before and had a reputation that he—and probably he alone—could be proud of.

"So how the hell have you been, petal?" he asked, leaning back in his chair and regarding me with a somewhat bemused expression. "It's been ages."

"I'm not the one who dropped off the grid decades ago," I snapped. "Do you know how long our father searched for you?"

"What did he care?" Puck scoffed. "He and Mother wrote me off centuries ago—long before we came here. I figured they'd be relieved when I disappeared."

I wasn't about to tell him that he'd pretty much hit the nail on the head when it came to our mother. Instead, I focused on our father's concern. "Dad has always held out hope that you'd make amends."

"Christ—don't give me that, 'Give me your hands, if we be friends' bullshit," he groaned. "There's too much water under that bridge for me to ever come groveling back to the high-and-mighty Mab and beg her for forgiveness."

"That's not why Dad searched for you," I insisted. "He just wanted to make sure you were safe and happy."

"And did he come to look for me himself?" When I hesitated, Puck sniffed derisively. "I should've known it was too much to ask the King of Fairies to come looking for his only son. Sent his ever-loyal toady after me, didn't he?"

"Gideon's a good man," I shot back. "His loyalty is one of his best qualities."

Puck lifted an eyebrow at me. "That wound still raw after all these years, baby girl?"

I pressed my lips together, reminding myself that I'd once idolized and adored the man sitting across from me. Even if he'd always managed to get me into trouble along with him. Luckily, our coffee came before I had the chance to tell him to fuck off.

"So, where've you been all this time?" I demanded instead. "Here in The Refuge?"

"Nah." Puck lifted his coffee cup to his nose and inhaled deeply, then took a tentative sip much in the way a wine connoisseur would sample a fine Cabernet. Apparently satisfied, he took a larger sip before finally saying with a shrug, "I just wandered here and there. You know, having a little fun along the way."

Causing trouble, I translated silently. "Dare I even ask?" I said, raising a disapproving brow.

He flashed me a smile. "Probably best if you don't."

"How'd you end up here?" I probed. "This is a bit prosaic for you, isn't it?"

He draped an arm casually over the back of his chair and gestured toward the window that looked out on Main Street. "It's actually right up my alley, when you think about it. A town full of Tales who couldn't give a flying fuck about the FMA's rules and laws about denying who and what they are? Are you kidding me? The minute I heard about it, I knew I belonged here."

"So, you just strolled into town and they made you mayor?" I said, my tone betraying my disbelief. "That stretches the imagination even where you're concerned, Puck."

He chuckled. "Wasn't quite like that," he admitted. "I met the right people, made the right friends. And it didn't hurt that I opened up a casino in the nearby town and made a killing."

Ponytail waitress sidled up to our table, the bodice of her uniform revealing more of her cleavage than when last I'd seen her. She bent forward more than necessary as she set a plate of food in front of Puck, giving him a good look at the valley between her breasts.

He didn't even bother trying to hide his interest and looked a little forlorn when she turned to place a plate in front of me as well (sans gratuitous cleavage).

"What's all this, sweetheart?" Puck asked, motioning toward the heaping plates of food as if noticing them for the first time. Which was probably true.

"Compliments of the chef," she bubbled. "Enjoy!"

I glanced toward the kitchen and saw Seth peering out through the Plexiglas window of the kitchen door, his eyes narrowed as he studied us. I felt the heat rising in my cheeks and offered a smile that was admittedly a little feeble—but whether because of the sudden fluttering in my stomach at the sight of him or because of the cold look in his eyes, I couldn't tell.

I'm not sure how he interpreted my sudden discomfiture, but he punched open the door and strode toward us, his shoulders taking on that predatory stance I was growing accustomed to.

"Well, well, well," Puck drawled. "If it isn't the Big Bad Wolf."

"Stop it," I hissed. "He's a friend."

Puck didn't bother keeping his voice down when he said, "Careful of the company you keep, Lav. People might get the wrong idea."

"Exactly what I was planning to say," Seth growled, grabbing a chair from a nearby table and setting it so close to me, his thigh was pressed against mine when he sat down.

Puck threw his head back and laughed, then leaned forward, moving a plate of toast to the side so he could put his forearms on the table. "Don't worry, Wolf," he said, sotto voce. "Lavender's my little sister. Even *I* draw the line somewhere."

"Sister?" The tension in Seth's shoulders eased up a little and he sat back in his chair, his hand coming to rest on my knee. I cast a startled glance his way, but I left his hand right where it was and tried to focus on the little spikes of pleasure his touch caused in the pit of my stomach and not the fact that my heart was pounding so hard I was certain he could hear it.

"So, I guess she can stay then," Seth said. "A few of the townspeople were ready to tar and feather her yesterday—if she was lucky."

Puck opened his arms wide. "Of course she can stay! I have more than enough room at my apartment in the casino. Or she can stay at the house I own here at The Refuge." He gave me a broad grin. "Be just like old times, eh sis?"

"She stays with me," Seth returned, his tone daring Puck to challenge him on it.

Puck's gaze darted between the two of us, his eyes asking questions I wasn't exactly prepared to answer. So instead I said, "Seth has saved my life twice now." I covered Seth's hand with mine, linking my fingers with his. This time it was his turn to send a guarded glance my way. "He protected me the night I arrived when a hellhound attacked me, and—"

"Attacked *you*?" Puck interrupted, his brows furrowed together in a dark frown. "What the hell?"

I leaned in, lowering my voice. "At first I thought James sent it to take me out for burning down the Charmings' mansion—"

"You burned down the mansion?" he laughed. "Holy shit."

I blinked at him. "Have you been living under a rock? It's been all over the Tale networks."

"I've been a little busy lately," he shot back. "So you don't think James had someone conjure it?"

"Not anymore." I turned toward Seth and whispered, "I found another body this morning. J.G.'s girlfriend, Brie."

"Jesus, Lavender," Puck hissed.

"What?" I snapped. "We can trust Seth."

Puck gave me a look that clearly conveyed he wasn't so sure, then muttered a curse under his breath.

"It was worse than the first," I told Seth, close to his ear so that none of the other patrons in the restaurant could hear me.

His fingers tightened around mine and the look in his eyes as I pulled back gave me a glimpse of his concern. "Are you okay?"

I nodded, although I wasn't entirely sure how I was going to be later, when the reality of what I'd seen actually hit me.

"Wolf!"

The three of us turned toward the kitchen where Gretel stood, her hands on her hips. "I'm not paying you to sit on your ass!"

Seth let out a long sigh, then turned to me. "I'll see you this evening at the town meeting," he said, giving my hand one last squeeze before heading back to the kitchen.

"Totally didn't see that one coming," Puck drawled after the kitchen door swung shut behind Seth.

"What?" I asked, picking up my fork and digging into the plate of food before me.

"You're banging the werewolf."

I choked on the scrambled eggs and reached for my coffee to wash it down.

"Holy shit," he continued, laughing. "Mother will lose her fucking mind! It's almost worth going to visit just to see the look on her face."

When I finally managed to dislodge the egg from my windpipe, I glanced around the restaurant to see if anyone had noticed Puck's loud pronouncement, but they were all too busy eating their breakfast or mooning over my brother to actually listen to what he was saying.

"What is *wrong* with you!" I hissed between clenched teeth. "I'm not"—I lowered my voice—"sleeping with him."

Puck held up his hands in front of his chest as if to ward me off. "Hey, I'm not one to judge when it comes to fuck-buddies. I'm just expressing brotherly concern for my little sister. You know what they say about lying down with dogs. . . ."

"And you would know!" I charged. "You're the biggest hound dog I've ever seen. You're lucky we can't catch the diseases the Ordinaries spread around!"

Puck shrugged. "I'm a manwhore. Guilty as charged. But all joking aside—I'm serious about being worried for you, Lav." He leaned forward and added quietly, "I don't trust him. For all I know, he could be committing these murders."

"Don't be absurd," I scoffed. "Seth hates magic. He'd never stoop to using it."

"Maybe not personally," Puck conceded, "but what if he'd given someone else the knowledge they needed to perform the blood rites?"

I shook my head. "No way he'd know anything about the rites."

"As far as you know." Puck took a long drink of his coffee, then pressed his lips together, mulling over what he wanted to say. "How well do you really know him? Do you even know his full story?"

I stiffened defensively. "I know enough."

Puck's brows shot up. "Do you? He's damaged, Lav. Hell, I can see that and I'm an insensitive asshole. The man hates what he is, what he's become. He's lost everyone and everything that was ever important to him. That kind of loss can push a person right over the edge and make him do things he'd never normally consider doing."

"Maybe," I conceded. "But—"

"Have you been with him every moment since you came here?" my brother interrupted.

"Of course not," I said with a shrug. "No one is ever together twenty-four hours a day. Besides, I was unconscious the first twenty-four hours I was here, thanks to the hellhound."

Puck pegged me with a serious look. "And has Seth ever acted suspiciously around you? Paranoid?"

I blinked at my brother, remembering my initial conversation with Seth. He'd acted suspicious and paranoid then, but his paranoia was easily understandable. He'd been hunted for most of his existence. That would tend to make anyone a little jumpy. But last night was a different story. I knew he was lying to me about what had happened. I just didn't know why.

Puck sighed, apparently sensing my uneasiness. "Come stay with me, Lav," he pleaded. "I'd feel a lot better knowing you're safe. And, what can I say—I've missed you, kiddo. Wasn't sure I'd ever see you again."

"You knew how to find me," I reminded him. "You made it very clear when you left that you'd cut your ties to us. And then when we all came over and had the chance to start over . . . you could have reached out, *Robin*."

He bristled at my use of his real name. "You were already in enough trouble," he replied. "Didn't want to add to it."

I gave him a wry look, letting him know he could peddle that bull-shit somewhere else. Puck had always done—and would always do—what was best for Puck.

"Speaking of trouble," he continued, his voice low, "your indiscretions with that werewolf aren't the only things I'm worried about. Anyone else finds out you know those symbols, petal, I don't know what they might do."

I set my fork aside, my appetite now gone at the reminder. "There are other Tales who know that magic."

"If they came over they're already in the FMA prisons or in the Asylum," Puck said, shaking his head. "That leaves only you, baby girl."

"You saw those symbols," I whispered. "They were amateurish, unpolished—not even remotely my style. You know it wasn't me."

He nodded. "Of course, *I* do. But I *know* you, Lavender. I know your style, your finesse. Hell, I've been jealous of your talent since we were kids! But everyone in this town knows you brought us to the Here and Now using a form of dark magic totally foreign to them." He reached across the table and took my arm, pushing up my sleeve. "And it looks to me like you've been using that same magic since you've been here. If someone makes the connection . . ."

He didn't have to finish. I knew what would happen. I glanced around the restaurant, wondering just how long it would take the townspeople to come after me with the proverbial torches and pitchforks if they discovered the truth about my knowledge of the crimes. Even with my brother's protection, there was no telling what might happen.

"I've got to get to the bottom of this," I told him, "figure out who's behind it before it comes to that."

"No," Puck insisted, "you need to stay the hell away from it, Lavender. I'll sort it all out. I'm your big brother—it's my job to protect you. Just leave everything to me."

Chapter 10

When Puck pulled into the parking lot of his casino, I couldn't help gaping in awe. With its bright white paint, wraparound porches, and pitched roofs with red shingles, the sprawling Victorian structure looked more like a luxury ocean-side resort than a casino. As I stepped out of the car, the soothing crash of the ocean waves upon the stretch of beach behind the casino and the scent of the salty air wrapped around my senses.

"My God, Puck," I breathed. "This is amazing!"

He grinned as he swaggered toward me. "You think this is incredible, you should see inside. Come on in and take a look."

He wasn't kidding. The interior of the casino was the most high-class establishment I've ever seen this side of Monte Carlo, and by the look of the Ordinaries and Tales milling about with complimentary champagne glasses, the clientele were not your average gamblers.

"I feel a little underdressed," I mumbled as Puck came to stand at my shoulder, his hands in his pockets as he surveyed his empire.

"Nah, don't worry about it," he said with a shrug. "No one will notice."

I frowned and started to ask what he meant, but then I felt it—the gentle, soothing tingle that started in my fingertips and slowly began to spread up my arms. In a matter of seconds it would reach my spinal cord and then my cares would drift away as the fairy dust took over my central nervous system.

"Oh, my God, Puck," I gasped. "You're drugging these people!"

Puck shrugged away my objection with a grimace. "What's a few airborne sedatives among friends? It's just to relax everybody, keep them happy and calm. I've never had a single belligerent visitor. I don't even need to hire a security staff."

I shook my head. "This is wrong," I admonished. "You are creating addicts! Like gambling isn't addictive enough—these people will keep coming here over and over again just to get a fix of D."

Puck spread his arms and inhaled deeply, filling his lungs with the sweetly scented air. "Ah, but isn't that a basic tenet of corporate marketing? Create a false need and keep them coming back for more!"

"We're not talking about convincing the public they need to buy brand-new cars every couple of years," I fumed. "What you're doing is dangerous and irresponsible."

"You'd know a thing or two about that, as I recall."

Furious and disappointed, I spun on my heel and stormed toward the door, but I'd barely gone three feet when my brother blocked my way. "Come on, petal," he cajoled. "Would you feel better if I told you I dilute the D so that it has pretty much the same effects as the oxygen Vegas casinos pipe in? The D just makes them a little . . . less inhibited."

"If our parents knew what you were doing . . ." I warned, leaving my sentence unfinished. Honestly, there's no telling *what* my parents would do if they found out their once-beloved son was now harvesting fairy dust on his own and foisting it upon an unsuspecting population. My mother was a nagging, meddling harpy and was certainly not a fairy queen you wanted to fuck with. However, she looked like a delicate little sprite compared to my father. Although he was usually mild-mannered, few people ever incurred my father's wrath and lived to tell the tale—which is why you'd never recognize his name even if I told you.

"Trust me," Puck went on, "I'm not even using the good stuff. Most of the time everyone just has a mild buzz."

"Still . . ." I shook my head quickly, trying to combat the effects of the D. I attempted to formulate my long list of objections, but they began to drift away along with all my other cares.

"Come on, Lavender!" my brother whooped, grabbing me around the waist and spinning me around. "Have a little fun!" He set me down again and swept his arm toward the bustling casino. "Go ahead and partake in the merriment—on the house."

"I can't," I said, laughing, although I wasn't sure what was funny. "I have stuff to do . . . important stuff." I frowned, trying to remember what exactly it was.

As one of the waiters passed by, Puck snatched up two flutes of champagne and held one out to me. "I'm sure there's nothing that can't wait a little while," he said, his grin as wide and as mischievous as always. "Come on, little sister—we haven't seen each other in decades! The least you can do is hang out with me for a couple of hours."

Although some still-coherent part of me warned that every time Puck and I hung out I ended up getting into trouble, I took the champagne flute and raised it in salute. "What the hell."

The worst part was the taste in my mouth—that dry, pasty, sour taste that I'd woken up with every morning for almost two hundred years. I rubbed my eyes with the heels of my hands and sat up, glancing around me. I appeared to be in a massive living room filled with white leather couches, plush white carpet, and rather racy modern art covering the walls. Draped over the various couches and easy chairs and passed out on the floor, were several naked men and women—some of them curled up together, others apparently having fallen asleep where they'd landed.

What the hell had happened?

Then it all came rushing back to me—fairy dust, champagne . . . general debauchery.

Shit.

I quickly looked down, reassuring myself that I hadn't participated in one of Puck's infamous orgies. My boots were missing as was the steampunk jacket I'd worn over my buckle dress, but the rest of my clothes were in place. A small comfort at least.

I ran my hands through my hair and went in search of my belongings and a bathroom where I could at least try to freshen up a bit before leaving. Considering how much champagne I'd probably imbibed, there was no telling what state my appearance was in.

Once I found the bathroom, I had to roll a busty blonde out before I could shut the door and have a little privacy. When I looked in the mirror, tears stung my eyes. The woman looking back at me was one I thought I'd shaken off over a year ago. Her eyes were bloodshot and swollen. Her hair was a ratty mess. And her lovely face looked haggard and worn.

Sniffing, I wiped at my eyes, clearing away the blur, then snatched a hand towel from the silver hook by the sink and wet down the corner so that I could wash my face and try to reduce the swelling around my eyes. But with each swipe, the tears in the center of my chest welled up higher and higher until they finally spilled over onto my cheeks. Covering my face with the towel, I sank down onto the floor and sobbed into the plush cotton. I'd betrayed Red and the promise I'd made to her to stay sober and get my shit together. But, worse, I'd betrayed myself and my hard-fought war for sobriety. I hated myself more at that moment than I had in all the long years I'd been in the Here and Now.

Finally, when the tears had at last subsided, I managed to pull myself together again and put my appearance into passable order. Then, taking a deep breath and squaring my shoulders, I went in search of a way out of Puck's apartment, hoping to get the hell out of there before any of his harem woke up and saw me skulking away. I'd just spotted what appeared to be the front door when I caught a sudden whiff of cloves.

"Leaving so soon? That was just Act One."

I turned an angry glare on my brother. "Bite me," I snapped. "I'm going home."

"To dog-boy?" Puck taunted, tying his bathrobe around his waist. "You can do so much better, Lav."

"I don't recall asking your opinion," I hissed, waving away the plume of clove-scented smoke he exhaled with such swaggering suavity it probably drove the women wild. I just found it annoying. "And I sure as hell can't stay here with you. You're just as bad an influence as ever. I love you, Puck, and I'll hang out with you in town or on my own turf, but I'm never coming back here."

He gave me a wounded pout. "Now, petal—"

"Don't *now petal* me," I shot back, spotting my boots and jacket on a rug by the door and snatching them up. "I should've turned around and left the moment I realized you were drugging your patrons. And don't give me that bullshit about a mild buzz from diluted D. If it affected *me* that much, it means you're using *pixie* dust."

Of all the fairy dust available on the market—black or otherwise—the dust harvested from pixies was by far the most potent. And the most addictive. Being a fairy myself, I couldn't become hooked on it, but that wasn't the case for the rest of the Tales. And God knew what it would do to Ordinaries. From what I understood, though, it was the Tale equivalent of LSD. There was a reason people always thought they could fly after a little sprinkle of pixie dust.

Puck rolled his eyes and took a drag off his cigarette. *"Please,"* he replied. "You're just sensitive after being so cut off for so long. For chrissake, Lavender—you're so out of touch with who you really are, you probably couldn't even produce a little dust on your own now if you tried. The pixies I have on retainer charge a fucking fortune. There's no way I'd use my most expensive product on the average asshole who waltzes in! Trust me—you only got a taste of my normal cheap stuff until we came to my little private party."

I pegged him with a pointed glare. "And what happened at the party?" I gestured to the naked partygoers scattered all over his apartment.

Puck gave me a cockeyed grin. "Well, you were a sad prude, unfortunately, so you missed most of the fun. One of our friends from the restaurant took quite a liking to you, but you were disappointingly uninterested, no matter how much she shook her lovely little pixie titties at you."

"Those girls are the ones you have on retainer," I deduced. "That's why they are so eager to please. It's not just because you're screwing them—you're paying them a fortune for their pixie dust!"

He let out a wistful sigh. "Exactly so. Giselle—with the green hair—offered to waive her fee for the evening if she could have you as her plaything. You could've at least let her get to second base and saved me a few dollars. And who knows—you might've even enjoyed yourself a little for once."

I shook my head in disbelief. "Wow. You unbelievable jackass. And here I thought your days of using me for your own amusement were gone. I guess next time you decide to pimp me out to save some money, you should let me know first so I'll know how far to go."

Beyond pissed now, I whirled back toward the door but felt his hand grasping my elbow before I could make my escape.

"I'm sorry," Puck said, his tone sincere. "I can be a total asshole sometimes. I'm so used to these people fawning all over me, I forget that every now and then I need to think of someone else. Forgive me."

I looked up at him, wondering if he was bullshitting me, but his expression seemed sincere. "Don't ever pull this kind of shit on me again, Puck."

He bent and gave me a kiss on the cheek. "You have my word, petal. I'll be on my best behavior with you from this point forward."

I narrowed my eyes at him, wondering where the catch was. But then I heard a pouty voice calling his name and decided not to bother sticking around any longer to find out. I snatched his cigarette out from between his fingers and stubbed it out in the ashtray stand by the door. "I'll believe it when I see it," I told him, then took off down the hall before he could stop me again.

I somehow managed to find the elevator and took it down to the main floor. When the doors opened into the casino, I made sure not to breathe except in short, small bursts until I'd made it to the main entrance, where a smiling doorman was more than happy to call for a car to take me home.

The sky was already dark by the time Puck's driver dropped me in front of Seth's little cabin. The house was quiet and dark but for the flickering candlelight I could see from the front porch. I started to knock on the front door, but thought better of it and instead slipped quietly inside, shutting the door gently behind me.

"Welcome back."

I started at the sudden sound of Seth's voice and spun around, probably looking as guilty as I felt. He was sitting at the table, a half-consumed glass of red wine in his hand, the food he'd prepared still on the table, untouched.

I closed my eyes and muttered a curse under my breath. "Seth, I'm so sorry," I said, coming a few steps toward him. "I went to visit my brother's casino and . . ." I paused, not wanting to divulge the truth of what had occurred. "Well, we just lost track of time."

Seth shrugged. "No big deal. When you didn't show at the town meeting—"

Ah, hell.

"—I explained that you were the mayor's sister and that he'd given his blessing for you to stay. Luckily, they agreed not to run you out on a rail."

"Thank you," I said, feeling like the most ungrateful bitch ever born. I forced a smile. "Dinner looks amazing."

"It would've been about two hours ago."

I glanced at the clock that hung on his wall. Eleven o'clock.

Shit.

"I'm sure it still is," I replied, trying to make amends. "Let me go change so I don't smell like casino"—*or booze and fairy dust*—"and I'll come join you."

I hurried off before he could object and came back a moment later, wearing the first thing I'd seen—which happened to be one of Seth's button-downs hanging on the closet doorknob. He was tall enough that the shirt came down to mid-thigh on me, so I didn't have to worry too much about my modesty. Plus, at that moment, the scent of him comforted me like nothing else could.

Wishing it was his arms and not just his shirt enveloping me, I pulled out the chair next to his and sat down, shifting the plate and flatware to that position at the table. His expression was mildly curious, but he didn't say a word as I cut a piece of chateaubriand and raised it to my lips.

Even though it had long ago cooled off, the steak was magnificent. I'd never tasted anything so delicious. I closed my eyes for a moment, savoring the taste. "My God, Seth," I sighed. "This is delicious!"

He grunted dismissively, but when I turned my eyes toward him, his look of pleasure and gratification as he watched me eat what he'd prepared was impossible to mistake. And the longer our gazes held, the hungrier his expression became. I felt the heat rising in my cheeks and suddenly found it difficult to breathe—let alone swallow the mouthful of delectable food.

"I really am sorry," I said softly, once I'd managed to force the food down past the pounding pulse in my throat. "Standing you up was unforgivable."

He shrugged. "Shitty, maybe, but not unforgivable."

"What can I do to make it up to you?"

A slow grin curved his lips, making me wonder what I'd just offered. "Finish your dinner," he said, "and then I'll tell you how you can make amends."

I huffed and turned my glare on Seth as he leaned smugly against the kitchen counter. "This is *so* not what I had in mind," I grumbled. I waved the scrub brush toward a pile of dishes on the countertop, flinging suds and water in a wide arc. "Washing this many dishes approaches cruel and unusual punishment."

He didn't bother to hide his amusement. "You're making it a lot harder than it needs to be. You obviously haven't washed many dishes."

I made a noise in the back of my throat as I began scrubbing anew at the cast-iron skillet in the sink. "Of course not! Why would I? That's what magic is for. In fact, there's a very simple spell that could take care of these in no time—"

"Oh, no." Seth laughed, shaking his head. "I've read that story. I know how it turns out."

I gave him a sour look. "What do you think I'm going to do—flood your kitchen after the mops and brooms go wonky? Come on! It's *easy*. I've been doing it since I was a little girl."

"Well, it's time you learned a new method." He pushed away from the counter with a chuckle, and motioned for me to get back to it. I felt him move in behind me, his body pressing into mine as he reached around to take hold of my hand. He began to move it in small, circular motions. "It's much easier this way," he said, his lips close to my ear. "See how much better that is?"

I nodded, unable to form a coherent thought with the warmth of him seeping through the thin shirt and into my veins, setting off an inferno in my body. He had to feel the rapid, shallow breath sawing in and out of my lungs, but his own was perfectly calm, perfectly controlled. The only indication that he felt the growing charge in the air between us was when his fingers tightened around mine and the small, circular motions he was guiding me through became even slower and more sensual. And when he turned his face into my hair ever so slightly and inhaled, the nearness of his lips to the curve of my neck sent a shudder through me that I didn't even bother to try to hide.

His fingers slipped between mine and then skimmed along the top of my hand and along the inside of my forearm—luckily not the one with the still-healing symbols. I let my eyes flutter closed as my breath left me on a gasp. But then he took a step back, abruptly putting distance between us.

"There," he said, his voice gruff, flustered. "I think you've got it."

Completely confused and disconcerted by my reaction to his touch, and still reeling from the heat coursing through my veins, I shook my head, clearing my throat when I tried to speak and no sound came out. But then I glanced out the kitchen window and caught sight of what it was that had distracted him.

The moon. It was just a sliver, but even the portion of it showing through the clouds in the sky was radiant and cast a soft white light on the forest.

With a sigh, I rinsed the skillet and set it aside to dry, then dried my hands on the nearby dishtowel before I turned around. Seth stood on the opposite side of the small kitchen, bracing himself against the cabinets, his head hanging low.

"Seth," I said quietly, coming toward him. "Are you all right?"

He nodded, but when he lifted his eyes to mine, I could see the tortured emotion there. I stepped closer, cautiously, not wanting to push him too hard. But when I took his face in my hands, he didn't flinch. And when I pressed my forehead to his, his hands came up to encircle my waist and pull me closer. And when I shifted to brush my lips against his, his own responded, clinging to mine, drawing out the kiss. I could feel the mutual desire, the heat building between us in that one simple kiss, but I also felt him holding back, not willing to give in, even though we both knew where we wanted things to go. After a moment, he pulled back, squeezing his eyes shut as if by closing his eyes he could will me away.

"I'm sorry," I said, my face flooding with heat. "I—God, I'm sorry. I shouldn't have done that."

I tried to move away, but he grabbed my hand and pulled me back to him. "It's not you, Lavender," he told me, his tone sincere enough to make me believe it wasn't just a line. Then he bowed forward, resting his forehead on my shoulder, poised on the edge of a precipice from which I couldn't rescue him because I wasn't quite sure why he was there.

I put my arms around him, twining my fingers through his hair. "Tell me your story, Seth," I whispered, desperate to understand the depth of his pain. "Tell me what happened to you."

Chapter 11

"Once upon a time, I was an honorable and gallant knight who traveled through Make Believe, performing heroic deeds and protecting those who couldn't protect themselves," Seth began as soon as we'd settled onto the sofa in front of the fire with our raspberry chocolate tortes and freshly brewed cups of coffee.

"One of the deeds I performed most often," he continued, his voice taking on a wistfulness I'd never heard from him, "was slaying horrible beasts that terrorized the Tales, stole from them, made off with their children in the night. What could be a more noble use of my skills and talents than that? Soon I gained a reputation as one of the most feared slayers in the land."

I rested my chin on the palm of my hand, studying his profile in the firelight. It didn't take a huge feat of imagination to picture him astride a great steed, his armor shining, his golden brown locks falling about his shoulders as he brandished a sword. I saw him racing into battle against a mighty dragon, taking it down with so little effort the dragon didn't even seen its defeat coming.

"But, as I'm sure you know, the greater your reputation becomes, the more often you're tested by those who would love to see you fail."

I nodded. "We Tales love to build each other up, then tear each other down. We can take a completely ordinary and banal event and gild it in golden lies until it becomes a story of legend. But then we celebrate when those very same legends are revealed as nothing more than products of our own imaginations, that they are fallible, imperfect."

Seth turned his gaze on me. "That sounds like it comes from personal experience."

I grunted. "Yeah, well, we all have our stories. I'll tell you mine another time. Right now, I want to hear the rest of yours."

He nodded slowly and took a sip of his coffee before continuing. "There for a while, I couldn't enter a town without some young upstart challenging me to a duel or a joust or demanding a demonstration. It was becoming tedious—and I felt I was losing my sense of purpose. So I decided to hide out in the woods for a while, to seclude myself for a time, maybe let my legend die down a little."

He sighed and took another sip of coffee.

"I met her on my second day in the woods," he said. "Her name was Meryn. She was so beautiful she took my breath away. She'd been gathering herbs and roots in the forest near my campsite and had come to investigate who'd taken up residence so near her home. I was enchanted by her gentleness, her beauty, I didn't hesitate when she invited me to her little cottage." Here Seth hesitated and he sent a rather uncomfortable glance my way.

"You became lovers," I supplied, sensing where that part of the story was going.

He nodded. "I was naïve, inexperienced. She taught me how to love a woman, how to give and receive pleasure. But that wasn't all she taught me. I learned about the forest, its beauties as well as its dangers. She taught me how to cook, how to incorporate the flavors of the world around me into the food I prepared."

"She sounds like an amazing woman," I said, feeling a little stab of jealousy.

"She was that," he said. "I loved her. And I loved our life together. She spoke of having family elsewhere—of a mother, brothers, sisters. . . ." He sighed. "But we never went to visit. We were devoted solely to one another. It seemed to be all that either of us needed. The only times we were apart were on those occasions when she slipped off alone at night. She always returned with fresh game for us. I suggested she let me go with her to protect her from harm, but she laughed off my concerns."

When he paused, his gaze intent on the flames dancing in the fireplace, I prompted, "So what happened?"

He let out a heavy sigh. "I could only hide from my reputation for so long. One day, three men from a nearby village came to our cottage looking for me. They'd been searching for me for the better part of a year. Their livestock was being slaughtered and they needed someone to slay the beast—or beasts—doing it before their families starved."

"So you came out of retirement," I guessed.

He nodded. "Meryn begged me not to. She was worried that harm would come to me." Here he paused and chuckled bitterly. "I should've listened."

I twined my fingers with his. He grasped them loosely, but his thoughts were clearly elsewhere.

"Just before nightfall, I took up position in the village near where the livestock was penned, but nothing came. I returned every night for a week, but whatever had been killing the livestock appeared to have moved on. That final morning, I assured the villagers that their troubles seemed to be over and then made my way home. But on the road I encountered a farmer from another village who complained of mysterious attacks on his livestock."

"The creatures had moved on to the next village," I surmised.

Seth nodded. "I told the farmer I'd do what I could to help him. So, off I went that night, intent on being the hero. I kissed Meryn good-bye, told her I loved her and that I'd see her soon. It didn't take long before the first creature appeared. It was humanlike, but not quite. Monstrous, hideous. It had horns and wings like a bat's. A demon of some sort, maybe—or perhaps a gargoyle. I've never known for sure. Then came another and another. In all, I believe there were eight of them. I was terrified—and woefully outnumbered. I was able to kill three of the creatures with my bow before they even realized I was there. Two others met their deaths at the point of my sword."

"And the others?" I prompted.

"Two of them attacked me, nearly killed me, while the third

looked on," he said. "They dragged me off with them into the woods to their lair. When I awoke, I was lying in my bed, my wounds clean and dressed. I immediately went in search of Meryn, terrified that she'd been hurt by the monsters that had attacked me. When I didn't find her in the cottage, I ran outside and was horrified by what I saw. Lying on the ground were the bodies of five people—three of them bearing wounds from arrows, two from a sword. They were women, men, even a boy who was only eleven or twelve years old."

"The creatures you'd killed—they were shapeshifting humans," I said.

"Not only that," he replied, his voice going deeper with sorrow. "One of them was my beloved Meryn. She'd been one of the first I killed. I'd been so desperate to prove myself worthy, to do my duty, it never occurred to me that I might be putting her in danger by my actions."

"Oh, Seth," I breathed, "I'm so sorry."

"Well, I got what was coming to me," he replied. "The creature watching from the sidelines was Meryn's mother Aurelia—who, as it turned out, was a very powerful enchantress whose five children I'd just slain in my arrogance. They'd all been cursed by a rival enchantress who was jealous of Aurelia's power. They had no control over their transformations, the need to kill, but they had learned to kill livestock instead of humans." He ran his hand down his face, the pain of what he'd done etched in every line of his features. "They were simply misunderstood. And I'd murdered them."

"I've never heard of this Aurelia," I said with a slight shake of my head. "And who was her rival? Did you ever find out?"

Seth shrugged. "Hell, back then you couldn't spit without hitting a witch or a sorceress or an enchantress of some sort."

I had to give him that one. "So what happened next?"

"In retribution for all I'd taken from her, Aurelia cursed me to be a werewolf so I'd spend the rest of my days being hunted and hated. She cast me out of my idiom of medieval romances and into the fairytales, where I was certain to be seen as a villain. And to the curse she added the bonus punishment of being unable to die except by silver bullet or a wound so grievous my body couldn't heal, thus forcing me to die slowly and painfully." Here he turned and offered me a bitter smile. "I thought that time had finally come the other night until you stepped in and took care of me."

"What did you do after you were cursed?" I asked, quickly diverting the conversation.

He shrugged. "I wandered, lost, heartbroken, hunted and hated—just as Meryn's mother had intended. For several years, I had no control over my transformations—or what I did while I was in wolf form. God knows what atrocities I committed during that time. Sometimes these flashes of images come to me—like half-remembered nightmares." He let his head fall back onto the pillows and pressed the heels of his palms to his eyes.

Seeing him so tormented, so tortured, made my heart ache. Not knowing how to comfort him, I scooted closer and laid my hand on his chest over where his heart beat so strongly. After several agonizing moments, he covered my hand with one of his as the other dropped onto his lap. His fingers curled around mine, and he finally opened his eyes.

"Anyway," he continued on a shaky sigh, "after a while, I settled down, built a cabin. I'd managed to gain enough control that I thought perhaps I could lead a normal life again. But it was lonely. Horribly lonely. Until one day I was hunting in wolf form and a beautiful young woman crossed my path. She was out walking, taking food to a sick aunt—not her grandmother as the story would have it."

"Red," I said, my stomach sinking.

At this, the corner of his mouth hitched up in a grin. "She was so striking, so unexpected, I stopped dead in my tracks when I saw her. I caught her gaze, and I couldn't look away. I thought she would scream or run—show some sign of fear at encountering a wolf in the woods. But she just stood there, blinking at me—fearless, strong, defiant—quintessential Tess." He chuckled at the remembrance and ran a hand over his haggard face. "I transformed then, right before her eyes, thinking that would be enough to scare her away, but she stayed there, her head cocked to one side as she studied me. 'You shouldn't be out here alone,' I told her. And do you know what she said?"

I shook my head, the pain in his expression stealing my voice.

He turned that crooked smile on me. "She said, 'I'm not alone anymore.' Then she gave me that look of hers—you know the one where it feels like she just sized you up in a glance and now knows all your deepest secrets—and said, 'And neither are you.' "

He chuckled again, but this time it sounded choked with sorrow, and he averted his eyes. "God, I loved her."

We sat in silence for a long moment before I could bring myself to ask, "If you loved her so much, why did you leave her?"

He exhaled a long sigh. "*She* was fearless," he said, "but I wasn't. I was a coward. I was so afraid of hurting her as I'd done Meryn, I let that fear rule me. For a while, I pretended Tess and I could have a normal life together. But when the villagers came after me, I realized I was a fool. I told myself I was protecting Tess, saving her from a life of sorrow and heartache when she deserved so much better. I figured that if I cut and ran, it would be easier for her. I realize now that deep down I was more concerned about what would be easier for me. I was terrified that if she came with me, she would someday realize she'd made a horrible mistake in loving me and would come to hate me."

"Why did you not tell her any of this after we came over?" I asked.

"I did," he admitted. "But it was too little too late." He sighed again. "Anyway, I guess it all turned out for the best in the end. Nate seems like a pretty good guy. Does he treat her right?"

I nodded, thinking of the way Nate and Red were when they were together and how much his love had changed Red's life. I hadn't known her very well before they met, but I'd heard of her and her various adventures. And since knowing her as a dear friend, I'd come to see just how rare and beautiful their love was. It gave me hope that maybe someday I'd find a love like that, too. "Nate adores her. He'd die for her."

"Good," Seth said, nodding. "Good. I'm glad she's so happy. She deserves it."

"So do you," I blurted, feeling my face go warm as he turned that soft, caressing gaze upon me. "I mean, don't you think you've tortured yourself long enough for what happened to Meryn and for your mistakes with Tess? It's time you let yourself be happy, too."

"I thought that way recently," he admitted, "but it didn't turn out well. I had a chance to find love again with a woman named Molly

O'Grady. She was a friend of mine—an Ordinary. She'd been good to me, knew the truth of my condition, what I was. I really cared about Molly and probably could've let myself fall in love with her eventually, but I didn't realize she was in love with me until it was too late. I never got the chance to tell her how much she meant to me. Hell— I'd never even kissed her."

"Molly was the Ordinary woman Sebille Fenwick killed," I said, remembering the stories in the Tale papers. "The one she murdered and tried to pin on you."

"Heard about that, did you?"

I shook my head. "I read about it like everyone else. Sebille was an evil, manipulative bitch. She was using anyone and everyone she could to further her own quest for power. Red told me that once Sebille was gone and they started digging a little deeper into what she'd been trying to pull off in Chicago, the FMA discovered she had her followers so brainwashed into believing she was some kind of deliverer that no one would even give up a lead to what might've happened to her corpse when it vanished from FMA headquarters. You can't be responsible for the actions of someone that freaking crazy, Seth. What happened to Molly was tragic, but it wasn't your fault."

Seth's frown deepened. "I know it was actually Sebille who killed Molly. But at the time, I wasn't so sure I was innocent. The thing is, Lavender, there's nothing to prevent me from actually hurting someone I care about. Hell—I turned on you the other night. I was so out of it I could've killed you."

"But you didn't."

He abruptly stood and snatched up his plate and coffee cup and strode angrily to the kitchen. I was on my feet in an instant, hurrying after him.

"Seth," I called. "Seth, wait—"

My words were cut off by the sound of his howl of rage and the shattering of one of the dishes lobbed against the wall. Then there was a clatter and a splash and a loudly roared curse. Concerned and a little afraid of what Seth might do in his sorrow, I ran into the kitchen. The moment I hit the tile, though, my feet slid out from under me and I came crashing down hard on the floor, landing in the water that had splashed out when Seth threw his dish in the sink.

"Motherf—" I bit off the curse and squeezed my eyes shut, curling into the pain in my recently healed ribs.

Seth was at my side in an instant. "Oh, shit," he muttered, his hand covering mine where it was pressed against my ribs. "I'm sorry, Lavender. I wasn't . . . *damn* it!"

"It's okay," I gasped, wiping at the beads of sweat that had popped up on my forehead as Seth carefully helped me to my feet. "It was an accident."

"Here, let me take a look," he said, gently moving my hand aside. Before I realized what he was doing, he'd unbuttoned three of the buttons on the shirt and had slid his hand inside.

My eyes snapped open at the warmth of his hand on my skin. "What the hell—"

"Just checking your ribs to make sure they didn't crack again," he explained, his brows furrowed in a frown. As he explored the tender area along my rib cage, I turned my face up to the ceiling, trying desperately not to think about what his touch was doing to me.

It had been ages since a man had touched me. And even though Seth's hand smoothed my skin in a purely clinical manner, it set my heart racing and ignited a prickling heat that started in the center of my stomach and quickly spread through my body. And when Seth's thumb grazed the underside of my breast, I couldn't stop the little gasp that escaped my lips.

"Doesn't look like there was any damage," he said, his voice a little deeper, rougher than I remembered. "You just . . . uh . . . I . . ."

I turned my gaze away from the ceiling and found him staring at me, his eyes glowing like radioactive fire. I swallowed hard as his hand slid around to the small of my back, the gentle pressure there bringing my body a little closer to his.

"You, what?" I breathed, my hands sliding up his abs to his chest, where I could feel his heart pounding as hard as mine.

"Don't know," he whispered, his eyes growing hooded. "Shit."

The next thing I knew, his lips were on mine, demanding, devouring. And I was kissing him back, my lips just as hungry for his. I didn't know what the hell had come over me, but I was like an animal, moaning and writhing as his hands roamed my back, the curve of my hips, my ribs. And when his thumbs brushed over my nipples, I nearly exploded.

With a feral growl, Seth grasped my hips and lifted me up, setting me down on the counter and stepping into the V of my open thighs. "This is such a bad idea," he muttered, ripping open my shirt and sending the remaining buttons flying.

I gasped as his mouth captured one of my breasts. I twined my fingers in his hair, letting my head fall back on my shoulders. "I know," I panted, wrapping my legs around his waist. "It's really late. We should be in bed."

His head shot up. "Good idea."

He wrapped his arms around my waist and carried me from the kitchen to the bedroom. We'd barely made it through the threshold before he was pressing my back against the wall, and his mouth was on mine again, his tongue plunging between my lips in a frenzied rhythm. Desperate to experience that dizzying rhythm elsewhere, I rolled my hips against him. He groaned in response, letting me know he was right there with me.

His lips still plundering mine, he carried me over to the bed and lowered me onto the mattress, his body stretched out over mine. Now that his hands were free, they began to roam again. And when his hand slipped between my legs, I thought I would shatter apart. I cried out, arching up into him.

"Jesus," he hissed. "You're burning up."

My head was spinning, pleasure and desire an intoxicating mix that I couldn't seem to get enough of. When my release came, my scream filled the room as my back arched off the bed. But it wasn't enough. I needed more. I needed him. At that moment, the only thing I wanted was to feel him inside me, to feel that blissful coupling I'd denied myself for far too long.

But before I could voice my demands, Seth had hastily stripped out of his clothes and his naked body eased down over mine. I felt the smooth head of his erection pressing in and retreating ever so slightly, teasing me, drawing out the sweet anticipation of what was coming.

I took his face in my hands and held his bright, feral gaze. My

God, I wanted him. I'd never wanted any man as badly as I did right then. It was insane. I didn't know him. Didn't even completely trust him. And he'd made it very clear just a moment before that he wasn't looking for another relationship. But I knew if I didn't feel him inside me in the next ten seconds, I was going to lose my mind.

As if sensing my desperation, Seth grasped my hips and plunged deep, filling me up with one long thrust. We both cried out with the sudden joining and lay there, perfectly still for a heartbeat. But then Seth began to move his hips in that incredible, steady rhythm I'd longed for.

"Don't stop," I panted, taking hold of his shoulders, my nails digging into his skin. "Dear God, don't stop."

Chapter 12

When I awoke, sunlight was streaming in through the bedroom window. I stretched languidly, my lips curving into a satisfied grin. I'd never in my life experienced a night of such unbelievable passion.

Seth was incredible. Gorgeous. Totally selfless. And he made me feel more beautiful than I'd ever felt in my entire life. There was something in the way he'd looked at me while we made love that made me want to show him just how beautiful he was, too.

It was just sex, Lavender, I chided, forcing myself to face facts. *Don't romanticize it.*

The realization hit me hard in the chest, making it difficult to breathe. What we'd shared had been mind-blowingly fantastic, but it was just two lonely people finding a little solace in one another. In light of what he'd shared with me the night before, I had a feeling he was probably going to totally regret every moment of it with the typical morning-after misgivings.

That's what I kept telling myself over and over again as I lay there looking at the exposed rafters, listening to Seth's steady breathing beside me. But when he rolled onto his side and pressed a kiss to my shoulder, my heart skipped a beat.

"Good morning," he said, his arm sliding around me and pulling me into the curve of his body.

I snuggled into him, my fingers lacing with his. "Good morning yourself. I didn't sleep for shit. You snore."

He chuckled, the sound vibrating through me. "Sorry. I haven't slept that well in a long time."

I took a deep breath and let it out on a long sigh. "Seth, about last night . . ."

I felt him draw back ever so slightly, suddenly on his guard.

Shut up, Lavender, an inner voice warned. *Just shut the hell up before you ruin everything.*

"I just want you to know that I don't expect anything from you," I told him.

Once an idiot, always an idiot.

"No?"

I shook my head. "I know it was just sex."

"*Just* sex?" Seth repeated, his hand smoothing down my thigh. "Then maybe I should try harder."

"Don't you need to go to work?" I asked breathlessly as he pressed a kiss to the back of my neck.

"Nope," he said. "It's Saturday. I'm off today."

I closed my eyes. "Well, in that case . . ."

Our sexathon during the night had been frenzied, animalistic, full of need and desperation to feel alive—on both sides, I imagine. But this time, Seth took things slowly, his hands and mouth exploring every inch of my body, taking his time. After a while I lost track of the number of times he brought me to ecstasy before he finally let go and joined me in my blissful haze.

For a while we just lay in each other's arms, not speaking, just content to hold one another and feel the warmth of skin upon skin. Eventually, though, Seth pressed a kiss to my temple and rose from the bed, pulling on the jeans he'd hastily discarded the night before.

A few minutes later, he sauntered back into the bedroom carrying two steaming cups of coffee. He grinned as he handed one to me and sat down on the bed, leaning back against the headboard beside me.

"So," he said, taking a sip of his coffee. "Did I do any better this morning?"

Still a little dazed, I turned my head to look at him. "I didn't think it was possible," I grinned, "but yeah."

He leaned over and pressed a lingering kiss to my lips. "You're beautiful, you know that?"

I narrowed my eyes at him. "I bet you say that to all the girls."

He shook his head, his expression serious. "No, I don't. In fact, I haven't said it to anyone since coming over. You're the first woman I've been with in the Here and Now."

Which meant since Red.

My eyes went wide. "Oh, come on." I laughed. "You can't be serious!"

He shook his head again, his expression growing sad.

I studied him for a moment, watching him retreat into his thoughts. When it was clear he wasn't going to say any more on the topic, I asked tentatively, "So, why me? I mean, you'd never met me before I showed up here. Why suddenly break nearly two hundred years of celibacy to have sex with the seriously fucked-up fairy who ruined your life by transporting you here?"

"Why do you do that?" he demanded.

"Do what?"

"Remind me of the reasons I shouldn't like you."

I blinked at him. "I'm just stating a fact. It was my fault the Tales ended up here. I was messing with magic I had no business messing with, and I fucked it up. Big time."

"You're not the only one who's made mistakes, Lavender," he said. "I've got a list a mile long. Hell—you heard the biggest ones last night!"

"Oh, so we're playing one-up now?" I snapped, throwing back the covers and rising from the bed. I stormed into the bathroom and slammed the door, then turned on the shower, letting the steam fill the room as I sat there and tried to figure out why the hell I was being such a bitch. What was the deal? I'd just experienced hours of the most incredible sex of my life. So why was I trying to sabotage whatever it was that was happening between Seth and me?

Because I honestly had no idea what *was* happening between us. Seth was afraid of getting close to someone again for fear he would be a threat even if indirectly. So, if it was just sex, as I'd told him earlier, why was it such a big deal? We were adults. We could screw each other and have some fun and then walk away. Right?

Yeah, right.

The problem was, I was falling for him—even if he wasn't falling for me. And that truth was so painful, I wanted to curl up in a ball on the floor and cry.

A quiet rap on the door brought my head up as Seth peeked his head in. "You okay?"

"You never answered the question," I said by way of response.

"What question?"

"Why me, Seth?"

"I don't know," he replied. "I just know in spite of my fears and misgivings, I've never wanted someone so badly in my life."

I cocked my head to one side, studying him. "When did you first feel that way?"

He shrugged, frowning. "I don't know. Why does it matter?"

I reached up to my chest, where my pendant should have been. For the first time I realized it wasn't there. "Where's my necklace? Did you take it off me?"

Seth nodded. "Yeah, when I was cleaning you up. Burned the hell out of my hand, too—must be pretty high-grade silver. Anyway, I put it in the soap dish."

I felt tears springing to my eyes and got into the shower, mostly to keep him from seeing the disappointment suddenly washing over me.

"Don't worry," he said, now standing just on the other side of the shower curtain. "It wasn't damaged in the attack."

I swiped angrily at my eyes and sniffed, my heart breaking. "It wasn't real."

"What wasn't real? Your necklace?"

"No, your desire for me," I told him, my voice catching. "None of it was real."

"What the hell are you talking about?" he asked, pulling back the shower curtain. "Of course it was! Hell, Lavender, I could throw you down on the ground right now and still not get enough of you."

I shook my head. "But that's not *your* desire you're feeling."

He reached for me, but I avoided his touch. "Lavender, what—"

"You're enchanted!" I blurted.

He gaped at me, his face going pale. "You cast a spell on me?"

"The necklace is my family's crest," I explained, deliberately refusing to answer the question. "It's woven with a binding spell that contains my true name. When a fairy gives her name to another, it binds him to her. Forever. It's not something we ever do lightly."

Seth looked horrified, his eyes going dull. "So when I took off your necklace and it burned my hand . . ."

My shoulders sagged. "My true name was written on your heart."

He leaned back against the wall, his expression going dark. "Are you sure?"

I nodded.

"Is there a way to break the enchantment?"

"The necklace has to be destroyed by the one who forged it," I told him. "This one was a recent gift from my father. I have no idea who forged it, but I can try to contact him and find out."

He ran a hand through his hair and turned his gaze on me, his expression so hurt, so filled with sorrow, it was killing me. Still, I knew I had to tell him the truth—all of it—if I was truly going to make amends. "There's more."

He blinked at me. "What other fabulous news could you drop on me?" he snapped. "Here I thought"—he bit off his angry words and instead ground out—"What else?"

I held out my forearm, the symbols now just pink marks on my skin.

"What are those?"

"Runes," I said. "Symbols that are part of a dangerous form of magic that only a few Tales are allowed to practice. I used them the other night. On you."

He was visibly shaken and for a full minute just stared at me. Then, finally, he breathed, "Why?"

"To save your life," I said. "You were hurt so badly you were slipping away. I had to do something to save you. You're too—I care about you. I couldn't let you die." His face slowly morphed into an expression of such rage, I thought for a moment that he might rip out my throat. "Seth, I'm so sorry. I can't imagine how you must feel right now. I know how magic has tainted your life all these years."

"You don't know anything about it," he snapped. "You're not cursed, forced to live on the fringes because no one trusts you."

I shivered at his cold tone in spite of the heat in the shower. "Aren't I?"

His lip curled a little away from his teeth, his anger almost palpable. I reached for him, wanting desperately to make him see that I understood what he must be going through.

"I can't be here right now," he snarled, flinching away from my touch.

My throat felt tight. "Seth, please . . ."

He let out a bitter little laugh. "You're a magical creature, Lavender. You and your kind are all alike—you don't give a shit whose lives you fuck up. I should've known I couldn't trust you."

When I got out of the shower, I dressed slowly, not eager to face Seth again. But as it turned out, my anxiety was for nothing, because when I went out into the living room I realized he was gone.

My chest was so tight with the tears welling up again, I rubbed it with my closed fist, trying to work out the knot of regret and sorrow. But it didn't help. I had to do something to occupy my thoughts and keep them off of Seth, off of what we'd shared, or I'd go crazy.

The problem was, I was more or less trapped in the house. I had no idea how to get anywhere except into town. I glanced through the front picture window to see if the truck was still here, thinking maybe I should just take it and drive straight to the airport and go home to take my chances with James Charming's vendetta against me. But the truck was gone. And if the depth of the skid marks was any indication, Seth had left in a hurry.

I huffed in disappointment, then wandered randomly around the little cabin, looking for some way to occupy my time. There were several books on the shelves in the living room, but none of them interested me as I skimmed their titles. They were mostly the classics from which a large number of Tales had come and some recent fiction, thrillers and crime novels from what I could tell. And there were several books on woodworking, gardening, architecture, haute cuisine. I had to give Seth credit—his tastes in reading were eclectic. I was about to abandon my search when I caught sight of a small volume without a title blazoned on its spine.

Curious, I pulled it from the shelf and opened it. It appeared to be a journal of sorts, but the strong masculine script had not been recording any kind of story or personal diary. To me the contents appeared to be random notes, thoughts hastily jotted down. There were snippets of recipes, notes on culinary techniques, and—most surprisingly—scraps of half-written poems. They were beautiful, lyrical, and heartbreakingly poignant. Suddenly feeling like I was betraying Seth's privacy, I started to close the journal but stopped when I caught a glimpse of something in the center pages.

I flipped back to the center of the volume, surprised to find a section of the pages had been cut away to create a tiny secret compartment. And in the compartment was a single silver bullet.

"Oh, Seth," I breathed, realizing what I was looking at. It was his out. His insurance. If things ever got too bad, he had one certain way to bring it all to an end.

"What are you doing?"

I started so violently, the book fell from my hands, the silver bullet clattering to the floor. The room went so silent, the sound of the bullet rolling across the hardwood floor might as well have been a tank plowing through his living room.

I spun around to see Seth framed in the open doorway. "I'm sorry . . . I just . . ." I really didn't have any explanation. I'd been snooping and had gotten caught. Pretty much end of story.

Scowling, he charged over and snatched up the bullet, placing it into its hiding spot and jamming the book back on the shelf.

"I wasn't sure when you'd be back," I said, by way of excuse.

"So you thought you'd just go through my personal things?" he spat. "You haven't violated me enough?"

His words stung so badly, tears immediately sprang to my eyes. I reached out to touch his arm, trying to convince him to look at me, but he dodged my touch. "Seth, can we talk?"

"Nothing to talk about," he called over his shoulder as he stormed into the bedroom. A moment later, he returned, dragging my suitcases with him. "Let's go."

"You're throwing me out?" I cried.

"I've made other arrangements for you," he said, heading for the door. I hurried after him, catching up just in time to see him lobbing my suitcases into the back of the truck. "Get in."

"No," I retorted, crossing my arms over my chest and planting my Mary Janes. "I'm not going anywhere until you talk to me."

"I think we've done enough talking," he mumbled, casting a furious glance my way. "Get in the fucking truck."

I lifted my chin. "Make me."

"Fine." With a shake of his head, he stormed over and scooped me up into his arms.

"Let me go," I ordered. "I'm not going anywhere with you! I'll call my brother!"

Seth dumped me into the front seat of the truck and leaned in, his face close to mine. "I refuse to let you stay with your brother," he ground out. "He's not good for you."

"What do you care?" I shot back.

He glared at me for a long moment, then abruptly turned away and dropped down onto the ground, leaning back against the truck, his eyes closed.

Slowly, cautiously, I stepped down and sat on the ground beside him. We sat there in silence for several minutes before Seth finally said, "I'm a total son of a bitch, Lavender."

I let that one hang in the air, half-inclined to agree with him.

He opened his eyes and turned his head toward me. "The thing is, I *do* care," he said. "I know I shouldn't. I'm pissed as hell right now. But I care about you. The problem is, I'm not sure how much of what I feel about you is genuine and how much is enchantment. And, honestly, part of me doesn't give a damn. But I think if we're going to sort this out, you should probably stay somewhere else for a while."

I nodded. "Okay."

He sighed and took my hand. Then a few moments later, he pulled me to him. When I straddled his lap, he put his hands on my hips and held my gaze for a long moment before he said, "You didn't have to tell me about the enchantment, you know."

I took his face in my hands. "Yes, I did. It wasn't fair to you. I couldn't let you think that you actually cared for me. That you actually *wanted* to be with me."

He gazed at me for a moment longer, his head cocked to one side as he studied me, his brows drawn together in a dark frown. Then he leaned in and pressed his lips to mine in a slow, languid kiss that made my heart trip over itself. His lips were so warm, so loving, it made my chest tighten, and tears slipped onto my cheeks. When he pulled back, he gave me a sad smile and wiped away my tears. "No magic spell made me want to do that, Lavender. That was all me. But I . . . I don't know what I can offer you. I don't know that I can give you what you need."

Unable to bear the sorrow and regret in his eyes, I pressed my lips to his again and again, each kiss lasting a little longer than the one before it until there was only one kiss, and Seth's arms came around me, holding me tightly. And when he released me to lift my skirt and run his hands up my thighs, I moaned, wanting so badly to feel him inside me again, to recapture what we'd shared before the truth had gotten in the way.

Apparently feeling the same way, Seth grasped my hips and ground them against his so I could feel the hard length of him. Then, in the next moment, he'd hefted me up and had set me on the truck's seat. For a brief moment, I thought he was going to tell me again how we couldn't be together, but then he was shoving up my skirt and pulling off my panties and thrusting deep inside me with a groan.

I gave myself over to the moment, not daring to hope what it might mean—or even caring if it meant anything at all. All I knew was the pleasure I craved, the fullness of him inside me, and the overwhelming love I suddenly knew I felt for this man.

The sex was quick, rough, and not nearly enough for either of us. A few moments later, we were back inside, shedding our clothes in desperation so that we could join our bodies once more. And we did. On the floor of the living room. On the dining room table. Bent over the back of his sofa. Against the bedroom wall. And, finally, back in his bed where we spent the rest of the day. As the sun began to set, we both collapsed, completely exhausted. At some point I must have fallen asleep because the next thing I knew, I felt Seth's fingertips gently running up and down my spine as I lay on my stomach.

I turned my head so that I was facing him. His expression was a mixture of sadness and some other emotion I couldn't quite place. "Is it time to go then?" I whispered.

He closed his eyes and sighed, his fingertips beginning to play along the curve of my ass and down the seam of my body until he reached the center of me. I gasped a little at his touch and writhed against his hand, finding it hard to believe I was so ready to go at it again.

"I don't know that I can let you go," he said, bending forward to press a kiss to my shoulder.

"Then you probably should," I said a little breathlessly as his fingertip began to caress the swollen bud of pleasure that was burning for his touch.

I felt him nod as he continued to kiss my back. "Probably," he murmured. "But not yet."

"No," I gasped as heat built rapidly, my body preparing to shatter apart. "Not yet."

Chapter 13

The next morning, Seth unloaded my suitcases from the back of his truck, then helped me unpack them.

"Are you sure about this?" I asked. "I want you to be sure. What if my father is able to destroy my necklace and you discover you don't want me here after all?"

"Won't happen," he said with a shrug. "Trust me."

I studied him for a long moment, wondering at his complete one-eighty. There had to be more to it than just incredible sex, right? I had to believe that after his initial shock and anger over the enchantment, he'd realized that what was truly in his heart had nothing to do with magic.

Right?

I smiled at him as I handed him the last of my shoes to line up on the floor of the closet next to his running shoes, work boots, and two pairs of combat boots. And suddenly I didn't give a shit if what he felt for me was enhanced by the enchantment. I knew that was selfish and unfair. And as soon as the enchantment was broken, I'd most likely find myself dejected and heartbroken. But right now I was happy. And I loved him. My God, I loved him. And I was going to cling to every single moment of that for as long as it lasted.

"So, are you off work again today?" I asked, trying to keep the conversation light.

He grabbed me around the waist and jerked me close, giving me that smile of his that turned my knees to jelly. "Why, hoping to stay in bed all day?"

I felt my face going hot and knew I must've gone about three shades of red. "I was just wondering what you had planned."

He kissed me briefly, then released me to stack up the empty luggage. "I was hoping to take you to meet a friend of mine. She'd planned on meeting you last night, but that obviously didn't happen."

"Was she the one who was going to take me in before we . . ." I paused, considering my words.

"Before we made up?" he supplied with a wink.

I nodded.

"Yes," he confirmed. "She was going to take you in for a while. I'd still like to introduce you, if that's okay."

I nodded, forcing a smile. I wasn't sure what he'd told his friend—whoever she was. I could only imagine the kind of greeting I'd receive if she knew the whole truth. And I was guessing she did if he'd talked her into putting me up indefinitely.

A little while later, we were riding down a bumpy, barely passable dirt road in Seth's pickup truck. I was more than a little queasy by the time we pulled up in front of a sweet little farmhouse with a white picket fence. It looked like something right out of the fabled American Dream shared by millions.

"Come on," Seth said, grinning as he extended a hand to help me down. "You're going to love her."

I grimaced and shrank back from his outstretched hand. "But what if she doesn't like *me*?"

"She'll like you," he assured me, taking my hand and pulling me toward him. "Trust me."

I gripped his hand as we climbed the few wooden steps to the porch and held back a little as he opened the door to poke his head inside. "Hello? Anyone home?"

"In here, Seth-baby!" came a cheerful voice that carried an unmistakable and yet impossible-to-place twang of the Deep South. "Come on in!"

He gave me a comforting wink and led me to a set of French doors that opened into a tiny little sitting room. As soon as he walked in, a buxom older woman with her gray hair pulled into a bun on top of her head hurried forward to envelop him in a warm hug.

"Give Mama some sugar, baby," she said, pressing a kiss to his cheek.

Seth returned the hug and kiss with a grin. "I brought someone for you to meet, Mama."

The woman turned to me and smiled, which caused tiny creases at the corners of her sparkling dark eyes, but the rest of her lovely dark skin was flawless, completely unlined in spite of her advanced age. "Well, I'll be," she said, clasping her hands together. "This must be Lavender Seelie. Come here, baby, and give Old Mama Hubbard some sugar."

I glanced at Seth, taken off-guard by the warm welcome. "Go on," he mouthed, motioning me forward.

Mama Hubbard came toward me, not waiting for me to go to her, and gave me a hug that was so warm and comforting, I felt like snuggling up against her and asking her to read me a bedtime story. "Now, come on," she said when she released me. She pointed to her cheek. "Gotta give Mama some sugar, baby. Can't come visit without it."

I laughed, my anxiety lifting. "Well, all right." I pressed a kiss to her cheek and only barely resisted hugging her again. She had to be one of the most charming and charismatic women I'd ever met. There was something about her that made me feel like I'd known her for years. Images of sitting in rocking chairs on her front porch, shelling beans, and sipping sweet tea came to mind even though I knew I'd never seen her before in my life.

She lightly patted my cheek. "Looks to me like you two managed to work things out without Old Mama's help," she said with a smile. "Warms my heart—it surely does. Never seen Seth so happy and so down all at once. When he showed up on my doorstep yesterday, I said, 'Seth-baby, you go right on back home and talk to that girl. Ain't nothin' gonna get fixed by runnin' away now.' Old Mama knows a thing or two, that's right."

I slipped my hand into Seth's and looked up into his eyes, glad to see him gazing back at me with that soft, caressing expression that made me feel so adored. "Thank you for sending him home, Mama," I said. "I guess I owe you."

Mama waved her hand in the air, brushing off my thanks. "Don't owe me nothin', baby. Now, come on in and have some sweet tea. Just made it."

We followed her into the kitchen, where I was shocked to see a hound dog sitting at the table reading the newspaper.

"What's up, Harlan," Seth said with a jerk of his chin.

The dog folded down his newspaper and peered at Seth over his spectacles. "Seth," he said, his deep voice a slow Southern drawl. "Good to see ya'll again."

"Anything exciting in the news today?" Seth asked, pulling out a chair at the table.

Harlan folded up the paper—rather dexterously considering his lack of opposable thumbs—and sighed. "More of the same ol' nonsense."

Mama Hubbard set down a tall glass of iced tea in front of Seth and then handed one to me. "Come on, honey, why don't you and I go out on the porch and sit a spell? Any minute now they're gonna start talking about portfolios and complaining about the stock market. It's too gorgeous a day to be mired down in the business of being boring."

Seth nodded to me, encouraging me to go, so I shrugged and followed Mama outside. She settled into a weather-beaten white rocking chair and motioned for me to take the other. For a moment we sat in companionable silence, just listening to the breeze rustling through the branches of the evergreens.

"Cold weather's coming soon," Mama said. "Not gonna be many more days like this one."

"How long have you lived near The Refuge, Mama?" I asked, genuinely curious.

Her eyes tilted up a little as she considered my question. "Well, now, let's see. I came here close to fifty years ago, I reckon. Much quieter here for an old woman and her dog."

Considering she had moved away from the South around the height of the Civil Rights Movement, I could well imagine that being the case.

"Do you go into town much?" I asked, not seeing a car or other means of transportation.

She nodded. "Oh, some. But mostly it's the townsfolk comin' out to see me."

I lifted my brows. "Oh? Why's that?"

"Well, don't many of them trust that weasely-eyed little doctor in town. They prefer Old Mama's remedies."

"You're the healer Seth told me about?" I guessed.

Mama gave me a knowing smile. "Is that what Seth called me?" When I nodded, she chuckled, her ample bosom rising and falling. "Bless him. I guess that's how he'd need to see it to make his peace. Truth is, honey, Old Mama knows the remedies for what ails a body beyond the hurt on the outside."

"Oh," I said, beginning to understand. "You're a witch."

She shook her head, chuckling a little again. "No, baby, not a witch. Sometimes people just need a little help from the spirits or maybe a special charm to help take care of a problem."

"Voodoo then," I deduced.

"Well," she drawled, "I don't really like to put a name to what I do for the folks in these parts. Sometimes folks just need to believe things will get better. Need a little hope, that's all."

"So, you've helped Seth before?"

Mama nodded. "Once or twice. I knew him before, when he lived down in New Orleans for a spell. Had a darkness around him then— a curse—that I couldn't lift. But what's haunting him, honey, is more than just what witchcraft was laid on him all those years ago."

"He's been through a lot," I told her. "He feels it's all his fault."

"Well, we all got a past, demons we gotta shake." She pegged me with a knowing look. "You know that, baby."

I nodded. "Yes, I do. I'm working on that. Being here..." I paused, sighing. "Well. Finding Seth was unexpected."

Mama smiled, her eyes crinkling in the corners. "I'd say he wasn't expecting you either."

I laughed. "I imagine not!"

Mama turned her gaze out into the woods and resumed her slow rocking.

"Mama," I said cautiously, "you said people often come to you for help. Has Bo Peep ever visited?"

Mama's rocking nearly stilled, but she faltered for only the briefest moment. "She came out once a while back . . . I reckon it was right around the time Seth arrived in The Refuge if memory serves. Why do you ask, honey?"

"She's disappeared," I told her, watching her reaction closely.

Mama shook her head slowly. "That poor, poor baby," she sighed. "Thought something like this might happen."

"Because of her fairy dust addiction?" I probed.

"Because she's been lost for a very long time," Mama replied.

I frowned. "I know she's had a hard time dealing with her relocation," I admitted. "But you'd think having a child to look after might have helped give her some purpose."

"Well, nobody knows where that boy came from, now do they?" Mama said, turning her dark gaze on me.

"You think something's wrong with Gareth?" I asked, disbelief bleeding into my voice. "He's a darling little boy!"

Mama nodded. "He sure enough is, but there's something not right there, baby. You best be careful."

I frowned, mulling over what she'd said. There *was* something different about Gareth. He was a Tale—that much I could tell. But there was something . . . *off* about his aura. It wasn't like the other Tale auras I'd seen, which could've been what made Tom look into missing Ordinary children. Was it possible that Gareth was a hybrid of some sort—the son of a Tale and an Ordinary? Or was there something wrong with him? Was that why his real mother was nowhere to be found?

"I know Tom Piper has tried to search for Gareth's real parents," I mused, "but maybe I'll say something to my brother about it, see if he has any better luck. Puck has the kind of connections Tom lacks."

"Mayor Puck is your brother?" Mama cried.

I nodded. "Yes, why?"

She whooped with laughter, slapping her knee. "Lordy, lordy. Don't that beat all?"

I frowned, puzzled by her reaction. "Is he that bad at being a mayor?"

She shook her head, still chuckling. "Oh, no, baby—he does just fine running things. In fact, everybody's so busy adoring him they don't think to question anything he says or does. But I've heard about that boy's escapades! What your poor parents must've been through with that one."

I couldn't help laughing at her assessment of my dear brother. "That's very possibly true."

When Seth and Harlan came out onto the porch a moment later, Mama and I were still smiling. Seth came up to me and took my hand in his. "Mama, do you mind if I steal Lavender away from you for a while?"

"No, no, baby," Mama replied, waving away his concern. "You young people go on and enjoy this fine day. Don't you worry about me!"

We bid Old Mama Hubbard and her famous dog farewell and made our way back down the bumpy road.

"Thank you for taking me to meet them," I told Seth after we'd made it through the worst of the journey. "How did you get to know her?"

Seth grunted. "Harlan went missing once while I was living in Louisiana. The FMA brought me in for questioning in his disappearance, thinking I had something to do with it."

"Why would you?"

Seth gave me a bitter smile. "I'm brought in for questioning whenever *anything* happens."

"So, where did they find him?"

Here Seth chuckled. "Turns out Harlan just needed to blow off a little steam, be a dog for a while. And there were a lot of bitches in heat in the area."

"Oh," I gasped. "Oh, God. Okay."

He laughed. "Yeah, it was a little embarrassing for the FMA folks when they found him. Anyway, Mama had told them all along that she didn't think I had anything to do with it, and after I was released from custody, she kind of took me under her wing for a little while. A few years later, I moved back to Chicago and she moved here."

"And, so . . . Harlan . . ." I began, trying to be delicate, but there was really no way of skirting around the obvious. "So, he's a talking dog."

"Not only that," Seth replied, "he's a financial genius! He's totally turned my stock portfolio around."

I frowned at him. "How did he get to be . . . you know, *that way*?"

"Don't know," Seth said, his brow creasing a little. "I guess I never asked. Magic spell maybe?"

"And that doesn't bother you?"

Seth turned his eyes away from the road for a moment to frown at me. "No. Why should it?"

"He's obviously a magical creature," I pointed out. "And Mama, she . . ." I didn't finish the thought. If Seth needed to rationalize his relationship to Old Mother Hubbard and her dog by believing them to be something other than magical, who was I to shatter his illusions? I gave him a tight smile. "Never mind. I really like them both."

We rode on in silence until we reached the main road. When he didn't turn to go back toward his cabin, I glanced around, trying to figure out where we were. "Where are you taking me now?"

He grinned. "It's a surprise."

Chapter 14

At some point along the drive, I'd dozed off, so when Seth finally pulled off the road and parked the truck, I was completely taken by surprise at the view before me. A small spring-fed lake surrounded by a field of crimson flowers and evergreens was framed by the peaks of ridges and mountains just beginning to accumulate snow.

"My God," I gasped, not sure what else to say. "What is this place?"

Seth was grinning when he came around and helped me out of the truck. We walked together, hand in hand, until we stood at the edge of the lake, which was so still in spite of the soft breeze that it almost looked fake.

"I came across this lake not long after I got here," he told me, putting his hands on his hips and surveying the beauty around us. "I remember that day I was feeling so . . . lost. I transformed myself and just started running. Didn't stop for hours. I finally ended up here. I don't know. . . . The minute I got here I just felt more at peace than I ever had before."

I watched him as he closed his eyes and inhaled deeply, breathing in the autumn air. He seemed like a completely different person. Gone was the hardened, jaded demeanor that had seemed his hallmark. This man was the true Seth—the man he'd been before tragedy and heartbreak had broken him down. I'd thought him unbelievably gorgeous and sexy from the moment I'd met him. But staring at him now, I realized he was ... beautiful. In spite of all he'd been through, there was a tenderness and a gentleness in his soul that was unlike any I'd ever seen before.

"I love you," I whispered before I realized what I was saying. It was said so quietly, I was sure he couldn't hear. In fact, I wasn't even sure I'd said it out loud. Until his eyes snapped open and he turned to me, the pained look returning.

I let out an embarrassed, bitter little laugh and closed my eyes. *Well, shit. Well played, Lavender. Smooth as always.*

"God," I groaned. "I'm sorry. I just ... that just ..." I shook my head, not really knowing what to say and feeling more humiliated than I ever had in my life. Not able to endure the look in his eyes, the apology I sensed was coming, I spun around and practically ran back to the truck.

"Lavender!" I heard him calling after me. "Lavender, wait!"

But I didn't wait. I couldn't. I knew if he opened his mouth and told me he didn't love me back, couldn't love me back ...

Damn it!

He'd brought me here to share something special and beautiful that meant a lot to him. And I'd ruined it. When would I learn just to shut the hell up and—

Suddenly the white wolf was standing in front of me, blocking my path. I slid to a stop with a startled cry. Seth immediately changed and took hold of my arms.

"Where are you going?" he demanded.

I covered my face with my hands, wishing a vast chasm would miraculously open up beneath my feet and put me out of my misery. "I'm sorry," I said, letting my hands drop. "I shouldn't have said that. I know you said you couldn't offer me anything. I know that. But you were standing there, looking so amazingly gorgeous, and all heroic-y and stuff. And I just couldn't help it." I let my head drop back and groaned again, my humiliation taking on a whole new level. But then Seth took my face in his hands and forced me to look at him. And he was grinning. No, not just grinning. Laughing.

Great.

"This isn't funny," I huffed.

His grin faded. A little. "No, it isn't," he said, shaking his head. Then he bent and touched his lips to mine. "Neither is that." Then he kissed my brow, oh so tenderly. "Or that." And then my cheek. "Or that." And the tip of my nose. "Or that."

"Okay, now *that's* a little bit funny," I grumped.

He chuckled and pulled back to peer down at me. "Come on," he said. "There's more I want to show you."

I nodded, still stinging a little from my misstep and took his hand as we headed back to the lake, letting him lead the way. Well, he hadn't exactly told me he loved me, too. But he hadn't told me to piss off either. I guess that was something.

The sun was sinking low on the horizon as I lay in Seth's arms among the flowers by the lake, our fingers entwined. The breeze was beginning to grow cold, but I didn't care. I hated to have to leave this place of peace where Seth was so uninhibitedly happy and relaxed. Had it been up to me, I would've built us a little stone cottage with a wave of my wand and never left.

But my wand was broken and in the custody of the FMA. My magic was shit. And whatever future Seth and I might have together certainly wasn't entirely up to me.

"Should we head home soon?" I asked quietly.

He pressed a kiss to my hair. "Probably. You have to be starving."

I shook my head, smoothing my hand over the tight coils of hair on his chest. "Not really."

He ran his hand up and down my bare back, then pulled me in closer. I could sense in his movements that there was something he wanted to say but was holding back.

I lifted my head and pegged him with a concerned look. "What is it?"

He reached up and tucked my hair behind my ear and gazed at me for a long moment. "You know all about me," he began. "Probably knew a lot about me before you even met me."

I nodded, confirming this to be true. "I'd heard stories. But none of what you told me the other night."

"Why have I not heard anything about you—aside from the fact that you brought all the Tales here?" He heaved a sigh and rolled up onto his side, propping his head up on his hand so that we were facing each other. "I'd say at this point I know every inch of your body, Lavender"—he grinned a little mischievously—"but I don't really know anything about *you.*"

"Sure you do," I said, dropping onto my back and staring up at the sky, avoiding his gaze. "You know I'm the daughter of the King and Queen of the Seelies. That Puck is my brother. You know I'm on the run from a vindictive little prick of a prince. You know I have trouble controlling my magic."

"I didn't know about your drinking problem until the other night," he said gently.

My eyes briefly darted to his face then away again. "I've been sober for a year," I mumbled. "I had a little lapse the other day when I was with my brother."

"Sorry I kept serving you wine at dinner," he said. "I wouldn't have been so insensitive had I known."

I shrugged. "It's okay. I have a feeling it'll always be a struggle. I tried to drown my sorrows quite literally for a long time. And Cindy and James were more than happy to keep it that way."

"How did you become Cinderella's fairy godmother in the first place?" he asked.

I sighed, thinking back on what were happier days. Or what at least seemed that way. "I was selected for the role," I told him. "I had a great deal of talent and my mother determined that being a fairy godmother would be the best use of it. I think she was perhaps a little afraid that I might try to take over as queen if I stuck around court too much."

"Would you have?"

I shook my head. "Who knows? Maybe. I was arrogant and condescending to pretty much everyone. I knew I was better than everyone else and was determined to prove it. I probably *would* have challenged my mother back then, just to make a point. She was right to send me away."

"How did Cinderella end up in your charge?"

"I chose her," I explained. "She was so mistreated, so downtrodden, I felt sorry for her. And, honestly, I saw the potential there—or, at least, the potential for me to be touted as a hero for rescuing her from her horrible life. And who does she choose for the husband she wants? The freaking prince of the kingdom! Talk about a challenge. But I was up for it. Of course, what the fairytale doesn't say is that Prince James was quite the defiler of young women—peasant maidens, in particular. He'd had his eye on Cindy for some time, but she wouldn't give in. So I swept in, turned her into a princess for the night and sent her off to the ball to have a little fun. My intention was to help her find someone more appropriate and worthy starting the next day."

"And the prince was so enchanted he knew Cinderella was the only woman for him?"

I laughed bitterly. "Not exactly. He seduced her that night, took her innocence without a second thought. She says now that it's what she wanted, but I have my doubts."

"He *raped* her?" Seth cried. "That little son of a bitch!"

"Hard to say for sure," I told him. "He might not have forced himself on her, but he certainly took advantage of her ignorance and most certainly made all kinds of promises to convince her to finally give up her maidenhood to someone so undeserving. When I found out what happened, I decided I wasn't going to let that little bastard get away with taking what he wanted from her, then dumping her on her ass."

"What did you do?"

I closed my eyes, my old self-loathing coming back with a vengeance. "Made a deal with the devil, as it turned out. I went to James and promised him I would use my magic to give him all his heart desired if he would marry Cindy and make her happy. He agreed."

"Just like that?" Seth asked, eyeing me suspiciously.

I squirmed a little. "Not exactly. He had a few other demands."

"So, he forced you to sleep with him, too?" Seth guessed.

I shook my head. "No, thank God! But he demanded that I belong to them exclusively or he'd tell Cindy about our deal. Every time I tried to refuse one of his requests for a spell to further his agenda, he'd bring up the fact that I'd betrayed Cindy by lying to her about how much the prince wanted to marry her. She did lose a shoe—but I manufactured the whole searching-the-kingdom-for-his-one-true-love thing. I didn't want her to ever find out—she was so naïve and innocent and so in love with him; I couldn't bring her that kind of pain. It was only after we came over that I began to truly rebel and refuse his darker requests, and so he outed me to Cindy. I hated to do that to her, but what was I supposed to do? In Make Believe his demands were mostly just self-serving—notoriety, wealth. There was really no harm to others. But since coming here . . ."

"Not exactly the case."

I shook my head. "But even while we were still in Make Believe Cindy began to see him for who he really was, and she changed, too. She wasn't the same girl I'd rescued from the ashes. She grew vain, mean-spirited, and completely unconcerned by how her actions affected anyone else."

"So how did you end up in that duel with the genie?"

"It started as a little good-natured boasting," I told him. "Cindy was having a soiree one night while James was away visiting another kingdom. By this point she was beginning to have some of her own liaisons and a few of her more questionable friends were more than happy to enable her romantic trysts. One of her lovers was the genie. And when Cindy began to tease him that I was more powerful than he was, he challenged me, wanting to prove himself to his lover."

"And?"

"And he was a tougher opponent than I'd anticipated," I admitted. "His magic was very different from any other I'd faced before. And, well, I was considered one of the most powerful fairies ever born. I couldn't let it get out that I'd lost a duel to a genie, for crying out loud. What would my family think?"

"So what happened?"

I heaved a heavy sigh. "I called upon the powers of a very dark magic—one I'd been entrusted to protect and employ justly and responsibly. I knew it was unstable. I knew it was dangerous. And yet I couldn't allow my reputation to be tainted. I'm not entirely sure what went wrong. I don't know how I lost control. But I did. The fabric of reality seemed to rip apart right before my eyes. The tear grew so quickly I couldn't stop it."

Seth nodded. "I remember that sudden electricity in the air. It was like the charge before a lightning strike. And then—darkness. Such impenetrable darkness."

I closed my eyes, hearing once more the terrified screams and chaos of that moment when we'd all been suddenly transported to this strange new world. "I tried to reverse the spell," I said, my voice growing tight with tears. "I tried. But something had happened. The spell had taken something from me, damaged me somehow. And there was nothing I could do."

A single tear escaped from my eye and slid slowly down my cheek toward my ear, but Seth gently wiped it away with his thumb.

"Thank God for Al Addin and his presence of mind that day," I continued, sniffing. "If he hadn't taken control of the situation, I don't know what would've happened. I owe him my life, that much I know. The Tales were ready to lynch me on the spot, but he insisted I be tried by a Tribunal."

"Did no one stand up for you?" Seth asked, his voice soft, gentle. "Your family? Anyone?"

I smiled a little at this. "There was one who tried," I told him. "His name was Gideon. He'd secretly been my lover for most of my adult life even though our relationship was forbidden. Gideon was my father's personal assistant, and assassin when called upon, and was considered too far beneath me to be a suitable husband. But Gideon is far nobler than any of the other fairies I've known, I can tell you that. He came to my defense, offered his own life in exchange for mine, confessed his love for me to my father—no small feat of valor, believe me. I think that alone was enough to move the Tribunal to show me mercy—well, that and fear of my father's wrath if they killed his beloved daughter. I was stripped of my titles, my wings, and my place among the Seelies."

"And what of Gideon?" Seth asked, no jealousy at all in his voice.

"He was made to choose between his love for me and his duty to my father," I explained.

"And he chose his duty over you?" Seth asked, his tone so incredulous it warmed my heart.

I shook my head. "No. He didn't. He was willing to stand by me through whatever trials and tribulations lay ahead. But I turned him away." Now the tears were coming unheeded. "I refused to let him share in my punishment. I couldn't forgive myself for what had happened and I didn't believe anyone else could either. And I loved him far too much to make him suffer with me."

Seth slipped his arm under me and rolled me toward him, holding me close, not saying a word as he smoothed my hair and pressed kisses to my head. Eventually, my tears subsided but we continued to lie there among the flowers, holding one another in silence until the sun slipped down below the horizon.

Chapter 15

When Seth helped me out of the truck after returning home to his cabin, he kept my hand in his and pulled me close, kissing me tenderly. Then he peered down at me, his eyes so full of emotion, my heart began to pound. I wanted so desperately to hear the words that I thought for certain I could sense in that expression. I wanted to hear him say he loved me, that he needed me, that he didn't want to ever be without me. Even if it was only the enchantment talking. I was fooling myself, living in a fantasy that might never come true—but I didn't care. I was no stranger to hoping for a fairytale ending only to be disappointed. I could handle it. Right now, just hearing the words would be enough.

I gazed up at him expectantly, holding my breath so that I didn't miss a single syllable. The corner of his mouth curved up a little in a smile and his lips parted. But before he could utter a word, a rustle close by brought his head up. Instantly, his demeanor changed and I heard a soft growl growing in the center of his chest.

"Seth?" I whispered. "What is it?"

He shook his head and held a finger to his lips, then swept me behind him, shielding me with his body as he slowly backed me toward the cabin. Once we were inside, he shut and locked the door, then took hold of my arms.

"Stay here," he whispered. "Keep the lights out and don't come outside no matter what."

"You're not going out there!" I hissed. "Something nearly killed you the other night. And don't give me any bullshit about a mountain lion. I saw through that in a fairytale minute, pal. You're not going out there alone!"

He pressed his lips together in an angry line. "Lavender—"

A creaking floorboard on the deck outside made him bite off his words, and just as we both glanced toward the picture window, a hulking shadow darted past. I gasped, covering my mouth to muffle the sound. Seth gave me a stern glare, then jabbed a finger at the floor, demanding I stay put. Before I could protest again, he slipped out the front door.

For a moment, I simply stared at the closed door, not sure if I should lock it or not. Then a scrabbling of claws on the deck sent me bolting forward. I slid the lock into place just as whatever it was slammed into the door.

Shit shit shit.

I slid down the heavy wooden door and glanced around the cabin, trying to get my bearings in the darkness. There was really no place to hide if something came after me. Maybe in a closet or under the bed, but those were so cliché, it'd only take a moment for a monster to sniff me out.

"Damn it, Seth," I muttered under my breath. "Where the hell are you?"

I pressed my ear to the door, hoping to hear some sign that he was coming back, but there was nothing. Even the breeze that'd been so warm and inviting earlier in the day had gone still. All I could hear was silence, thick and deadly. Something was waiting just on the other side of the door. I could feel it. There was a heaviness that alerted me to a presence there. My fingertips began to tingle as fear injected my system with adrenaline.

I closed my eyes, trying to calm myself. It sure as hell wasn't the time for my magic to come out and say hello—and very likely burn down Seth's home in the process.

"It's okay, it's okay," I murmured, trying to ignore the bead of sweat snaking down my spine. I blew out a long, quiet breath, trying to slow my pulse. The tingle in my fingertips began to dissipate. Then, suddenly, the heaviness on the other side of the door vanished.

I exhaled in a sharp burst. "Thank God—"

The sudden impact against the door startled a scream from me. I scrambled to my feet and spun around, relieved to see that the door had held and was still firmly in place. Another impact, though, and the wood creaked, threatening to give way. A low growl on the other side of the door sent a violent shiver through me.

I sprinted into the kitchen and snatched a knife from the butcher's block, then crept back into the living room, wincing with each little creak of the floorboards. I glanced toward the picture window, wondering why the creature hadn't tried to break through the glass. Was it just toying with me? Taunting me?

"Come on, Seth," I whimpered, clutching the knife until my knuckles went white. Little sparks of purple light began to dance around me as my magic once more surged to the surface. I swallowed hard and listened, hoping to get a bead on where the creature was. Suddenly, I heard a heavy thud above me.

My head snapped up, my eyes searching the ceiling. I turned a slow circle in the middle of the room, not sure where to go or what to do and rapidly losing control over my magic. A sudden rhythmic pounding on the door startled a lightning bolt of purple light from me. It shot across the room, shattering a soup tureen sitting on the shelf. I yelped and ducked as shards of porcelain flew everywhere.

"Lavender!" More pounding on the front door. "Lavender! Are you okay?"

Seth. Thank God.

The moment I heard his voice, there was more scrabbling of claws on the roof. I wasn't sure if that meant the creature lurking there was scared off by Seth's presence—or was coming for him.

I rushed to the door and unbolted the lock, pulling Seth inside and slamming the door behind him. I threw my arms around his neck and hugged him tightly, relieved to have him safe and in my arms again. He was muddy and bloody, but I didn't care. I kissed him over and over again, reassuring myself that he was alive.

After a moment, he gently set me away from him and took my face in his hands. His brows drew together in a worried frown as his searching gaze held mine. "Are you okay?"

I nodded. "Are you? Is this your blood?"

He shook his head quickly as if my question was unimportant. "A little, but I'm fine."

"Was it the same thing that was on the roof?" I asked in a rush.

His frown grew darker. "I didn't see anything on the roof."

"It was there," I insisted. "And something else, something big, tried to break down the door while you were chasing down its pal. Did you get a good look at whatever it was?"

Seth didn't immediately answer but went to the picture window and peered through the blinds. "Yeah," he said after a moment. "I got a good look at it."

"What was it?"

He turned away from the window and when his gaze met mine, I didn't like the worried look I saw there. "A hellhound. And it was a hell of a lot nastier than the one that went after you the other night."

I sat on Seth's lap in Tom Piper's kitchen, my head resting against Seth's shoulder, his arm encircling my waist protectively even though the immediate danger had passed.

"Thanks, Tom," Seth was saying as he took a cup of coffee from the sheriff and set it down on the table to cool. "I appreciate you letting Lavender and me stay here tonight."

Tom gave him a curt nod. "Think nothin' of it, Wolf. You're welcome to stay as long as you want."

"We'll head back to my cabin tomorrow morning," Seth assured him. "I just didn't want to take the risk of those things coming back tonight."

"I'll go with you," Tom told him, "check things out, see if I can gather any evidence to find out who's sending them."

"Who in town would be able to summon hellhounds?" Eva asked, dunking her teabag in her cup as she joined us at the table. "And why would they be targeting Seth and Lavender?"

Seth squirmed a little at the question and once again I got the impression he was hiding something when he said, "No clue."

At that moment, there was a soft *slap, slap, slap* of tiny feet on the linoleum and all of us turned to see Gareth padding into the kitchen in yellow footie pajamas, rubbing his eyes. "I heard voices downstairs," he explained as Eva came around the table to scoop him up and plant a kiss on his chubby cheek.

"There's nothing to worry about, love," she murmured, her voice taking on a soft lilt that I hadn't heard there before. It reminded me of the accent of the Celtic fairies I'd known in Make Believe. "Mr. Wolf and Ms. Seelie are going to be spending the night here, that's all."

Gareth gave me a wide, sleepy smile. "You can stay in my room, Lavender," he said. "It's blue!" He laughed and then started singing, *"Lavender's blue, dilly dilly. . . ."*

I took his hand and pressed a kiss to it. "Thank you, *céadsearc*," I said, using the Gaelic endearment. I met Eva's surprised gaze evenly as I added, "But I wouldn't want your sweet dreams to be disturbed by my snoring."

When Gareth giggled, Eva gave me a tight smile, then pressed another kiss to his cheek. "Come on, little one," she said. "Let's take you back to bed."

I watched them go, wondering again at the strangeness of Gareth's aura. There had to be a very simple explanation. No matter how hard I tried to reconcile myself to Mama Hubbard's misgivings, I just couldn't see it. As soon as they were out of sight, I turned and pressed a kiss to Seth's temple. "Do you mind if I turn in while you and Tom talk?"

He shook his head and then ran the back of his fingers down the line of my jaw. "I'll be there soon."

I climbed the stairs and went into the guest room that Eva had prepared for us, running a hand over the lovingly stitched quilt with the Celtic knot design disguised in the pattern.

"Hello, Eva," I said, sensing her presence in the doorway. I turned and offered her a knowing smile. "Or is it Aoife?"

"How did you know?" she asked, coming into the room and crossing her arms. "Was it the accent? So many years in the Here and Now and it still slips in now and then."

"Why hide it?" I questioned. "There are any number of us who've retained the accents from the country where our stories originated."

"Sometimes it's just best to leave the past behind." She heaved a sigh. "I am not just *an* Aoife," she explained. "I'm *the* Aoife."

My brows shot up as I took in the seemingly serene wife of The Refuge's sheriff. "The warrior from Irish mythology?"

She gave me a sad smile. "My warrior days are long gone," she admitted. "I decided that even before I came to the Here and Now. Having my darling boy murdered by his own father took all the fight out of me."

"I'm so sorry," I told her sincerely. "I can't imagine what that must've been like for you."

Her lips trembled a little when she attempted a brave smile. "Little Gareth reminds me so much of my son, sometimes it makes my heart ache. Tom and I have tried to have one of our own, but haven't been able to. I know it hurts him that I've been so unhappy about not having a baby—he'd do anything for the people he loves. I'm just glad you've let Gareth stay with us. I feel like I've been given the chance to love and protect him as I couldn't my Connla."

"Everyone deserves a second chance," I told her.

"I guess I have you to thank for my own," she said. "If not for the relocation, I never would have met my Tom. He's such a dear man, you know. I've never known anyone so kind in all my days."

I blinked at her, taken aback by someone actually *thanking* me for transplanting them into the Here and Now. "I'm glad you've managed to find happiness here. There are many Tales who feel otherwise, trust me!"

She nodded. "Do you think that's why they're sending hellhounds after you?"

Frowning, I sat down on the edge of the bed. "I don't know. It's almost as if . . ." I paused and let out a frustrated sigh. "It doesn't make sense to me, Eva. When those things came after us tonight, they easily could've broken into the house. Seth doesn't know magic—he hasn't placed any protections on the place. It's almost as if they were only meant to scare us, to warn us somehow."

"But who would be wanting to warn you, now?" she asked, coming to sit beside me on the bed. "And why?"

I glanced out into the hallway. "I'm not entirely sure I was the one being warned."

Her brows shot up. "You think the hellhounds are meant to be a warning for *Seth*?"

I nodded. "There's something he's hiding from me, Eva," I whispered. "And I don't know why. He's shared everything else with me. What could he possibly be keeping from me that would cause someone to send hellhounds after him?"

Eva squeezed my hand. "Perhaps you'd best ask him, darlin'."

As if on cue, Seth strolled into the room, glancing between Eva and me, his eyes narrowing a little. "Ask him about what?"

Eva smiled, then patted my hand. "Well, I'll let you two get some rest. Sleep well."

Seth's gaze remained trained on me as Eva left the room and shut the door behind her. "What's going on?" he asked as soon as she was gone.

I took a deep breath and let it out slowly before rising to my feet to pull back the covers on the bed. "I was just telling Eva that I think the hellhounds were sent as a warning."

He crossed his arms over his chest. "Okay."

I began stripping off my clothes, waiting for him to say more. When I'd pulled on the nightgown Eva had loaned me and he still hadn't spoken, I pegged him with a frustrated glare. "What are you keeping from me, Seth?"

He instantly turned that penetrating gaze away and busied himself with stripping down to his boxers. "What are you talking about?"

"You're not telling me everything," I charged. "I can tell you're holding something back."

He got into bed and stared up at the ceiling. "Lavender, what would I possibly be keeping from you?"

I slipped in beside him and scooted closer so that I could peer down into his face and force him to look at me. "I think you know more about these hellhounds than you're letting on." When he huffed and started to turn his head away, I put my hand on his cheek and turned his face back to me. "It was a hellhound that attacked and nearly killed you the other night, wasn't it?"

He blew out a sharp breath. "Yeah."

"Why didn't you tell me?" I demanded.

"I didn't want to worry you."

I grunted and flounced down on the pillow.

Now it was his turn to be on the offensive. He propped himself up on his elbow and looked down at me, his eyes beginning to glow. "You're pissed because I was trying to keep you from worrying?"

"No," I snapped. "I'm pissed because you think I can't handle it. I'm not some delicate flower that needs to be protected, Seth."

"Really?" he drawled. "Because, as I seem to recall, the night I met you, you were running for your life from one of these hellhounds and couldn't protect yourself because your magic was too fucked up to be of any use!"

I blinked at him, too shocked to speak. Then I threw back the covers and started for the door. "Fuck off."

"Lavender, wait," Seth called, lunging from the bed to intercept me.

I pulled open the door, but he pushed it shut before I could leave the room. "Get out of the way, Seth," I told him, forcing my voice to remain even and calm. "I don't want to look at you right now."

He sighed and ran a hand through his hair. "I'm sorry. I shouldn't have said that. It wasn't fair. I didn't mean to imply that you aren't strong enough to handle what's going on."

I lifted my eyes to him. "So what *is* going on?" I demanded, my tone daring him to try some other line of bullshit. "And don't lie to me again, Seth."

He pulled his hand down over his face with a groan, then his mouth opened and closed as if he was on the verge of imparting the truth I sought. He seemed to think better of it at the last minute.

"Screw it," I mumbled, reaching for the doorknob again, but he caught my arm.

"Lavender, I just . . . I can't tell you everything right now," he told me haltingly. "There are reasons why. You just have to trust me, okay?"

I stared at him, waging an internal debate between my head and my heart. The logical, rational side of me wanted to tell him to either spill it or get to stepping. But then my heart started to do its little fluttery thing as I looked up into his pleading eyes and it became very clear which one was going to win the battle. He grasped my chin lightly between his thumb and forefinger and tilted my face up to receive his kiss. It was just a light brush of his lips against mine, but it was enough.

Damn it.

"All right," I huffed. "I'll trust you. For now. But I swear, Seth . . ."

He pulled me into his arms and held me tightly, resting his cheek on the top of my head. "That's all I can ask."

Chapter 16

When we arrived at Seth's cabin the next morning with Tom Piper, it was evident to all of us that we'd made the right decision by leaving. The front door had been ripped off its hinges and lay on the deck. The contents of Seth's house were strewn about the front yard, many of them shredded beyond recognition. For a full minute Seth could only sit in the cab of his truck, staring at the devastation.

I reached over at some point and took his hand, giving it a comforting squeeze. This seemed to snap him out of his stupor. He turned his gaze to me and blinked several times.

"Do you want to go in and see what's left?" I asked gently.

He sighed, then nodded. "Might as well."

We let Tom take the lead as we carefully stepped around the pages of books, shards of smashed dishes, and scraps of clothing that littered the front yard and deck. He motioned for us to stay outside while he went into the house, gun drawn, to check for anyone—or anything—that still might be on the premises.

A few minutes later, he came back out and holstered his gun, his expression sympathetic. "Sorry, Wolf. It looks like there's not much left inside to salvage. Whoever did this was pretty damned thorough."

"Do you think it was the hellhounds, Tom?" I asked, knowing the answer before I even asked the question but needing to make sure.

"Looks like," he said with a nod. "Claw marks on the cabin walls and it looks to me like it was claws that tore up the furniture. If you two want to head back to my place, I'll see what kind of evidence I can gather and—"

"Don't bother," Seth muttered, stepping over a frying pan in the doorway and going inside. "I just want to start cleaning up."

I gasped when I entered the cabin. Tom hadn't been kidding about the intruder being thorough. All of the cabinets in the kitchen had been emptied, the contents smashed on the floor or against the wall. The dining room table and chairs were broken apart and lay in pieces, good for nothing now but kindling. The living room furniture had been shredded, the stuffing tossed about. When we went into the bedroom, the bed was in similar shape, and all of Seth's clothes had been ripped to shreds. Curiously, mine were all carefully hanging in the closet, my shoes lined up on the floor right where we'd set them when we unpacked.

I peeked into the bathroom and saw it, too, had been destroyed. The mirror over the sink had been shattered, creating a surreal funhouse image of my reflection as I stepped inside, my boots crunching on the shards of broken glass that littered the floor. Thankfully, the creatures hadn't torn out the plumbing to add a flood to the other destruction.

My heart breaking for what Seth must've been feeling at seeing his home so violated, I bent and picked up the lone hand towel that was left intact, and stood to hang it up on the rack when something hanging from the handle of the medicine cabinet caught my eye. The cabinet door was hanging precariously on a single hinge, but the cabinet was still attached to the wall. And hanging from the small decorative knob was my necklace.

I cocked my head to one side. Seth had put it in the soap dish when he'd rescued me the night of my arrival, and I hadn't bothered to put it back on after discovering he'd been enchanted by my family's magic. But seeing it hanging there now, it was clear to me that the necklace had been placed on the knob deliberately. And whoever had done it wasn't a demon-dog.

Frowning, I waved a hand over it, trying to pick up some kind of trace of who might've touched it last. But nothing happened. My frown deepened as I called my magic to the surface, letting the tingle in my fingertips spread through my body. Slowly, I released the mental dam against my power, letting it flow out of me in a wispy stream. The little trail of sparkling purple light wound about the charm on my necklace until it was completely encased. Then I added just a tiny bit of force with my mind. The light exploded outward in a minute burst, sending sparkles of my own fairy dust into the air.

I gasped and laughed a little, startled by the fact that it seemed to be working without disastrous effect. The fairy dust spun about, creating a tiny cyclone in the air before my eyes, and then slowly an image began to form. A woman's hand passing across the pendant's moonstone—the eye through which I was now viewing what had occurred. Slowly the pendant began to rise as the woman lifted it up by the chain.

"That's it," I muttered, "take a good look at it. Let me see your face. . . ."

Bosom . . . neck . . . chin . . . lips . . . nose—

"Lavender?"

I started at the sound of Seth's voice and the fairy dust image burst apart, my control over it lost. "Damn it!"

He peeked into the bathroom. "You okay?"

I heaved a disappointed sigh. "Someone was here, Seth," I told him. "A woman. She hung my necklace on the medicine cabinet."

He frowned. "How do you know it was a woman?"

"I saw her," I said. "The moonstone can reveal to me the image of the last person to touch it. I could tell it was a woman, but her face was just coming into view when you startled me and I lost it."

"Can you call it up again?"

I shook my head. "No, it only works once." I took down the necklace and undid the clasp to put it on. I started to ask Seth for his help, but stopped myself, remembering how the silver had burned his hand when he'd touched it before.

"Seth! Lavender!" Tom called from the living room. "You might want to come see this!"

When we came out, Tom was standing by the fireplace. As we approached he pulled out a handkerchief and a small evidence bag.

"Looks like someone left you a message," he said, jerking his chin toward what sat on the mantel.

A silver bullet.

"I'd say the message is coming through loud and clear," Seth drawled.

"My God," I breathed, remembering the bullet Seth had hidden in his journal. Had the intruder known about the bullet all along and set it out for Seth to see in hopes that he would take the hint? Or was this another bullet that she had brought with her to leave as a threat of what was coming? Both options made my heart pound with fear for Seth's safety. I took his hand and stepped in front of him so he was looking directly at me. "Let's go," I pleaded. "Just leave all this mess and come with me."

"Where, Lavender?" he replied. "This is my home. I built this cabin with my bare hands. I'm not going to let someone run me out of town."

"Seth, there's nothing left here," I told him. "They've destroyed everything you own."

He shrugged. "I came here with almost nothing. I can replace all the stuff I've lost."

I took his face in my hands. "But what if next time it's not just a warning?" I said. "What if next time whoever it is decides to use that silver bullet instead of leaving it on your mantel? What if—" Tears caught in my throat, choking off my words.

Seth bent and pressed a kiss to my forehead and then wrapped his arms around me, holding me close. "I'll be fine," he whispered against my hair. "Don't worry about me."

Yeah, right. Might as well tell me not to breathe. . . .

My arms tightened around his waist, and I buried my head in his chest, the thought of losing him too much to bear. At some point, Tom drifted outside, giving us some time to just hold one another.

Finally, Seth heaved a sorrowful sigh. "I guess we should start cleaning all this shit up."

I nodded, not wanting to leave the warmth of his arms but eager to help him salvage what he could. We managed to find a box of trash bags that hadn't been destroyed and a broom that was still in the front closet. We were just setting the sixth trash bag out on the deck when a box truck pulled up in front of Seth's cabin. A moment later, Hansel and his sister climbed out of the cab.

"Hansel. Gretel," Seth said with a nod to each. "Sorry I couldn't be at work today. I meant to call, but—"

Gretel grunted. "Sheriff Piper called to tell us what happened. Hansel decided to give you the day off."

I suppressed a smile, getting the impression that Gretel had needed a little persuasion from her brother to go along with his charity.

"We brought you a few things to replace those you lost," Hansel said, gesturing toward the truck.

Seth blinked at his employers, clearly astonished by their kindness. "Thanks," he stammered. "I . . . I don't know what to say."

"Say you'll help my brother unload everything before he has a coronary," Gretel snapped. "We have to get back to the restaurant before we lose *all* our business today."

Seth and Tom immediately started to unload the contents of the truck while Gretel and I went back into the cabin to finish clearing out the debris. By the time we'd set out the last trash bag containing the debris from the main part of the cabin, the guys were bringing in a small wooden dining set and four chairs. The furniture was a little beat up and appeared to have been something Hansel and Gretel had used in their restaurant at some point but had put in storage long ago. But the table was sturdy and all the chairs matched.

Next were boxes of plain white restaurant dishes, stainless steel flatware, cooking utensils, and pots and pans—again from the restaurant's storage, but the way Seth beamed about having them you'd think they were the finest money could buy. Gretel and I washed and put everything away in silence as the men dragged the ruined living room and bedroom furniture out into the yard and loaded what trash they could into the empty box truck to be hauled away.

I put the last plate on the shelf and offered Gretel a smile. "Thank you," I said sincerely. "I know Seth appreciates your kindness."

She grunted. "Just see to it that he's at work tomorrow," she retorted. "He's the best chef we've ever had—has spoiled the palates of all the townspeople. Our customers will forgive his absence for one day now and then, I suppose, but no one will come to our restaurant if he leaves."

I nodded, knowing that was about as good as conversation was going to get with Gretel. "You got it."

"Gretel!" Hansel cried from the doorway. *"Kommst du mit?"*

She rolled her eyes. "Of course, I am coming with you, idiot! Do you think I am walking home?" She continued to grumble to herself in German as she stomped out of the house.

"Thanks again!" I called, waving at Hansel. He gave me a tight smile and hurried after his sister.

I followed them out, eager to tell Seth that the appliances still appeared to be in working order, when a red pickup truck bounced down the logging road, passing Hansel and Gretel on their way home.

"Who's that?" I asked, frowning.

Seth shrugged. "No idea."

"Looks like Ted Walsh," Tom said.

I frowned in their general direction, waiting to be brought up to speed. "Who?"

Seth glanced at me, clearly surprised to have more visitors. "The Farmer in the Dell. He's one of the guys who tried to throw you out of town."

"Oh," I said, remembering well the hulking farmer in overalls who'd been one of my biggest fans the day I'd been murdering birds and frightening small children. I stepped a little closer to Seth, wondering why exactly Farmer Ted was paying a visit now.

But my anxiety was laid to rest when Ted got out of the truck and gave us a nod in greeting. "Tom, Seth, Ms. Seelie."

"Hello, Ted," Seth said, his voice wary. "What brings you by?"

"Well," he drawled as he made his way to the bed of the truck. "Tom thought you could use a few things." He took out a crate of canned green beans, peaches, and other food that his family had no doubt raised themselves and canned for winter. Another crate held a baking dish covered in foil that smelled like it held a casserole. There were also fresh-baked biscuits and homemade jam, a tub of butter, and a glass quart of milk.

"Not much," Ted said, readjusting his well-worn John Deere hat.

"But it'll get you by for a day or two until you can replace what was lost."

Seth was struck speechless, so I stepped forward and offered my hand. "Thank you, Mr. Walsh," I said, grinning. "We appreciate your kindness."

Ted looked at my hand warily, obviously still not trusting me entirely, but after a brief hesitation, he clasped it in a firm handshake. "Think nothin' of it, Ms. Seelie," he replied. "Just bein' neighborly."

And so it went on for the rest of the day. Old Lady Patterson came by with three of her five sons and two of her eight daughters to help where she could. The boys set to work boarding up the windows while the girls and I hauled out the last of the trash from the bedroom and bathroom. Then as the Pattersons were loading into their Suburban, another group of townspeople showed up to see where they could help, bringing more covered dishes and a peach cobbler.

By late in the afternoon, someone had brought a grill and set it up on the deck and had pressed Seth into cooking what I came to discover was his famous grilled chicken and pork chops. And several of the townspeople who had shown up earlier in the day returned, having somehow found out before we did that we were hosting a barbeque.

I was just polishing off my dinner when I glanced Seth's way, marveling at the change that had come over him. He stood chatting with Tom, beer in hand, looking so casual and happy, he was hardly recognizable. The only other time I'd seen him so relaxed and content was when we'd been at his lakeside refuge. He must've felt my gaze upon him, for he turned and winked at me, making my heart flutter with happiness.

The sound of tires coming down the logging road made me turn away from him and I instantly wished I hadn't. Slowly and carefully creeping toward the cabin was a black Mercedes SUV. It only took a moment for me to figure out who was driving it.

"Excuse me," I said to the Tales I'd been sitting with. I dumped my paper plate and cup into the trash can as I walked out to meet the SUV. It came to a stop several yards away, unable to navigate any further because of the number of vehicles clogging the dirt road.

"Having a party and didn't think to invite your brother?" Puck

asked as he tucked his sunglasses into his suit pocket. "I'm hurt beyond measure."

I rolled my eyes, seriously doubting it. "What are you doing here,
Puck?"

"Town's buzzing with news of what happened last night," he said.
"I came as soon as I heard."

I glanced to where the sun was sinking toward the horizon. "Gee,
thanks for rushing here so quickly—your show of concern is overwhelming."

He pressed his lips together and gave me an irritated look. "I had
a late night," he spat. "I didn't wake up until a couple of hours ago. I
came right over—after I rescheduled a few meetings."

I nodded, trying not to picture the drunken, drug-fueled orgies
that were most likely the source of his sleep deprivation. "Well, as
you see, I'm fine," I said, turning to go. "Thanks for your concern."

"You're *not* fine," he insisted, grabbing my arm. "You're in danger, Lavender. That's been made very clear. Whatever is happening
here is going to end up getting you killed."

"If it makes you feel any better, I don't think those things that tore
Seth's house apart were after me at all," I told him. "If you want to be
concerned about anyone, worry about Seth. You've already got two
missing Tales and two dead Ordinaries. Help me make sure Seth
doesn't become one of the statistics."

"Come with me so I know you're safe," Puck insisted, "and then
I'll do what I can for dog-boy."

"Puck—"

"Just come stay with me for a few days," he interrupted. "Give me
some more time to look into things."

"No," I said firmly. "I'm not leaving Seth. He needs me right
now."

"I don't give a rat's ass what *he* needs," Puck shot back.

I put my hands on my hips, squaring off. "I'm not leaving here,
Puck, and that's final."

He shook his head. "I can't believe you'd choose him over your
own family."

"Why are you so against me being with him?" I demanded.

Puck straightened, eyeing me closely. "So, you *are* fucking him?"

I sent a glance over my shoulder, making sure no one had heard him, but they were all still laughing and enjoying their dinner. "I *love* him," I hissed. "And I'm not going anywhere."

Puck shook his head. "You always were so damned stubborn, Lavender."

I crossed my arms over my chest. "Then you shouldn't be surprised."

He stared at me for a moment, then a wide grin broke across his face and he laughed. "Shit. No, I guess not."

"Now, do you think you can stop being a pompous, condescending ass long enough to join us?" I asked. "Seth's cooking, so you know it'll be amazing."

"It's still a little early for dinner for me," he said. "Maybe next time."

"Suit yourself."

I turned to go, but Puck grasped my elbow again, bringing me to a halt. "Do you have everything you need?" he asked, sotto voce. "I heard it was a total loss."

I shrugged. "We have enough. Eventually Seth will have to buy new living room furniture and a bed, but we can camp out on the floor until then."

Puck cursed under his breath. "No sister of mine is sleeping on the floor. Christ, Lavender, you're a *Seelie*."

"So?"

"So whip something up with your magic, for God's sake!" he grumbled. "You can create a freaking carriage out of a pumpkin and you won't make a bed for you and your lover?"

I glared at him in warning. "My magic has been a little *off*, remember? The last thing I want to do is create a bed that's going to come to life in the middle of the night and gobble us up."

He gave me an exasperated look and reached into his suit pocket, withdrawing a wallet. "Then take this and go shopping."

"I don't want your money," I told him.

He flipped the wallet shut. "Last time I checked, you didn't have a job without Squiggington around, baby girl. And I know Wolf doesn't make shit at the restaurant. How do you anticipate refurnishing his little shack if you won't use magic?"

I narrowed my eyes at him. "I have money, thank you."

He nodded sagely. "Dad set you up when you left Chicago, huh?"

"What do you care?" I snapped.

He sighed. "Look, I'm just trying to help, okay? I want to make sure you have what you deserve. I sure as hell don't think it's that fucking—" He bit off his words and closed his eyes, holding up his hands in a conciliatory gesture before the furious words on my lips could come out. "Let me do something nice for you. Please?"

With that, he made a subtle wave of his hand. Golden fairy dust burst forth in a little cloud and swept toward the house, swooping down the chimney and disappearing.

"What was that?" I asked.

He bent and pressed a kiss to my forehead. "Consider it a housewarming present, I guess." He put his shades back on and turned to go, but paused before getting in his SUV. "Oh, and Lavender, I suppose you and your . . . *boyfriend* should have dinner with me or something."

I smiled. "Sounds good. When?"

"Friday night," he said. "Let's say around eight o'clock?"

I nodded. "See you then."

As I was waving good-bye, Seth came up beside me and slipped his arm around my shoulders. "What was that all about?"

"My brother dropped by to see if we needed anything and to invite us to dinner Friday evening," I said, polishing the truth more than a little.

Seth's brows came together, but he didn't say anything more about it. "Everyone seems to be ready to head out," he said, his tone distracted. "Do you want to help me wrap up the leftovers?"

I started toward the cabin, but turned back when I realized he wasn't with me. He stood staring down the road watching my brother's careful departure. "Seth, are you coming?"

He nodded. "Yeah," he called. "Yeah, I'm coming."

Later that night, Seth and I lay together in the newly christened bed my brother had magically produced as a housewarming present, having already broken in the sofa after all the guests had left.

"Today was pretty amazing," he said, running his fingertips lightly up and down my arm. "I never would have expected any of the towns-people to help out like they did."

I pressed a kiss to his chest. "You're not used to the kindness of others," I reminded him. "But those people care about you, Seth. And if they didn't before, they do now that they're getting to know you and see what an amazing man you are."

He inhaled deeply, his breath a little shaky. "I just . . ." His words trailed off and he pressed the heel of his hand to his eyes for a moment before continuing. "For the first time since my story began, I feel like I have a home, Lavender. I feel like I *belong* somewhere."

I shifted so that I could press a lingering kiss to his lips. My heart swelled with happiness, knowing that this man who had suffered so much for so long had finally found his place in the world. And that—at least for now—that place included me.

"I love you," I whispered softly.

He reached up and gently lifted the pendant that hung between my breasts. His skin instantly began to grow red, the silver searing the point of contact, but he didn't move his hand away. Instead, he curled his fingers around the pendant and pulled me down to him to receive his kiss. When he let go of my necklace to run his hands along the curves of my body, I felt the imprint where the silver had branded his skin.

I straddled his waist and sat up to remove the necklace before it did any more harm, but he sat up with me, stilling my hands. "Leave it."

I shook my head. "But if it hurts you—"

He grasped the nape of my neck and pulled me to him, claiming my lips and cutting off my protest. He managed to avoid my necklace as we made love again, but as I shattered apart, he clasped me tightly against him, my breasts flattened against his chest, and cried out with me as his own release came. When I pulled back to brush a kiss to his lips, I caught a glimpse of the angry burn in the shape of my pendant on his chest just above where his heart still beat rapidly.

"Oh, Seth," I lamented. "I'm so sorry!"

He shook his head, still a little breathless, then pressed his forehead to mine. "Don't apologize," he insisted. "It's part of you, Lavender, part of who you are. And now it's part of me."

Chapter 17

I shook my head as Seth rolled up the legs of his jeans, looking like a little boy playing dress-up in his father's clothes. "That looks ridiculous," I chuckled. "I'm going shopping for you today."

Seth frowned as he stood and surveyed the too-baggy shirt and jeans he'd borrowed from Tom Piper. "What? I'm going to work—not a fashion show."

"Tom has about three inches and fifty pounds on you," I reminded him. "You can't keep borrowing his clothes until you have time to go to a shopping mall. I'll just go today and buy you a few things to get you by for a while."

"Can't you just . . ." He wiggled his fingers in the air.

I laughed. "Can't I just use magic to create new clothes for you?"

His face flushed a little with what I presumed to be embarrassment that he'd asked me to use my magic. "Yeah, I guess that's what I'm asking."

I smiled at his naïveté. "It doesn't quite work that way. You have to have something to start with—you can't just make something from nothing."

"Then how did your brother create the sofa and bed for us?" Seth questioned.

I worked my mouth from side to side, trying to figure out how to explain it. "Each fairy has a particular strength. My brother's is transformations. He can transform himself, someone else, or any kind of object into pretty much anything he wants. But even *he* has to start with something. Considering our location, I'm betting the bed and sofa were taken from trees in the forest—hopefully fallen ones."

"So . . ."

"So," I explained, "while I could maybe spruce up the train wreck of fashion you're sporting today, the effect would be temporary, a few hours at most. Remember, my spells for Cindy only lasted until midnight. My brother's spells, however, are indefinite until he chooses to reverse them."

"So sometime while we're making love he might decide to turn our bed back into a rotting log?"

I grimaced a little, wrinkling my nose. "Knowing Puck, that's not totally out of the realm of possibility."

"Good to know," Seth drawled, giving me a wry look. "So, do you want the keys to the pickup? I can always run to work."

I shook my head, still hating the piece of shit he drove—even though it now had some rather steamy and fabulous memories attached to it. "Your new pals from town saw my Jag on the side of the road and fixed it for me yesterday. I'm all set."

"Ah, well . . . okay, then." He came to me and kissed me until I finally had to push him away with a laugh.

"I promised Gretel I'd make sure you were at work on time today," I admonished. "Now get out of here before she comes to hunt your ass down."

He groaned as he gave me another quick kiss and then was out the door. I waited until I heard the truck's engine roar to life and then shut myself in the bathroom and turned on the shower, letting the steam fill the tiny room. It didn't take long before the newly replaced mirror was covered in a fine mist. I put my call through, anxiously waiting for my father to answer. But there was no response.

"What the hell?" I murmured. He should've been able to pick up no matter where he was as only the fairy initiating the call needed the mists to create the connection. I wiped the mirror clean and let it cloud over once more so I could try again. I was about to wipe the mirror again when a face suddenly appeared to me, but not the one I was expecting.

"Gideon?" I said, not bothering to hide my surprise. "Where's my father? Why isn't he answering my call?"

Gideon's normally impassive expression took on a softer edge. "Lavender . . . there's been an accident."

I blinked at him, dread seizing my heart. "What do you mean 'accident'? Where's my dad?"

"He's in the Tale hospital here in Chicago," Gideon informed me. "The doctors think he'll be okay."

I leaned against the sink, my knees feeling too weak to support me. "What happened?"

Gideon shook his head. "We're not sure. He was sleeping and started to thrash around. Your mother believes he was being hexed, that someone was trying to harm him remotely."

I frowned. "Hexed? Who would want to hex Dad? That's opening up a really dangerous door."

Gideon's face went dark again. "I don't know, but when I find out who it was, there's going to be hell to pay. I'll rip the fucker's head off his shoulders for harming your father."

I nodded, knowing Gideon meant what he said. "Is there anything I can do? Should I come to Chicago?"

Gideon sighed. "I don't know if that'd be the best idea, Lavender. Your mother is pretty upset that your father helped you recently. And she's seriously pissed off that he sent me to see you."

I blinked at him, regret once more twisting my heart. Although my father had been moved by Gideon's love for me during my trial, my mother had been furious. The knowledge of my secret affair was enough to seal the deal on my being cast out of the family. I nodded, though, understanding that my showing up at my father's bedside—as hard as it was to stay away—would just end up in a screaming match that nobody needed right now.

"Will you keep me posted on things, Gid?" I asked. "And, when you have a private minute with him, could you let him know I'm thinking about him and that I love him and . . ." I wiped my eyes, trying not to let my emotions take over.

"Of course," he said. "Is something else wrong—is that why you wanted to talk to your father?"

I stared at Gideon, unblinking, for a long moment, trying to decide what to say next. Finally, I closed my eyes and let out a long, slow breath. "I need a favor, Gid. Do you think you can meet me somewhere? I'll explain everything then."

I waited at the coffee shop in the mall, several bags of clothes from Nordstrom sitting at my feet. I took another sip of my latte, wondering if Gideon would actually show up. He'd agreed to meet me that afternoon, but knowing my father was in danger, I wasn't sure Gideon would be able to tear himself away for long enough to perform the task I'd asked.

I checked the clock on the wall of the coffee shop and was just beginning to doubt that Gid would show, when I felt a heavy presence at my elbow. As I glanced up, he was standing there, gazing down on me.

"Hello, Gideon," I said softly. Then I pushed back my chair and stood, my heart hammering in my chest, a warring mixture of feelings stealing whatever words I'd prepared to say when I saw him again. So instead of saying anything, I threw my arms around his neck and hugged him tightly, glad that he hugged me back after a moment's hesitation.

With a relieved sigh, I released him and stepped back, feeling a little awkward. I sat down again and motioned for him to join me. "Thanks so much for coming," I said. "It means a lot to me. Really."

"I told you before, anytime you need me, I'll be there," he said, his voice low. "I wish it could be for a different reason, though."

The pain in his eyes made the center of my chest ache. "I'm so sorry for everything, Gideon," I told him. "The way I left things . . ."

"Don't," he interrupted. "I've moved on, and I'm guessing you have, too."

I nodded. "Only just recently—since I left Chicago. His name is Seth Wolf."

Gideon's brows lifted in surprise. "The Big Bad Wolf?"

I chuckled a little. "He's not nearly the villain he's been painted."

"Do you love him?"

I nodded. "Yeah, I do. But..." I paused, feeling a little strange talking to Gideon about my love life, but I needed someone to talk to, and being a fairy, he'd understand the way no one else could. "I'm not sure his feelings for me are genuine. He took my necklace off me and the silver seared his flesh before he understood what it meant."

"So you think it might just be the enchantment?" Gideon surmised.

I nodded, frowning. "I need to find the one who forged the pendant and have him destroy it."

"If you're happy, though, why not leave well enough alone?"

"Because I love him," I replied. "And I want whatever our future holds to be based on truth and choice—not a magical bond he didn't intend to accept."

Gideon sighed, then held out his hand. "Give me your necklace."

I jerked back a little, surprised by his request. "But it will bind you to me as well."

"Lavender, I've been bound to you once before," he reminded me. "And even after the first pendant was destroyed, my love for you remained unchanged. Your true name will always be written on my heart—the pendant can do nothing to alter that for good or ill."

A fresh wave of pain and regret washed over me as I unclasped my necklace and handed it to him. "Do you think you can figure out who forged it without anyone growing suspicious?"

"There's nothing to figure out," he said, his hand closing around the pendant. "*I* forged it—a gift to you to replace the one we'd shared and as a reminder that there are those who still love you."

"Gideon, I—"

"I'll destroy this as soon as your father is out of danger," he interrupted, tucking it into his suit pocket. "And I'll make you a new one—out of something other than silver so that you can share it with this werewolf of yours if he proves worthy."

"Thank you," I said simply, knowing it wasn't nearly enough.

He glanced up at the coffee shop clock and sighed. "I should go before someone notices my absence. Plus, it's going to take me a while to find a secluded place to slip through the dimensions unnoticed."

He then looked around, making sure none of the other patrons was watching, and put his hand under the table. When he brought it out again, he held a fragile, tattered book. He slid it across the table to me.

"Be careful with this, Lavender," he said just above a whisper. "Someone's definitely been messing with it. I have no idea how they managed to bypass the defensive magic I put up around it, but if they were able to neutralize those spells—even just long enough to catch a few glimpses now and then—they've been doing their homework on the book and what it can do. And if your mother finds out I gave this to you . . ."

I nodded, understanding well the risk he had taken in bringing the book to me. I rose with him as he stood to go, the book held closely against my chest. "Thank you again, Gideon. For everything. I wish . . ."

He gave me a rare smile, then bent and pressed a kiss to the top of my head. "Take care, petal."

I watched him walk away, his long strides taking him too quickly beyond my line of sight. Then, with a sigh, I tucked the book into one of the Nordstrom bags and gathered my things, ready to go back to Seth's cabin and do what I needed to do to keep him safe—whether he liked it or not.

Chapter 18

The rain was coming down in a gentle drizzle by the time I turned off onto the logging road that led to Seth's cabin. I flipped on the wipers in my Jag, praying I wasn't going to have a repeat of the night I'd arrived. I cursed under my breath as I felt the tires struggle to grab hold of the softening earth. "This is bullshit," I muttered, bringing the car to a stop. With a determined huff, I threw open the car door and slammed it shut to keep the rain from ruining the interior. I stared at the car for a moment, trying to get a feel for what I needed to do. I took a deep breath and let it out slowly, then shook out my hands. "Okay, okay, okay. . . . Here goes nothin'."

I waved my hand with a flourish, sending out the same bit of magic that had made me famous. There was a bright flash of purple light and my beautiful Jag groaned and creaked, slowly contorting. My eyes went wide as I watched it shift again, trying to transform. "Damn it!" I hissed. "Where's Puck when I need him? Son of a bitch!"

I waved my hand again, quickly trying to correct the hot mess I was making of my car, straining to control the magic as it wrapped around my Jag. The metal began to shriek as it strained and twisted, making my back teeth cry out in agony as the harsh sound assaulted my ears. But to my astonishment, there was a sudden pop and burst of light and where my Jag had been was now a beat-up white pickup truck with peeling paint and rust spots around the tire wells.

I gaped at the piece of shit in front me. "Are you fucking *kidding* me? It was supposed to be a goddamn Lexus!" Now feeling the damp on my clothes from the persistent drizzling rain, I stomped to the pickup, grumbling. "Seriously? After all that, I get stuck with a replica of Seth's jacked-up truck?"

I jerked open the door and climbed in, glancing down on the floor to make sure my shopping bags were at least intact and hadn't morphed into neon-orange velour track suits or something else equally offensive. Fortunately all was well from a fashion standpoint, so I shoved the stupid truck into gear and started out for home.

As much as I hated to admit it, the truck handled beautifully on the muddy road and I didn't have a single moment of concern as I made my way along the logging road, giving me a chance to scan the woods as I drove, searching for any unwanted fauna lurking in the shadows. Although I didn't see anything, the hair on the back of my neck began to rise as I approached the cabin, but whether it was from a genuine perception or just paranoia, I couldn't tell. Regardless, I didn't waste any time unloading my shopping bags and hurrying inside.

There were still a couple of hours before the restaurant closed, so I grabbed the book Gideon had smuggled to me and curled up on the couch, eager to search for one spell in particular. As I held the volume, my hands began to tremble. It had been nearly two hundred years since I'd been allowed to touch the treasured tome. And Gideon's apprehension hadn't been unfounded—if anyone were to discover that I had it now, there was little doubt of the outcome. There'd be no leniency for me this time, no matter who my father was.

I blew out a sharp breath, steeling my nerves, then lifted the cover. Instantly, a bright flash of light assaulted my eyes, making me wince and avert my gaze. But then the light dimmed and on the blank pages the ancient symbols of the Tales began to appear, faintly at first, but then gradually darkening. I hadn't been sure if the symbols would reveal themselves to me, all things considered, so when they did, tears of joy and relief stung my eyes. I quickly blinked them away and began to turn the delicate pages.

I couldn't remember exactly where the protection spell I was looking for fell in the sequence, so I had to skim the pages one at a time until I'd reached the end and then go back through. The information wasn't static as in a normal book; the more times you paged through, the more spells the book revealed—if you were deemed worthy.

I was turning through the pages for the eighth time, my frustration growing, when I finally came across the one I'd been searching for. "Finally!" I muttered, letting my fingers skim across the symbols on the page to absorb their essence into my memory. After stroking them lovingly this way for several minutes, I closed my eyes and let the power of the words drift through my thoughts, reassuring myself that they were there and ready for me to call upon when the time came.

Then, unable to resist the draw of reacquainting myself with the power I'd once wielded so effortlessly, I continued to page through, marveling anew at the loveliness of the ancient symbols. I remembered the first time I'd seen them and how awestruck I'd been. The incredible honor that had been bestowed upon me as their guardian hadn't been lost on me. Nor had I failed to feel the incredible loss when that responsibility was revoked.

I was perhaps three more trips through the volume when an unusual arrangement of symbols caught my eye. I paused, wondering where I'd seen that particular pattern before. I frowned, my thoughts racing. I traced the symbols with my fingertip, but the secrets of their power were difficult to grasp. Not willing to let the spell slip away, I pressed my lips together, determined to discover its true power.

Suddenly, there was a blinding flash of light and the symbols abruptly faded, replaced by ones similar but more refined, more precise—the differences so minute only the most experienced fairy would notice. I gasped, realizing the ones I'd been trying to decipher had been decoys, phonies used to mask the true spell hidden beneath.

As I read through the symbols, translating them in my head, a heavy mantel of dread settled upon my shoulders. *Oh shit.* The spell was one of necromancy—its symbols used in a ceremony to raise the dead, to reclaim a Tale's soul from the mists of the Great After.

No wonder the spell had been disguised and difficult to penetrate. Such an undertaking as reclaiming a spirit was nothing to be trifled with. It was dangerous to the one casting the spell, for one slight misstep could result in the caster's soul being exchanged with the one she was trying to reclaim. For that reason, the caster had to use a substitute, a sacrifice of another being to buffer and protect her own soul and that she would exchange at just the right moment for the already deceased.

"My God," I breathed, as the remaining elements of the spell became clear. Not only was there a bloodletting involved and the murder of another needed to ensure the caster's survival, but the ceremony was also gruesome, brutal, barbaric. Necromancy was forbidden, I knew, but until reading this spell I had never so fully understood why.

My stomach began to churn as images of the ancients performing these heinous acts flooded my thoughts, snatches of the spell's history imprinted upon the page along with the symbols. I tried to look away, but the power of the spell had enveloped me, refusing to release me. The images came faster and faster, the agonized screams of those sacrificed for such a dark purpose raking through my brain like monstrous claws.

I could feel a scream of terror building in the center of my chest, could feel it burning my throat as it was ripped from me, but I couldn't stop it. I squeezed my eyes shut and clutched the sides of my head, the pain of the images tearing me apart. But then a sudden calm came over me, and I felt a distant, pale purple light building from deep within me. It spread slowly from the center of my soul, pushing away the searing pain, replacing it with healing warmth. The air around me began to move gently, lifting my hair and the loose sleeves of my sweater as I rose to my feet.

I pressed my palms together as if in prayer and raised them until they were level with my chest, the air now a cyclone spinning faster and faster about me, whipping my hair into my face until it stung. Then with a sharp command, I pulled my palms apart and shoved forward. There was a loud crack as the spell's hold abruptly released me and a shower of fairy dust rained down in a perfect circle around my feet.

I gasped and glanced down at the book. It had tested me. And I had passed. I was once more a guardian of its secrets, welcomed back into the depths of its mysterious past. I laughed, elated that the strength and skill I'd thought lost to me forever had returned. I felt energized as if I'd suddenly been reborn.

But my elation was short-lived. As I regained my composure, I remembered the final image of the spell's history that had been revealed. Brie, the Ordinary girlfriend of J. G. Squiggington, lying on her bed, arms and legs bound, terror in her lovely eyes as she shook her head, pleading for her life. I still heard her screams of agony as I raced to the bathroom to heave the contents of my stomach.

When there was nothing left to vomit, I dropped onto my ass and pressed my back to the wall, the magnitude of what I'd just discovered hitting me like a fist to the center of my chest. There was now no doubt that whoever was committing these murders was attempting to wield the same ancient necromancy spell that was in the book— although there were elements that were wrong, missing. Whoever it was hadn't been able to fully penetrate the spell. The murders that had taken place so far were just practice, I realized, a warm-up for what was coming.

But who could be doing it? And why?

Puck had told me losing everyone and everything a person cares about could push him over the edge, insinuating that Seth could be guilty of the murders. But I refused to believe that. Whom would Seth be trying to resurrect? Meryn—the beloved lover he'd killed by mistake? Never happen. Not with Seth's aversion to magic.

Of course, Seth wasn't the only one who'd lost someone. Bo Peep was high on my list, especially as she was still MIA. And what of Eva, the infamous warrior who'd lost her darling boy so tragically? Hell, for all I knew, there were countless others in the town whose losses were so heartbreaking they could drive a Tale to commit murder. Then again, maybe the murderer was just plain crazy. Always a possibility. And if being mucho loco was the motivation, I was laying my money on ultra-creepy Doctor Dreadful.

The problem was, I had no idea where to even start digging into the pasts of the other Tales to discover who could be capable of such a thing. And Tom had limited resources at his disposal. There was magic involved, no doubt about it. But anyone could attempt to harness magic; it didn't have to be a creature born of magic. And, considering what I'd seen of the carvings on Brie's body, it was clear that while the perpetrator might know of the spell, he or she didn't have the skill to back it up.

I ran my hands through my hair, my head spinning. Who in town would know the histories of the other Tales? Where could I start looking to uncover the truth? My stomach suddenly dropped, almost making me heave again.

J.G. had told me on the day we'd met that he only published his tabloid for the money, that his true passion was in investigative reporting. He'd also said he was on to something big, something that would "knock the Tale world on its ass." Had he been on to the person committing the murders? Was that why Brie had been chosen as a victim and J.G. was now missing?

I needed to find out. And the only way to do that was to go through J.G.'s things.

The sound of a car door slamming made me jump. I scrambled to my feet, realizing Seth must be home, and ran into the living room, snatching up the book and racing into the bedroom, frantically looking around for a place to hide it. Not finding anywhere that wouldn't be obvious, I grabbed a sweater from the closet and wrapped it around the book, then stashed it in one of my empty suitcases. Not ideal, but probably not the first place someone would look.

Then I darted to the bathroom and flushed the toilet again, hoping Seth wouldn't pick up on the fact that I'd been so violently ill. I heard the key rattling in the multiple locks on the front door as I quickly brushed my teeth. I was just rinsing my mouth when Seth poked his head around the doorframe. I attempted a grin around the mouthful of water, making him chuckle.

"Everything okay?" he asked with a bemused grin.

I nodded, then spit and wiped my mouth, now offering him a genuine smile. "Everything's great."

"Did you enjoy your shopping trip?"

"Oh, yeah," I said, backing him out of the bathroom as I came toward him. "I have some great new things for you to try on."

"Yeah?" He cocked his head to one side, studying me as if picking up on the fact that I was hiding something—or maybe it was just my guilty conscience reading into things.

I nodded then pressed a kiss to his lips. I began unbuttoning his shirt, looking up at him through lowered lashes. "But, you know, before you can put on your *new* clothes, we're going to need to get you out of these."

His lips curved into a slow smile as I slid his shirt from his shoulders. And he was still grinning when I pulled his T-shirt over his head and tossed it aside. But when he pulled my sweater over my head, his smile abruptly faded, replaced by a deep frown.

"Where's your necklace?" he asked, his hand instinctively going to the scar over his heart.

"I'm having it repaired," I said—which wasn't *exactly* a lie. . . .

"Repaired?" he repeated.

I nodded, undoing his belt and letting the too-baggy borrowed pants fall to his ankles. When he started to ask another question, I captured his mouth with mine, letting him know that the time for talking was over. And whatever he'd intended to say died on a groan, the absence of my necklace completely forgotten.

Chapter 19

Later that night, when I was certain Seth was sleeping soundly, I slipped naked from bed and tiptoed to the kitchen, where I grabbed the same paring knife I'd used before, then made my way to the front door. I winced when the locks clicked as I disengaged them, and cast a glance toward the bedroom door, holding my breath. But after a few seconds I heard Seth's soft snoring and let my breath out on a relieved sigh.

As much as it seemed he was beginning to come to terms with the fact that he had a magical being for a lover, I didn't want to press my luck by letting him know I meant to place a spell on his cabin. Plus, he didn't see that he himself was in serious danger. His concern was more for me and *my* well-being. And while that made me go all warm and fuzzy, there was no way in hell I was going to let his stubborn male ego prevent me from protecting him. End of story.

The night air was cool on my bare skin as I stepped outside and shut the door firmly behind me. Wouldn't do much good to cast a protection spell on the cabin if something walked right through the front door while I was doing it.

I glanced around me, the hair on the back of my neck standing up. I couldn't quite shake the feeling that someone was watching me from the shadows, but as I surveyed my surroundings, letting my senses reach out into the darkness, I found nothing to confirm my fears.

"Pull it together, Lav," I muttered under my breath. I had to be able to concentrate to pull this off. There were certainly other, easier spells I could have cast that didn't involve any of the darker magic of the ancient Tale symbols, but they were also weaker. And considering these hellhounds were some seriously nasty mothers, I wasn't planning to half-ass it. I'd fallen back on what was safe and easy for far too long.

I closed my eyes and cleared my mind, focusing on the spell I'd absorbed earlier. When I felt a persistent hum just beneath my skin, I opened my eyes and looked down at my hands. I was glowing, the light I'd lost touch with for so long finally coming back to me like a long-lost lover. My skin went translucent, taking on the pale lavender shade that it had been at my birth. I knew that if anyone were to look on me at that moment, my eyes would also be glowing, having gone from lavender to bright purple. The magic was ready to pour out of me; all I had to do was let go.

I walked out to beyond where Seth's truck was parked, making sure that it, too, would be included in my protection, then murmuring the words that would keep him safe, I ran the edge of the knife across my palm, gratified when the blood that appeared was not red as it normally would have been, but a psychedelic purple version that spoke of the potency of the magic coursing through my veins. Just then, the clouds covering the moon parted as if to allow that magnificent orb to grant her own blessing upon the spell to protect my beloved—one of her own.

I squeezed my hand into a fist, letting the blood trickle down onto the ground as I slowly walked the circumference of the cabin. The trail I left behind flared brightly as the spell began to take hold. As I walked, the unshakable feeling of being watched kept trying to creep into my thoughts and distract me from my purpose, but I pushed the feeling away, ignoring it so that I could concentrate and ensure the success of my spell. I raised my voice, which was no longer *my* voice, but the voice of ages, of the ancients who had come before me, all in chorus. The voices entwined themselves about the wind, letting the breezes carry them to the forces that would lend their potency, reinforcing the spell against attack.

When I at last reached the beginning of the protective circle, I stepped inside and sealed it with my blood, locking it in place. The chorus of voices grew louder and louder, filling the night. My own voice joined them now as the one who'd forged the spell, and for a brief moment I worried that the sound might wake Seth, but I had only one last duty to perform.

Just inside the spot where the circle closed, I drew a symbol that represented my true name, disguised as nothing more than a random design, marking the spell as my own doing. Then I held my palms up to the moon, reciting the last of the sacred words. As the final word passed my lips, the circle of protection blazed brightly to life, searing its power deep into the ground and high into the sky. And then it was gone. There was no evidence at all of what I had done, save for a small area of the grass that was imprinted with my signature.

I let out a heavy sigh. Now only those with pure intentions could cross it. No one who held malice in his heart toward Seth could cross the circle. It was done. I laughed a little in relief and exhaustion. The force of will it had taken to wield the power after so long had left me trembling and weak but finally feeling alive again.

Satisfied with the work I'd done and grinning from ear to ear, I turned around to go back inside the house, but my feet suddenly turned to stone, stopping me where I stood, my grin vanishing with a startled gasp. For there on Seth's deck, filthy and bedraggled and huddled into a fetal position and shuddering violently, was J. G. Squiggington.

In spite of my nakedness, I bolted up the deck steps as best I could on my wobbly knees and crouched down next to J.G. He was rocking a little, his arms wrapped around his tattered clothing, mumbling incoherently under his breath. If I hadn't known any better, I would've thought he was going through fairy dust withdrawal, but when I'd met him before I'd seen no evidence of his being an addict.

I cautiously laid a hand on his arm. He shrank from my touch with a startled cry as if he'd been severely beaten, but there again I saw no evidence of that fact—at least, not outwardly.

"What's happened to you?" I whispered. Knowing I couldn't exactly leave him there on the porch but not wanting to give away my activities to Seth, I quickly slipped back inside the house and pulled on the button-down shirt from earlier that night when I'd been ripping off Seth's clothes. Because it was Tom's shirt, it came down to my knees, providing an acceptable amount of modesty. Then I quickly washed the blood from my hand and the mud and grass stains from my feet. Once more presentable, I crept out to the bedroom.

"Seth," I said, shaking him gently. "Wake up."

He rolled toward me with a puzzled frown. "Lavender? What's wrong?"

"You have to come with me," I told him. "Right now."

He immediately threw back the covers and grabbed his pants. "What's going on?"

I hesitated a moment, my mind racing to come up with how I'd found J.G. "I heard a noise outside," I said, hurrying toward the front door, "and I found—"

"You went outside without me?" he snapped, cutting me off.

"Just come see this," I shot back before he could ask any other questions. I grabbed his hand and pulled him outside onto the deck where J.G. still lay in a strung-out heap.

"Holy shit!" Seth cried, as taken aback to see the missing gossip peddler as I'd been. "How the hell did he get *here*?"

"I don't know," I said, shaking my head, "but we have to help him. Should we drive him into town to Tom?"

Seth shook his head, crouching down to try to help J.G. to his feet. "No, there's nothing Tom can do. Help me load him into the truck. We'll take him to Mama's. She might be able to at least calm him down so we can try to talk to him and figure out what happened."

When we got to Mama's house, Seth and I tried to coax J.G. from the cab of the truck, but he recoiled, crying out in fear and mumbling incoherently.

"J.G.," I said, gently. "Please, you have to come out. We're trying to help you."

As I kept talking to him, trying to persuade him to come with me, Seth slipped around the back of the truck and silently crept up to the passenger door where J.G. was cowering. He nodded at me from over

J.G.'s shoulder, then jerked open the door, catching the man under his arms as he fell backward out of the cab.

J.G. struggled and screamed, trying to break away from Seth's hold, but even with the strength of fear working for him, he was no match for Seth. But as J.G. became more violent, Seth let out an exasperated sigh and clocked him, knocking him out cold.

"What the hell?" I cried. "Don't you think he's been through enough?"

Seth tossed J.G. over his shoulder in a fireman's hold and gave me an irritated look. "Would you have him hurt Mama with all his flailing around? Besides," he said as he climbed the porch steps, "he's yelling so loudly, he could draw the attention of whoever—or whatever—has had him all this time."

Damn. He had a point.

It hadn't even occurred to me that by bringing J.G. there we might be putting Mama and Harlan in jeopardy. I rapped on Mama's door, wondering how it was possible that she hadn't already been awakened by our less-than-discreet arrival.

A moment later, she came to the door, fully dressed, hair in place, as if she hadn't slept a wink the entire night. And yet she looked completely refreshed and rested. "What in the world brings you by at this hour, babies?" she asked, but her question was quickly answered when she saw the man draped over Seth's shoulder. "Oh, Lord! Bring him on in. Quick now."

Mama motioned us in with a wave of her hand and glanced out into the darkness as if expecting to see some monstrous creature lurking in the shadows. She shut the door behind us, then peeked out through the glass, searching the night again, the jovial, unflappable woman's sudden uneasiness making me want to scratch my skin off to reach the creeping, crawling apprehension wriggling just below the surface.

"I'm sorry to barge in on you, Mama," Seth told her, looking around for a place to put the unconscious J.G. "I didn't know where else to take him for help."

"Never mind that," she said, waving away his apology. She bustled past him in the entryway and motioned for him to follow. "You bring him on back here now and let Mama take a look."

Seth dropped J.G. on Mama's tiny guest bed, which was just wide enough for her to take a seat on the edge next to the tortured man. She put her hand on his forehead and closed her eyes for a moment, then shook her head.

"Darkness," she said, her voice gruff. "So much darkness in this boy."

I came up beside Seth, glad when his arm circled my shoulders and pulled me close against him. "Can you tell what happened to him, Mama? Can you tell how he got this way?"

"Somethin' nasty been tearing at his mind," she said, patting him lightly on the cheek. "Poor boy—not much left there to draw out. It's just scattered images—and not pretty ones neither. Been tortured somethin' awful."

"When I found him he was acting like he was going through fairy dust withdrawal," I told her. "He was muttering and shaking. But when I tried to help him, he pulled away like he'd been beaten."

She nodded. "He's definitely had the dust," she agreed. "Forced into him, most like. But there's more. Something's been in his head, tore out the memories they didn't want him to have."

"My God," Seth breathed. "Who the hell would do that to him? Who *could* do that to him?"

"Nothin' to torturing," Mama said with a sad shake of her head. "Anyone can push a body till he breaks. Don't have to be nothin' special to tear someone's soul apart—just evil."

I had to concede that point, but somehow I had a feeling it was related to the murdered Ordinaries and the story J.G. had been ready to break wide open. And now, with J.G.'s mind compromised and little more than a jumbled mess of terrifying images, I wondered if I'd ever know what that story was.

"Seth baby, come help Old Mama," Mama called, getting to her feet and bustling toward the bedroom door. "Gonna need to get this boy cleaned up. Can at least do that much for him."

Seth cast a questioning glance my way, but I nodded, assuring him I'd be okay. As soon as they'd gone, I sat down on the edge of the bed where Mama had been and scowled down at J.G., my heart twisting with regret and sorrow at seeing him in such a state. I felt responsible for his condition, somehow. Although I hadn't been the one to pump him full of fairy dust to the point of a debilitating overdose, it was my kind who'd started shilling our magic for profit. The Seelies especially were to blame. We were supposed to be benevolent, helping the less fortunate and looking after our nonmagical brethren. That had changed somewhere along the way. As a race of Tales we were perhaps the most culpable for every single fairy dust addict out there.

With a bitter sigh, I reached out and smoothed J.G.'s hair from his eyes, wishing there was something I could do and knowing there was absolutely nothing that could help the man at this point. He was too far gone and—

I cried out as J.G.'s hand suddenly grasped my wrist and jerked me forward so that I was half on top of him, my face only inches from his. His eyes snapped open, darting wildly until finding mine. His pupils and irises were indistinguishable, and the whites of his eyes were blood red, the vessels having burst from the massive dose of D he'd been given.

"Get out!" he ground out, his voice shot to hell—from screaming, I guessed. "Get out now!"

"J.G.," I said, my voice quaking, "it's Lavender Seelie. You're safe now."

He shook his head, frantically, his eyes beginning to dart again. "Not safe. Nowhere's safe."

"J.G.—"

"They killed her," he interrupted, his voice thick with tears. "Dead, she's dead."

"Oh, honey, I know," I soothed, glancing nervously at the door. "Tell me who it was. Tell me who hurt you and Brie."

"The mother, the mother," he screeched, his eyes going wide with fear. "I found her."

My God—did he mean Bo Peep? Was it Gareth's *pseudo-mother he was talking about?*

"Not what you think!" His eyes were losing focus and rolling wildly in his head. "Not really a mother."

"I know, J.G.," I assured him. "Tom told me. Just tell me where she is and I'll take the bitch out."

He shook his head slowly, his gaze finding my face once again.

"You can't," he said, his voice so saturated with sorrow and hopelessness it was little more than a squeak. "The plans are in motion."

"Plans?" I repeated, frowning. "What plans?"

His gaze suddenly became intense to the point of deadly. I tried to pull back, but his grip on my wrist tightened, keeping me where I was. "You can't stop her."

Yeah, well, we'd see about that.

"Let me worry about it," I said, my voice firm. "Just tell me— what is she planning?"

He began to shudder violently as his lucidity slipped away. His teeth were chattering so hard a piece of one front tooth broke off as he snarled, "To kill you."

Chapter 20

"Lavender."

My eyes fluttered open at the sound of Seth's voice near my ear. I gave him a groggy smile as I stretched out my legs, stiff after having been curled up in one of Mama Hubbard's chairs for a few hours of sleep. "Hey."

He smoothed my hair from my face and kissed my forehead. "I've made breakfast if you want to eat."

"How's J.G.?" I asked, letting him pull me to my feet and into his arms.

"Sedated. Whatever Mama gave him has helped keep him quiet. Harlan's watching over him right now so Mama could get a little sleep."

I slipped my arms around his waist and rested my head against his chest, wondering for probably the thousandth time if I should tell him what J.G. had said in his fevered ramblings. Every time I pictured the look in J.G.'s eyes, or remembered the terror in his voice, it turned my blood to ice water in my veins. But as much as I wanted to share the information with Seth and let him soothe away my concerns, I knew him well enough to know he wouldn't just sit back and wait for something to happen. Ever the slayer of monsters, he'd run off to do battle, intent on protecting me, and probably get himself killed in the process.

And, well, that just wasn't an option.

"Are you going to be okay?" he asked softly against my hair.

I took a deep breath and let it out slowly. "I will be."

His arms tightened around me. "Have I mentioned how much I—"

A sudden pounding on the door cut off whatever it was he'd been about to say. *Damn it!* Something told me it would've been good, too. I tried not to shoot laser beams of death out of my eyes in the general direction of the unknown visitor. "Who the hell is that?"

Seth released me and started for the door. "I called the FMA last night to let them know about J.G.—"

"You what?" I screeched.

"—so that they could send someone from the Asylum. I'm guessing it's one of their agents."

I hurried after him. "Why did you call them?" I demanded, noting that my voice held an edge of anxiety that sounded suspicious even to my own ears.

He paused and frowned. "I had to report this, Lavender. J.G. needs help—what would you have had me do?"

I blinked at him, my breath coming in shallow, panicked gasps. There were FMA Investigators. Here. Where some fucking psycho was killing and torturing people with magic that had been entrusted to me to keep safe once upon a time. Fuck. Me.

Stay calm, Lavender, for God's sake.

I forced a smile and knew my lips were trembling a little. "I just wasn't expecting the FMA to investigate with Tom already on the case."

The visitor pounded on the door again, less patiently this time.

"I'm sure Tom will understand," Seth called over his shoulder as he reached for the doorknob.

Yeah, right.

Probably about as much as my brother, who had expressly forbidden FMA interference. I ran my hands through my hair as Seth opened the door, wondering just how things could get any worse.

"Jesus Christ—you bring me out into the middle of fucking nowhere and then take your sweet-ass time opening the door?"

Oh . . . that's how.

"Tess?" Seth cried. "What the hell are you doing here?"

"Good to see you, too," she drawled, shouldering past him wearing a dark scowl. "I traveled all fucking night to pick up your emergency whack-job. You might at least say 'hello' before you start giving me shit."

"Sorry," he said quickly, stepping forward and wrapping his arms around her in a hug. "It's good to see you." Her arms hung limply at her sides for a moment, but then she hugged him back, clinging to him a little more than I would've liked.

There was a soft cough behind them from on the porch, and they stepped apart, revealing the other visitor. Trish Muffet offered a slightly uncomfortable smile, then extended her hand to Seth. "Hi. Trish Muffet."

"Seth Wolf," he said, shaking her hand. Then he came to me and slid an arm around my shoulders. "Trish, do you know Lavender Seelie?"

"Yeah, I do. Hi, Lavender." She gave a little wave and offered me a smile in greeting, but it was edged with uneasiness as she cast a look at Red, whose head was cocked to one side, her eyes narrowed as she studied Seth and me.

"What *the hell* is going on?" Red ground out.

"We're not sure," Seth said with a shake of his head. "J. G. Squiggington just showed up on my porch—"

"That's not what I'm talking about." She waved her hand back and forth in the air between Seth and me. "I'm talking about *this*. I sent her here so you could look after her—not take advantage of her!"

Seth jerked back at the harsh accusation. "What?"

"No, no, Tess," I interjected, stepping between them. "It's not like that."

Ignoring me, she jabbed a finger at Seth. "You. Outside. Now."

He shook his head with a huff and pressed a kiss to my cheek. "Back in a sec, princess."

My fingertips drifted up to my cheek as I watched him follow Red outside, completely floored. He'd called me "princess" before, but this was the first time as a term of endearment. I practically floated to the picture window in the sitting room to watch what was happening between him and Red outside. For a moment I forgot Trish was still standing there but then I heard her clear her throat politely and turned away from the window, blinking at her as if she was an apparition.

We exchanged awkward glances and tight smiles. Then Trish puffed up her cheeks and worked the air in her mouth for a moment before blowing it out in a soft burst. She offered me a sympathetic smile. "Don't take it personally," she said. "Red's in a seriously shitty mood every day until she's had some coffee."

I nodded. "I can totally relate."

I heard Trish heave a little sigh. "And I think she's freaking out about the baby."

My head snapped toward her. "She told you?"

Trish nodded. "Yeah."

"I thought she'd be happy," I said. "Tales can't conceive a child unless we *want* to. It's not like we have accidents."

"She is happy," Trish confirmed. "From what I can gather, Red never thought she'd be a mother, never thought she'd settle down, but then she found Nate. . . ."

"And everything changed." I grinned, knowing just how finding the right guy can make you rethink everything you thought you'd always wanted. I'd avoided thinking about the future at all since coming over, but since arriving at The Refuge—since knowing Seth—I was beginning to wonder what my future might hold.

"Guess so," Trish said, turning her attention back to the window. "But when she told Nate about the baby, he freaked. She didn't tell me much of what he said, but whatever it was, it pissed her off enough to kick him out of Gran's. Since he sold his house to move in there, he didn't have anywhere to go and has been crashing on my couch for the last few days."

I turned my gaze back to the picture window, watching Seth and Red a lot more closely now. She was running her hand through her long black hair, much calmer than she'd been a few moments before. Seth stepped forward to wrap his arms around her in a comforting hug and pressed a kiss to her forehead.

My eyebrows snapped together as a spike of jealousy lanced through me. *What the—*

"So, you and Seth . . ." Trish said cautiously, interrupting my mental rant.

I pressed my lips together, bringing to heel the ferocious green-eyed monster that was beginning to growl in the center of my chest. "Yep."

"That must be a little awkward," Trish said. "You know—with him being Red's ex." There was a pause. "I mean . . . *is* it awkward?"

Well, no, actually it hadn't *been. But it sure as hell was beginning to feel that way now.*

I turned my frown on her. "Why do you ask?"

She shrugged and shook her head. "No reason. I just—well, you know, Red's kind of a hard person to forget. Guys have a hard time getting over her, from what I understand."

Well, shit. That really didn't help appease my nasty little monster.

I started to make a bitter quip about Red's trail of brokenhearted lovers, but bit back my words when I noticed the small square of linen Trish held in her hand. Her thumb lovingly smoothed the monogrammed "N. B." in what appeared to be black silk thread.

"So," I said, drawing out the word as understanding began to dawn, "which of Red's exes are *you* in love with?"

Trish's head popped up and she guiltily tucked the handkerchief into her pocket. "Oh, I'm not in love with him—" she broke off her words, shaking her head. "I mean, no one. There's no one."

I felt a little stab of sympathy. Based on the initials, I was guessing she had it bad for Nicky "Little Boy" Blue, the Tale crime lord who'd been attacked by Sebille Fenwick during her killing spree. Unfortunately, Nicky's wife had been one of the casualties. I wondered how Trish knew him, seeing as how they didn't exactly travel in the same circles, but I'd have to ask about it later—Red was stomping back into the house, Seth strolling after her, hands in his pockets.

"Everything okay?" I asked, my tone stiff. I forced a smile, trying to appear nonchalant, but it felt grotesque and distorted, so I can only imagine what it looked like.

Seth sighed and came toward me, his frustration seeming to melt away with each stride. He slipped his arm around my waist and pulled me to him, dropping a tender kiss on my temple. "It is now," he murmured softly.

"So where's the guy we're supposed to be transporting to the Asylum?" Red asked, her words clipped. She was still angry, but whatever Seth had said must've at least lessened her hostility.

We took her and Trish back to the guest room where J.G. tossed and turned in a fevered sleep. Harlan snorted as our entrance jolted him awake, but he quickly recovered his composure and bid us hello with a good-natured, "G'morning, y'all."

"So, somebody want to fill us in on exactly what happened to this guy?" Red demanded after Harlan padded out of the room to go grab his morning coffee.

"Seth didn't tell you anything over the phone?" I asked cautiously.

"I didn't talk to Red at all," Seth announced, fidgeting a little. I eyed him, wondering why that admission would make him uncomfortable. "I just called it in—an anonymous tip—and gave them Mama's address."

My God, he's lying. But why?

"Al's actually taking a vacation for once in close to two hundred years," Red explained, "so the tip came to my desk—and, lucky you, I decided to take this one myself."

"All we were told is that there was a possible pickup for the Asylum," Trish told us. "There's been a situation at the Asylum in the past couple of days which has taken up the director's time, so I came to certify that the Asylum is the appropriate place for the patient. We can't admit him without cause, so I'll need to know something about his case."

Seth and I glanced at one another. I wasn't sure how much he was planning to say, and I sure as hell wasn't planning to share any more than I had to.

"Or we can take you all in for questioning," Red snapped, sensing our hesitation. "That's fine. I've got room on the plane."

Seth gave her an irritated look. "I don't think that'll be necessary, Tess," he said, his voice a controlled calm. "J.G. disappeared a few days ago, but we have no idea where he's been or what's happened to him. Mama Hubbard tried to get a good look at his thoughts, but all she was able to see were disjointed images of violence and gore. He's been tortured, that much we know, but we can't be certain by whom or why."

I glanced at Seth, wondering if he was going to mention Brie's horrific death, but he shoved his hands deep into his pockets, rocked a little on his heels, and said nothing more. He was keeping it back from Red—probably the one person in this world he seemed to actually trust. What the hell was that all about?

Red turned that penetrating gaze of hers on me, making me squirm a little, but she didn't press for more information. For the moment. However, there was something that passed between us that made me realize she'd be chatting with me later. She then turned her gaze on J.G. "Poor bastard," she murmured. "He had a lot of potential once."

"Did you know J.G.?" I asked.

Red nodded slowly. "Yeah. He worked with me on a few cases for the FMA early on as an informant, fed me tips now and then. But then he realized he could make better money in the scandal business. There were more than a few people who've paid him hush money over the years."

I frowned, sinking into my own thoughts as Trish came over to J.G. and began to examine him. Was it possible that the story J.G. was about to blow wide open had involved one of the people who'd been paying him off? Was he about to betray the confidence of the person behind the murders, causing her to persuade him otherwise—first by butchering his girlfriend before his very eyes and then by driving him insane with torture and fairy dust?

"I'm starving," Red grumbled, breaking into my thoughts. "Mind if I go eat something while you take a look at him, Trish?"

Trish grinned and cast a conspiratorial glance my way. "Not at all. I know better than to come between you and food."

Something about the Forensic Investigator's quiet, intelligent gaze made me like her in spite of the fact that she was probably the one person who could make a lot of connections about the dead Ordinaries that I didn't want anyone to make. I'd known of her by reputation for decades. She was competent, dogged, and had a no-bullshit attitude about her that immediately made it clear why she and Red were friends.

We'd just polished off our breakfast when Trish came into the room, her expression looking a little grim. I had no idea what her examinations involved, but I was guessing it wasn't just a matter of checking his vitals. She pulled out a chair next to me and grabbed a slice of bacon.

"What'd you find?" Red asked.

Trish let out a long sigh. "Definite signs of fairy dust abuse. And what Seth said about the images of his torture is pretty much dead-on. I couldn't glean anything more than Mama Hubbard could. He's going to need intense therapy to recover from the psychological damage that's been inflicted upon him."

"And the D?" Red prompted.

Trish shook her head. "Nothing I can do about that one. We might be able to get him some help from a fairy therapist, but it doesn't look good. It would take someone better than the two-bit hacks they have on staff at the Asylum." She cast an apologetic glance at me. "No offense, Lavender."

"None taken," I said, knowing well that the best fairy dust therapists were hired for the private sector, not for the strung-out junkies who were one sprinkle away from their brains turning to mush and draining out their noses. The ones who worked at the Asylum were those who hadn't made the cut under my father's very stringent certification program and weren't even good enough to work at one of the cheaper, less respected distribution clinics. With my conscience niggling at me about the fairies' elitist attitudes concerning who was worth helping and who wasn't, I said, "I could make a call. See if I can line up someone better."

Red lifted a single dark brow at me. "Yeah? And why would you do that, Lav? You barely knew J.G., right?"

I shrugged. "No one deserves to go through what he's going through. I wouldn't wish that on anyone. Let me see if my sister Poppy is available. She's one of the best."

Red gave me a slight nod, still eyeing me suspiciously. *Damn it, that stare of hers was unsettling!*

"Okay," she said. "If you can line up Poppy as a therapist, I won't say no. The sooner we start treatments, the better. Trish and I will take J.G. back today and then your sister can start on J.G.'s sessions right away."

"Actually," Trish piped up, "I think I'd like to stick around a while, do a little more investigative work. There were some things I saw that I want to look into a little closer."

The food in my mouth suddenly turned to ash as Red gave Trish a tight nod. "No problem. Just let me know what you need and I'll requisition it." Then Red turned her attention back to Seth and me. "Who else knows about J.G. turning back up?"

I cast an expectant—and rather miffed—look at Seth, wondering who the hell else he might've called without my knowing about it. He blinked back at us, looking a little cornered. "No one," he said quickly. "Except Mama and Harlan, of course."

"Good," Red said, pushing back from the table. "Let's keep it that way. No one else is to know he turned up, you feel me? If anyone asks, Trish is here to look into his disappearance—end of story."

We all gave her obedient nods and murmured our acquiescence.

She stood then and grabbed one last scone. "This is damned good, by the way," she said to Seth. "You haven't lost your touch living out here in the sticks."

He was grinning at her as we all headed out of the kitchen, and my little green monster reared her ugly head again. But before she could trip my bitch switch, there was another knock on the door—this one much more hesitant and cautious than Red's had been.

"Who's here *now*?" I demanded of Seth, throwing my arms up in the air. "I thought you didn't call anybody else."

"I didn't." He shrugged and strode to the door, swinging it open.

There, in a long trench coat and fedora, was Nate Grimm, the shadows hanging around his face darker than they'd been the last time I'd seen him. "Wolf," he said with a tight nod. "Mind if I come in?"

"Yes!" Red snapped, storming up behind Seth and trying to shut the door in Nate's face. When Seth stuck his foot in front of the door to keep it open, she huffed and leaned around him to glare at her boyfriend. "I told you, I don't want to see you right now, Nate!"

"Come on in," Seth said, pegging Red with a chastising look.

Nate gave Seth an appreciative nod, then turned to Red, his expression pained. "Tess, sweetheart, we need to talk."

She made a sweeping motion with her arm, gesturing toward the rest of us. "Little busy, Nate."

"It won't take long," he assured her. He then gave Seth a pleading look. "Could we have a minute?"

We started to shuffle back into the kitchen, but Red stepped in front of us, blocking the path. "You're not going anywhere," she ordered. "If you have anything to say to me, Nate Grimm, you can say it in front of everyone."

He blew out a harsh breath, then held his arms out to his sides. "Fine. You want to do it this way, I'm game. We didn't finish our conversation the other night."

"Oh, this conversation's over as far as I'm concerned," she hissed. "There's nothing else to talk about."

"The hell there isn't!" Nate shot back. "Now will you shut up for one goddamn minute and let me say what I came to say?"

She crossed her arms in a huff. "You have one minute. Go."

He glanced around at us, looking a little cornered, but then he squared his shoulders and pegged Red with a pained look. "I've missed you, Tess," he started out in a harsh whisper as he stepped closer to her. "Everything I am, everything I have—none of it means anything without you."

She rolled her eyes. "So help me God, Nate, if you say, 'You complete me,' I'm shoving my fist down your throat."

Nate's mouth lifted at one corner. "I wouldn't dare," he drawled, taking another cautious step toward her. "But I *will* say I'm sorry for freaking out on you about the baby."

"Baby?" Seth whispered, near my ear. "What baby?"

I waved him away, wanting to hear what was coming next. "Shh. I'll tell you later."

"I should've just told you what I was so afraid of instead of making it sound like I wasn't happy about having a baby with you," Nate continued.

She blinked at him, her expression becoming a little less aloof. "What are you afraid of?"

"I'm worried that it won't be . . . normal. That it'll be like me."

This seemed to weaken Red's defenses a little. Her brows were drawn together in concern when she asked, "What do you mean? You're worried it'll be a Reaper?"

He took a deep breath and then glanced at the rest of us again. "No," he said, his voice low. "I was afraid it wouldn't be a Tale."

Red's gaze darted between us quickly, no doubt sensing our collective shock. Or maybe it was Seth's, "Holy shit."

"Nate's not a Tale?" Trish whispered, putting the concrete words to Nate's confession.

"None of that matters to me," Red told him, her tone softer than I'd ever heard it before. "You know that."

"But it matters to *me*." Now that she was within reach, he took hold of her arms and pulled her close. "Did you ever wonder why I'm so attached to the forties?" he asked. When she shrugged, he said, "Because that's when I was given this assignment and could finally be with you, Tess. I never wanted to lose that."

Trish made a little choked noise and stepped closer to me. "Oh, my *God* . . . that's so romantic."

I nodded, feeling like I was watching one of those chick flicks that were a little over the top with the melodramatic love story but made me cry anyway.

"Nate—"

"Tess, I want this. I don't ever want you to think otherwise. But I'm scared shitless that if our child isn't like you . . ."

"Nothing's going to take you away from me," she said, taking his face in her hands. "Not ever. It'd have to be over my dead body—and you'll be there for that call anyway."

Oh, yeah. Totally going to cry. Apparently, Trish was right there with me—she had her handkerchief out and was dabbing at her eyes.

I sniffed and glanced at Seth, who was grimacing at Trish and me like we were nuts. *Men.* I turned back to the love scene before me, waiting breathlessly to see what would happen next. When Nate dropped down on one knee, I covered my mouth to keep from squealing with delight and Trish gripped my hand, squeezing in excited anticipation.

Nate took off his fedora and gazed up at Red, his expression so full of love, I had to blink some more to banish the stupid tears from my eyes.

"Marry me, Tess," Nate said. When her eyes went wide, he grinned up at her. "You know if you don't say yes, I'll just keep asking, so you might as well give in now."

A slow smile spread across Red's face and then she gave a choked little laugh. "Well, if you're just going to annoy the hell out of me about it . . ."

"Is that a yes?" Nate asked.

She rolled her eyes. "Yeah, I guess."

He launched himself to his feet, sweeping her up into his embrace and kissing her over and over again until she laughed with joy.

Unable to resist any longer, Trish and I rushed forward with ridiculously girly squeals and added our own hugs and kisses of congratulations to the mix. I'd never seen Red so radiant with happiness. It'd been a damned long time since I'd witnessed a truly happy couple, since I had felt the warmth and scintillation of being so near to complete and unconditional love. The fairy godmother in me wanted to twirl and dance as I'd done in happier days, letting the love in the room seep into the very center of me and fuel that ancient, primal light that gave my magic strength.

"What's all this hoopin' and hollerin'?"

We turned to see Mama Hubbard in the room with us, her dark eyes sparkling. I quickly introduced her to Red and Nate and she clapped her hands with delight. "Oh, babies! Well, don't that beat all? A proposal right here in my own little house. I always say, gotta have some happiness to balance out the sorrow. Let me give you both some sugar!"

As Mama enveloped Red and Nate in her cushiony embrace, I looked for Seth, surprised not to see him anywhere in the room. Then I noticed the front door was still open and slipped outside onto the porch. He sat on the steps, his shoulders rounded, his hands hanging limply between his knees as he stared out into the surrounding forest.

I sat down next to him, not saying a word, just listening to the excited talk inside the house. After a moment, I nudged him with my shoulder. "You okay?"

"Of course," he said too quickly. "Why?"

I shrugged. "Well, it's one thing to know the person you used to love loves someone else. It's another to actually see the evidence of it."

"So, Red's pregnant?" Seth asked by way of response.

I nodded. "Yeah."

He laughed a little bitterly. "Wow. I didn't think . . . well, I hope she and Nate will be really happy. He obviously loves her a great deal—even if he's not really a Tale."

I blew out a sharp breath. "That was kind of a shocker, huh?"

He grunted. "No shit."

"So I guess he's the real deal then," I mused. "I mean, an actual Reaper."

"Yeah, I guess so," Seth said, his brows knitted together in a frown. "But I don't understand—why would he want to pretend to be one of *us*?"

I blew out a long breath, mulling over his question. But there was really only one reason I could fathom based on the conversation we'd just witnessed. "For Red," I told him. "It sounded like he'd waited a long time to be near her, and I guess when that chance finally came, he took it."

Seth ran a hand down his face. "The whole thing is totally fucked up."

"You know, it says a lot that Nate and Red were willing to trust the three of us with the truth," I told him. "If Al Addin were to find out that his most trusted Investigator isn't really a Tale, Nate could lose everything."

"It's not like he's the first non-Tale to join the fold," Seth pointed out. "Look at Brie."

"J.G. dating Brie was one thing," I said. "She was a cocktail waitress from a casino and only knew about what was going on here in The Refuge. Nate, on the other hand . . . he knows all our deepest, darkest secrets, has access to the Tale registry, to—hell—pretty much everything. Not to mention, he has the power to kill every single one of us if we went after him. That kind of showdown could go very wrong, very fast. It's no wonder he's been keeping the truth a secret."

"Well, I guess we're all keeping some secrets, aren't we?" Seth sighed, finally turning to look at me.

"Guess so." I met his gaze evenly, letting him know that I was on to the fact that he was hiding something from me, too.

He held my gaze for a long moment but was the first to blink.

"You still love her, don't you?" I asked, my heart breaking a little.

He nodded. "Red was an important part of my life. I'll always care for her."

I took a deep, ragged breath and started to stand up, but he grabbed my hand. "Lavender, I may still love her..." He paused a moment, the look in those ice-green eyes making me shiver. Then he said, "But I now know I'm not *in love* with her anymore. I realized that when I found you."

My breath left me on a gasp. For a moment, I just stared down at him, my heart pounding. "What are you saying?" I finally managed to whisper.

Seth slowly rose to his feet, then slid his hand around to the nape of my neck and pulled me to him, answering me with a kiss that spoke more than any words ever could.

Chapter 21

After loading a sedated J.G. into Red's SUV and sending Red and Nate off with more congratulatory hugs, we wished Mama and Harlan good-bye and drove Trish into The Refuge so she could find a place to stay. Seth, of course, had offered to let her stay with us when we'd stopped at his cabin to shower and change clothes, but she had insisted on staying somewhere in town where she could search for possible leads in J.G.'s kidnapping and escape. Old Lady Patterson was more than eager to offer Trish a room at her boarding house—free of charge for a friend of Seth Wolf and Lavender Seelie.

After leaving her there so she could rest for a while before beginning her official investigation, Seth and I drove to Das Gingerbread Haus where he was well overdue for his shift.

"Why didn't you tell Red and Trish about the murders?" I asked, adjusting my purple and black striped thigh-highs as we drove, not missing the hunger that was coming into his eyes as he watched me.

He swallowed hard and shifted a little in his seat before forcing his eyes back to the road. "Whatever's going on is completely fucked up. I'm already worried about you being in danger," he told me. "I didn't want to put Red and Trish in danger as well."

"You know the first person Trish will go see is Tom, to find out what she can about J.G.'s disappearance," I said. "He's going to have to tell her about the murders."

Seth nodded. "Yeah, I know."

"She's going to wonder why we didn't say anything to her about them," I pointed out.

He nodded, his mouth turned down in a grim frown. "We'll just have to say we were trying to protect her until we were able to find out something more."

I pressed my lips together, wondering how exactly we were supposed to go about finding that elusive "something more."

"I'm going to J.G.'s office to see what I can find," I announced.

Seth sent a startled glance my way. "Like hell you are! It's a crime scene—Tom would shit if he found out you were rummaging around in there."

I gave him a wry look. "Better me than Trish," I insisted. "My brother forbade Tom to involve the FMA, and—"

"He did?"

I nodded. "Puck was very clear that he wanted this handled internally. He's not a huge fan of the FMA or their rules and procedures. I think he's worried that Al Addin will clamp down on The Refuge and impose FMA oversight."

"I'm sure that wouldn't help Puck's casino operations, either," Seth guessed. "Al would shit if he knew Puck was running a business that catered mostly to the Ordinaries."

And that Puck was drugging those Ordinaries with fairy dust, I added silently.

Seth was quiet for a minute, then sighed. "Damn it. All right— slip in if you can. If not, though, leave it to Trish to sort out. I don't want you putting yourself in unnecessary danger. Get in and get out."

I nodded. "You got it."

When we pulled into a parking spot in front of the restaurant, Seth undid my seatbelt and pulled me across the seat to him, giving me a deep kiss, his hand slipping under the hem of my short skirt. His fingers played along the edge of my thigh highs, making me ache with need and wish we weren't sitting in a parking spot in the middle of town. I groaned and broke our kiss. "You sure you have to work?" I asked, breathlessly.

"Why?" he grinned, his hand smoothing over the curve of my ass. "Did you have something else in mind?"

I gasped as his finger slipped teasingly under the edge of my panties. "God, yes."

His chuckle was dark as his questing fingers slipped inside me. "Something like this?" he murmured, pressing a kiss to my neck.

I nodded, swallowing hard as need threatened to overtake reason. "What if someone sees us?"

He suddenly released me and threw the truck into reverse. The next thing I knew, we were parked in the alleyway between the restaurant and the bakery next door and Seth was sliding out from behind the wheel and pulling me onto his lap. A moment later, he was filling me, loving me, bringing me to ecstasy quickly and then capturing my mouth with his as he gripped my hips and pistoned rapidly, bringing me over again twice more before finally shuddering to a violent release of his own. Breathless, I stayed on his lap, kissing him languidly, loving the feel of his lips on mine as his hands once more began to roam, teasing and caressing lazily as if we had nowhere else to be.

"God," he murmured, "I love being inside you. I could do this all day."

I ground my hips against him. "I'm ready whenever you are."

"I should go to work." He let his head fall back and closed his eyes, and I felt him growing rock hard again.

I grinned, moving my hips against his, noticing his hands weren't any less insistent in their mission to know every inch of my body. "Are you sure?"

He moaned, gripping my hips and moving with me, slowly and deliberately—not hurried at all. "Hell, what's another few minutes. . . ."

When I finally kissed Seth good-bye and left him at the restaurant, I was so buoyant, I could've floated down the street. As it was, there was a bounce in my step that was completely at odds with the mission I was planning.

As I neared J.G.'s office, I began to glance up and down the street, making sure that no one else was around to see where I was going. Then I sent a gentle unlocking spell toward the door, relieved when it didn't explode into a million splinters but merely swung open, letting me in without resistance.

I glanced around once more before slipping inside and shutting the door behind me. The air in the building felt heavy, burdened by the horrible violence that had occurred there. I shuddered, remembering the scene of Brie's death. I forced my feet to take the stairs and walk down the hall. I peeked inside the room. Brie's body and the sheets had been removed for Doc to investigate, so only the debris on the floor and the blood on the mattress remained. I let my senses drift out into the room but found no evidence that there was more to discover here.

Relieved, I left the room and headed downstairs to J.G.'s destroyed office. It looked like everything was still as I'd found it days before. I carefully stepped through the debris field, my eyes scanning the room for anything that might help me understand what J.G. had found.

Most of the papers were loose receipts, invoices, copies of stories from the days before computers had allowed for electronic copies to be kept instead. I shook my head, not finding what I was looking for.

But there had to be something somewhere. J.G. didn't strike me as the kind of person who would keep everything in his head. He'd have too much going on—too many lies for his tabloids—to keep everything straight without writing it down. I looked for J.G.'s computer, hoping to discover something there, but the CPU was missing, apparently having been taken by the murderer—or perhaps taken by Tom as possible evidence.

"Shit," I hissed under my breath. I ran my hands through my hair and frowned at the mess on the floor. I was just about to give up and go see if maybe I could interest Seth in taking a lunch break in the alleyway sometime soon, when I saw a glint of metal sticking out from under a pile of scattered paper.

I squatted down and gripped a piece of paper with my fingernails, moving it aside so I could take a better look. It was a smallish, spiral-bound notebook like the one J.G. had given to me to record my notes from the town meeting.

My heart began to hammer. If J.G. had expected me to gather my info the old-fashioned way, perhaps it was because that was his style as well. Not caring about what fingerprints I might be leaving behind, I grabbed the notebook and flipped it open.

Bingo.

The notebook was filled with notes. Unfortunately, they were all for stories I'd already read in the *Daily Tattletale*. But I knew I was on to something. I began to sift through the papers more urgently now, using the toe of my Mary Janes to poke around in the debris. In a matter of moments, I'd found three more notebooks. I flipped through the first two but found nothing that would point to knowledge of who was murdering the Ordinaries with pilfered magic.

I opened the third notebook and began flipping through the pages. I was only a few pages in when a loud thud in the front of the house startled me, making me fumble the notebook. A jolt of fear kicked my pulse into high gear.

I silently grabbed up the notebook I'd dropped and lifted my skirt, tucking the notebook into the top of one of my thigh highs and letting my skirt fall back into place. Then I waited, listening intently for any movement. I was just beginning to think that maybe I'd imagined the earlier noise when the floorboards on the stairs creaked. Once. Twice.

Footsteps.

Oh, shit.

I whirled around toward the open office door, wondering how long it would take me to reach the front door. Fifteen seconds, maybe, at a dead run, but I'd have to go past the bottom of the stairs. I waited, listening as the intruder continued up the stairs and wishing not for the first time that I could pass through space and time as Gideon did, but that was the one fairy ability that had always eluded me.

Finally hearing the tread of footsteps above my head, I decided it was now or never. I took a deep breath and crept down the hallway, wincing with each step. A tiny bead of sweat trickled down my back, but I resisted the urge to shiver, afraid that even that little rustle of movement would give away my presence. When I reached the bottom of the staircase, I paused, listening. When I heard nothing, I swallowed hard, then sprinted toward the door and freedom.

I was within a couple of feet of the door when it suddenly swung open. I slid to a halt, my heart in my throat. "Tom," I croaked, my mind racing as I glanced over my shoulder, fully expecting to see some horrifying creature come bounding down the stairs to rip out our throats.

"What are you doing here?" Tom demanded.

"I saw someone come in," I lied in a hushed whisper. "I came in to check it out."

Tom's brows snapped together, and he drew the gun at his hip. "Where?"

"Upstairs."

He gave me a tight nod, then motioned for me to stay where I was. I wasn't wild about being left to watch the door—if there was a murderer upstairs, there was only one way out of the building. But a few moments later, Tom came back down, holstering his gun.

"There's no one here, Lavender," he said, his voice edged with irritation. "So, you want to tell me again why you were in here?"

I shook my head, now perplexed. "No, there was someone upstairs—I know it. I heard her walking around."

"Her?" Tom said, his tone uncharacteristically patronizing. "You get a good enough look to identify who it was?"

I shook my head. "No, no. I just assumed . . ."

He sighed, then crossed his arms over his chest. "Because I'm grateful for all you did for me once, I'm not going to arrest you right now, Lavender—"

"*Arrest* me?" I cried.

"—but I'm afraid if I catch you in here again, I won't have any choice."

I shook my head, not believing what I was hearing. "What? But, Tom—"

"Now, it looks like we have an Investigator from the FMA in town," he drawled, interrupting me again. "She's over at my office right now chatting with Eva and having some lemonade. I told her I'd bring her on over to look around in here after Doc lets her examine the bodies."

"The bodies?" I repeated, my throat going tight. "She knows about the murders then?"

Tom nodded. "Yep. And she was mighty surprised. Especially when I told her you're the one who found 'em. She thought it odd you didn't tell her about the bodies when she saw you this morning."

I froze, not sure what to say. I couldn't mention finding J.G. So instead, I just blinked at Tom, my knees beginning to go a little weak.

"Don't worry," Tom said, "I told her we'd already cleared you of any involvement."

"I *wasn't* involved," I told him. "You know that."

Tom neither confirmed nor denied his belief in my innocence, instead continuing with, "Thing I don't understand is why Ms. Muffet's here to begin with. Your brother gave instructions for this to be handled internally. I thought it was pretty clear he didn't want the FMA getting involved."

I gave him a tremulous grin. "Well, it wasn't like J.G. kept a low profile, was it?" I said. "I imagine it was only a matter of time before someone noticed he had disappeared."

Tom eyed me for a long moment and then gave a contemplative nod. "True."

I tried not to let my breath burst from me in a relieved sigh. "Well, the good news is with Trish here, perhaps we'll figure out who's behind the murders a little quicker," I said, forcing a smile that I knew was weak. "You're only one man, after all."

Tom returned my smile, his good-natured geniality suddenly returning. "That I am," he agreed. "Never gonna turn down an offer of help."

He held open the front door and ushered me out, locking the door behind us. As we walked back to his office, Tom's arm came around my shoulders and he gave me a quick squeeze. "Sorry if I scared you."

I shook my head. "No problem."

His arm was heavy across my shoulders, but I didn't mind. At first. But the longer his arm stayed there, the more uneasy I became.

"So, how's Eva?" I asked, trying to keep my voice nonchalant.

Tom looked down into my face and gave me a kind smile. "She's enjoying having Gareth with us. It warms my heart to see her so happy."

"Has there been any sign of Bo Peep yet?" I probed.

Tom's face went a little dark at this, but he rallied quickly. "No, nothing."

"Perhaps Trish can help you with that as well," I suggested. "She's amazing at analyzing a crime scene, from what I understand."

Tom gave me a tight smile. "Maybe so."

I really felt for the man and understood completely his reluctance to track down the drugged-up head-case who'd been masquerading as Gareth's mother when his own wife, who so desperately wanted a child, had already proven to be a better guardian for the boy.

"Mind if I tag along while she investigates?" I asked, giving him the most innocent smile I could muster.

Tom shook his head with a laugh. "No way. You've already been involved enough."

I blew out an exasperated huff. "Tom—"

"Sorry, Lavender," he said, looking stern for the first time since I'd met him. "This one's a little more complicated now that the FMA's involved."

I thought I detected a slight note of bitterness in his voice. "But I don't see—"

"Come on," he interrupted, steering me toward his SUV. "I'll drive you home."

I tried to slip out of his hold, but he shifted his grip to my arm and wasn't about to let me talk my way out of it. The passenger door closed with a thundering finality.

Damn it.

I wanted to be there when Trish looked at the bodies, gauge her reaction to what she saw. Yet at least back at Seth's place I'd be able to look through J.G.'s notebook without worry of being discovered—or eaten by some hellhound.

Tom and I sat in silence for the drive to Seth's but when he pulled up in front of the house, he offered me that wide, boyish smile of his. "Well, here were are—safe and sound."

"You want to come in and have a cup of coffee or anything?" I offered. "We never have had the chance to sit and catch up."

His answering smile was one of gratitude. "You know, a cup of coffee would be nice. Thanks." As we made our way toward the house, Tom said, "I'm sorry about back in town. I just want to make sure you're safe." He took hold of my upper arm and pulled me to a halt. "You are a very special woman, Lavender."

I was completely taken aback by the compliment. "Thanks, Tom. It means a lot to hear you say that."

His hand lightly caressed my arm, but then dropped to his side. He stared at the ground for a moment, frowning as if debating his next words. I was just about to remind him about sharing coffee when he shoved his hands deep into the pockets of his fatigues and let out a sharp sigh. "I know you've had a rough time of it since the relocation and everything and that the townsfolk weren't exactly welcoming at first," he said, "but they've warmed up to you. And I think you could be a real asset to this town, to our family. Because when you get down to it, Lavender, we're one big family here. And we take care of our own."

I blinked at him, dismayed by his words and wondering what exactly he was worried about happening to me. Was he still not convinced of my innocence?

"I appreciate that," I replied, my tone wary enough to bring his head up. I offered him a smile, trying to cover my growing curiosity. "Now, how about that coffee?"

He nodded and was heading toward the path that led to the house when he abruptly stopped. "You know," he said, "on second thought, I'd better get back to town, check on Ms. Muffet. I probably should be there when she goes through J.G.'s office. Your brother will have my ass in a sling if I don't stay on top of this one. I'm damned sorry, Lavender. Trust me, I'd much rather be enjoying your company."

"Another time then?" I suggested, hoping my relief wasn't too evident.

He gave me a tight nod as he backed toward his SUV, then gave a short wave before hopping in and driving off. I watched him go, wondering at the strange exchange, then headed toward the door. Instantly, I felt the warmth of my spell's protective power and closed my eyes for a moment, just letting it seep in. Then I slipped J.G.'s notebook out of my thigh high and hurried inside, determined to finally get some answers.

Chapter 22

Trying to decipher J.G.'s notes was like trying to learn some ancient alien language while shit-faced. Saying the man's handwriting was sucktastic was being generous. And then add in his totally jacked-up brand of shorthand, and it wasn't hard to see why several hours later as the sun was beginning to dip low on the horizon, I was just finally beginning to crack the code.

My eyes aching from squinting for so long, I decided to take a break and make good on what I'd promised Red. I went into the bathroom and turned on the shower, letting the steam fill the room. A few minutes later, I heard a playful little twitter on the other side of the mist.

"Stop it! *Seriously*," came the mildly chastising giggle. "I have to take this call."

Afraid of what I might be interrupting, I started to wipe the mirror clean when my sister's flushed face and rather mussed pink hair suddenly appeared.

"Lavender!" she said, smoothing her hands over her hair. "Oh, my God! I totally can't believe you're calling right now. It's *so* not a good time, you know?"

"Sorry, Poppy," I said, feeling my cheeks grow a little warm. "I'll keep it quick. I just wanted to let you know I'm sending a new patient to you. His name is J. G. Squiggington. Red Little is bringing him in to the Asylum."

She swatted irritably at whoever it was that was trying his best to divert her attention. "So like, why doesn't he just see one of their therapists? My schedule is like massively booked."

"Someone did this to him, Pops," I told her. "He's pretty far gone, and you're the only one I know who's good enough to help him, the only one I'd trust."

She dropped her head over to one side and gave me a bright smile. "Aww, that's like so totally nice, Lav! Thanks."

"Just do what you can, okay?" I said. "He's had a really rough time."

She nodded and started to speak again, but her words were cut off by another giggle.

"So, how's Dad?" I asked, trying not to think about what might be going on outside my line of sight. "Any improvement?"

She gasped and leaned closer. "How did you know about Dad?"

"Don't worry about that," I said quickly. "How is he?"

She sighed a little. "Better, thanks to Mom and some of the others' magic, but nothing seems to be bringing him out of it. Mom says it's like a hex, something remote." She glanced around quickly, then whispered, "Mom's talking about calling for *the book*."

My eyes went wide. "Oh, shit."

She nodded furiously. "I *know*. It was getting way too intense at the hospital. I had to get away for a while and release some tension, you know?"

I frowned at her. "What was going on at the hospital?"

She let out an enormous sigh, then took a deep breath before saying in a rush, "Mom was like totally storming around, demanding justice and all, and one of the elders was all like, 'Summon the book, Mab,' and then Gid kept trying to calm everybody down and was all like, 'You don't need to go to those lengths' and—*Stop it!*" She swatted at her companion and cast an irritated scowl his way. "I'm like *totally* serious. Don't make me turn you into a toad or some junk." She then rolled her eyes and turned back to me. "Sorry. Mermen—they're so horny!"

"Um, yeah. So . . . I won't keep you from—well, *whatever*," I stammered. "Call me if anything changes with Dad, okay?"

She nodded and then vanished. My heart heavy with concern for my father, I wiped the mirror clean. I should've been there. I should've been the one treating him, using my magic to help him. And if anyone was going to wield the magic of the ancients to combat whatever was attacking him, it should've been me. And yet it had been made very clear to me that my magic was never going to be needed again, that the fairies were better off without me, fuck-me-very-much.

And then there was the wee little problem of the book, which happened to be wrapped up in a sweater in a suitcase in the closet I shared with my werewolf lover. I needed to figure out what the hell was going on here so I could return the book before anyone went apeshit and came looking for it.

"Damn it," I muttered, glancing back toward the bathroom door and wondering when Seth might be getting home. Deciding to risk it, I let the mirror cloud over again and waited. It took a couple of minutes, but Gideon's face eventually appeared as I'd hoped.

"I can't talk long," he said in a hushed whisper. "The shit is seriously hitting the fan here, Lavender."

"So I heard," I whispered back. "I talked to Poppy a minute ago and she told me that they're thinking of calling on the book to help Dad."

Gideon nodded. "Yeah, and that idea's gaining popularity. Problem is we're a little short on Guardians in the Here and Now."

"What are you talking about?" I said with a confused shake of my head. "You're a Guardian. I figured they were trying to press you into calling the magic."

He glanced around to check for anyone nearby, then leaned forward. "That's the thing—I'm *not* a Guardian. I lied, Lavender. When they took it away from you, I couldn't let some random asshole step in and take your place. So I went through the trials and made it look like the magic chose me. But now there's really no one who can do it. We'd have to summon all of the fairy Tales and let the magic choose someone else."

I swallowed hard. "It already has."

His eyes went wide. "It accepted you back?"

I nodded, not even bothering to try to hide my excitement. "Oh, God, Gideon—it was incredible. I feel completely revitalized, even stronger than before. If I can get my head back into the game, I think . . ." I hesitated to even put my hope into words, but he knew what I was thinking.

"Ah, Lav—I'm so happy for you." He pressed his palm to the glass. "You deserve this."

I placed my palm against the image of his. "Thanks, Gid—I couldn't have done this without you bringing the book to me. I know you took a huge risk. And as soon as I figure out what's going on here, I'll give it back to you, I promise."

At this, his brows came together. "I don't think I can wait much longer."

I nodded solemnly. "Maybe if they know it's chosen me . . . maybe they'll let me come back and help Dad. If you come pick me up, I can just—"

"What the hell's going on?"

My head snapped around and I stumbled back away from the mirror, nearly tumbling into the bathtub behind me. "Seth."

He strolled into the bathroom, his jaw clenched so tightly I half-expected to hear his molars cracking under the strain. He cast a furious glance my way, then turned toward the mirror where Gideon still stared back.

To Gideon's credit, he assumed his trademark stoic expression, refusing to be engaged in a testosterone-infused stare-down. "Greetings," he said with a slight incline of his head. "You must be Seth Wolf. Lavender has told me a great deal about you."

"Yeah?" Seth said, his shoulders beginning to take on his attack stance. "Who the fuck are you?"

"My name is Gideon."

I carefully approached Seth, feeling the anger emanating from him. "Seth . . ."

When he slowly turned to me, the look in his eyes was like a knife in the heart. There was so much hurt it brought tears to my own eyes, which probably didn't make me look any less guilty of doing something I shouldn't have. "How long?" he asked, his voice catching.

"It's not what you think," I said firmly. "I swear it's not. There's more going on here—"

His bitter laugh interrupted me. "That's pretty fucking clear."

When he pivoted to storm out of the room, I grabbed his arm, but he jerked away from my grasp and strode away before I could stop him. "Damn it, Seth! Will you just listen?"

"There's nothing to hear, Lavender," he called over his shoulder, heading for the front door. "You're still in love with him. Fine. I won't stand in the way."

"In love with him?" I echoed, hurrying after him. "I'm not still in love with him! I'm in love with *you*, you son of a bitch!"

He stopped abruptly and turned around. "Then why the hell are you talking to your former lover—the one you gave your necklace to *willingly*?"

I stood staring at him for a moment, trying to figure out what I could say quickly enough to convince him to stay. "I needed his help," I said after that brief hesitation. He pegged me with his glowing gaze, waiting for me to further explain. I swallowed hard, then said, "I know the magic that's killing the Ordinaries. It's the same magic that brought all of us here."

Seth shook his head a little, looking confused. "What?"

"The symbols," I said. "They're the same magic that I was Guardian of—someone else has found out about the symbols and is using them. They're necromancy spells, Seth."

"Why didn't you tell me any of this?" he breathed. "You didn't trust me? You didn't think *I* could help you?"

I took a step closer. "I didn't want to put you in danger. And . . ." I wrapped my arms around myself, feeling suddenly cold. "And I was afraid."

His brows drew together. "Of what?"

"Of what you've been hiding from me."

This seemed to take him off-guard. He blinked rapidly, taking a step back. "What do you mean? You think I committed these murders?"

I shook my head. "No. But you're involved somehow. I know that. Just tell me how, Seth. Please, I need to know."

He ran a hand down his face. "Shit."

"Seth, please. Whatever it is, we can work through it. I'm sure you didn't know what you were getting involved in. Trust me—"

"I can't do this right now," he interrupted, sounding exhausted. "I have somewhere I need to be. I'll talk to you about this later."

I rushed toward him and would've thrown my arms around his neck and begged him not to go, but the look he gave me brought me up short. "Don't run away, Seth," I called after him as he turned to go. "Not this time."

He paused, his hand on the doorknob. "I'm not running away."

"The hell you aren't!" I charged, my voice thick with the tears building in the back of my throat. "You're *this close* to cutting and running and never looking back. Don't you dare do that to me, Seth, goddamn it! Not to *me*."

He cursed under his breath, then suddenly turned and closed the gap between us in two long strides to press a harsh kiss to my lips. "I'm *not* running away this time," he ground out, grasping me at the nape of my neck. "I swear to you." He kissed me again, softer this time, then pressed his forehead to mine. "I'll be back later tonight. Then we can talk all of this out, okay? But I want to know it all, Lavender. Not a single secret left between us."

I closed my eyes. "Let me come with you."

"I can't," he insisted. "You have to trust me on this. Please, just believe in me a little longer. I need you, Lavender . . . you mean more to me . . ." He paused and pulled back just enough to peer down into my face. "Please, just stay here. Be here when I get back."

"Just make sure you come back."

He kissed me again, and then he was gone in a shimmer and a soft padding of paws. As soon as he was gone, I drifted back to the bathroom, surprised to see Gideon still waiting there.

"You okay?" he asked.

I nodded. "Yeah, I'll be fine. Just try to stall everyone a little longer."

"I don't know how much time I can give you," Gideon said, his tone hesitant.

"I don't need much, Gid," I told him.

"Samhain's approaching," he pointed out. I could sense the apprehension in his voice. He knew as well as I did that although the day was sacred, there were those who took advantage of the power of the celebration for their own dark purposes.

"I know," I said. "I have a feeling that if something's going to happen, it's going to happen then. And I've got to figure out how the hell Seth is involved before he gets himself killed."

Chapter 23

I took a deep breath and let it out slowly, trying to ignore how constricted I felt in the black leggings I wore instead of my customary skirt. But if I was going to go tramping through the woods after a werewolf without being noticed, I didn't want to take the chance of his hearing the rustle of my skirts beneath the murmur of the wind.

Forcing myself to focus, I lifted my hand and blew gently across my palm, sending out a sprinkle of purple fairy dust. "Seth Wolf," I whispered as the dust floated down toward the ground. As it settled, I could see his footprints illuminated with a soft purple light. "Alrighty then, here we go."

I followed the footprints for several miles, sending out another sprinkle of fairy dust to track him whenever the trail went cold. I knew I was close to The Refuge, but beyond that, I was hopelessly lost. The woods here were dense, thick with overgrowth. It was tough to navigate in the same path Seth had taken, his wolf form making him much more agile than I could ever hope to be, but I could still see the glowing footprints stretching out before me. The toe of my boot snagged on a root and I tripped, nearly face-planting in the weeds.

"Son of a bitch," I muttered, wondering just how far I was going to have to go before I finally reached Seth's destination. "Where the hell is he going?"

I was just coming out of an especially thick blackberry patch when I heard a murmuring in the distance. Voices. Rhythmic and even—as if chanting. And Seth's footprints led in that direction.

What the hell?

I crept forward as silently as possible, crouching low, now using the irritatingly dense foliage as cover. The closer I got, the louder the voices became, but I still couldn't quite make out what they were chanting. The words were all monotonous, flat, and ran together in an unintelligible stream of sound.

"Damn it," I hissed under my breath. How the hell was I supposed to protect myself or Seth from whatever they were calling upon if I couldn't understand them? I came closer, slower now, my senses on edge. I began to feel a tingle, a low-frequency hum of warning just beneath my skin that made me want to turn and run. But Seth was there. I forced myself to keep moving forward, ignoring each anxious twitch of my muscles, focusing instead on the cadence of the chanting.

As I came closer, I also picked up on the smell of wood smoke and then saw the soft glow of a small bonfire in a clearing. I took cover behind the wide trunk of a nearby tree and peered out from behind it, watching the scene before me.

Gathered around the campfire were numerous figures cloaked in dark, hooded robes. Their hoods hid their faces in heavy shadows, so I couldn't determine their identities. I was going to need to get closer. I moved in, my senses raging in warning now, but I had to know what was going on. I ran to another tree that was just on the edges of the clearing.

I could now hear them clearly, the words starting to take shape. The chant was an ancient one, something I hadn't heard in centuries. It'd been part of a ceremony of praise and reverence once upon a time. Whoever these people were, they were worshiping someone— or something—calling upon the entity to protect them, guide them, deliver them.

I squinted, trying to see if I could recognize anyone now that I was just a few yards from where they stood, but their hoods hid all their faces in shadow, obscuring their identities.

Damn it.

I studied each of those present, looking for any sign as to which one—if any—was Seth, but I didn't see him among them, and I'd lost track of the trail of footprints when I'd made my dash toward the clearing. It was a relief in some ways to know he wasn't one of the worshipers, but that fact left me with even more questions.

Suddenly, one of the worshipers stepped forward, arms spread wide. "Come forward." It was a man, his voice deep and gravelly. It was familiar, but sounded intentionally distorted, making it impossible for me to place. "Bless us, wise one. Show us the path to truth."

At that moment, another figure emerged from the darkness. It, too, was clothed in a hooded robe, its identity a mystery. The figure moved slowly but purposefully, erect and commanding, if unsteady. It was smaller in stature than the man who appeared to be the leader, but I still couldn't tell if it was male or female. The moment the figure took its place near the leader, all the others in attendance dropped to their knees, bowing their heads in deference.

"We are in danger," the leader explained. "There are those who would interfere with our plans, thwart our mission."

"This must not happen," the figure spoke, the voice little more than a whisper but somehow loud enough for me to hear with perfect clarity. Only speech infused with powerful magic would be able to achieve such an effect. "You know what you must do."

"But, Mother—"

Holy shit. Was this *the mother J.G. was talking about?*

"—what you ask . . ."

"Must be obeyed," she hissed. "You all are bound to me. You have given your allegiance. You know the price for disobedience. I have shown you what I do to those who would interfere with my plans."

The leader pressed his palms together and bent at the waist. "Yes, Mother."

"I sense the presence of one who would harm me," she said, surveying her followers. "You must protect me, my children. You know what you must do. We are nearly there, my own. Tomorrow night, we will initiate the final rite."

I swallowed hard. I'd been dead on about their using Samhain to make a move.

The leader turned back to the others and spread his arms wide. "Come, receive our Mother's blessing."

The followers rose and began to converge around Mother. She reached up to grasp the edges of her hood—her hands covered by black gloves, not even giving me that much of a hint as to her identity. I leaned forward, my heart pounding with the prospect of seeing her face.

Suddenly a strong arm wrapped around me and a hand clapped over my mouth, dragging me back into the shadows. I bit back a startled scream and drove my elbow hard into my attacker's ribs. His breath shot out on a gasp, but his grasp only tightened. Then he hissed in my ear, "Be still or you're going to get us killed!"

Relief flooded over me, making my knees weak.

Seth.

I nodded and he let me go, then grabbed my shoulders and turned me around to face him. "I told you to stay at the cabin."

Before I could explain myself, one of the followers suddenly barked, "Hey!"

"Fuck," Seth hissed under his breath as three of the robed figures charged toward us. He grabbed my hand and pulled me after him. "Run, go!"

We raced through the woods, tearing through the brambles and blackberry bushes, heedless of the thorns and branches ripping our clothes and tearing into our flesh. My lungs were burning with each labored breath as I tried to keep up with Seth, his graceful strides outpacing mine. As he leapt over a rotting log, I clambered to keep up with him, but the tree's pulpy flesh crumbled under my boots and I stumbled, falling hard on my ass.

"Seth!" I cried, scrambling to my feet to hurry after him. But I suddenly flew backward as one of the followers grabbed a handful of my hair and jerked me off my feet. I spun in midair, landing in a crouch. I lunged upward in the next instant, driving my fist into the chin of the attacker and sending him stumbling back. I then swung, connecting with his jaw with my left hook. I reared back to clock him again, but a powerful hand closed over my fist and spun me around.

I reflexively swung with my free hand, catching the second attacker in the temple. I heard a decidedly female grunt as the hooded figure reeled from the blow. I shoved hard, sending her stumbling back over the same log that had slowed my escape. As she ass-planted, her hood fell back, giving me a glimpse of spiky green hair.

"Giselle."

Her lovely face changed in an instant, her teeth suddenly two rows of tiny, razor-sharp spikes. She launched forward, sailing through the air and tackling me before I could respond.

"Hello, Lavender," she hissed, her hand closing around my throat. "It's too bad you didn't make friends with me." I struggled against her viselike hold on my throat as she ran her free hand roughly over my breasts, then slid her hand inside my shirt, copping a feel. "We could've had a lot of fun. I certainly had a lot of fun using your father to sneak past Gideon's spells to steal glimpses at the book." Her lips curled into a wicked grin. "Who knew such a powerful Tale as the great Fairy King was so easy to control in his sleep? We had some deliciously naughty dreams, he and I. And after he fucked me, Lavender, we always took a trip to see the book. . . ."

"Fuck off," I ground out in spite of her crushing grip on my windpipe.

Suddenly a great mass slammed into us, taking her down. There was a dark growl and a shrill scream and then silence. And then Seth was standing over me, blood covering his face and chest.

"Come on!" he barked, grabbing my arm and jerking me to my feet. "Quit messing around."

I resisted the urge to send an angry retort his way and raced after him instead, wondering where the hell the other robed pursuer was. I glanced over my shoulder, half-expecting him to pop out of nowhere and tackle me. I could hear someone crashing through the underbrush, and I could feel him growing closer, the hairs on the back of my neck rising with the feeling that I was being watched. No, not watched. Tracked.

"Oh, shit," I gasped. "It's not just the followers chasing us."

"This way," Seth gasped, dragging me after him. "Mama's isn't far."

"No, not there," I managed to say in spite of the fire in my lungs. "Not safe. Your cabin."

Seth cast a perplexed glance my way, but immediately shifted direction. The heavy footfalls of the hellhounds pursuing us grew louder, signaling how rapidly they were closing the distance.

Shit.

We were still miles from Seth's cabin. We'd never make it in time to reach the safety of the protective spell I'd placed around it. Hoping that my recent good luck with magic would hold in spite of my panic, I waved my arm in a great sweeping motion. Immediately, the winds responded, sending up a flurry of forest debris behind us, following in our wake as we continued to run. The tree branches groaned and creaked ominously, several smaller ones snapping like twigs in the tornadic winds. And yet I could still feel the hellhounds coming for us. I slid to a halt and turned around.

"What the hell are you doing?" Seth cried, coming back for me.

"Buying us some time," I murmured. Then I brought my open palm to my lips and blew gently across it as I'd done when I'd sent out my fairy dust in search of Seth's tracks. But this time, my breath became a tendril of mist, just a wispy trail at first, but rapidly growing in just a matter of seconds, enveloping the entire forest in an impenetrable fog.

"Lavender?" Seth called. He was standing only two feet from me but could no longer see me.

I reached out and took his hand when I heard the frustrated howls of the hellhounds. They too were disoriented, furious at having lost their quarry. "Come on," I said softly, although there was no need for silence—the fog would disguise and distort the sounds of our escape now.

Seth gripped my hand tightly as I led him through the fog, not letting go until we finally reached the edge of his deck and he could feel his way to the front door. Once inside, he closed and bolted the door, then shed his shirt and went to the kitchen to wash off Giselle's blood. When he returned he came to a sudden halt, his expression unreadable.

But I knew what emotions were raging in me now that we were both safe. Furious, I shoved him, knocking him back a few stumbling paces. "What the hell is going on!" I roared. "What were you doing out there with those people? Who the hell are they? You'd better start talking right fucking now, Seth Wolf!"

He blinked at me, his mouth turning down in a frown. "I've never seen your eyes do that before."

"What?" I snapped, not willing to let him derail the conversation. "What the hell does that have to do with anything? How are you involved in all of this? In the *murders*?"

He grabbed my hand and held it up to my face. "Why are you glowing?"

I snatched my hand away. "That's from my fairy light," I said, my tone terse. "Now it's your turn. Spill it."

He put his hands on his hips and regarded me for a long moment. Then he blew out a long exhale and ran his hand through his hair. "I don't guess it matters now," he muttered. "My cover's blown."

I shook my head, confused. "What? Your cover?"

"Yeah, Lavender," he retorted, "my *cover*. I've been working undercover for the FMA since I came here."

My knees felt weak and when I started to slip to the ground, Seth caught me up in his arms. He lowered me to the floor and sat down beside me, pressing his back to the door. "I don't understand," I murmured.

He pulled his hand down his face, suddenly looking haggard. "When I left Chicago after everything happened, I wandered around for a few months, working my way west. Then one day Tess showed up at my door, asking if I would be willing to go undercover for the FMA in a place called The Refuge. They'd received intel that something big was about to go down and they needed someone believable as a refugee on the inside to find out what was going on."

"After all they've done to you over the years, why would you possibly help the FMA?" I asked. But I pretty much knew the answer before I'd even asked the question.

"Because it wasn't the FMA asking, it was Tess."

Yep.

"Why didn't you just tell me about all of this?" I pressed.

He turned his eyes toward me and I was startled to see guilt there. "I wasn't sure I could trust you at first." He gave me that adorable half-grin of his and reached up to tuck a lock of hair behind my ear. "But then it was because I was worried about your getting hurt."

"If it was so dangerous here," I mused, "why would Red send me in the first place?"

"I wondered the same thing," he admitted. "So when she showed up at Mama's, you'd better believe I asked her."

"That's what you two were arguing about in the front yard."

He nodded. "Yeah, that and the fact that she wasn't thrilled about us sleeping together. She thought I was taking advantage of you while you were emotionally vulnerable. When I accused her of being the one using you, it really didn't go over well. She explained that she'd hoped maybe whoever was behind everything might make an effort to welcome you into the fold and that I'd finally have the answers I needed before the situation got out of control."

"Little too late for that," I drawled.

"She realizes that, trust me," he said. "She was pretty pissed at herself for putting you at risk and was ready to take you away that day." He took my hand and smoothed my skin with his thumb, averting his gaze. "I assured her you'd be fine, that I'd make certain nothing happened to you, that I was close to figuring everything out and needed you here." He lifted his eyes, his gaze holding mine. "I needed you, that's for damned sure. But it was all about me—not the case. I was selfish. I should've let you go."

"I'm glad you didn't," I told him. His answering grin was relieved. He slipped his arm around my shoulders and pulled me close. I settled in under his arm, letting him hold me for a few moments in silence before I finally said, "So what *is* going on in The Refuge, Seth?"

His chest rose slowly and lowered at the same rate. "There's a faction of the Tales in The Refuge who're convinced we have the right to be who and what we are and not have to hide our true identities. They believe the Tales should be the ones calling the shots in the Here and Now and that the Ordinaries are ignorant and arrogant and have forgotten the stories that have taught them and empowered them."

"They were planning a hostile takeover," I deduced. "A war against the Ordinaries."

He nodded. "Exactly. The movement started here, but it's gaining popularity outside The Refuge. Red told me that Nicky Blue had been on to something back in Chicago, but that he'd been unable to find out much. People are afraid of whoever the leader is."

"You think it's this Mother person who was at the meeting tonight."

"That's what my gut's telling me," he said, "but I'm still not entirely sure. Hell, I'm not even entirely sure who's part of the more militant faction and who just likes the idea of living freely, completely separate from the Ordinaries. Everything's been shrouded in such secrecy, it's been tough to make any inquiries. Because of my past, it's been a struggle to convince the militants to trust me enough to reveal themselves. When someone set out the silver bullet after the cabin was ransacked, I worried that my cover was blown. But I don't think they had anything to do with that."

I blinked at him. "Who was it then?"

Seth shook his head. "No idea."

I frowned. "So how are the murders connected to the impending revolution?"

"I was hoping to find out at the meeting," he said. "I was just about to come out and join in when you showed up."

"Shit," I hissed. "Sorry. I seriously screwed up."

He shook his head. "No, if I'd just been honest with you, none of this would've happened."

"So who invited you to the meeting?" I asked.

Here Seth's expression went dark, his face clouding over with sadness. "Hansel," he said on a sigh. "He pulled me aside at work, told me that he considered me to be a true friend, that he was glad the rest of the town finally seemed to accept me, and then he told me about the revolution—just hinted at it at first, gauging my response, I'm guessing. Of course, I pretended that I was totally onboard with the idea."

"Not much of a stretch of the imagination considering what you've been through," I told him.

"Exactly."

"So was he the leader at the meeting?" I asked, even though I hadn't picked up on Hansel's accent at all when I'd been eavesdropping.

Seth shook his head. "No, from what I can gather, Hansel's just another follower—no leadership role really."

"And what of Mother?"

"No clue. I didn't even know anything about her before tonight."

I let out a short sigh, realizing that now it was my turn. "I did."

When he gave me a bewildered frown, I scrambled to my feet and went to grab J.G.'s notebook. When I handed it to him, he flipped through it and looked up at me expectantly. "Is this in Russian? I can't even read it."

My lips twitched a little in amusement. "I'm glad I'm not the only one who has trouble deciphering his handwriting," I said, sitting beside him and crossing my legs. "I think J.G. was Red's source. She mentioned at Mama's house that she and J.G. had worked together before, that he'd shown a lot of potential as an informant, remember? And J.G. told me he was on to something big before he disappeared. I think he knew about the revolutionaries and was about to out them to all of Tale society."

Seth nodded. "Makes sense so far. What else did you find?"

"When you and Mama left me alone with J.G., he told me that he'd found the mother, that she wasn't who we thought, and that the plans were in motion. At first I thought he meant Bo Peep."

"Gareth's mother."

"Except she isn't really his mother, remember?" My hands were shaking a little when I started flipping through the notebook. "And I think J.G. figured out who is. It's just random notes, but he knew, Seth. He refers to Gareth here." I pointed to a group of notes toward the end of the collection. Seth glanced down, then back up at me. I tried not to huff before I summarized, "He knew as well as all of us that there was something *off* with Gareth. J.G. thought the boy was a spirit made flesh."

"What, like a ghost? Or a zombie?" Seth asked. When I nodded, he continued, "But wouldn't he have some memory of his previous life? And how would someone have accessed his soul from the Great After? Only Nate Grimm can go there, right?"

I closed the notebook. "Not necessarily. There are times when the veil between the living and the dead is very thin. And one of those times is Samhain, which takes place tomorrow. If someone is going to try to access a soul that's particularly hard to regain, Samhain would be the day to do it."

"And you think that's what someone is planning?"

I nodded. "The symbols carved on the bodies we've been finding—they're part of a necromancy spell as I mentioned earlier. But they're not quite right. The technique is poor and so the spell isn't going to be as powerful as it would be if done correctly. It's probably been enough to animate a corpse, or to keep someone on the verge of death from slipping away, but not to truly give a corpse a soul, especially since the person behind it has been using Ordinaries. It will take the sacrifice of a Tale to make the spell powerful enough to make up for sloppy magic. And whoever's behind it has been waiting until the veil is at its thinnest to bring forth the intended soul."

"What does this have to do with Gareth?" Seth asked.

"I think Gareth might've been an early attempt—a successful dry run," I explained. "He's just a boy and probably had a pure soul that was easy to reach and coax back. And it wouldn't take much in trade to persuade the Lord of the Dead to give up the soul of a child of no consequence. But I have a feeling the one they're after now won't be so easy."

"That still doesn't answer who this mother is."

"I think Gareth's 'mother' is the woman who was being worshiped at the meeting. I think she is the one who brought him back to life. I think it's an honorary title of sorts; her followers call her that as a show of respect."

"And?"

I shook my head. "I have no idea." My shoulders slumped and I pressed my back against the door next to Seth. "Without knowing who they're trying to bring back, it's impossible to determine who's behind it. All I know is that J.G. said the plans are in motion." I slipped my hand into his and clasped it tightly. "And, Seth, I think I'm meant to be the Tale sacrifice."

His head snapped toward me. "What?" he breathed, his face going slack. "What are you talking about? Why would you think that?"

"J.G. told me that the mother planned to kill me," I told him. "If they're needing a meaningful sacrifice, who better to use than one of the most powerful fairies ever born? Even though my magic is still a little sketchy, my soul would be quite a prize for the Lord of the

Dead. Not to mention, it would get me out of the way so I couldn't pose a threat to their plans."

Seth cupped my cheek and forced me to look into his eyes. "I won't let anything happen to you," he assured me. "I swear on my life, Lavender, no harm will come to you."

My heart began to hammer in my chest when I saw the determination in his eyes. "You forget, they know you were there tonight," I reminded him. "I have a feeling they're going to be coming for you, too. And this time it won't just be a couple of them chasing after us in the woods."

"I will fight to the death for you," he ground out between clenched teeth. "Lavender, you are everything to me. I will not lose you. Not ever."

I smiled and covered his hand with mine, my heart swelling. Still, for all his protestations, it was only the two of us, and even though my magic seemed to be coming back online, I wasn't about to count on its saving my ass and his when we were so woefully outnumbered. We were going to need some backup.

Chapter 24

I opened the door to the cabin when I heard the sound of tires on gravel but waited inside the doorway at Seth's insistence, with him standing at my side surveying the night for any threats.

"Christ," Puck muttered as he stepped out of the third car I'd seen him driving since coming to The Refuge—this one a bright yellow H2. "What the fuck is up with this fog anyway?"

"That's mine," I admitted. "We needed cover. Come inside and I'll tell you everything."

His brows drew together in a scowl and he came forward but stopped abruptly, his surprised gaze darting up at me. Then his lips curled into a proud smile. "Very nice, baby girl. Gonna let me in?"

I blinked at him. "You should be able to cross it—unless you want to do harm to Seth."

"What can I say—I'm still not thrilled about you two hooking up."

With a huff, I made a casual gesture, creating an opening wide enough to let him through.

Still smiling, he stepped across the barrier of the protective spell I'd placed around the cabin. "Haven't seen your magic work that well in a long time."

"What's he talking about?" Seth grumbled.

I sent a sheepish glance Seth's way. "I placed a spell around the cabin to protect you after the hellhounds tore it apart."

His brows shot up, and then he shook his head with a bitter little laugh. "Wow. We seriously need to get past our trust issues."

"Sounds like you have bigger issues than that," Puck drawled. "Want to fill me in on what the hell is going on?"

As soon as we were safely inside once more, I brought Puck up to speed on all that Seth and I had learned in our separate snooping and what we'd encountered tonight in the forest near The Refuge. Puck listened, his expression difficult to read. When I told him that one of his precious pixies had attacked me, he ran a hand down his face and shook his head.

"Is she dead?" he asked, his voice carrying a hard edge.

I gaped at him. "After all I've just told you, the first thing you ask is if she's dead?"

He got up from the easy chair his magic had created just days before and began to pace around the living room. "You know, I was worried something like this would happen."

I shook my head a little, not following. "What are you talking about? You worried something like *what* would happen? That we'd uncover how the Tale revolution brewing in The Refuge was linked to murdered Ordinaries?"

"I said you were in over your head, Lav," he snapped. "I told you to leave it all to me!"

I rose slowly from the couch, studying him closely now, watching how his shoulders were stiffening up and supplanting his roguish, carefree attitude. "What's going on, Puck?" I breathed. "Did you . . . did you know all of this was going on? Did you know about the plans for revolution—for *war* against the Ordinaries?"

He halted his pacing and turned toward me. "Of course I knew about it," he hissed. "I planned to lead the charge."

"What?" I blinked at him in disbelief and felt Seth launch to his feet to stand guard at my shoulder, his body half-curling around mine.

Puck blew out an exasperated breath. "Who do you think began to foment the idea in their straw-brained little heads?" he spat. "Idiots.

All of them. They would've gone on living in this little corner of nowhere, cowering in obscurity, if I hadn't inspired them to consider the possibilities."

My stomach tightened into a painful knot, twisting with fear, disgust, and heartbreak. "Oh, my God," I whispered, my voice catching. "How could you have killed those people?"

He gave me a disappointed look. "Don't be ridiculous! I didn't kill anyone. All I did was plant the seed of revolution. The Ordinaries are asses, but I don't want to kill them—just command their respect and reverence."

"You want us to believe you had absolutely nothing to do with the murders?" Seth drawled, his tone betraying his disbelief.

"I don't give a shit what *you* believe, dog-boy," Puck retorted. "My sister's the only one I care about. I'm a lot of things, Lavender, but I'm not a murderer."

I crossed my arms over my chest, trying to contain my fury. "And what exactly is it you'd have me believe?"

"That there's someone else behind the murders," he assured me. "Someone else who has a much more militant stance on things than I have. You know me—I'm more about being worshiped and adored and having the most fabulous, raucous orgies known to man. Why the hell would I want to kill my potential fuck-buddies?" He gave me his golden smile and spread his arms wide. "What can I say—I'm a lover, not a fighter."

I frowned, fighting back tears and wanting so desperately to believe him. "You're the one who's been messing with the book, aren't you?"

He rolled his eyes and began to wander again. "Well, one can't have a revolution without the magic to back it, can one?"

"What about Dad?" I charged, my anger seeping through. "Are you why he's lying in a hospital bed dying?"

This brought him up short. "What are you talking about? I never attacked our father. I would just slip in now and then and take a quick peek at the book but it would only give me glimpses. I never had time to try to go deeper into the layers."

"Someone has," I fumed, charging toward him, my hands balled into fists at my sides to keep from unleashing all hell on him. "Who else were you sending? Giselle, obviously—she admitted she used Father to look at the book. She got in his head and fucked with his mind, Puck!"

At this, Puck looked uncharacteristically guilt-stricken. "She and Elise—the pixie with white hair—they both knew what I was doing, what I was planning. They were two of my biggest supporters. I guess Giselle decided to take a more drastic approach when she joined up with the Mother and her followers."

"Who is the Mother?" I demanded. "And don't give me any bull-shit, Puck!"

He eased down on the arm of the chair. "I don't know. And that's the God's honest truth. For a while now I've known that another faction was splintering off, that they were planning something far more militant than what I'd intended. It wasn't until you found the first body, though, that I began to have some inkling as to how serious it was. That's why I tried to warn you away."

I narrowed my eyes at him. "Warn me away?"

"*I* was the one who sent the hellhounds to tear up the house," he said as if I was a total idiot, but I didn't have time to dwell on his con-descension. Hearing what Puck had done, Seth lunged forward, teeth bared in a vicious snarl, knocking Puck over the back of the chair and pinning him to the ground, his fangs centimeters away from ripping out Puck's throat.

I strolled over to his side, glaring down at my brother. "Why would you do that to Seth's house?" I demanded. "You destroyed everything he had."

"Not quite everything," Puck spat, pressing as flat as possible against the floor to avoid the powerful jaws that could snap his neck in an instant. "He had my sister, didn't he? And that's more than some fucked-in-the-head werewolf deserves." When Seth's growl deep-ened, Puck added quickly, "But I wasn't trying to hurt anyone—just scare you badly enough that you'd come stay with me where I could keep an eye on you. I had Elise hang your necklace where you could see it to remind you of who you are, where your loyalties should lie."

"Why did you send the hellhound after me the night I arrived?" I asked.

"I didn't," he protested. "I didn't even know you were here." He turned his eyes to peg Seth with an accusing glare. "Apparently, I wasn't the only one who was suspicious of dog-boy here. It's a little curious when someone who has taken great pains over the years not to be noticed suddenly shows up and tries to become part of a community. Of course, when all the townspeople came to help after I'd ransacked this place, I figured Seth was in on whatever insurrection they've been planning."

"Why'd you invite us to dinner if you thought Seth was involved with Mother and her followers?" I asked.

He gave me a smile that was edged with a dark malice I'd never seen there before. "I think you know, sister dear, once you are in my home, it's rather hard to leave."

"You planned to drug me," I realized. "You were going to dose me up and—what?—lock me in the dungeon just to keep me away from Seth?"

"Don't be ridiculous!" he scoffed. "I don't have a dungeon. They're so passé."

Disgusted, I shook my head. "Just let him go," I said to Seth, waving him off. He gave me a questioning look but eased off and changed back into his human self, his eyes still glowing with deadly threat should Puck even flinch in the wrong way.

Puck got to his feet and brushed off his shirt and slacks, grumbling under his breath.

"If there's anything else you need to get off your chest," I said to my brother, "now would be the time. I won't be speaking to you after this."

Puck gave me a wounded look as if he couldn't understand how I could be so unreasonable. "There goes my dream of ever being one big happy family again," he drawled. He patted his pants pocket, then delved in and drew out his cigarette case.

"I'd rather you not smoke," Seth said, his tone an even calm that belied his deadliness.

Puck gave him a mocking grin. "I'd rather you not fuck my sister." He pointedly stuck one of his clove cigarettes between his lips, then drew out a silver lighter.

A chill cut through me as Puck flicked open the lighter and lit his cigarette, holding Seth's gaze in challenge. "Where did you get that?" I breathed.

Puck glanced down at the lighter, frowning. "Hell, I don't know. Why?"

I took a step back, suddenly wary. "That's J.G.'s lighter."

"So?"

I felt Seth take a step closer to me. "What the hell did you do to him?" he demanded. "His brain's totally fried from D—that much we know. What else did you do to him, you son of a bitch!"

Now it was Puck's turn to look wary. He spread his arms out in a conciliatory gesture. "I have no idea what the hell you're talking about, Wolf. I haven't seen that little prick since before his girlfriend bought it. I didn't have a damn thing to do with his disappearance."

"Oh, Puck," I breathed, tears seeping into my voice. "I so wanted to believe you."

He took a step toward me, stretching out a hand. I didn't even think. My magic surged forth in a violent rush, fueled by my devastating sense of loss at my brother's betrayal. It sent him sailing backward, slamming him into the cabin wall with such force, the rafters creaked.

"Fuck me," he groaned, attempting to get to his feet.

"You were always jealous of my powers," I reminded him, my voice shrill as I stalked forward. "You said so just the other day. You lying son of a bitch! At least have the courage to tell me who you're using the book to resurrect."

He shook his head vehemently, holding up a hand to ward me off. "Lavender, be reasonable—"

I screamed in rage, cutting him off and sending up a shower of purple sparks. I saw Seth flinch and bring up an arm to protect his eyes from the light. "Damn it! I loved you, Puck! I looked up to you!"

He threw open the front door, but I pursued him as he hurried out into the fog. It was dissipating now, but I still couldn't see him. Puck was a master of disguise, able to transform himself into anyone or anything with a simple thought.

"Was your life as a transplanted Tale so bad that it would come to this?" I demanded, my heart shattering at the thought that I was responsible for what he had done. "Was it so horrible that you would betray who you are?"

"You've got it all wrong," I heard him respond from a distance, although the fog made it impossible to tell how far—or near—he was. "I am guilty of a lot of things, Lavender, but this is *not* one of them."

I waited, listening intently, but I heard only silence—thick and heavy. I jumped when Seth's hand pressed gently into the small of my back.

"Come inside," he whispered. "The others will be coming for us, Lavender. We need to get out of here—go somewhere safe until we can call in some FMA backup to help Trish sort it all out."

I nodded and backed slowly toward the cabin door, scanning the night one last time looking for some sign of Puck, but I didn't sense him anywhere. He'd fled. Like the selfish coward he was.

Chapter 25

"Just leave it," Seth said, grabbing my hand and pulling me toward the front door. "We need to get the hell out of here."

"I'm not leaving without the cane you made me," I protested, straining against his hold. "Trust me—we're going to want this."

Seth exhaled on a sharp sigh. "Fine, but then we're leaving. The fog's clearing out now that the sun's rising and I want to move you to somewhere safe."

I grabbed up the cane that I'd enhanced a little on the sly and followed him out onto the deck. "I still think this is a mistake, Seth. We can't leave now—who's going to stop Mother?"

"As soon as Red gets our message, she'll be back," Seth assured me, scanning the woods surrounding the cabin, his shoulders visibly bunching up. "Your safety is what's most important to me right now."

He opened the truck door and motioned urgently for me to climb in. I started forward but stopped, planting my feet firmly. I pressed my lips together, preparing for the argument I knew was coming. "I can't leave."

Seth ran a hand down his face and gave me an exasperated look. "I'm not doing this right now, Lavender. I want your ass in this truck. You know I'll pick you up and throw you in there if I have to."

"And then what?" I said. "Are you telling me that *you're* going to walk away from this, Seth? You're just going to take me to some hotel and stay there with me until the cavalry arrives?"

He blinked at me, his eyes beginning to glow a little and I knew I'd hit on the mark. "Not everyone in town is in on this," he insisted. "They can't be. Would you have me just abandon them when all hell's getting ready to break loose?"

"Who are these Tales that aren't in on it?" I demanded, knowing full well he had no better idea than I did. "Tell me, and we'll go warn them right now."

"What about Mama Hubbard and Harlan?" he asked, throwing his arms up in frustration. "We know they're not involved."

"Do we?" I shot back. When I saw the conflicted expression in his eyes, I stepped forward and rested my hand on his chest. "I know Mama means a lot to you, Seth, but has it occurred to you that 'Mother' could be Old Mother Hubbard? She told me once that Tales came to her, that she offered them hope."

"She meant potions and charms," Seth said, shaking his head. "She's a friend. I trust her."

"You trusted Hansel, too," I reminded him, my voice gentle.

He closed his eyes and bowed his head forward, my point hitting closer to home than he could deny. "Even so, someone needs to stay behind and protect the innocent."

I immediately thought of little Gareth, the blameless soul who was such an unwitting pawn in Mother's plans. "Then I'm staying, too. End of story."

He huffed and put his hands on his hips, ready to square off with me, and something told me I probably wasn't going to win. "Damn it, Lavender, I—" His head snapped up and whipped around toward the road. "Someone's coming."

As soon as he said it, I heard the sound of tires on gravel as the car approached. The fog was thin enough now that in the next instant I recognized the outline of Tom Piper's SUV coming toward us. "It's just Tom."

I could feel Seth's tension as Tom drove up and parked his vehicle directly in front of Seth's truck, blocking our exit. "I don't like this," he muttered as Tom got out of the car along with Trish Muffet. They both wore carefully guarded expressions, Trish looking like she'd swallowed something foul and acidic that had turned rancid in her stomach and now threatened to lurch back up at any moment.

"Tom," Seth said with a tight nod. "We were just heading out. What brings you by?"

"Not a social call, I'm afraid," Tom replied, ducking his head a little in an obvious effort to avoid meeting our gazes. "When Ms. Muffet took a look at the bodies and J.G.'s office yesterday, she found some evidence as to the identity of the murderer."

"That's fantastic!" I cried, relief washing over me. "We've come across some evidence as well that I think you'll find interesting. The Ordinaries were murdered by an ancient form of Tale magic that only a few people know, and—"

"People like you?" Tom interrupted.

"Well, yes, actually, I *am* one of the people who knows that magic," I said, waving his words away with an impatient motion. "I'm sorry, Tom—I know I should've told you sooner, but—"

"Why don't you tell us what Trish found, Tom," Seth cut in, grabbing my hand and pulling me close. He edged a little in front of me, putting himself between Tom and me. It was only then that I noticed the handcuffs Trish was holding. They weren't ordinary handcuffs, I knew. I could see the aura surrounding them that identified them as the enchanted handcuffs the FMA used to block the magic of beings they considered too dangerous to subdue in any other way.

"What the hell's going on?" I demanded.

"I'm so sorry, Lavender," Trish said, her mournful grimace sincere. "But your magical signature was all over the bodies and in J.G.'s office."

I felt the air burst from me as if someone had punched me in the gut. "What?" I managed to gasp. "There's been a mistake."

"Please don't make this harder than it needs to be," Tom said, his ultrareasonable tone serving only to piss me off. "We'll just head down to the office, and I'll put you in lockup until you can hire an attorney to help you sort this out."

Trish stepped forward with the handcuffs, but Seth knocked them from her hands with a vicious snarl, his teeth bared, his face half-transformed by his anger. "Stay the hell away from her!"

Tom sighed. "I was afraid it might come to this." He motioned with his hand and several of the townspeople emerged from the woods, shotguns trained on Seth and me. I recognized several of them, including two of Old Lady Patterson's sons and the Farmer in the Dell, Ted Walsh. "Every one of those guns has a silver bullet in it, Seth," Tom explained. "If you so much as twitch, I'll have them take you down."

A low growl began to build deep in Seth's chest as his shoulders hunched forward, preparing to attack. "Not before I rip out your throat," he threatened, his voice a deep snarl that made the color drain from Tom's face.

"Damn it, Seth," Tom ground out, "I don't like this any more than you do! But I have to do my job."

Seth's growl grew louder, and I saw his features growing sharper and knew he was barely restraining his transformation, his rage so violent, he was beginning to shudder with the effort to hold it in.

Gently, I placed a hand on his shoulder. "It's all right," I told him, keeping my voice soft. "It'll be all right, Seth." His gaze flicked to me, but only briefly before returning to Tom's jugular. Carefully, I cupped his face and forced him to look at me. "We know it's all a big mistake and we'll sort it out."

He tried to look away, but I held firm, forcing his gaze back to me.

"Listen to me," I whispered urgently. "I need you alive if you're going to help me."

At this he closed his eyes and exhaled slowly, then pressed his forehead to mine. After a moment, I felt him nod. Then the next thing I knew, all hell was breaking loose around me. Tom had stepped forward and grabbed my arm, his threat to me breaking the hold Seth had on his rage. With a snarl that split the air like a roll of thunder, Seth lunged at Tom, taking him down. Then there was a crack of bullets and a howl of pain as one of them struck Seth in the thigh and another in the shoulder.

"Stop!" I screamed, rushing forward. "Stop!" I saw Trish hit the ground and cover her head as I ran toward Seth to shield him from any additional hits. I instinctively threw out a blast of purple fire that melted the remaining bullets in midair, sending tiny drops of molten silver raining down.

"Hold your fire! Hold your fire!" I heard Tom order as I gathered Seth into my arms and cradled him against me.

"Are you hurt?" Seth rasped.

"No," I told him. "No, I'm fine." I sent a frantic glance around me to make sure no one else was going to get trigger-happy, but they all seemed a little wary after nearly being incinerated by my magic. My skin was glowing with fairy light, the symbols I'd accepted from the book blazing brightly all over my body.

Convinced we were safe for the moment, I looked down at Seth's wounds and could see the smoke rising from each bullet hole where the silver was searing his flesh. Without thinking, I placed my hand over the hole in his thigh and whispered a sharp command. He let out a scream of anguish as the slug zipped back to the surface of his leg and into my hand, cauterizing his flesh and stopping the bleeding as it exited. I tossed the bullet aside then repeated the extraction in his shoulder, forcing the shattered bone to knit back together at the same instant. Tears streamed down my face at his agonized screams, but a moment later, the second silver bullet was in my hand and he sagged against me. His face was drawn and pale from the pain I'd just put him through, and tears made their way down his cheeks as he fought to catch his breath again.

I lifted my face then to the crowd and saw Trish rising to her feet. I pegged her with an accusing glare and was gratified to see her shrinking a little. "I'll come with you quietly," I hissed, "but at least give me a minute to tell him good-bye."

Tom got to his feet and wiped the blood from his cheek. He looked like he was about to protest, but then gave a terse nod. "Make it quick."

I turned my gaze back to Seth and was glad to see some of the color returning to his cheeks. "I need you to let me go," I told him, caressing his cheek. "I promise everything will be okay."

He shook his head. "No fucking way," he rasped, his voice still weak but growing stronger.

"I'm not letting you die for me," I insisted, wiping my cheek against my shoulder with a sniff. "That's not nearly as romantic as the Willies would have you believe."

He laughed in a short burst, but it died on a groan. I helped him sit up, then wrapped my arms around his neck, holding on tightly, not sure how I'd let him go to make good on my word to surrender quietly.

"I'll see you soon," he whispered near my ear. "I swear it."

I nodded, my arms tightening. "You'd better."

"Lavender," Trish said gently. "We should go."

I pulled Seth's arm around my shoulders and helped him to his feet, then pressed my cane into his hands. "Hang on to this for me," I commanded. I held his gaze and hoped he caught my meaning when I added, "I think you'll need it more than I will, Sir Knight."

His brows twitched together in a confused frown, but when he glanced down at the cane, I pulled back the veil of my enchantment just enough so he could see the truth. His head snapped up, his eyes wide. Then he gave me a tight nod. "It's perfect."

"Lavender," Tom prompted, holding out his hand and motioning for me to come away.

I nodded but then turned back to Seth. "I love you," I whispered fiercely.

Seth grasped the nape of my neck and pulled me to him, his kiss harsh, desperate. His lips held mine until Trish gently took my arm and closed the handcuffs around my wrist, then brought my other arm behind me, fastening the other cuff. The moment it clicked into place, my magic vanished in such a rush it left my knees weak. I gasped as my legs crumpled beneath me, but Seth caught me up and brought me back to my feet.

He pressed another kiss to my lips and then another but didn't protest when Trish took hold of my upper arm and gently pulled me away. But when Trish opened the back door to Tom's SUV and started to help me inside, Seth called, "Wait! Just wait a goddamn minute!"

Trish took a half-step toward him as Seth limped forward, but he ignored her as he cradled my face in his hands. "I love you," he ground out, his voice taut with emotion. "I should've said it sooner, but I was too afraid of what it meant. But I'm saying it now—I love you, Lavender. With all my heart."

I closed my eyes and let the words wash over me, fill my heart until it was overflowing. But before I could respond, Trish was bending me forward and easing me into the backseat. "I'm sorry, Seth," she apologized quietly. "I really am."

As Tom drove away from the cabin, I turned around and looked out the back window, fixing the sight of Seth in my mind as he stood there, his clothes torn and bloody, his waves of golden brown hair lifting in the wind. The early morning sunlight broke through the last remnants of fog and glinted off the deadly blade of the enchanted sword I'd fashioned from the wooden cane he'd carved for me. And as the townspeople began to back off into the woods, Seth twirled the sword with a practiced flick of his wrist, his grim purpose unmistakable, his expression deadly.

And I knew he'd be coming for me. My knight in shining armor. My slayer of monsters. My Big Bad Wolf.

Chapter 26

"I thought we were friends, Tom," I said, staring pointedly into the rearview mirror, daring him to meet my gaze. He did. Briefly.

"I wish it could be different," he replied. "I really do. You know how much I admire you, Lavender."

"You know I had nothing to do with these murders," I protested. "Trish, I don't know how you found my magical signature on the bodies—I'd never even seen the first man until Seth and I found him on the side of the road. And I never touched Brie—never so much as even shook her hand."

Trish turned in her seat, her expression pained. "Magical signatures are unique, Lavender—like an Ordinary's fingerprints. All I had to do was send a sample through the FMA's database with my phone and a match came back in seconds. Faking something like that isn't possible."

I gave her a sardonic look. "We're fairytales who were magically transported to the mortal world. Call me crazy, but I'm pretty sure *any*thing's possible at this point, Trish."

"Fine," she conceded. "For argument's sake, let's say it's possible. Explain to me how someone managed to pull it off."

I shook my head. "I don't know how she did it, but she lifted my magical residue from something else and planted it," I insisted. "I *did not* do this."

Trish gave me a pitying look. "We have no other suspects at this point, Lavender. Maybe we shouldn't talk about this anymore until you have an attorney."

"Sorry, but I don't have a whole lot of faith in the FMA's trial system," I drawled. "That didn't really work out so well for me last time around. I would've been executed if you all weren't so afraid of my father."

"Well, I don't think his reputation will do you much good this time," Tom sniped. "From what I hear, he's not quite what he used to be."

My brows came together and I searched for his gaze again in the mirror, but he didn't so much as glance my way.

"Well, if you're going to worry about anyone in my family," I said, "it ought to be my brother."

Now he did glance up into the mirror. "Puck? What are you talking about?"

"He's involved in all of this," I said, watching Tom closely. "He's the one who sent the hellhounds to scare us off and who ransacked Seth's house—he admitted as much to Seth and me. Unfortunately, he took off before I could bind his magic. And he knew about the location of the book."

"Book?" Trish echoed, glancing between Tom and me. "*The* book? You didn't say anything about the book being here, Sheriff."

"Because he didn't know," I told her. "No one did except for the Tale who brought it to me at great personal risk. It'd been hidden away after the relocation. Only another fairy could access where it was being housed, and even then finding it wouldn't have been easy. Puck would've had an edge because he knew of the book and who was chosen to watch over it after I was deposed as its Guardian. If Puck himself wasn't able to sneak in and read the book on the sly, then one of his little pixie whores was popping in for a quick peek and reporting back what she found."

"Why?" Trish questioned, her intelligent gaze searching mine, no doubt analyzing every minute change in my expression, searching for any sign of deception.

"Puck thinks Tales should be living out in the open, doing as they please," I explained, "not hiding in the shadows too afraid to be who we truly are. He claims that there is a faction of Tales in The Refuge, though, that are far more militant in their goals—they want to subjugate the Ordinaries, wage war against them until they bow down to our superiority. But I think he's just trying to save his own ass. One of his pixies, Giselle, was among the followers who attacked us the other night when we witnessed their secret meeting."

"Hold on just a *freaking* minute," Trish said, her voice taking on a sharp edge that I found oddly comforting. "What the hell are you talking about—followers? Meetings? I thought this was just one person acting alone. There are more?" She sent such an angry glare at Tom it would've melted his face off if she'd had laser beams for eyes. "You care to explain how I'm just hearing about all of this, Sheriff? You can't tell me you knew nothing about this cult."

Tom adjusted his customary black ball cap and shifted a little in his seat. "Refuge business is Refuge business," he said by way of response. "There are things that shouldn't be shared with outsiders."

"Like what happened to Bo Peep?" I pressed.

Trish looked expectantly at Tom. "Sheriff?"

He exhaled a sharp sigh. "Bo Peep is a fairy dust addict. She went missing a few days ago. It's hardly a loss to our town."

Trish ran her hands through her hair, creating a buttercup yellow disarray. "Unbelievable," she muttered. She reached into her jacket pocket and pulled out her phone. "I'm calling all this shit in. I can't believe—"

We suddenly hit a massive pothole that knocked me hard against the door and sent Trish's phone flying. She quickly tried to recover it, but it fell down into the crevice between her seat and the center console.

"Damn it!" she hissed, pushing at the side of the seat to peer down into the darkness where the phone had fallen. "I can't see it. Sheriff, do you have a light?"

My eyes went wide at her words.

"Sure," Tom said with a shrug. He grabbed a small flashlight that hung at his belt and tossed it to her.

The sinking feeling in the pit of my stomach opened up like a chasm as I watched the flashlight sail toward Trish in a gentle arc as if in slow motion. A barrage of other images floated to me, and the truth hit me like a punch in the gut.

My God, how could I have been so blind?

"You gave Puck the lighter," I breathed, closing my eyes as all my assumptions fell apart in one fell swoop.

"What?" Tom said with a glance back at me. "What lighter?"

I opened my eyes again and caught a glimpse of my expression in the mirror. Heartbroken didn't even begin to cover it. "When we were at J.G.'s," I replied. "Puck was planning to smoke a cigarette, but he couldn't find his lighter, so you tossed one to him and told him to keep it."

"So," he said with a shrug.

"It was J.G.'s lighter," I explained. "When Puck had it last night, I accused him of taking it from J.G. while he was holding him captive and dosing him with enough D to fry his brain."

Tom's face suddenly became impassive, impossible to read. "You found J.G.? Where is he now?"

"How'd you get it, Tom?" I asked, ignoring his questions and not even trying to keep the disappointment out of my voice.

He laughed a little as the corner of his mouth lifted. "You know," he said with a shake of his head, "you're making some pretty wild accusations there, Lavender."

"No wilder than those you've made against me," I shot back.

"Sheriff," Trish interjected, her voice strained with the effort to keep it calm, "I'm afraid I'm going to have to ask you to pull over."

He nodded. "Of course." Then, in a blur of motion, his powerful arm shot out and grabbed the back of Trish's head, slamming it against the console before she could even react.

"Jesus Christ!" I cried, my heart hammering in my chest. I scooted forward and peered around the edge of Trish's seat. She was out cold, blood gushing from the huge gash over her left eyebrow. "Pull over right now, Tom! She needs medical attention."

"I'm afraid I can't do that, Lavender," he said, using that damnably reasonable tone that made me want to clean his clock. "I have my instructions."

"Your *instructions?*" I echoed, my mind racing as I surveyed the inside of the SUV, trying to figure out a way to get the hell out of there. But even if there was a way to escape, I wouldn't go very far with my hands cuffed behind my back. Besides, there was no way I was going to leave Trish behind. "Why don't you tell me who's calling the shots, Tom?"

But I realized the answer before I'd even finished asking the question. It was Mother. And now I knew why I'd recognized the voice of the ceremony leader the night before. Maybe I hadn't wanted to face the truth then. I sure as hell didn't want to now.

"I wish you could've just left well enough alone," Tom said, shaking his head with what appeared to be genuine regret. "I'd told them all that if they would just give me some time, we could win you over, help you see things our way. You'd been persecuted more than any of us, I told them. I assured them that after you got to know us, after you saw how much of a family we could be to you, you'd be one of our greatest allies. But the spell wasn't working. We were going to have to sacrifice a Tale to bring her back—and we couldn't allow you to interfere with that, Lavender. I'm sorry."

I swallowed hard, wondering just how many shades of crazy I was dealing with here. "I could still be your ally, Tom," I said, forcing my voice to maintain the same reasonable tone he'd used. "I don't know who this Mother is, but she's misleading you."

"Mother has a plan," he insisted. "Puck had the right idea, but we still would've been beholden to the rules and laws the FMA imposes on all of us. We still would've had to scrape and bow and kiss ass and not realize our full glory."

Okaaay . . . so apparently it was all *shades of crazy.*

"You're right," I said, nodding. "But whoever it is you're trying to resurrect with that spell Mother appropriated, it's not going to work. She's doing it all wrong."

His brows came together in a frown. "Mother is more powerful than any other Tale I've ever met—she has already shown us what life could be like."

"She might be powerful," I agreed, "but she's fucking up the spell big-time. The symbols are wrong. They're sloppy. I was right about Giselle, wasn't I? She was the one sneaking in to look at the book and then reporting back."

He nodded. "Yes, she assured us that her information was accurate."

I laughed, making it sound as condescending as I could. "Of course she would *say* that, Tom! She's not a Guardian like I am. She's not able to see the true spell. The book wouldn't give up that kind of spell to just *any*one."

"But we were able to raise Gareth from the dead," he pointed out. "No one can even tell he was a corpse I dug up from the local cemetery for Mother to reanimate."

"But he was an Ordinary, wasn't he?" I asked. "That's why his aura is so off. He's an Ordinary reanimated with Tale magic. It doesn't surprise me that you were able to cobble something together in that case. But it's different with Tales, Tom. Our souls aren't like those of the Ordinaries."

This seemed to trouble him. "What happens if we sacrifice a Tale and use the information Giselle gave us to perform the rites?"

Hell if I knew—nothing good, I imagined. But if my plan was going to work, I needed to make it sound even worse than it probably was.

"It will have the opposite effect," I said with as much authority as I could manage. "The soul you're trying to reclaim will be lost forever—but not before it has been rent asunder by the horrifying claws of hellhounds, raped and mutilated by the Lord of the Dead, and forced to undergo all manner of indignities. Only then, when the soul has been tortured to the point of madness, will it be granted mercy."

Tom's face went visibly pale and I saw him swallow hard. "Could you do the spell the right way? I mean, your magic kinda sucks."

I made a scoffing noise and shrugged. "Of course. I was just out of practice, that's all."

He nodded, his expression solemn. "I will make your case to Mother then," he agreed. "I will explain to her that you're willing to help—"

"Hang on, now," I drawled, scooting back and settling casually into my seat. "I didn't say that. I'm not doing jack until I find out who this Mother is and what's in it for me."

"She's planning to kill you, Lavender," he reminded me. "I don't think you have a lot of room to bargain."

I shrugged again. "Fine, she can kill me. But then she'll really be fucked."

He pressed his lips into a grim line and I could see him weighing his options. Finally, he let out a short sigh. "Okay. I'll take you to meet her. But I can't make any guarantees."

"Duly noted."

Fortunately, we didn't have to drive for very long before Tom pulled off onto a gravel road that tapered into a dirt road and then barely a road at all by the time I saw a squat little cottage in the distance. Its windows were overgrown with ivy and the door was clogged with the remnants of weeds that had been half-cleared away. But something told me the appearance of abandonment was mostly for show—something about it seemed far too deliberate and staged.

Tom helped me out of the backseat with surprising care, but when he began to lead me toward the cottage, I planted my boots firmly and strained against his hold. "Wait, Tom," I pleaded. "Please don't do this."

Tom gave me a pained look, then took me by the shoulders. "You'll see that this is for the best, Lavender," he insisted. "I wandered around for decades, nothing more than hired muscle—or a hired gun—until I came here. I bought into what your brother was preaching, but it wasn't until Mother came to show us all the way that I truly saw what I could become."

"And what is that?" I asked, the center of my chest aching as I looked into the face of the man who had treated me with such kindness, who had been my friend. I wanted to believe that he had been coerced, that he had been threatened. But I could see in his eyes that particular gleam of zealousness that was the hallmark of a fanatic. "What happened to the boy who would do anything to protect his family? Where is that boy I saved from the villagers who would've killed him?"

"I would still do anything for the ones I love," he assured me. "I finally was able to give my beautiful Eva a son, wasn't I?"

I shuddered, wondering what Eva would think if she knew Gareth was little more than an adorable zombie. "Does she know what you've done?" I asked, my voice just above a whisper. "Does Eva know what Gareth is? Does she know about Mother's plans?"

Tom let his hands fall to his sides. "No," he admitted. "All she knows is that she has a son now—the second chance she's always wanted."

"But she loves you, Tom," I told him. "That would've been enough for her. She believes in you. She thinks you're a good man."

"I *am* a good man!" he bellowed. "Do you think I've *enjoyed* what I've had to do? It was the only way for us to truly be safe and happy forever. We couldn't keep living in fear, Lavender, always looking over our shoulders, hoping there were no Ordinaries around when we slipped up. I'm helping to liberate my friends and family. Can't you see that?"

"You're being used," I replied, my words coming out swiftly now. "Mother doesn't care about you or any of the other Tales—she only cares about the power she can obtain."

He shook his hand and took hold of my arm again. "You're wrong, Lavender," he said. "You'll see."

"Wait," I said, digging in my heels. "What about Trish? We can't just leave her in the car—she's wounded. She needs help!"

He blew out a sharp exhale, then released me and opened the car door. Trish listed to one side and would've fallen to the ground had he not caught her up. He hefted her a little higher and cradled her against his broad chest, his careful handling of her completely at odds with the brutality that had caused her injury in the first place.

"Tom," I said, moving to block his path. "There's still time to do the right thing."

"I am." He gestured toward the cottage with a jerk of his chin. "Go on."

Not knowing what else to do to persuade him, I obeyed. The moment I stepped through the cottage door, my skin prickled with uneasiness, the hairs on my arms standing on end. I didn't need to have my fairy senses in perfect working order to sense the dark, twisted evil that lurked inside.

Instinctively, I turned and would've made a break for the door, but at the same moment Trish moaned as she began to come to, and my conscience kept my feet firmly rooted where they were. As Tom made his way to a rickety little bed in the corner, I slowly surveyed the interior of the cottage. The foliage that had assaulted the façade had infiltrated the walls and wound its way around the sparsely furnished room in which I stood. There were grimy sheets draped over several of the larger pieces of furniture but a few had been uncovered at some point and appeared to have been used recently. And in the air was a musty, repugnant stench like nothing I'd smelled before, but I thought I caught a trace of damp earth, mildew, moldy leaves . . . and rotting flesh. I gagged just a little and tried not to breathe it in.

"Good morning."

The sudden voice jolted a startled scream from me, and I spun so quickly toward the sound that I nearly toppled over. For a moment, I couldn't see where the voice had come from, but then I saw the shadows part as a figure dressed in a dark hooded robe slowly rose from a bent wood rocking chair and came toward me, the horrible stench growing stronger as it approached.

I swallowed hard at the figure's approach, my heart hammering so hard I could feel my pulse beating frantically at the base of my neck. "Oh, I don't know that I'd call it a *good* morning," I drawled, my voice little more than a rasp in spite of my attempt at insolence.

Her answering chuckle felt like sandpaper on my skin and sent a violent shudder through me before I could stop it. And if that hadn't been enough to put every nerve ending on edge, the way she studied me, her hooded head cocked to one side in mocking contemplation, would have done the trick.

"So, you are the infamous Lavender Seelie," she said after making a full circle. She clasped her gloved hands in front her and continued to peer at me from within the shadows of her hood. All I could see of her were luminescent green eyes, eerie and flat—dead somehow—in spite of the light emanating from them. "I thought someone with your reputation would be much harder to subdue."

I gave her a mocking smile. "Sorry to disappoint."

There was a flash of white as she returned the smile with what looked like genuine amusement. "Well, my disappointment will be short-lived, I assure you." She then strolled haltingly toward where Trish lay, and peered down at her for a moment. With a shake of her head, she reached out her gloved hand and placed it over Trish's wound.

"Get away from her!" I barked, rushing forward to knock her

away from Trish, but Tom grabbed me around the waist and lifted me off my feet to swing me away.

The figure turned her head only slightly, completely unconcerned. Then a soft glow zipped across Trish's wound, sealing the skin, and from her pained grimace, I imagine it was also knitting together the fracture in her skull. When the glow faded, the figure drifted back to her place in the shadows.

I shook my head, not understanding. "You just healed her."

"Of course I did," she said, her matter-of-fact tone indicating I clearly was a moron. "Why would I let her die when her essence might be needed later tonight to complete the rites if that of one Tale is insufficient? Besides, we can't have that troublesome Reaper showing up too soon, now can we?"

I blinked at her. "You mean Nate Grimm?"

"Do you know another Reaper?" she snapped, her voice infused with bitter venom. "Of course I mean Nate Grimm. He and I have a score to settle and I intend to do just that when he arrives tonight."

I felt my heart hop up into my throat and tried to swallow past it. "What could you possibly have against Nate? He just collects the souls—it's not like he's the one who actually kills them."

She launched herself from the chair with such stunning speed, I didn't even have time to gasp before she was standing before me, her shadow-shrouded face just inches from mine. "No?" She snatched the hood from her head. "Then I guess I was the exception."

My stomach retched before I could stop it, a mixture of revulsion and terror generating a violent reaction, the source of the horrible rotting stench now clear. I heaved, gagging and sputtering as I tried to stumble away. But she pursued me and in the next instant, her gloved hand grabbed me under the jaw and slammed my back against the cottage wall, sending a cloud of plaster into the air.

"Look at me," she hissed. "Look at the putrid, festering monstrosity that I am because of that bastard Grimm and his little whore!"

I squeezed my eyes shut and shook my head vehemently, determined never to look at her again, but her grip tightened, squeezing my jaw so hard, I was sure I heard the bones fracturing beneath her punishing fingers. She gave me a hard shake and slammed me against the wall again.

"Look at me!"

I choked back a whimper and opened my eyes—just a small slit at first and then wider, forcing myself to look her in the eyes and see nothing else. But it was no use. I couldn't help but see her. What I imagined had once been a beautiful face was now a festering mass of flesh and bone, her body a half-decomposed corpse that had only been preserved as well as it had through the sacrifice of who knew how many Ordinaries. Her skin had begun to peel away in moldy chunks, revealing the rancid muscle and decaying tendon beneath. Her lips were cracked and dry, oozing with blood and pus. The odor of her rotting flesh was overwhelming, but what made my stomach spasm again was the sight of the countless maggots that squirmed in a pathetic frenzy, attempting to feed on flesh that refused to completely yield to the ravages of time. The only part of her that seemed to be unaffected was the luxurious locks of coppery hair that hung about her shoulders.

In a flash of understanding, I suddenly realized who she was. "You're Sebille Fenwick," I managed to mutter.

Laughing, she tossed me casually to the ground, where I landed hard against my shoulder without my arms free to catch me. As I fought back the tears of pain, she crouched down as much as her rigor-mortis-ridden joints would allow, her face twisting nightmarishly with hatred.

"Clever girl," she mocked. "But not as clever as you thought, eh? Nate Grimm will come rushing here to collect the poor, tortured Tales I've sacrificed to reclaim my soul—and will find himself securely in my clutches."

"You can't kill Death," I assured her, looking at her askance from where I lay on the floor.

"Believe me, my dear, a soul can experience things far worse than death." She put her foot against my shoulder and pushed, rolling me onto my back. "And thanks to your distress call to Red Little, my revenge will be complete in one glorious moment."

My eyes went wide. *How the hell did she know about the call we'd made?*

"Ah, yes—I have my little spies everywhere." She grinned, apparently guessing my thoughts. "I used rats last time to gather information for me, but I find birds to be so much easier. And they told me such a story about your little exhibit in town with some of their friends." She cackled, clapping her hands. "Oh, how I wish I'd been there to witness *that* stunning display of ability. Really, to think *you* were the one who brought us here! Simply astonishing. But, lucky for me, your little magical mishap provided enough residue to plant on the bodies and in Squiggington's office to frame you for all the murders if the FMA came snooping around before I could steal your essence to complete the rites. Gotta have a backup plan, right?"

"Mother," Tom said, coming forward sheepishly, his head bowed in deference—or maybe just to avoid looking at her. "Perhaps we shouldn't use Lavender as the sacrifice. Perhaps she could help advise you on the spell where you have been unable to fill in the gaps."

Sebille's head snapped up with a hiss; then she slowly rotated her head toward him, her lips peeled back in a snarl. "You would question my power?"

Tom ducked a little further into his shoulders and took a step back. "Of course not," he said in a rush. "You are our Mother, the one who will give birth to the future. We are but children who seek your wisdom, understanding, guidance...."

Wow. No brainwashing here, folks.

"... I was merely suggesting that she already possesses the knowledge that has been kept hidden from your eyes, and that she could *speed* the acquisition of the rest of the spell that you—no doubt—would obtain on your own, of course. I think only to have you restored to your former beauty and glory sooner."

Sebille went toward him slowly as if trying to ascertain the sincerity of his words. After a moment, she offered him a smile and caressed his cheek. "Dear Tom," she purred. "My most fervent follower. You shall be rewarded for your loyalty." She let her hand drift down to his chest. "Such a magnificent specimen of manliness." She grasped his shirt and pulled him down so that her lips were near his ear. "I will enjoy offering you my gratitude."

I saw Tom swallow hard. "But Eva—"

"She is nothing to me," Sebille hissed. She suddenly grabbed his crotch and squeezed, making him wince. "And when I finish with you, Tom, she will be nothing to *you*."

Tom cast a glance toward me, and I saw in his eyes his indecision. I shook my head. "Don't do this, Tom," I said. "She's lying to you. The kind of future you want for you and Eva and little Gareth—it's not through her!"

Sebille suddenly whirled on me with a snarl and kicked, her foot landing soundly where my ribs had been broken just days before. "I grow tired of you, Lavender Seelie," she ground out, ignoring my groan of pain. "But Tom may be right about one thing—you are worth more to me alive and under my power than dead." She lifted her eyes to where Trish was beginning to stir. She jerked her chin. "We will use that one instead."

Fear sent such a spike of adrenaline through my body that my fingertips tingled in spite of the enchanted handcuffs around my wrists. It was a damned good thing for Sebille they were firmly in place. But at some point they'd have to come off. And then I was going to serve up her rotting ass on a platter.

"Take them to the cellar, Tom," Sebille ordered. "I have preparations to make for tonight."

As soon as Sebille disappeared once more into the shadows, Tom gathered Trish up and draped her over one of his broad shoulders.

"You can still let us go, Tom!" I called, scooting myself around so that I could see what he was doing. He lifted the trap in the cottage floor, not even acknowledging me with so much as a glance. "Tom! Trish is completely innocent—at least let *her* go!"

But he merely turned his back on me as he made his way down the wooden ladder that led into the cellar. A few moments later, he emerged from the darkness and came toward me. I didn't bother trying to resist as he threw me over his shoulder and headed toward the ladder once more. As we descended into the damp darkness below, I felt him sigh—a mournful sound that seemed to come from the very depths of his soul.

"This isn't what I wanted," he mumbled, taking me to a corner where several crates were stacked. "I hope you know that."

I strained to see him in the dim light coming from the open door.

"I'd be much more inclined to believe you if you'd undo these handcuffs and let us go."

He pressed his lips together, regarding me for a long moment before he put a hand on my shoulder. "I have always admired you, Lavender," he said. "I wanted us to be friends. Once—before I met Eva—I'd dreamed that maybe I'd find you and . . . I don't know, maybe we'd have a chance to be more than just friends. I just . . ." He paused, sighing again. "I realize I've disappointed you, and that saddens me more than you know."

To my surprise, he bent forward and pressed a kiss to the top of my head, then turned and climbed the ladder. A moment later, the cellar door closed with a loud thump, making me jump. As his heavy tread strode out of the cottage, a sprinkling of dirt rained down, illuminated by what little light streamed through the cracks in the floorboards.

As soon as I was sure he was gone, I surveyed our makeshift prison, looking for any tools that might help break me out of the handcuffs—or at least get Trish the hell out of there so she could go for help.

"Trish," I called. "Trish, can you hear me? Are you awake?"

I heard her moan and then a rustling as she shifted. "Lavender?" she replied, her voice weak. "What the hell happened?"

"Tom cracked your skull," I said. "And then Sebille Fenwick healed it so you wouldn't die yet."

"What?" Trish cried, stronger now as consciousness took hold. "Sebille Fenwick—she's dead."

"Yep," I agreed. "She sure as shit is. But her corpse has been animated by the Ordinary sacrifices. It's her soul that they're planning to resurrect tonight."

"We can't let that happen," Trish insisted.

"Damn straight." I looked around again now that my eyes were adjusting to the dim light. "Don't suppose you have a handcuff key on you?"

"As a matter of fact, I do," she said. But before I could feel the full jolt of excitement and relief, she added, "But Tom has bound my hands and I can't get to it."

"Lost, lost. All is lost. . . ."

Trish and I both yelped at the sudden sing-songy voice. "Who the hell else is in here?" I demanded.

There was a girlish twitter and a rustle of movement. And then a pale, dirty face emerged from the darkest of the shadows. I gasped, the familiar visage impossible to mistake even in the meager light.

"Good God," I breathed. "Bo Peep."

Chapter 27

"*Little Bo Peep has lost her sheep* . . ." she sang, wandering aimlessly about the room, twirling a grimy lock of her bedraggled hair around her finger. "But they didn't come home. They never came home. All is lost. . . ."

I glanced at Trish. "She's been through a lot," I explained. "She's a little . . . out of sorts."

Trish gave me an incredulous look. "Out of sorts? She's a freaking loony."

"She's been overdosing on D for who knows how long. I'm betting it was Tom keeping her doped up." I sighed and shook my head. "God, I owe my brother a massive apology."

"I don't think any of us could've predicted this little turn of events," she assured me. She then glanced at Bo. "So, do you think we can convince her to help us?"

I shrugged. "Bo," I called gently. "Bo, honey, can you help Trish? She's tangled up in ropes—"

"It's actually some kind of linen—a cotton fabric perhaps," Trish corrected. "Not an overly expensive weave, but still decent quality."

I rolled my eyes. *Scientists.* "Sorry—she's tangled up in some sort of *cotton fabric* and needs your help."

Bo continued to wander, her head bobbing from side to side as if it were too heavy to hold erect. *"Leave them alone, leave them alone..."* she murmured. "Have to leave them alone. Sheriff Tom told me so. Have to leave them alone or very bad things happen."

"What very bad things?" Trish questioned. "Can you tell us, Bo?"

Bo slowly sank into a crouch in the middle of the cellar, gripping her head with both hands. "Bad, bad things!" she groaned. "So many bad things! I will never see him again. Never see him. She will not let me go back if I am a bad girl."

"Go back?" I echoed. "Go back where?"

"To Make Believe," Bo wailed, her voice thick with tears. "I have to go back! I have to see my husband again!"

I closed my eyes and shook my head. "Honey, Sebille lied to you," I told her as gently as I could. "She can't send you back. No one can."

Bo suddenly scrambled toward me on all fours, her freaky-wild, crazy-ass eyes open wide, her face inches from mine. "Yes, she can!" she screamed. "She can! She promised if I took care of the boy, she would send me back! She *promised!"*

Oh, yeah. This chick was officially Queen of Quacktown.

I blinked at poor, pathetic Bo, my mind racing. If Sebille had been tapping into the book's power in order to reclaim her own soul, had she also been trying to discover the spell I'd used to open the rift between Make Believe and the Here and Now? Hell's bells—*I* didn't even know how it'd happened. If she was trying to pull off something like that by dicking around with magic she only half-understood, God only knew what kind of shit storm she'd unleash.

"Lavender," Trish said, her voice hard with apprehension, "what happens if—"

"No freaking clue," I interrupted before she could finish her thought. Putting it into words out loud was way too much of a bitch-slap to the face of Fate, and considering we were pretty much royally screwed already, I wasn't willing to risk making things worse.

After hours of listening to Bo Peep's deranged ramblings, it was actually a relief when I heard heavy footsteps on the floorboards above us. Trish and I had long ago given up trying to wiggle out of our bindings. I couldn't maneuver enough to get into Trish's pocket to reach the handcuff key, and the knots in whatever Tom had used on

Trish were so tight, I'd been unable to loosen them even after trying until my nails split and my fingertips bled.

At the sound of the footsteps, I turned my face up, watching the dirt filter down with each step, marking where the person stood.

"Do you think it's Tom?" Trish whispered.

She sat with her back to mine, so I cast a glance over my shoulder. "Yeah."

I felt her inhale, then let it out slowly. "Guess it's time then."

I grasped her fingertips, giving them a comforting squeeze. "Guess so."

At that moment, the cellar door opened, letting in just enough light that I could make out Tom's hulking form at the top of the ladder. He didn't say a word as he joined us belowground, but he cast a sheepish glance at Trish and me before he went to Bo and took her hand. "Come on, Bo," he said gently. "It's time to go."

"Where are you taking her?" Trish demanded.

Tom had to place Bo's foot on the ladder as she seemed to have lost control over even basic coordination. She was mumbling to herself, her head twitching in a pronounced tic. "Don't worry," Tom called over his shoulder. "You'll find out soon enough."

As soon as they were out of sight, I managed to get my legs under me and hurried over to the ladder to peer up into the cottage. "Shit," I muttered. "It's dark. My guess is they're taking us to the clearing to perform the rites."

"Someone will come," Trish assured me. "You called Red, right? She and Nate will be here. They'll come for us."

"That's what I'm afraid of," I said. I was also worried that Seth would show up, fangs and claws bared, ready to give his life to protect mine. He might be able to bring down a few of Sebille's fan club before Sebille took him out, but there was no way he'd be able to take on both Sebille and her freaktastic followers on his own.

Before I could consider just how many horrifying ways she might react to someone interrupting her little Samhain soiree, Tom started back down the ladder and gave me an apologetic look as he stepped past me to help Trish to her feet and hefted her over his shoulder. As Tom carried Trish toward the ladder, she lifted her head enough to meet my gaze. I read the fear in her eyes, but there was also grim determination and strength shining there. She wasn't going down without a fight, that was for damned sure.

I waited for Tom to come back down for me, but several minutes passed and he hadn't reappeared. I frowned, staring up at the entrance to the cellar.

What the hell?

Not hearing anyone moving around upstairs, I squatted down and wiggled and contorted until I'd managed to maneuver my bound hands in front of me instead of behind me, then warily made my way up the ladder. When I reached the opening, I peered out over the floorboards, checking for anyone lurking in the shadows. The cottage was eerily empty; not even the wind rustled through. I was just pushing myself through the cellar opening when a glint of metal on the floor caught my eye.

That couldn't possibly be . . .

I picked it up and raised it to my eyes. *Holy shit.*

It was a small key—just the right size to belong to a set of enchanted handcuffs. Glancing around quickly, watching for any movement in the shadows, I maneuvered the key around and was able to slip it into the lock. I held my breath, praying like hell it would work.

There was a soft click as the first cuff popped open.

Thank God.

My breath burst from my lungs in a gasp. I immediately unlocked the other cuff, sending mental hugs to Trish for somehow managing to leave the key behind for me to find. As soon as the second cuff popped open, I felt a rush of energy surge through my body and a low-level buzzing under my skin that started at the very center of my chest and spread out until it reached my fingertips. Suddenly, the surge of magical energy sent purple sparks showering down onto the dried leaves covering the cottage floor, setting them ablaze.

Son of a bitch.

I quickly stomped them out, not eager to burn down yet another house in the span of a couple of weeks and probably half the forest with it. As much as I would've enjoyed destroying Sebille's shitty little hideout, a raging forest fire was exactly the kind of attention I didn't want just then.

As soon as I was sure I wasn't going to have Smoky the Bear

hunting down my ass, I crept from the cottage and surveyed the forest surrounding me. There were tracks where Tom's SUV had driven away, but I had no idea where we were in relation to the ceremony site—and that was if they were even heading to the same place.

I worked up a little fairy dust and blew across my palm. "Sebille Fenwick," I whispered, hoping it would pick up on her trail. But nothing happened. "Damn it!" I tried again. "Trish Muffet." Still nothing. "Shit!"

I blew out another sprinkle of fairy dust, this time whispering, "Reveal." As I suspected, there was the glow of another magic beneath my purple haze. Sebille couldn't have known I would try to track her, but she was worried enough that *someone* would to leave behind a spell to mask her route. "Oh, you're a smart girl," I murmured. Too bad for her, I was even smarter.

I started out into the woods, following what was tantamount to a magic-laden trail of breadcrumbs that would lead me directly to where Sebille was hoping to make her move on Ordinaries and Tales alike. And, if I was lucky, I might actually get there in time to take down her rotten, moldy ass before she hurt anyone I cared about. At least, she'd better hope I did, or she was gonna wish she'd stayed dead.

Chapter 28

I heard the chanting first. It was low, rhythmic, as it had been the night before when Seth and I had come upon them. But this time I could understand what they were chanting. It was a spell, calling upon the forces of darkness and evil to infuse their magic with the power they needed to pull off a resurrection. They called upon the Lord of the Dead, the leader of the Wild Hunt, begging him to bring with him the soul of their Mother in trade for the sacrifices they were prepared to make.

I crept forward slowly, silently, not about to tip them off to my presence this time around—especially without Seth at my side. My heart hitched at the thought of him and I found myself missing him so desperately, it was as if I hadn't seen him in months, years. I wanted him there with me at that moment so badly my throat grew tight with tears. I wanted to feel his calming presence at my side. I wanted to feel the strength and warmth of his love as I went into battle, hear his assurances that everything would come out right in the end because he loved me and would make it so.

I gave myself a little shake, forcing my head back in the game. I wasn't going to do anyone any good if I let myself be distracted.

When I finally reached the tree line, I was able to see what was going on in the clearing. As before, the robed figures stood together as they chanted, but this time a sacrificial bier stood in the center of their circle. Constructed of stone with a single sheet of wood serving as a platform, it was simple, but would be enough to serve its purpose—and based on the dark stains upon the stone and wood, had done so in the past. But it wasn't the presence of the bier that bothered me so much as that Bo Peep was already stretched out on the platform, her clothes having been stripped from her body, her hands and feet tied down, even though she was so far gone, odds were good she wouldn't have tried to fight back.

A sudden angry voice brought my eyes up from Bo Peep to the fringes of the circle. "Get your hands off me, you asshole!"

Trish.

Two of Sebille's followers were struggling with Trish, trying to strip her clothes from her body, but they'd made the mistake of untying her hands. She swung her arm, connecting solidly with a right hook and sending one of them to the ground. When the other grabbed her around the waist and threw her down, she rolled over whip-quick, her foot catching the other follower in the side of the head. She was scrambling to her feet when a blast of green magic struck her in the back, sending her flying forward.

Giselle—Puck's pixie concubine—grabbed Trish by the hair and jerked her to her feet. The traitorous pixie's face contorted with fury and she tried to speak, but her voice failed, the white bandage wound about her neck apparently covering the wounds Seth had delivered the night before that had robbed her of her voice.

"Enough of this!" came the raspy, otherworldly, magic-infused voice of Sebille Fenwick. The chanting instantly died as she stepped forward, her face still hooded. I wondered what her followers might think if they saw her for what she really was. She held a hand out to the follower at her side—Tom, I presumed. "It is time to begin."

He hesitated, but reached into his robes and withdrew a wicked-looking dagger. He handed it to her, then moved back as she approached the bier where Bo Peep lay in blissful ignorance of what Sebille intended for her.

The enchantress spread her arms and began to murmur the words of the necromancy spell. In response, the air in the clearing swirled gently and the shadows seemed to grow darker. She had at least that much of the spell right, but there was far more to it than what she imagined. One misspoken syllable, one misplaced symbol, and we were all going to be in a fuckload of trouble.

Guess it was now or never.

I called up my light, drawing upon the deepest recesses of my being to protect me and guide me. Then, as Sebille lowered the dagger to make the first cut in Bo's pale skin, I took a deep breath and stepped into the clearing.

"I can't let you do that, Sebille," I announced, infusing my voice with the same power she had so that it carried across the clearing like a roll of thunder.

Her head came up, her surprise evident even though I couldn't see her face. She cast a quick glance at Tom.

"I'm sorry," he said, taking a step back and pushing his hood from his head. "I won't be a part of this any longer."

With an enraged snarl, Sebille lunged at him, slicing down with her dagger. The blade cut a horrifying gash across his chest, sending him to his knees with a startled gasp.

"No!" I screamed, rushing forward, but before I'd even gone a few steps, Sebille whirled around, throwing out a wave of power that struck me square in the chest, lifting me from my feet and sending me flying into the trunk of a nearby tree.

My breath shot out of me with the impact, but I was back on my feet in an instant and raced forward, this time bringing up my defenses before she could strike again. The next wave of power she sent my way was deflected, knocking down three of her followers who'd been rushing to intercept me.

But four others were on me in seconds, tackling me from behind. I rolled, grabbing one by the face and sending a jolt of magic through his head—not enough to kill him, but enough to give him one hell of a headache. I was struggling against the others, ready to tear them apart with my bare hands, if necessary, when Sebille split the air with a deafening cackle.

"Enough, enough," she chided, pulling one of her followers away. "Lavender was supposed to be safely locked away in the cellar until I called upon her, but since she's here, let's have her say hello to our very special guests, shall we?"

Sebille gestured toward where her flunkies had finally subdued Trish. But now Trish wasn't the only one in their clutches. Standing there, wide-eyed and confused, was Eva Piper, her arms protectively encircling Gareth and holding him close to her. And as I looked on, two others dumped Tom at Eva's feet. With a cry of anguish, she dropped down beside him.

"My God!" she cried, her hands pressing his chest, trying to stanch the flow of blood. "Tom! What the hell is going on?" She lifted her eyes, pegging the horde of hooded figures with a murderous glare. "What the hell have you done to my husband?"

It was Sebille who stepped forward to answer. "I'm afraid he is not nearly as loyal to me as I'd believed," she said. "An example must be made. His wound is not mortal—just a flesh wound, although a rather nasty one. But I can certainly rectify that. So, I will put before him a choice. He can renew his loyalty to me—and see you live, my dear. Or, he can maintain this stubborn insistence upon being loyal to you and watch you—and the boy—die before I kill him. Really, I can't imagine it's a difficult choice. Tom?"

Tom managed to get to his feet with Eva's help, then turned to his wife, his expression so filled with regret and sorrow, it was painful to witness. He took her face in his hands and kissed her tenderly. "I love you, Eva. Remember that."

She shook her head vehemently as he backed away. "Tom, what are you doing? There has to be another way!"

When Tom reached Sebille's side, his shoulders sagged. "I just wanted a better life for us," he explained. "I just wanted to give you a son—the family you always wanted and deserved. I'm so sorry, Eva. I hope you can forgive me."

She shook her head in confusion as Tom untied his robe and let it fall to the ground. "Forgive you?"

Before any of us knew what was happening, Tom drew his gun from his holster and stuck it in his mouth. Eva's scream was punctuated by the sharp crack of Tom's gun as he made his choice.

Sebille's roar of rage made the ground tremble. Her arms shot out to the nearest follower and shoved him toward the bier. "Help me!" she ordered. "We don't have much time—the Reaper will be here any moment!"

But the follower shoved back his hood and offered her a cocky wink. "He already is."

My eyes went wide. *Fuck. Me.*

Sebille stumbled back at the sight of Nate Grimm and backed into one of her other followers. She spun around with a gasp as that hooded figure threw off its robe. *"You!"*

Red's arm shot out, the heel of her hand driving into Sebille's nose with a sickening crack. "In the flesh," Red drawled. She shook her hand, flinging off a rancid glop of goo with a grimace. "More than I can say for you."

Sebille glanced around frantically. "Take them!" she screeched. "Kill them! Kill them all!"

As her followers broke their circle and rushed forward to obey, several others threw off their robes—they were faces I recognized, FMA agents who'd been there at the Charmings' the night of the fire.

Suddenly, there was a flurry of motion as the loyal attempted to protect their leader, their numbers threatening to overwhelm the others in spite of the FMA's superior weapons. Sebille stood in the center of it all, enjoying her reign as the queen of this chaos. Taking advantage of the melee around her, she strode toward where Bo Peep still lay and raised the dagger.

"Sebille!" I roared, the force of my voice knocking her back as the shockwave struck her. I strode forward, my eyes narrowed, intent on my target. Around me the action slowed, time coming to a crawl for everyone but me and the enchantress.

"You cannot stop me," she taunted. "You aren't what you once were, Lavender Seelie. You are *nothing*. You are *worthless*. You are *refuse*—tossed aside by all those who once loved and cared about you." She lifted her arms, gesturing toward the slow-motion battle raging around us. "Why, your love isn't even here. Where is that pathetic werewolf now that you need him most? Even *he* has abandoned you."

I can't pretend that her words didn't cut through me. I *had* noticed Seth's absence—but I wasn't concerned that he had abandoned me. I was concerned that he was in danger, that it was *he* who needed protection.

Using my limited skill with space and time, I burst forward in a blur of motion and grabbed her around the throat, taking her down to the ground. "You are the one who's pathetic, you hideous fucking corpse!"

She merely chuckled. Her eyes blazed brightly for a split second and then the ground shook, rattling me to my bones. I started to turn to see what she had just conjured when the hair on the back of my neck suddenly stood on end and a burst of warmth hit me in the back, the thick, choking odor of brimstone filling my nostrils.

Oh shit.

I rolled off of Sebille as the dragon's teeth gnashed together where my head had just been. I scrambled back quickly, scooting my ass across the ground as fast as I could, not wanting to turn my back on the creature again. The dragon reared back, its chest filling with air in preparation to turn me to ash.

Well, wasn't this a bitch. . . .

I lifted my arm in front of my face, bringing up a shield of magical energy, hoping it was enough. But just then, a loud battle cry brought the dragon's head up as a massive sword flew through the air, burying itself in the soft spot of the dragon's chest. In the next instant, Seth leapt from the bier, sailing through the air and rolling as he landed, coming to his feet in front of the dragon and wrenching the sword from its chest in the same motion. He swung the sword, its enchanted blade slicing the beast's head from its neck in one clean cut. As the dragon burst into a bright flame, instantly reduced to ash, Seth whirled around and rushed toward me, dropping the sword and gathering me into his embrace.

I kissed him hard. Twice.

"Sorry I'm late, princess," he said with a cockeyed grin. "Had one more person to pick up."

I glanced in the direction he'd jerked his head and had to blink several times before I believed what I saw. My brother was walking casually through the melee, randomly snapping his fingers and grinning at the resulting transformations. As I watched, Ted Walsh suddenly brayed like a donkey, his head now that of an ass. Puck shook his head with a laugh and turned to Seth and me. "No matter how many times I do it, that one never gets old!"

My answering laugh was shaky with relief. I blew him a kiss, then turned back to Seth and gave him the real thing. "Come on," I said. "We've got some ass to kick."

His lips curled into that sexy grin of his. "God, I love you."

My joy at having him at my side once again was cut short when I saw Sebille rushing into the woods, retreating into the darkness. "Come on!" I yelled, snatching up his sword and tossing it to him. "We have to stop her."

Seth and I ran after her, tearing through the underbrush as it grew thicker upon her command, cutting into our flesh. "We're losing her!" I panted, pulling at the winds, sending them swirling after the enchantress. I called down the rain and the lightning, searching each brief flash of light for Sebille.

Just when I thought she was going to slip away into the night, I saw her slide to an abrupt stop. It was only as Seth and I burst through the last of her magical brambles that I saw the reason for her sudden halt. Blocking her path was a stunningly beautiful woman— tall, magnanimous, her flawless mocha skin and dark eyes somehow familiar.

"My God," Seth muttered, his own feet refusing to move. "I don't believe it."

The woman lifted her eyes and met our startled gazes. "Hello, babies."

"Mama Hubbard?" I gaped.

"Idiot," Sebille hissed. "She was never that old bat! That was just a ruse—I should've seen it sooner!"

Mama gave a nod of acknowledgment. "A disguise," she said, her Southern accent completely gone, replaced by that of Make Believe. "A useful pretense that allowed me the means to monitor Sebille's machinations and rectify some of my own mistakes." Here she turned to Seth, her expression apologetic. "What I did to you, Seth Wolf, was a horrible act of grief and vengeance. I have long regretted what you have had to endure because of my broken heart."

I glanced between Seth and the enchantress, my mind racing. *Was she saying—*

"I forgave you a long time ago, Aurelia," he said. "It's me I couldn't forgive."

Aurelia gave him a sad smile, then turned her gaze on Sebille.

"The pain we've all experienced can be traced to one person," she said, taking a threatening step toward Sebille. "It was *she* who took everything from us and again would destroy those we love in her quest for power."

"It was Sebille who cursed your children," I deduced. "She was jealous of you and couldn't battle you directly, so she cursed you in a way she knew would cause you the most pain."

Aurelia nodded. "I lost my family once." She cast a meaningful glance at Seth and me. "I won't let you destroy the new one I've created, Sebille."

Sebille laughed bitterly. "Ever noble, Aurelia," she hissed. "But naïve. I've learned a thing or two since then." She suddenly sent out a blast of magic that knocked Aurelia to the ground, and was on her in a heartbeat. At the same instant she sent up a loud command—one that I recognized.

"Get down!" I screamed. Seth dropped to the ground with me as the very fabric of reality split apart, revealing a great, swirling black hole before our eyes.

"What the hell is going on?" Seth yelled over the roar of the winds that were sucking us toward the abyss.

I dug my feet into the ground, wrapping my magic around us, straining against the force drawing us in. "I don't know!" I ground out. "This isn't what happened last time!"

Aurelia and Sebille wrestled with one another as the black hole sucked them closer. Aurelia managed to pin Sebille beneath her and grabbed her rival's ears, slamming her head hard against the ground. But Sebille bucked, sending Aurelia tumbling back end-over-end in a series of somersaults.

Aurelia cried out as she caught hold of a tree root, struggling as her body was lifted off the ground. Worse yet, it wasn't just the four of us, fighting against the pull of the tear in reality. The others we'd left behind were being swept toward it as well, tumbling and rolling through the forest—some of them slamming into trees before being sucked into the darkness, their horrified cries echoing after they'd disappeared.

"You have to stop this!" Seth shouted. "You're the only one who can!"

I shook my head frantically. "I can't! I don't know how!"

My gaze darted about me where trees were snapping now like toothpicks and the people I'd called friends—whether they deserved that designation or not—were being dragged toward their doom, for all I knew. As I looked on, panicked, I felt the tendrils of self-doubt begin to wrap around me, strangling me with uncertainty. *What if I tried to stop the rift and made it worse?* I swallowed hard, my thoughts pinging around my head in indecision. What I'd done before had been an accident. I hadn't been in control of the magic of the ancients—it'd been in control of me.

"Lavender!" Seth said, his tone sharp. "You have to do *something.*"

I shook my head, wanting to curl up into a little ball and cover my head while the chaos raged around me. "I can't. I just can't."

He grabbed my shoulders, his grip painful. "Look at me!" I tore my eyes away from the sight of Gretel flying by, her arms and legs flailing wildly as she screamed in terror, and met his gaze. His beautiful, soothing, ice-green eyes were glowing, his whole body shuddering with the effort to maintain his human form and not change into the wolf that wanted to break free and protect him from harm. He was holding it together for me, I realized, because I was falling apart. "You can do this," he ground out. "I love you. And I believe in you."

I closed my eyes for a moment, then took a deep breath and nodded. I'd let down everyone I cared about for long enough. There was no way in hell I was going to let Seth down, too. I grabbed his sword and with a loud cry, drove it into the ground. "Hold on to that."

He frowned. "What?"

"It's infused with my love for you—that's the strongest talisman against harm I can give you." I caught a glimpse of him taking hold of the sword's hilt as I hurried away, racing toward the enchantress. The woman stood with her arms aloft, cackling with malicious glee at what she had wrought. "Sebille!"

She turned toward me, her gruesome grin turning my stomach. "You're too late, Lavender!" she taunted. "You can't stop me! I feel my soul approaching! The Wild Hunt draws near, and the Lord of the Dead has heard my plea!"

She was right. I could feel it, too. The veil between this world and the Great After was thinning and any moment now, Sebille's plan would be complete. I didn't have time to battle it out with her. It was now or never. With a sharp command, I held my hand to the heavens and called down the lightning. With a deafening crack, a single bolt lit the darkness. I grasped it in my hand and broke it in two. With an enraged battle cry, I rushed Sebille, burying my lightning bolts into her body.

Her eyes went wide in surprise. "What have you done?"

"No body," I snarled, "no soul." I forced my energy into the lightning bolts with a single muttered word. She had only enough time to gasp before her body exploded into millions of pieces. The resulting ash was sucked into the void, scattered across the dimensions by the rift she'd created.

I struggled to my feet, still holding my lightning bolts, and gazed into the rift, its winds still howling. *What the fuck?* Sebille's death hadn't had any effect at all! It really *was* up to me. I waved my hands, eliminating the bolts, then closed my eyes and let out a long, slow breath, forcing my thoughts to calm. Slowly, warmth began to spread through my body as the ancient magic roared to life. I knew my skin was glowing, that the symbols I'd absorbed were becoming visible on my flesh. A brief flash of doubt entered my head and I felt the magic falter, but I quickly shoved it away.

No! I wasn't going to lose it. Not this time.

I opened my eyes and looked into the void, the images on the other side of the darkness coming into focus. Whatever force was behind the opening was staring back at me, daring me to try to stop it. A barrage of images, glimpses of my failures, my mistakes, assaulted me, trying to distract me. I pressed my lips together and forced them from my mind. Then I lifted my arms to my sides, my fingertips stretching to encompass the width of the opening. Slowly, I brought my arms together, groaning with the effort it took to shrink the breach. As it grew smaller, the resistance grew, and my groan became a moan and then a scream, but I wasn't letting go. My voice was hoarse, my arms shook with the effort, but I wasn't about to stop now. These people needed me. They were counting on me. There was no way in hell I was giving up. I felt tears stinging my face as white-hot pain washed over me.

Smaller, smaller, smaller...

I managed to force the opening down to the size of a melon, but it wouldn't shrink any further, the resistance too great and my strength at its end. "Oh, God," I wailed. "I'm losing it! I can't hold on!"

In an instant, someone's hand covered mine. I glanced up, sweat running into my eyes, but I didn't need to see his handsome face clearly to know who it was. Seth gave me a tight nod, then pushed, the veins in his neck straining with the effort. Then there was another hand, pushing from the other side. *Aurelia.* The void began to close, now the size of a grapefruit.

"Puck!" I hissed through clenched teeth. "I need you, goddamn it!"

My brother rushed to my side. And the void shrank down—smaller, smaller. ...

One last scream tore from my throat as I felt the barrier begin to give and then my hands slammed together, sending up a thunderous clap that shook the ground and echoed through the forest. The resulting shockwave knocked everyone but me on their asses and flattened the trees for nearly half a mile.

I blew out a sharp breath and turned to thank those who'd come to my aid, but the world suddenly spun and my head lolled back as I crumpled. Seth caught me as I fell, and sank down to the ground with me, holding me close and smoothing my hair away from my face.

"You did it," he said, his face beaming. "You did it, Lavender."

I was shuddering violently as my muscles began to protest and the magical inferno raging within my body began to fade, but I managed to nod. "How many?" I rasped. I tried to lick my parched lips, but my mouth was too dry. "How many did we lose?"

Seth shook his head, his expression grim. "I have no idea, but—"

A blood-chilling scream suddenly cut him off. I sat up with a jolt, my exhaustion forgotten as adrenaline shot through my body. Eva knelt nearby, her face and arms a bloody mess from being dragged through the forest, but she was more concerned about the little body lying on the ground before her.

"What's happening to him?" she screamed. "Help him! Please!"

Gareth.

I bolted over to where the boy lay, his chest caving inward as he gasped for breath. His eyes had rolled back into his head and his skin was growing alarmingly pale, withering before my eyes. "No, no, no," I whispered frantically, patting him on the face. "Gareth, I need you to look at me, baby. Look at me!"

"He's dying," Eva keened, her voice so full of despair the words hung heavy in the air. "Please, no . . . not him, too . . ."

I didn't have the heart to tell Eva that Gareth had always been dead, and that by killing Sebille Fenwick, I'd blown apart the only force animating his little body. There was nothing I could do but watch him fade away. I was helpless. Utterly, pathetically helpless.

"Lavender," I heard Nate Grimm say gently from over my shoulder. "You need to let me take him."

I was hit in the gut by fury so violent, I let forth a roar that sent out a wave of energy along the ground in purple ripples, shocking those not quick enough to jump out of the way, and sending them hopping. Grinding my teeth together so hard my jaw ached, I knocked Nate's hand away as he reached for Gareth. "Bullshit!" I spat. "Not happening."

Gareth's breaths grew more frantic as the spirit that had brought him back from the dead began to slip away. His chest sucked in so deeply with each breath, the rest of his body arched off the ground, fighting desperately, clinging to the second chance at life.

"Gareth!" I barked. "Gareth—look at me, goddamn it!"

His lids fluttered and then his eyes rolled, focusing on me. "Lavender," he gasped. "I'm dying."

I blinked back the tears. "Like hell you are, kiddo." But even as I said it, his skin began to turn gray and dark patches of decay appeared and spread before my eyes.

He lifted his pudgy hand and touched the tears on my face. "Don't . . . be sad."

"Damn it, Gareth!" I growled, taking him into my arms. "You're a dragon slayer, remember? They don't stop fighting!"

"Lavender," Puck said, crouching at my side and placing a comforting hand on my arm. "You can't help him. You'd need a blood sacrifice to replicate the magic Sebille used."

"*I* don't," I snarled, my voice thick with tears. As Gareth's lids fluttered closed and his chest ceased to heave, I held him close, rocking his limp little body, calling upon the spell deep within the hidden recesses of the ancient tome, the ones that were only revealed to the worthy—to a Guardian.

Please, I pleaded silently. *Please . . .*

My skin burned as the magic flooded through me. This was different from anything I'd felt before—harsher, more powerful, more intense. It was as if the very essence of the elements, of all that bound us together, was coursing through my veins. Slowly it spread through my body and then began to seep into Gareth, encompassing us both in light so bright I could see it even through closed eyes.

"Come back to us, Gareth," I murmured. "Come back."

I opened my eyes and pulled back enough to peer down at the little boy. His skin was glowing with my magic, the symbols that seared my skin now etched into his as well. But his chest was still as he hovered on that precipice between life and death.

Still nothing. It hadn't worked. He was really and truly gone.

"What's happening?" Eva demanded. "What's going on?"

I lifted my eyes to her. "I'm so sorry," I whispered. "I'm so very sorry."

"No!" she ground out. "No—you have to do something else. Try something else!"

I turned my gaze back to Gareth. My heart breaking, I smoothed his auburn curls, then bent and pressed a kiss to his forehead. And as the light faded and the magic ebbed away, I heard Eva's hysterical cries and let my own sobs come as I handed his little body over to her.

Seth reached out for me, but I brushed his hand away. I didn't want to be comforted. I didn't want to be told I'd done everything I could, that no one could've saved him. I was the most powerful goddamn fairy ever born, for fuck's sake! What the hell was the point of being able to wield that kind of power, to be that blessed with the abilities others could only dream of, if it didn't do a damn bit of good?

I rose to my feet and began to walk aimlessly through the devastated forest, surveying the damage. What was left of Sebille's followers looked dumbfounded, lost. Some of them were injured, some of them probably even dying. I caught a glimpse of Red Little barking out directions to her people, motioning for one of them and yelling at him to get on the phone to headquarters and call in support. Her head was bleeding and a nasty bruise was forming on her cheekbone, but when she caught my gaze she gave me a tight nod, letting me know she was okay. Nate joined Trish as she went from Tale to Tale, doing triage to see who could be helped and who was lost. I saw Nate shake his head and draw out the soul of one of the Tales who was beyond help.

"Oh, my God!"

Son of a bitch. What now?

I closed my eyes with a sigh, not knowing if I could bear any more sorrow today.

"Lavender—come quick!" Seth called.

My eyes snapped open, and I whirled around, my heart pounding. But when I saw why he'd called me, I swear it stopped beating. Sitting there, a broad—albeit rather bemused—grin on his adorable face, was Gareth, patting Eva on the back as she sobbed tears of joy and relief. "It's okay, Mrs. Eva. It's okay."

I hurried over to them and dropped to my knees, taking the boy by the shoulders and turning him to face me. Even as I looked upon him, the glow of vitality returned, his cheeks growing rosy with life—all signs of decay having vanished. "You're alive," I breathed, taking his face in my hands, such indescribable joy filling my heart. "Gareth, you're alive."

He laughed and nodded. "I know! You used your magic on me."

I nodded. "Yeah, kiddo. Yeah, I did."

He scrunched up his face, wrinkling his nose. "But I thought fairy godmothers were only for girls."

My laughter was shaky with tears as I kissed him on the cheek. "No, Gareth," I told him, "fairy godmothers aren't just for girls. And I'll be yours as long as you need me."

Chapter 29

Bemused and still reeling from what had happened two hours earlier, I started when Seth dropped down beside me. He took my hand in his and pressed a kiss to my fingertips.

"Nate has taken the last of them," he announced, his tone solemn. "Fortunately, it looks like the rest of the injured will pull through. Trish is going to set up a makeshift office in town so that she and the FMA doctors have a place to treat everyone for the next couple of days."

"How's Eva holding up?" I asked as I caught a glimpse of an FMA agent loading the black bag containing Tom's body into the back of a van.

Seth gave my hand a squeeze. "I think she'll be okay eventually. She's strong. And she has Gareth. Thanks to you."

I turned toward him, gratified to see such love and pride shining in his eyes, but my happiness was tainted by the guilt I felt that I hadn't been able to do more. "How many did we lose—do we know yet?"

Seth shook his head. "Hansel and Gretel, Bo Peep, Ted Walsh—I saw them all go, but I'm not sure about the rest. It'll probably take a few days to sort it all out."

"What's going to happen to those who were here today?"

He sighed. "Most of them are being arrested and taken to the

Portland facility for their trials. I'm not sure who'll be left in The
Refuge once all the dust settles."

"Well, I'll still be around!" my brother announced, dropping down
beside us with a grin. "That is, unless my most beloved sister decides
to accuse me of murder again."

I felt my cheeks growing warm at the reminder of how I'd mis-
judged him. "Just because you're not guilty of murder doesn't mean
you're completely without fault. Your ideas for Tale revolution need
to die here, Puck."

He inhaled deeply, looking uncharacteristically pensive. "I wish I
could say that was up to me, petal, but as we know, Sebille wasn't
working alone back in Chicago any more than she was here. She had
allies, partners, sowing the seeds of dissent elsewhere."

"You mean Tales like Dracula?" I guessed.

He shrugged. "Among others."

Seth cursed under his breath. "This could be much bigger than
anyone thought. Who knows how many other groups she'd been cul-
tivating over the years before things came to light in Chicago?"

"Well," Puck drawled. "I guess there's one less group to worry
about. And I give you my solemn vow that you have no reason to be
concerned that I will take up the cause again. I am finished with making mischief."

I gave my brother my best sardonic look. "Really."

He held up his hand and donned a very serious expression that
bordered on mockery. "I swear that from this day forward I shall de-
vote my time only to providing a fully legal gambling facility to those
who would *willingly* partake in such activities, and channeling my
charm and talent to building an empire of the fiscal variety." But even
as he spoke, his gaze drifted over my shoulder and a slow grin curled
his lips.

I turned to see what had caught his attention and saw Aurelia
walking toward an FMA vehicle waiting to take her home. She
caught Puck's gaze and gave him a flirty wink. "On just the casino,
huh?"

"Well," Puck muttered as he scrambled to his feet. "Maybe I
won't give up *all* my mischief just yet."

I watched him hurry to catch a ride with Aurelia and shook my head. "That was something of a surprise."

"Aurelia or Puck?"

"Well, both, actually. How did you find my brother?"

Seth tapped his nose. "There are definite advantages to being a wolf."

"So, now that Aurelia has forgiven you, do you think she'll remove the curse?" I asked, not sure how I felt about that possibility.

He nodded. "She offered."

"And?" I held my breath, waiting for his answer.

"I told her thanks, but no thanks."

I shook my head, frowning. "But you wouldn't have to suffer anymore. You'd no longer be hunted and hated."

Seth shrugged, turning his face away to watch the last of the FMA agents loading up to head out. "Hell, I'm used to all that now. Besides, kinda tough for the FMA to be dragging in one of their own agents all the time."

My heart hitched at the reminder that he hadn't come to The Refuge to start over like I had. His stay here had been an assignment. And the feeling of family and community he'd grown to appreciate had been nothing more than an illusion. Technically, there was nothing keeping him here now.

"So what's next?" I asked.

Seth scrubbed the stubble along his jaw, considering my question. "Think I'll head home."

"To Chicago?"

His eyes narrowed as he turned his gaze back to me. "Is that where you're heading?"

I shook my head. "No. In Chicago, there's a pint-sized prince with a massive chip on his shoulder who still has it out for me."

Seth chuckled. "I have a feeling once word gets out about your little display here today, he'll think twice about coming after you."

He had a point. Still . . . "Even so, I think my place is here," I told him. "Someone's going to need to stick around and help put the town back together—and keep Puck in line."

He nodded. "Well, then, I guess you'll probably need a hand with that."

I blinked at him, praying he was saying what I hoped he was saying. "What about the FMA?"

He stood and held out his hand. "They can call me when they need me. In the meantime, the town is going to need a new sheriff. And seeing as how I know the mayor's sister . . ." I laughed and took his outstretched hand, letting him pull me to my feet. He put his arm around my shoulders and pulled me close as we started walking toward home. "You sure you don't mind about the wolf thing?"

I slipped my arm around his waist and shook my head. "Nah. I think it's wicked sexy. Werewolves are the new vampire, you know."

He chuckled. "Lucky for me. Especially with the full moon coming."

I frowned up at him. "But I thought that was all bullshit—you can control your transformations. What effect does the full moon have on you?"

He gave me a wicked grin, then leaned down and whispered something in my ear that set my cheeks on fire. I swallowed hard, extremely naughty images drifting through my head. "Really?" I said, my voice sounding a little raspy.

"Let's just say that 'make up sex' has nothing on 'full moon sex'," he drawled, his eyes getting brighter as he spoke. "If you think I couldn't get enough of you before . . ."

"Dear God," I breathed. "And when does that start?"

He pulled me into his arms and pressed his lips to mine in such a slow, sensual kiss it left me breathless. When he finally lifted his head, he gave me meaningful wink. "How quick do you think we can make it home?"

"I'm a fairy freaking godmother," I said, throwing him a saucy smile. "I can get you home as fast as you want. All it takes is a little magic."

Seth gave me a wary look. "Is this ancient, reality-rending, soul-ripping magic," he asked hesitantly, "or is it *your* magic?"

I cocked my head to the side, puzzled by his question. Then a sudden thought struck me—did recovering my mastery of the ancient fairytale magic change the way he felt about me? Was he still distrustful of magical beings, even after all we'd been through? My throat was tight with worry when I asked, "Does it make a difference?"

His mouth lifted at one corner as he gestured toward the woodland debris field. "I was just wondering if I should step back or take cover."

I groaned and gave him a hard shove. "Just for that, funny man, you can walk home."

Laughing, he jogged after me. "Lavender, wait!"

I spun around to face him, crossing my arms over my chest and looking at him expectantly, ready to be defensive and angry, but he looked so damned handsome and sexy with that cockeyed grin, that I knew it wouldn't last. And when he took my face in his hands and claimed my mouth with that combination of tenderness and hunger that set my heart to thumping, I let my arms fall to my sides and leaned into him. And when he drew the kiss to a close, I sighed, my lips—still warm from his—curving into a contented smile. "Now *that* was magic."

His answering chuckle was heavily laden with the promise of more to come. "Well, if you think that was magical, just wait until I get you home." He nuzzled at my ear, his breath bringing all my senses to life and awakening that ache that only he could relieve. "Now," he muttered with a playful nip at my skin. "About that ride home . . ."

I glanced around—admittedly a little frantic—and spotted a squirrel peeking sheepishly out from behind a tree stump. It wasn't a mouse, but it'd do. I waved my hand, ditching the fancy flourish I'd normally use when I was about to totally show off. No time for that. This was obviously an emergency of the most carnal variety.

There was a sparkle of purple light and a little dash of fairy dust thrown in for good measure, and where the squirrel had been now stood a magnificent stallion, complete with flowing mane—a creature truly worthy of a fairytale romance.

"A horse?" Seth said, blinking in astonishment. "You turned a squirrel into a horse?"

"It's the best I had to work with," I snapped impatiently, striding toward the rather bemused-looking steed. "Now get on."

"It's been quite a while since I've ridden a horse," Seth complained, his face twisting into such an adorable grimace, I was tempted to throw him up on the back of the damned thing myself.

Instead, I grabbed the horse's mane and swung up on onto its back. Then with the sweetest smile I could muster, I batted my eyes at Seth and extended my hand. "Now, Sir Knight, I suggest you get your seriously sexy ass up here or you won't be riding anything—or any*one*—anytime soon, if you catch my meaning."

Seth didn't even bother with my hand as he leapt onto the horse's back. As soon as his arms were wrapped around me, he rested his chin on my shoulder with a grin and murmured, "What are we waiting for?"

Chapter 30

One month later . . .

"Elise, could you bring me that mistletoe?" I called from my perch on the stepstool. The white-haired pixie scurried to obey my request, offering me a bright smile as she handed it up to me.

"There you go! Anything else I can do, Lavender?" she asked, practically bouncing with her eagerness to please me.

I sighed. "Really, sweetie, you don't have to keep kissing my ass. I know you weren't in on Sebille's plans. And you're the best waitress Seth has here in the restaurant. I'm not going to turn you into a toad." She nodded but looked up at me with wide eyes, still waiting. "Okay then. How about you help Eva and Aurelia decorate the tree in Town Square? I know they'd appreciate the help."

I heard the bells chime on the door as she hurried outside to join the others and chuckled to myself. Over the last month I'd had a hard time shaking the little pixie—but I couldn't tell if it was her attempt to make amends for her role in the attack on Seth's house and prove her loyalty or if she was hoping I'd put in a good word for her with my brother who, in a shocking turn of events, had fallen head over heels for Aurelia and sworn off all other women.

I smiled, wondering just how the beautiful enchantress had managed to turn such a confirmed bachelor and bad-boy into a fawning, love-struck suitor. I hopped down from the stepstool and strolled to the restaurant window to watch the group of townspeople decorating the Christmas tree I'd insisted we erect in the center of town as soon as Thanksgiving was over.

It was beginning to snow, fat flakes drifting down and already coating the ground with a fine powder. Gareth was skipping and running, catching snowflakes on his tongue while Harlan trotted along at his side. Eva and Aurelia were handing out ornaments to a dozen or so of the remaining residents who'd been drafted to help decorate. And Puck was in the thick of things, laughing and smiling with his citizens, finally embracing the role of mayor and leader.

I'd hoped to see Trish Muffet among them—she'd extended her stay in The Refuge to help me try to determine where the rift had deposited the missing Tales—but just the day before she'd been called away to investigate an urgent case. In the month she'd been in The Refuge, we hadn't come any closer to solving the mystery of where the Tales had gone, but Trish had become a close and trusted friend. And I hoped that someday she would find the love and happiness she deserved.

"How's it going out there?"

I turned from the window to see Seth coming from the storeroom carrying a box of holiday decorations, my heart skipping a beat as it did every time I saw him. "Good," I said, coming over to inspect what was inside the box. "I think it's starting to feel like a community again."

"Thanks to you," he said, setting the box on the nearest table and pulling me into his arms. "You're not just Gareth's fairy godmother, you know. The tension here, the distrust and unrest that was simmering just below the surface—that all has vanished."

I shook my head. "I think that's more because the people instigating everything have gone, not because of anything I've done."

Seth pressed his forehead to mine. "Not because of anything you've *done*, Lavender, but because of everything you *are*. You've given us hope that we all can be something more than just Tales who've lost their way."

I kissed him then, my lips clinging to his. But when his hands slipped under the hem of my shirt and smoothed along the small of my back, I moaned and let my head fall back a little. He pressed a line of sultry kisses along the curve of my throat and nipped playfully at the sensitive spot where neck and shoulder met, making me laugh.

"Why, Mr. Wolf," I murmured as he nipped again, "what big teeth you have."

He chuckled. "Come back to the kitchen with me," he drawled, his voice going dark with promise, "and I'll show you what else is big. . . ."

Grinning, I slid my hand down the front of his jeans. "Oh, I *know* what's—"

A polite cough behind me cut off my words and brought Seth's head up. When his brows snapped together in a frown, I turned to see who had intruded upon our private moment.

"Gideon?" I said, pulling away from Seth. "What brings you here? Is my family okay?"

Gideon gave me a tight nod. "All is well. Your father sends his love and promises he'll visit next week as requested." He looked a little uncomfortable as he added, "Your mother asked me to repeat her concerns about your decision to stay in The Refuge, but I will not trouble you with the entirety of that particular message. However, I will share this missive she requested I deliver."

I took the scroll he held in his hand and unrolled it, my heart hammering. " 'Dear Ms. Seelie,' " I murmured, reading aloud, " 'we are pleased to inform you that by virtue of your recent heroics in defeating the enchantress Sebille Fenwick and thwarting her unsanctioned use of sacred texts, you are hereby reinstated as a Guardian with all the powers, duties, and responsibilities assigned thereto.' " I rolled my eyes. "As if I needed *their* permission when the magic had already selected me."

"But their recognition of that fact must count for something," Seth insisted.

"It counts for a great deal," Gideon agreed. "Keep reading."

I skimmed down further. " 'We also restore your title as Fairy Godmother'—also didn't need their blessing. Already doing it—'and forthwith reinstate you as' "—I swallowed hard, forcing down the sudden lump in my throat—" 'as heir to the Seelie throne.' " I held the parchment up to Gideon. "Mother reinstated me?"

He nodded, a smile curving his lips, then dropped down on one knee, his closed fist over his heart. "It is my pleasure to serve you again."

"Please don't do that, Gid," I admonished. "It's *me*, for crying out loud." As touched as I was by Gideon's show of devotion, I no longer needed people to fawn and grovel to assure me I was worthy of respect and admiration. For the first time in my life, I truly believed it in my heart.

When Gideon rose, he reached into his suit pocket and extracted a small bundle wrapped in the finest silk. "I have one last thing to give you." He handed me the bundle, his smile doing little to hide the glimpse of sorrow I saw in his eyes.

I untied the ribbon and gasped when I saw what lay inside. "My necklace. Gideon—it's breathtaking. It's the most beautiful I've ever seen."

His smile widened at the compliment. "Sorry it took so long to create. It's platinum this time. I wanted it to be perfect for you." His gazed flicked to Seth, and he inclined his head in recognition. "And your beloved. Although, from what I can see, you don't need it to bind this man to you."

"Thank you, Gideon," Seth said, extending his hand.

Gideon hesitated for the briefest moment, then shook Seth's hand. "Good luck to you both," he said. "If you have need of me, I am at your disposal." He bent forward in a slight bow, then turned and slipped between the dimensions.

I lifted my necklace before my eyes, marveling at the exquisite workmanship. It was truly a work of art, the detail unmatched. I undid the clasp and started to put it around my own neck, but Seth stilled my hand.

"If I remember correctly," he said, "that is supposed to go around *my* neck."

I blinked at him. "Seth, you don't have to accept it. I'll understand if you want to think about it a while. The bond is very powerful."

He nodded. "Yeah, I know. I felt it before, remember? But the thing is, Lavender, I feel that bond anyway—and no amount of waiting or thinking is going to change that. My heart belongs to you and always will."

My own heart soaring, I slipped the chain around his neck. The moment the clasp came together, there was a rush of energy that sent a tingle through my entire body—and by the look on Seth's face, it did his as well.

"Damn," he breathed. "That was . . . just . . . *damn*." He blinked at me a few times and then asked, "So, is that it? Is that all we have to do?"

I grimaced a little. "Well, not entirely. I have to actually *tell* you my true name to make the bond complete."

He cocked his head to one side, his brows furrowing in a frown that barely masked a smile. "It can't be *that* bad. Can it?" I wrinkled my nose, then leaned in and whispered my true name in his ear. He jerked back, smothering a smile. "Seriously?"

I rolled my eyes. "I'm a Lavender fairy—so Lavender is what my family has always called me, but, yes, what I just told you is my actual name."

He nodded. "I think I'll just stick with Lavender, if that's okay with you."

"God, yes!"

He was chuckling as he took my hand in his. "So, do you think we should go ahead and make things official?"

I shook my head a little. "What do you mean?"

He turned his eyes down to where his thumb lazily caressed the back of my hand. "I can't promise that my current popularity will last forever—there's a lot of stuff in my past that could still come back to haunt me, including a huge misunderstanding with a certain set of porcine brothers—but I love you, Lavender." He lifted his eyes, his intense gaze meeting mine. "And I can't imagine my life without you."

I took his face in my hands, hoping the joy and love I felt for him was shining in my eyes. "Don't worry, my love, you won't have to."

Read on for an excerpt of Kate SeRine's next
Transplanted Tales novel,

Along Came a Spider,

available in August.

I remember darkness—deep, impenetrable. Not even a hint of ambient light in the void that had consumed me. And falling. I was tumbling through space and time in a nauseating spiral that forced the blood to my feet and sent another sort of blackness rushing toward me. Clinging desperately to consciousness, I curled into myself, wrapping my arms around my abdomen in an attempt to stop that sickening rush that made me want to vomit and sob at the same time.

A scream of terror surged up from the center of my chest, but I bit it back, forcing myself to remain in control. I had to keep it together, could not let the fear consume me. That's what my father had drilled into my head time and time again.

You must control your fear, Beatrice, or your fear will control you. Never let your mind slip into the abyss where chaos reigns. . . .

I'd been there once before and had clawed my way out of the chasm one agonizingly pitiful inch at a time. And now I was falling again—but this time the abyss was not of my own making.

One moment I'd been playing on the floor of our cottage with my niece Mariella, and the next, my body had been snatched away from all I'd known and loved. I'd heard my family's cries of surprise, caught the look of horror and panic in my father's eyes as his arm shot out to grab my hand, but his fingertips had just barely brushed mine before I'd been jerked into the void.

And then I was falling. In darkness.

Suddenly there was light. A blinding flash that made me wince even though my eyes were already squeezed shut. Then a sudden impact jolted the breath from my lungs. I had to blink several times before I realized I was lying on my back in a field, staring up at a sky that was not familiar, at stars that didn't shine nearly as brightly as they should have.

Slowly, I sat up and looked around, seeing others nearby—just as dazed and disoriented as I was. They were Tales, some of whom I recognized from my little village. But we were no longer in Make Believe. That was clear. Gone was the scent of dew-kissed roses and sunshine on daisies. The air that now filled my lungs was stale, thick, heavy. The wind that whispered through the trees did not bring with it the laughter of fairies or the secrets of the pixies flitting about in the night. And the grass beneath me was no longer the velvety soft bed I'd lain upon as a child, watching the clouds drift lazily into fluffy white knights on pudgy steeds as they leisurely made their way to battle. Coarse and savage, *these* blades poked through my muslin dress, stabbing my skin like a thousand Lilliputian swords.

"Are you hurt?"

My gaze darted toward the sound of the voice. The man standing over me was devilishly handsome, his chiseled features stark and sharp, giving him an air of danger, but his dark amber eyes were kind as he gazed down at me.

"Are you all right?" he asked, phrasing the question differently in response to my blank stare.

This time I nodded and took the hand he extended, letting him pull me to my feet. "I think so."

"Good," he said, the corner of his mouth hitching up in a mischievous grin that completely altered his countenance. He lifted his hand and wrapped one of my buttercup yellow ringlets around his index finger. "Hate to see harm come to a girl as pretty as you."

I felt my cheeks growing warm at the intensity of his gaze and quickly looked away, not wanting to look too deeply into those amber eyes for fear of what I might see. "What has happened?" I asked, glancing around the crowd as confusion and panic began to make them uneasy, their frightened voices growing louder. "Where are we?"

The man at my side shrugged and shoved his hands deep into his pockets. "Not in Make Believe, that's for damned sure."

I let my gaze drift over his shoulder, and saw a tall Tale I recognized from the story of Aladdin trying to take control of the rapidly deteriorating situation, his deep voice booming over the din of sorrow. "My friends—please! You must remain calm!"

A woman with long black hair and eyes as blue as robins' eggs hurried past me, glancing my way and giving me a terse nod before joining Aladdin as he tried to herd the crowd toward a series of carriages drawn by black horses. "That was Tess Little," I breathed.

"Little Red Riding Hood?" my companion asked, his brows arching with interest.

I nodded. "Yes, but . . . well, it can't be! She disappeared almost a hundred years ago with the others." My heart was beginning to pound. "Have we been transplanted, too?"

He shook his head. "No idea, but I'll tell you one thing—I'm not letting them haul me in like a criminal just so I can find out. If I've broken out of Make Believe, I'm making the most of it."

At this, his eyes met and held mine. I felt the connection beginning and started to look away, but his gaze was so unguarded, so unapologetic, I let it come. And in that glimpse, I saw a soul so steadfast, so dauntless and true, that I gasped at the beauty of it.

It was rare that a Tale let me past his defenses, rarer still that I was so taken with what I saw. But here was an intensely intelligent and quietly courageous man who could command respect from his friends and instill fear in the hearts of those who weren't. He was also capable of genuine kindness and the deepest and most profound love. But I was shocked to see that he had absolutely no idea what a remarkable man he could be.

"Want to come with me?" he asked, grasping my hand in his and severing the connection between my soul and his.

I blinked at him, hardly daring to believe what he was saying. But even more surprising was that I *did* want to go with him even though logic and reason warned me that such a thing was reckless and foolish. I swallowed hard, hating what I was about to say. "I cannot," I told him, wishing I had the courage to flout propriety and take my chances with a man whose name I didn't even know. "It wouldn't be proper."

He chuckled and pressed a kiss to the back of my hand. "Well, maybe some other time." He backed away, grinning a little sadly as he released my hand, his fingertips touching mine for just a moment before he gave me a wink and turned away.

"Wait!" I called, hurrying a few steps after him as he sauntered toward the tree line. "What's your name?"

He turned and offered me a rakishly charming grin that held more than a hint of mischief. "Nicky Blue."

"You there—with the curls!" I started at the voice behind me and whirled around to see Tess Little striding toward me, her long black duster flapping around her dark skirt and cherry red high-button boots. "Time to go."

I obediently moved toward the carriages with her. "Is it true?" I asked. "Have we been transplanted?"

"Afraid so," she replied. "But don't worry—we have people with the FMA who will help you settle in."

"The FMA?"

"Fairytale Management Authority," she explained. "I'll tell you everything on the way to headquarters. By the way—I'm Tess Little. But everyone calls me Red."

"Beatrice Muffet," I replied, attempting a smile. "Everyone pretty much just calls me Beatrice. Or Ms. Muffet." I chuckled a little. "Except my niece Mariella—she has trouble pronouncing my name." My voice caught in my throat, the words lodging around the lump of sorrow that had rapidly developed at the thought of never seeing little Mari again. I coughed, forcing my emotions away, and blinked rapidly to clear the tears that pricked the corner of my eyes. "She calls me Trish."

Tess motioned me toward the last remaining carriage. "Well, welcome to the Here and Now, Trish."

I placed my foot on the step, but paused and turned to search for Nicky Blue, hoping that perhaps he had changed his mind and had decided to come with the rest of us after all. But my heart sank when I didn't see him. I sighed, a part of me already regretting that I hadn't gone with him. But it was too late to change my mind. Nicky Blue had vanished, having faded deep into the shadows like a spider in the night.

About the Author

Kate SeRine (pronounced "serene") faithfully watched weekend monster movie marathons while growing up, each week hoping that maybe *this* time the creature *du jour* would get the girl. But every week she was disappointed. So when she began writing her own stories, Kate vowed that *her* characters would always have a happily ever after. And, thus, her love for paranormal romance was born.

Kate lives in a smallish, quintessentially Midwestern town with her husband and two sons, who share her love of storytelling. She never tires of creating new worlds to share and is even now working on her next project. Please visit her at www.kateserine.com.